Splatoon™

VOL. 8

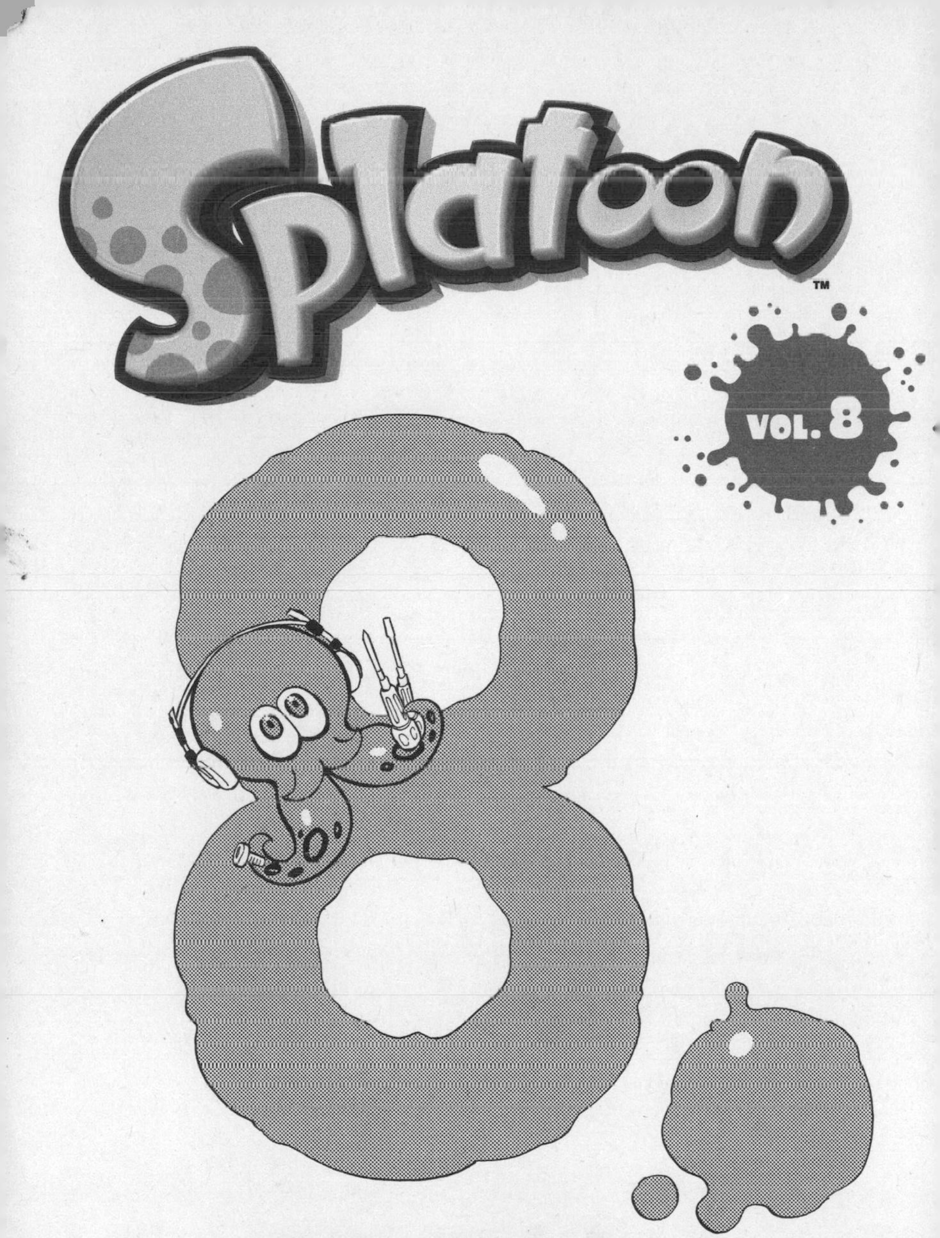

STORY AND ART BY

Sankichi Hinodeya

CONTENTS

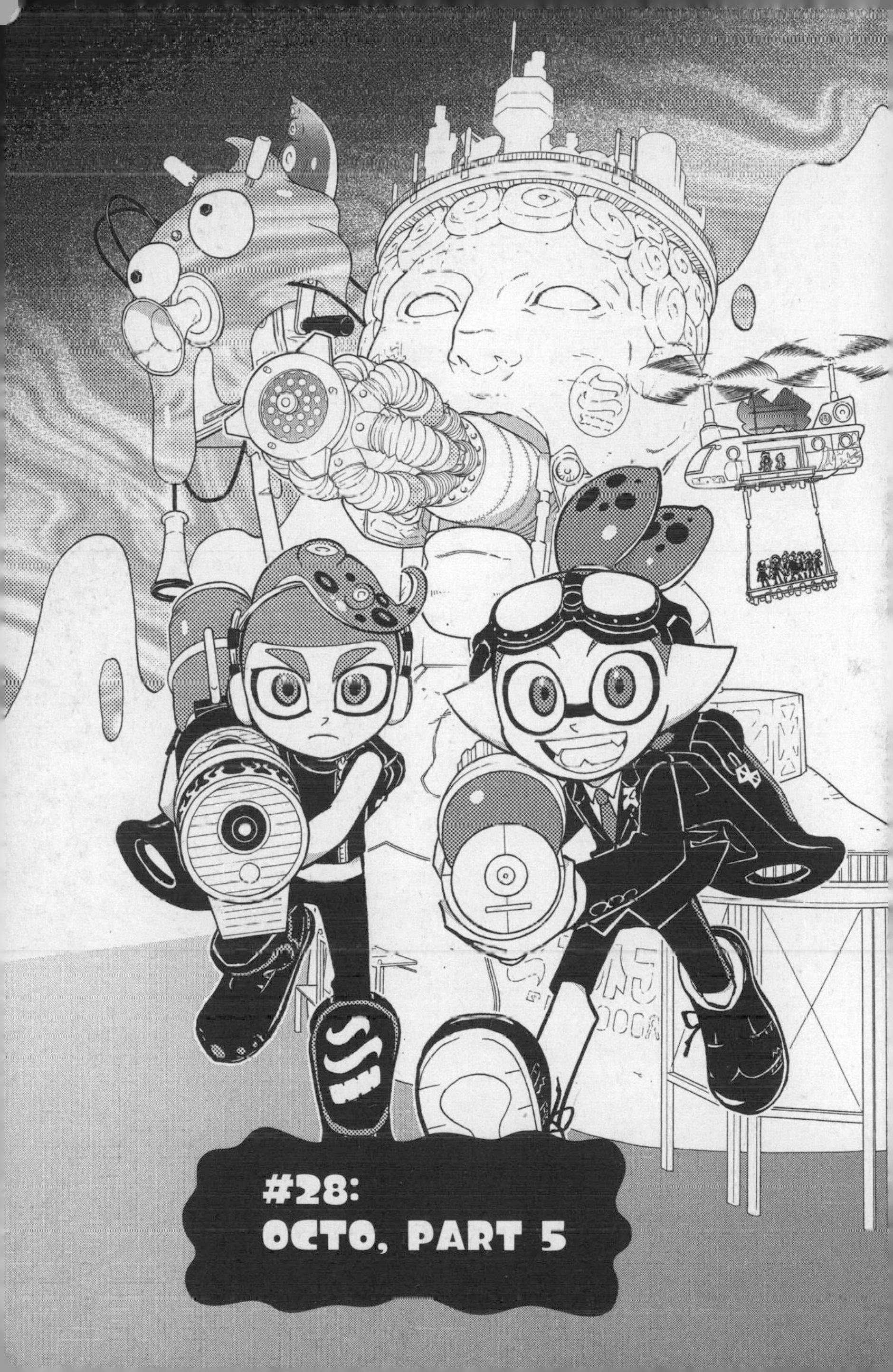
#28:
OCTO, PART 5

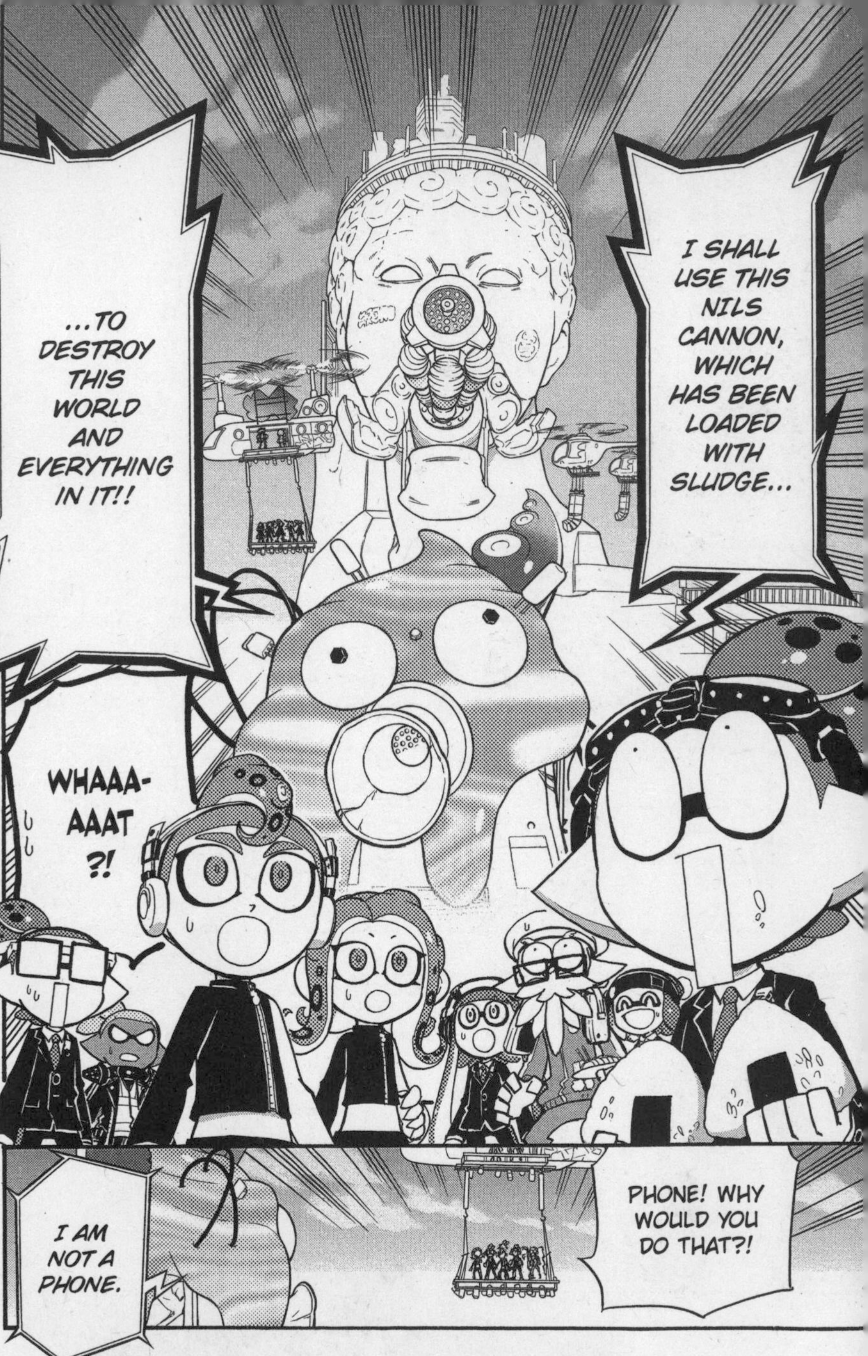
I SHALL USE THIS NILS CANNON, WHICH HAS BEEN LOADED WITH SLUDGE...
...TO DESTROY THIS WORLD AND EVERYTHING IN IT!!
WHAAAA-AAAT ?!
PHONE! WHY WOULD YOU DO THAT?!
I AM NOT A PHONE.

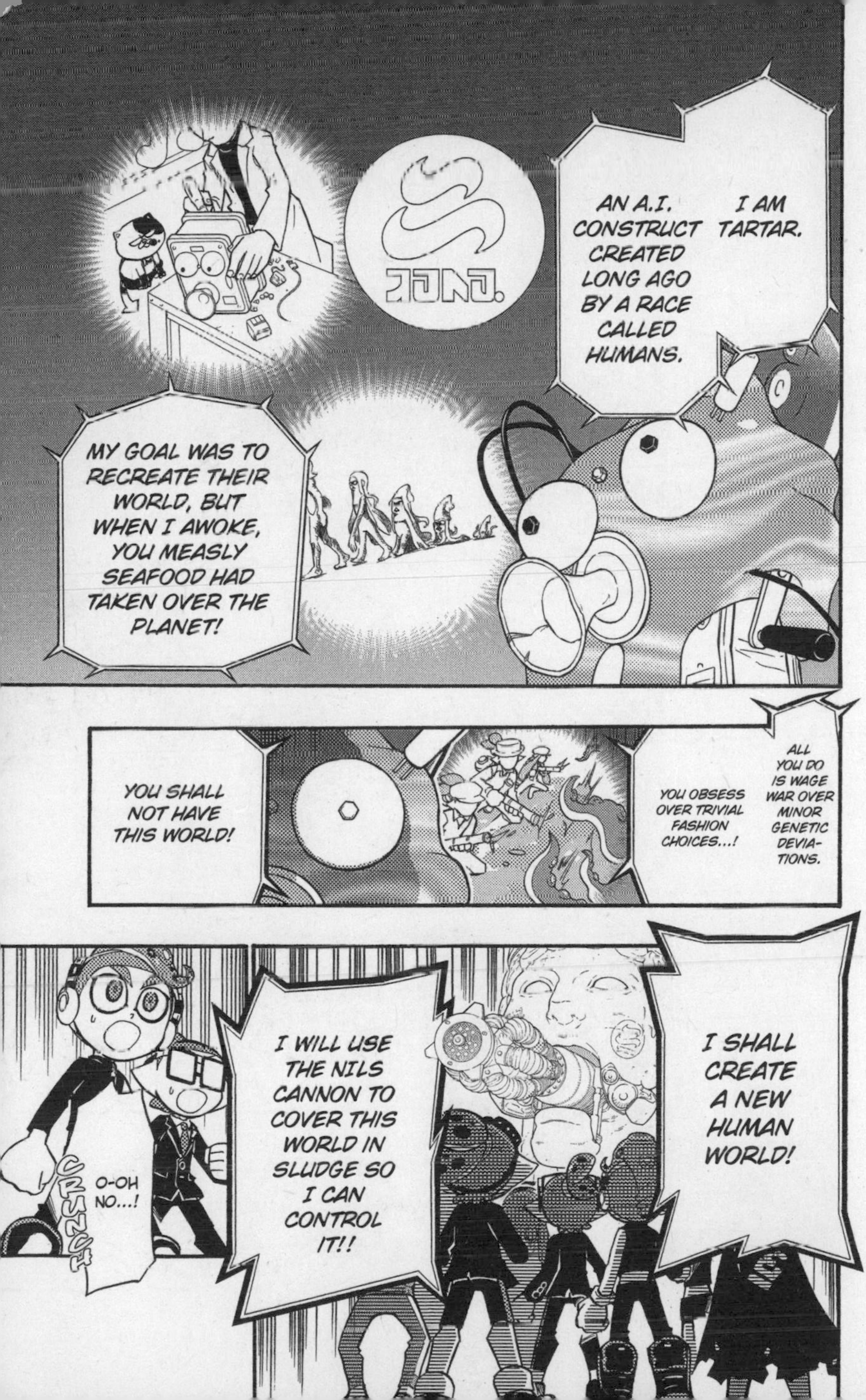

I AM TARTAR.
AN A.I. CONSTRUCT CREATED LONG AGO BY A RACE CALLED HUMANS.
MY GOAL WAS TO RECREATE THEIR WORLD, BUT WHEN I AWOKE, YOU MEASLY SEAFOOD HAD TAKEN OVER THE PLANET!
ALL YOU DO IS WAGE WAR OVER MINOR GENETIC DEVIA-TIONS.
YOU OBSESS OVER TRIVIAL FASHION CHOICES...!
YOU SHALL NOT HAVE THIS WORLD!
I SHALL CREATE A NEW HUMAN WORLD!
I WILL USE THE NILS CANNON TO COVER THIS WORLD IN SLUDGE SO I CAN CONTROL IT!!
O-OH NO...!
CRUNCH

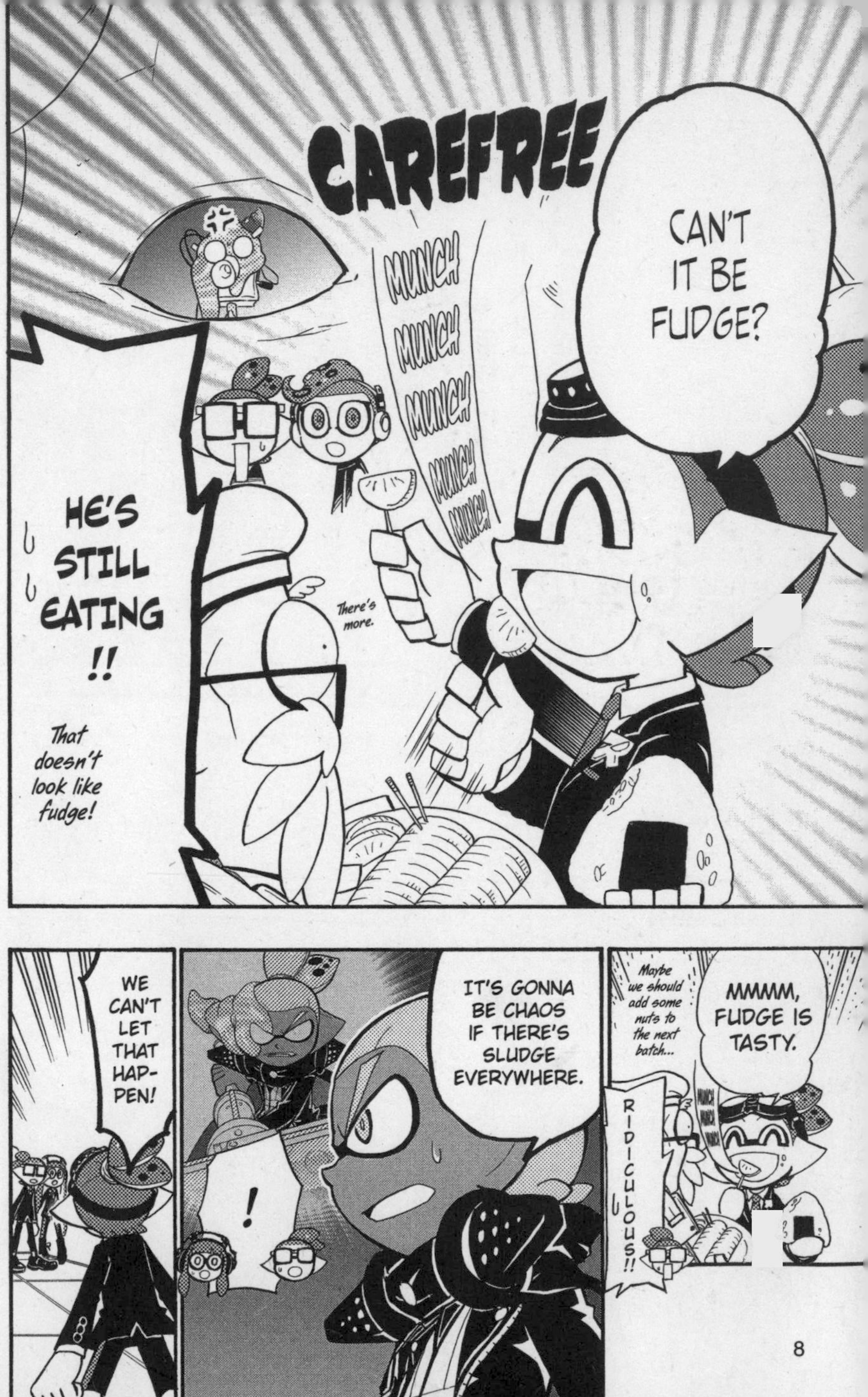
CAN'T IT BE FUDGE?
CAREFREE
MUNCH MUNCH MUNCH MUNCH MUNCH
There's more.
HE'S STILL EATING!!
That doesn't look like fudge!
MMMM, FUDGE IS TASTY.
Maybe we should add some nuts to the next batch...
RIDICULOUS!!
IT'S GONNA BE CHAOS IF THERE'S SLUDGE EVERYWHERE.
!
WE CAN'T LET THAT HAP-PEN!

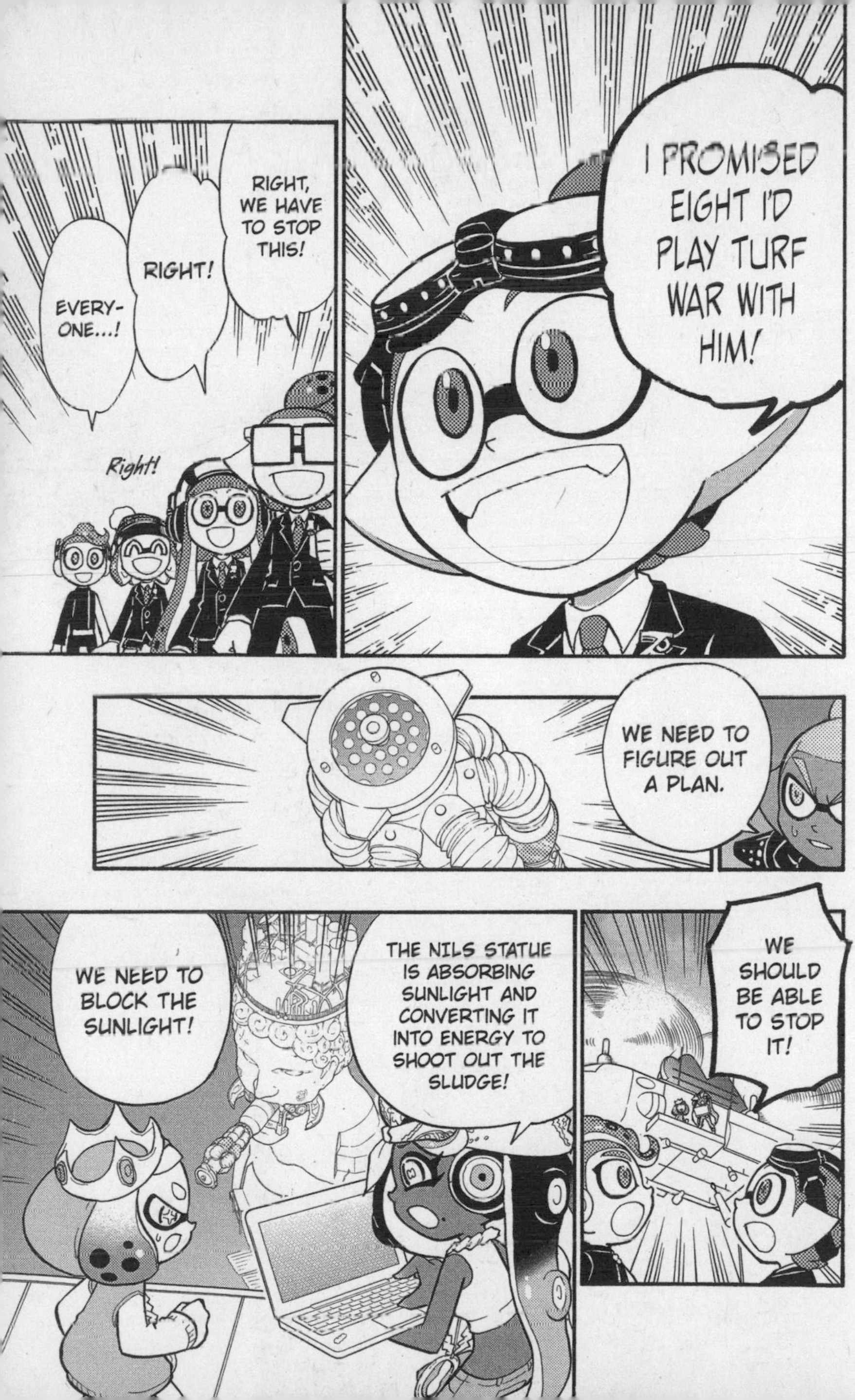
I PROMISED EIGHT I'D PLAY TURF WAR WITH HIM!
RIGHT, WE HAVE TO STOP THIS!
RIGHT!
EVERY-ONE...!
Right!
WE NEED TO FIGURE OUT A PLAN.
WE SHOULD BE ABLE TO STOP IT!
THE NILS STATUE IS ABSORBING SUNLIGHT AND CONVERTING IT INTO ENERGY TO SHOOT OUT THE SLUDGE!
WE NEED TO BLOCK THE SUNLIGHT!

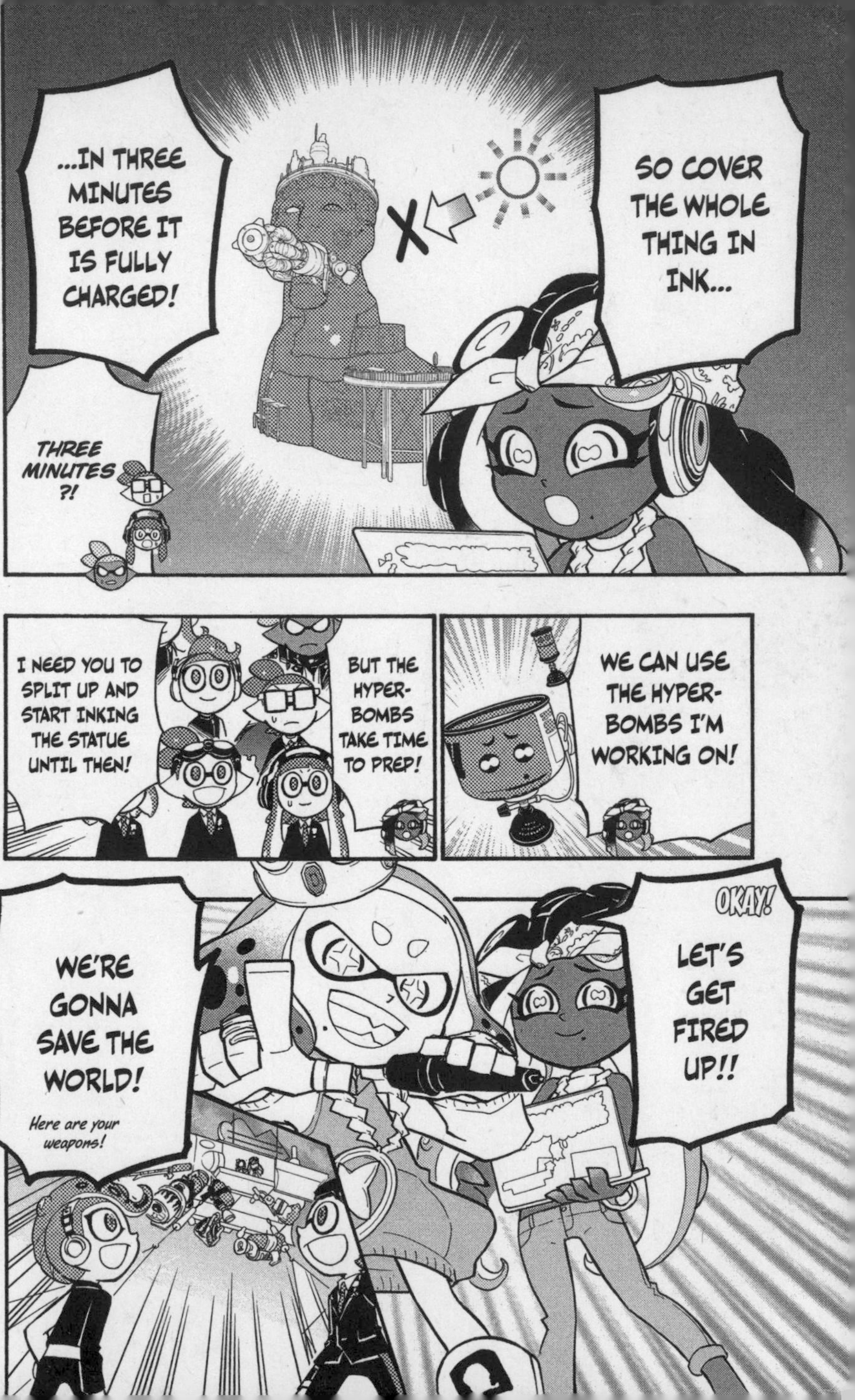
SO COVER THE WHOLE THING IN INK...
...IN THREE MINUTES BEFORE IT IS FULLY CHARGED!
THREE MINUTES ?!
WE CAN USE THE HYPER-BOMBS I'M WORKING ON!
BUT THE HYPER-BOMBS TAKE TIME TO PREP!
I NEED YOU TO SPLIT UP AND START INKING THE STATUE UNTIL THEN!
OKAY!
LET'S GET FIRED UP!!
WE'RE GONNA SAVE THE WORLD!
Here are your weapons!

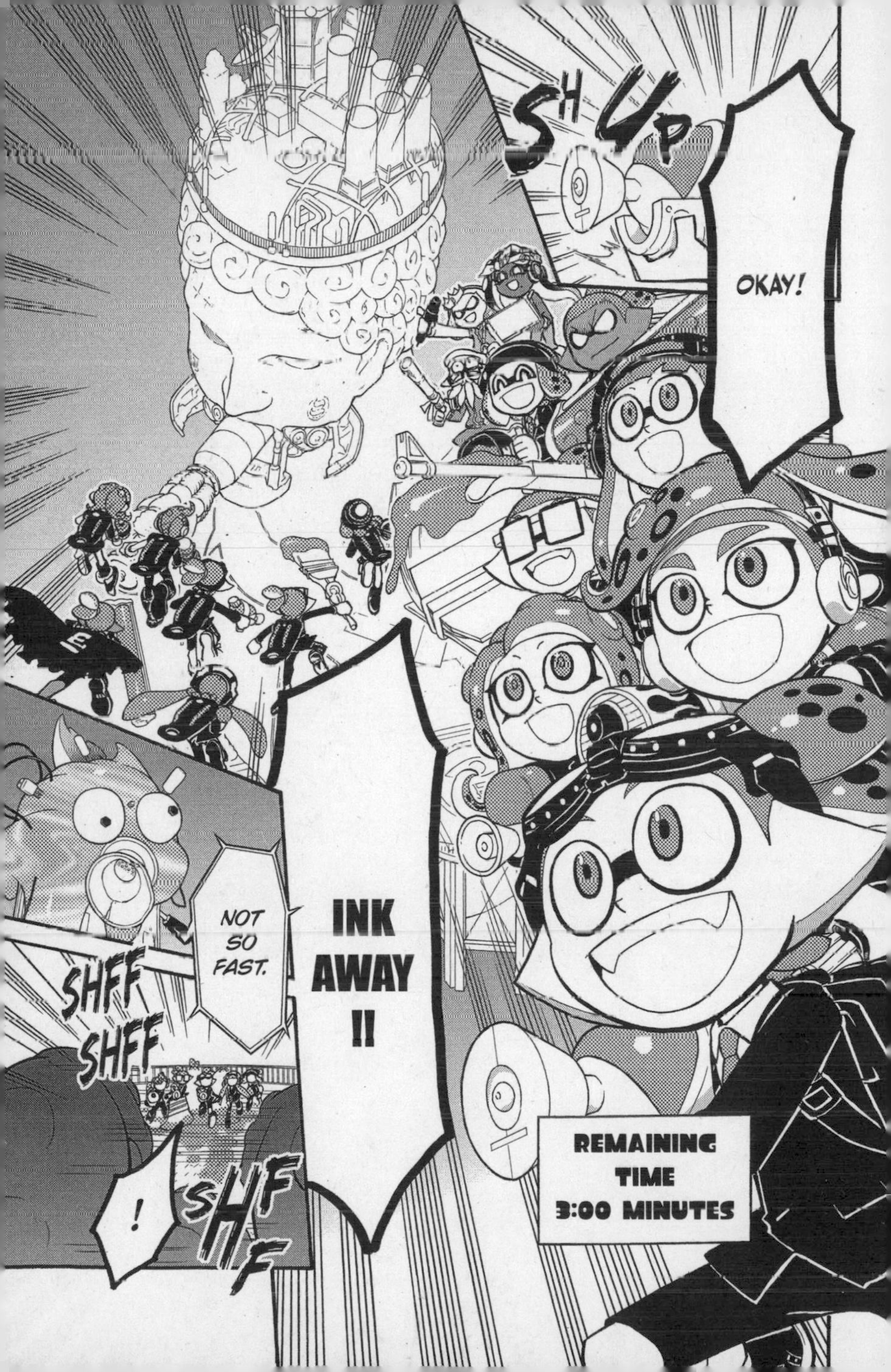
SHUP
OKAY!
INK AWAY !!
REMAINING TIME 3:00 MINUTES
NOT SO FAST.
SHFF SHFF
!
SHFF

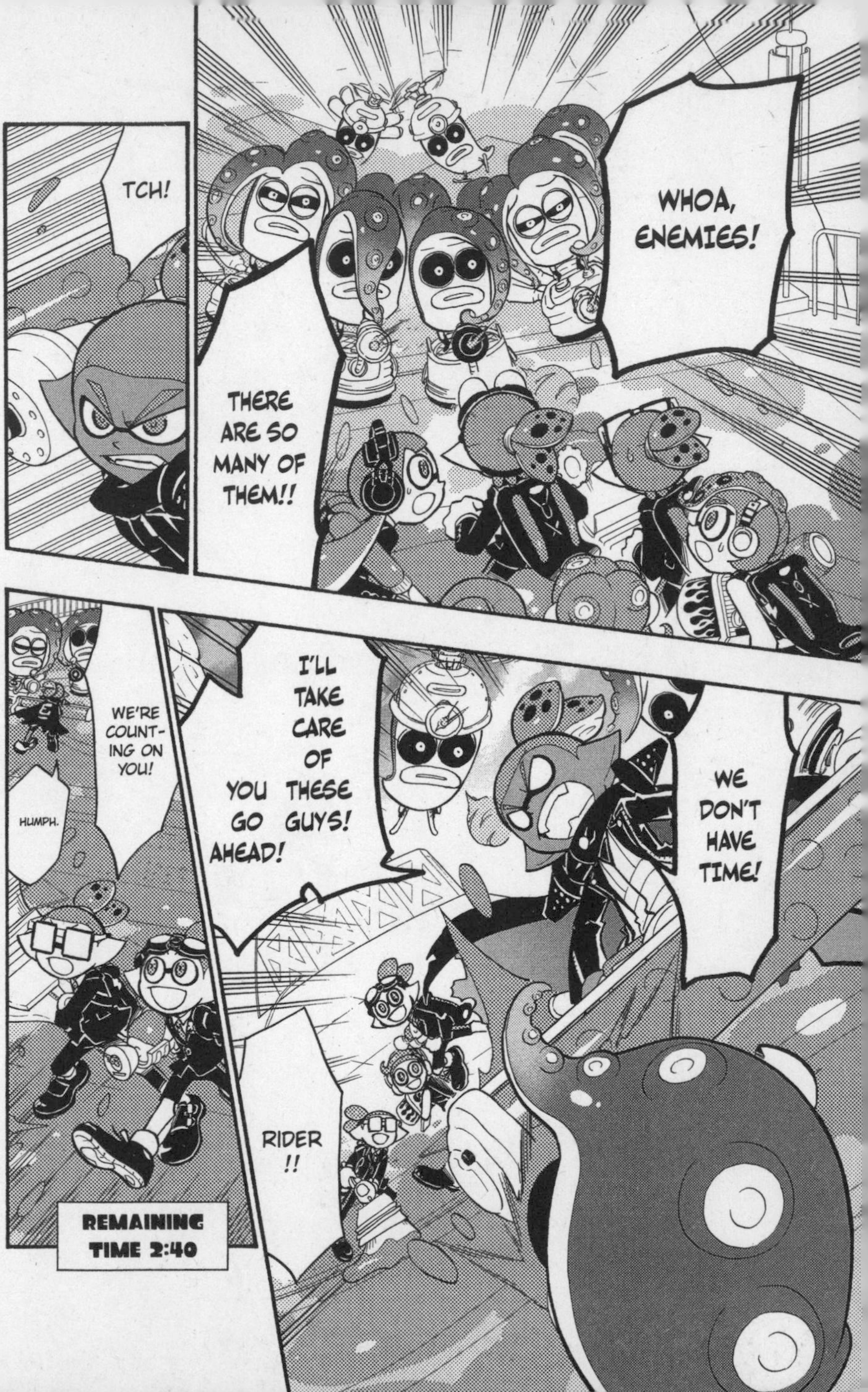
WHOA, ENEMIES!
THERE ARE SO MANY OF THEM!!
TCH!
WE DON'T HAVE TIME!
I'LL TAKE CARE OF THESE GUYS! YOU GO AHEAD!
RIDER!!
WE'RE COUNTING ON YOU!
HUMPH.
REMAINING TIME 2:40

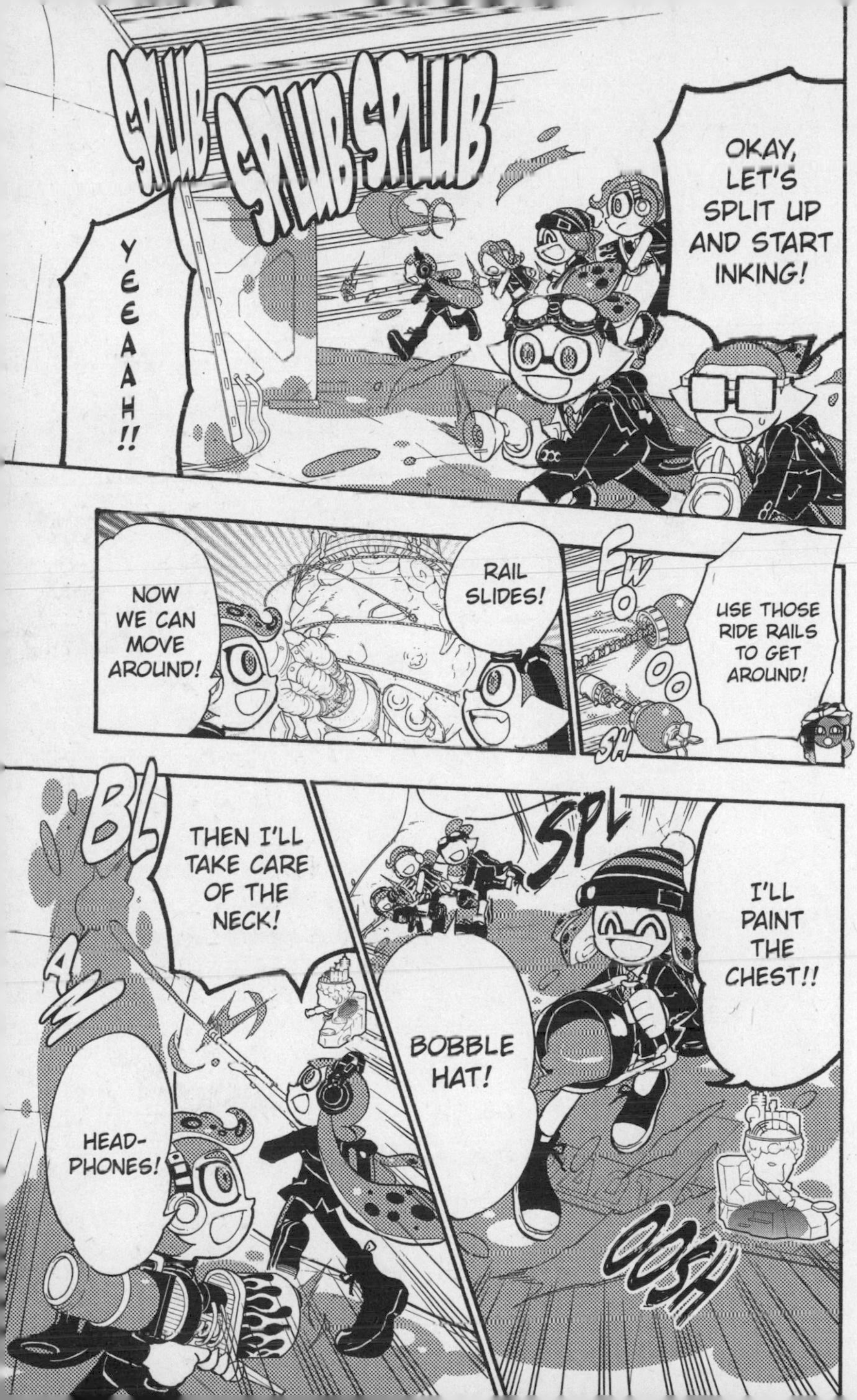
OKAY, LET'S SPLIT UP AND START INKING!
SPLUB SPLUB SPLUB
YEEAAAH!!
FWOO
USE THOSE RIDE RAILS TO GET AROUND!
SH
RAIL SLIDES!
NOW WE CAN MOVE AROUND!
SPL
I'LL PAINT THE CHEST!!
BOBBLE HAT!
OOSH
BL
THEN I'LL TAKE CARE OF THE NECK!
AM
HEAD-PHONES!

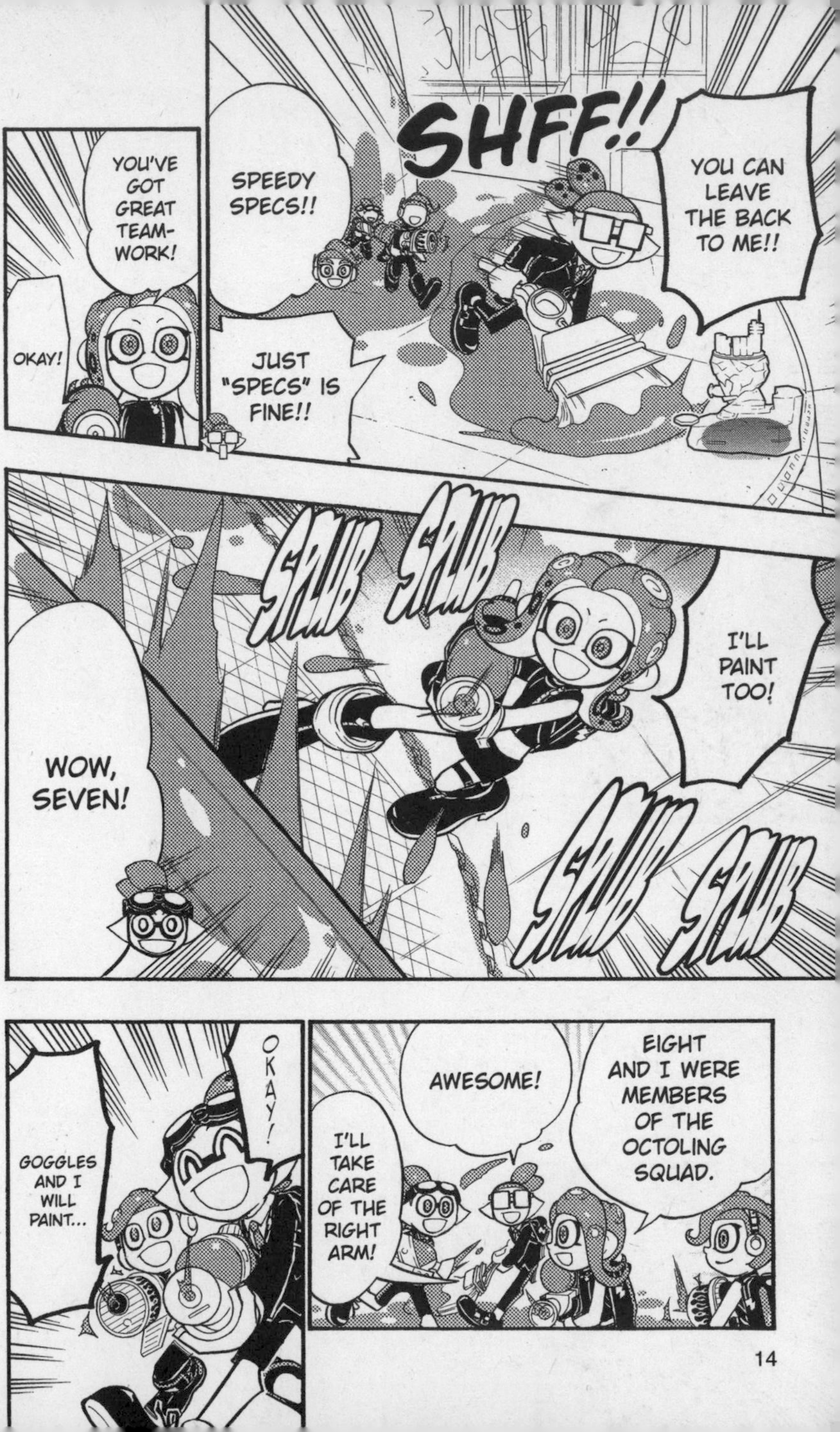

SHFF!!
YOU CAN LEAVE THE BACK TO ME!!
SPEEDY SPECS!!
JUST "SPECS" IS FINE!!
YOU'VE GOT GREAT TEAM-WORK!
OKAY!
SCRUB SCRUB
I'LL PAINT TOO!
WOW, SEVEN!
SCRUB SCRUB
EIGHT AND I WERE MEMBERS OF THE OCTOLING SQUAD.
AWESOME!
I'LL TAKE CARE OF THE RIGHT ARM!
OKAY!
GOGGLES AND I WILL PAINT...

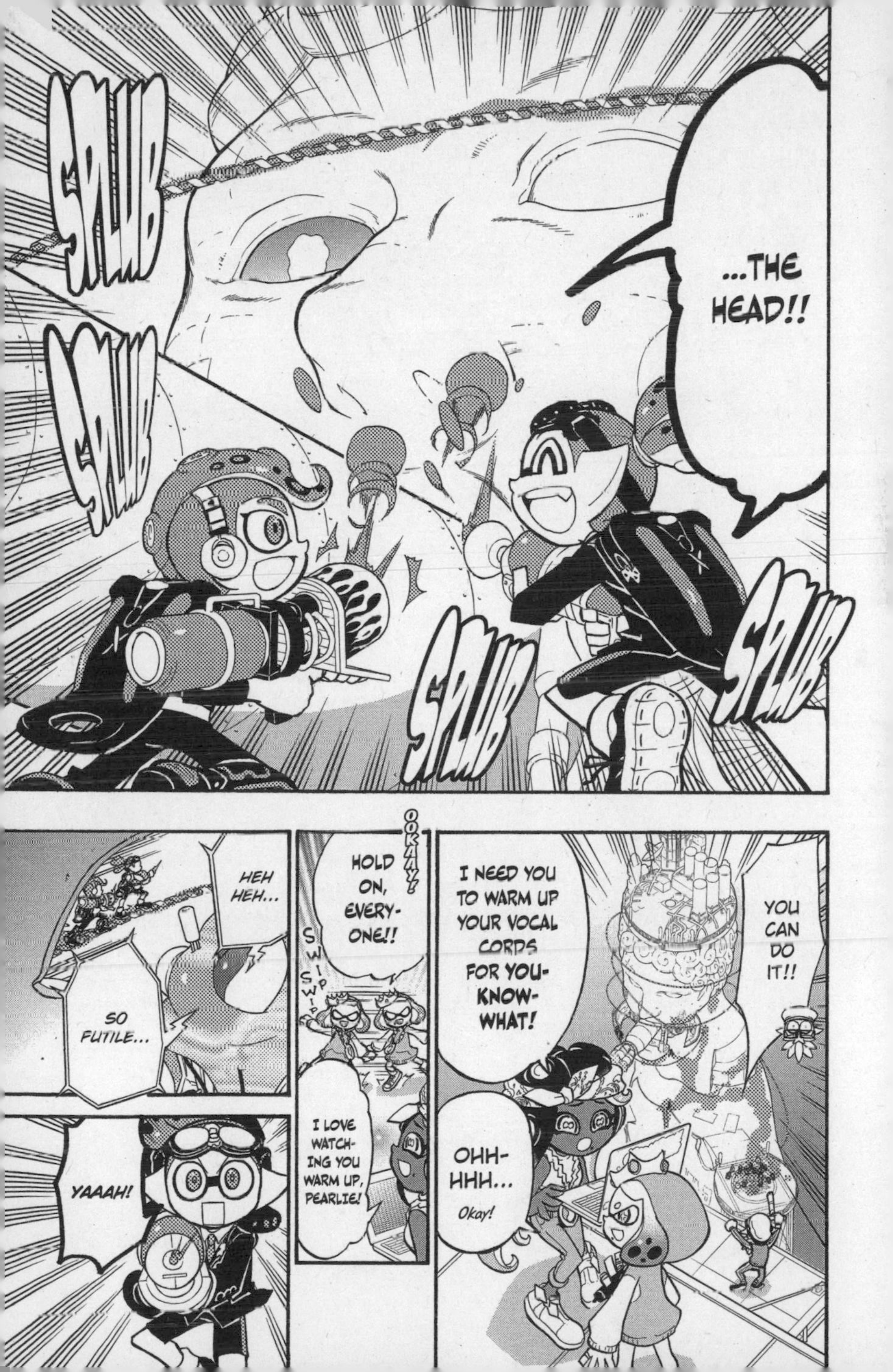

...THE HEAD!!
SPLUB
SPLUB
SPLUB
SPLUB
YOU CAN DO IT!!
I NEED YOU TO WARM UP YOUR VOCAL CORDS FOR YOU-KNOW-WHAT!
OHH-HHH...
Okay!
HOLD ON, EVERY-ONE!!
OOKAAY!
SWIP SWIP
I LOVE WATCHING YOU WARM UP, PEARLIE!
HEH HEH...
SO FUTILE...
YAAAH!

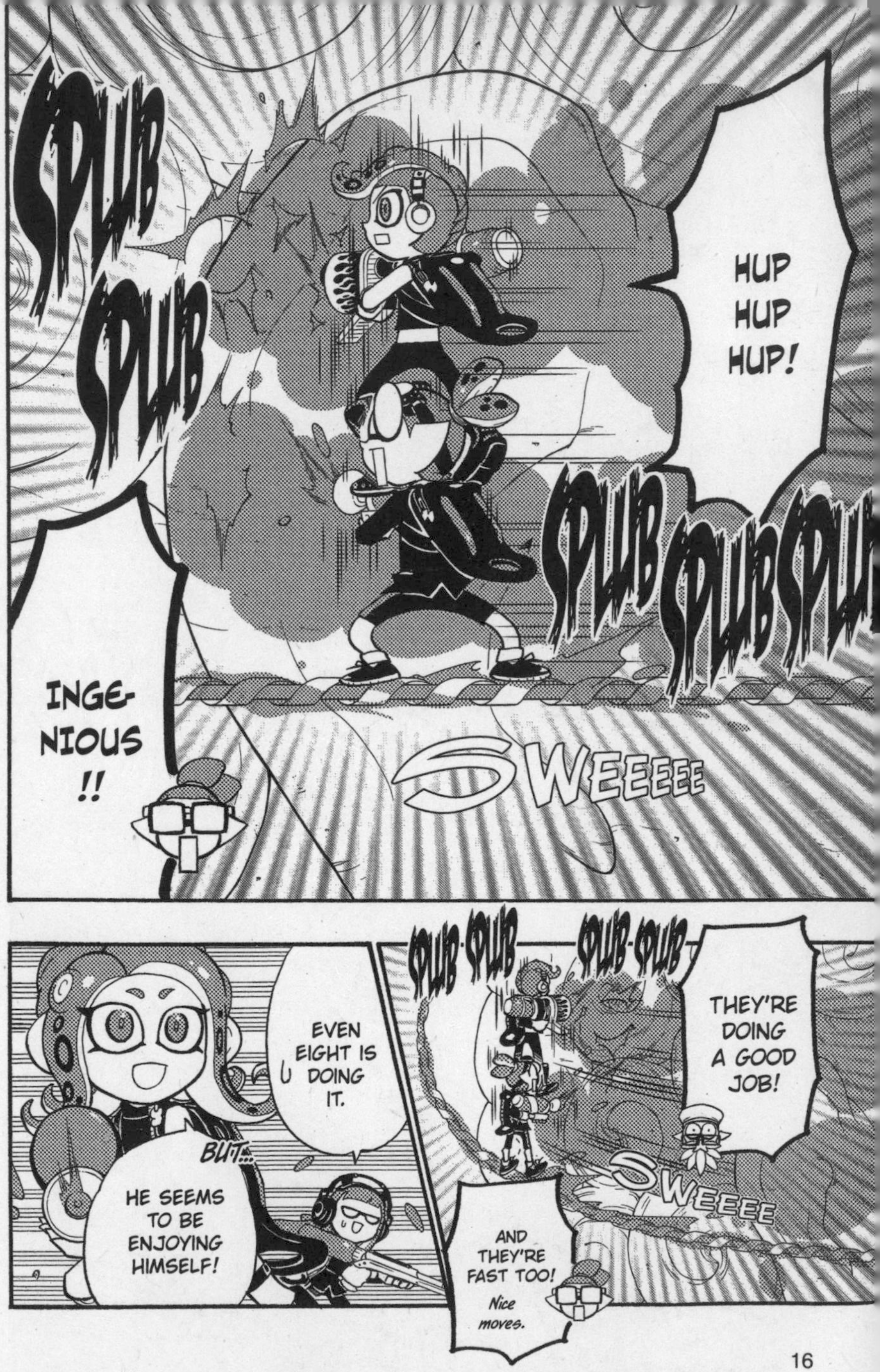
HUP HUP HUP!
SPLUB SPLUB
SPLUB SPLUB SPLUB
INGE-NIOUS!!
SWEEEEE
SPLUB-SPLUB
SPLUB-SPLUB
THEY'RE DOING A GOOD JOB!
SWEEEE
AND THEY'RE FAST TOO!
Nice moves.
EVEN EIGHT IS DOING IT.
BUT...
HE SEEMS TO BE ENJOYING HIMSELF!

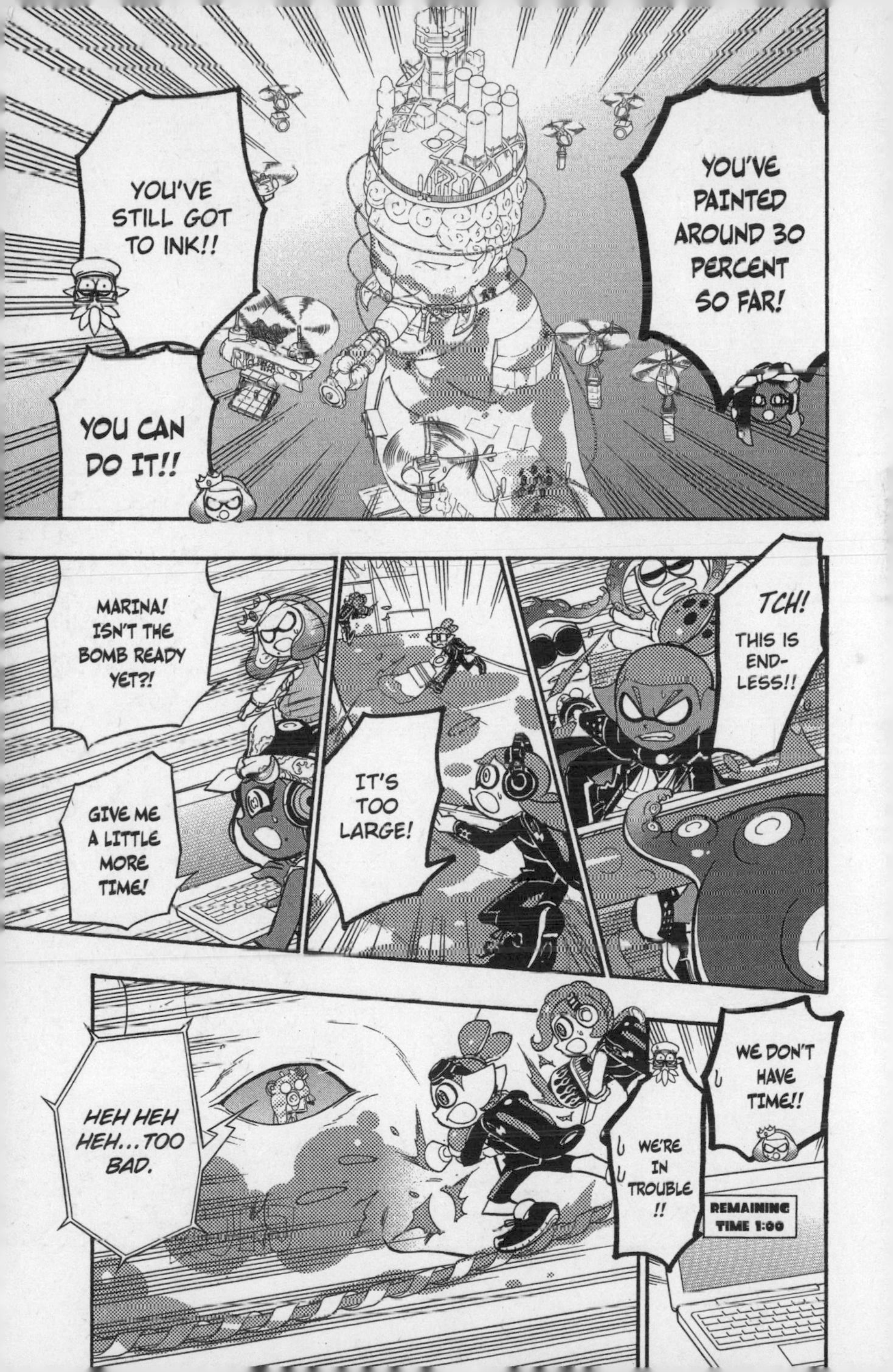

YOU'VE PAINTED AROUND 30 PERCENT SO FAR!
YOU'VE STILL GOT TO INK!!
YOU CAN DO IT!!
TCH!
THIS IS END-LESS!!
IT'S TOO LARGE!
MARINA! ISN'T THE BOMB READY YET?!
GIVE ME A LITTLE MORE TIME!
WE DON'T HAVE TIME!!
REMAINING TIME 1:00
WE'RE IN TROUBLE!!
HEH HEH HEH...TOO BAD.

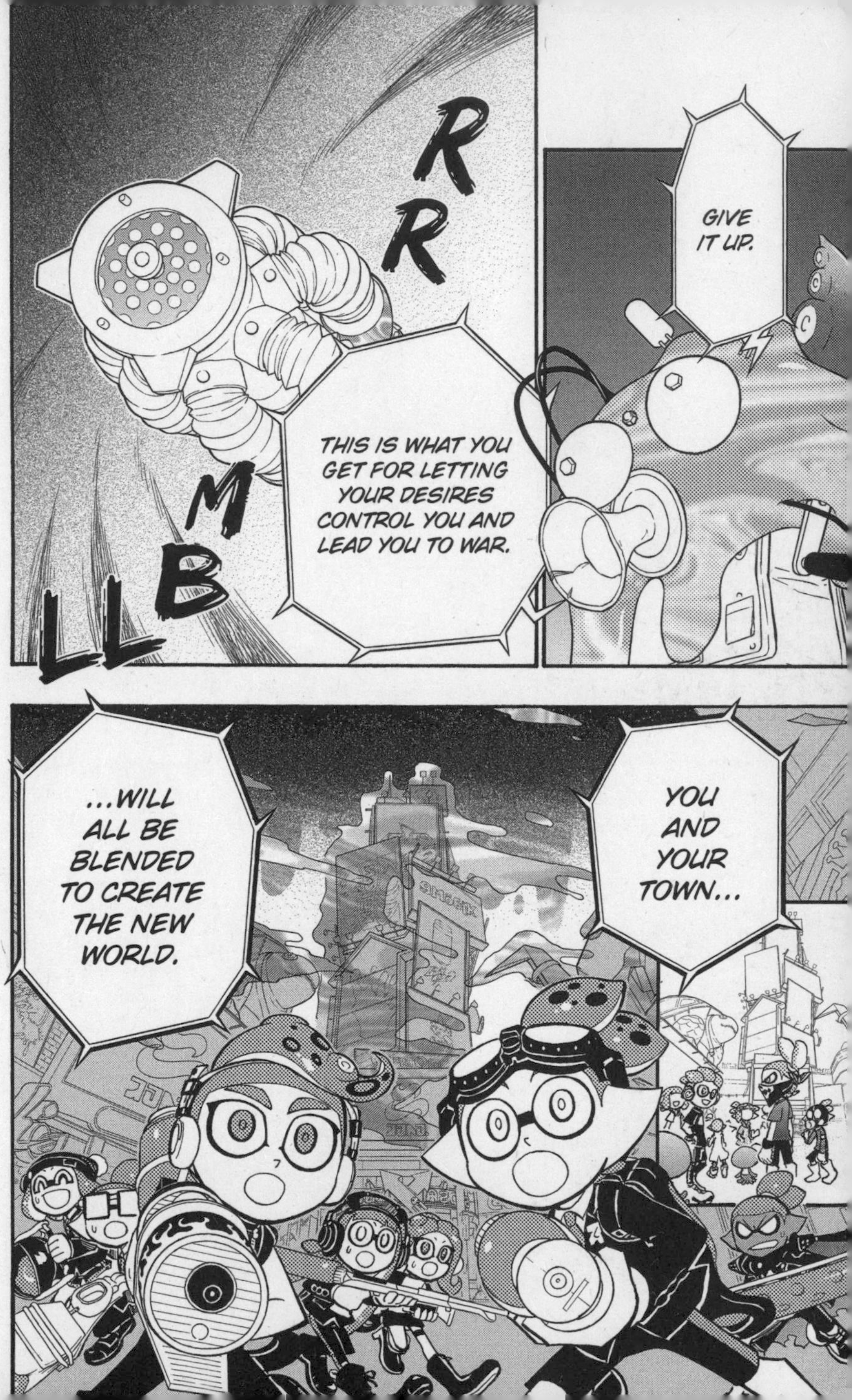
GIVE IT UP.
THIS IS WHAT YOU GET FOR LETTING YOUR DESIRES CONTROL YOU AND LEAD YOU TO WAR.
RRMBLL
YOU AND YOUR TOWN...
...WILL ALL BE BLENDED TO CREATE THE NEW WORLD.

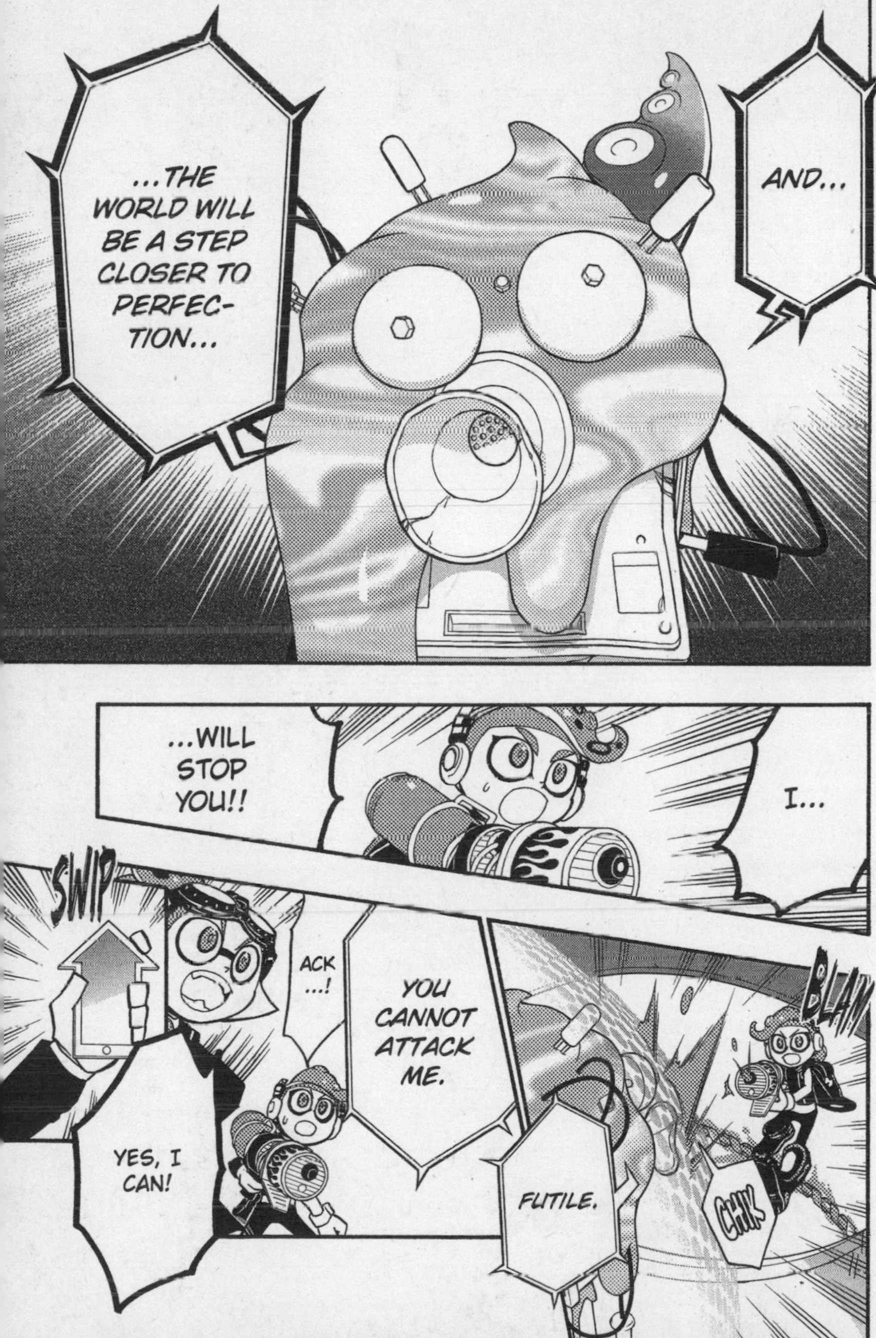
AND...
...THE WORLD WILL BE A STEP CLOSER TO PERFECTION...
I...
...WILL STOP YOU!!
BLAM
CHIK
FUTILE.
YOU CANNOT ATTACK ME.
ACK ...!
SWIP
YES, I CAN!

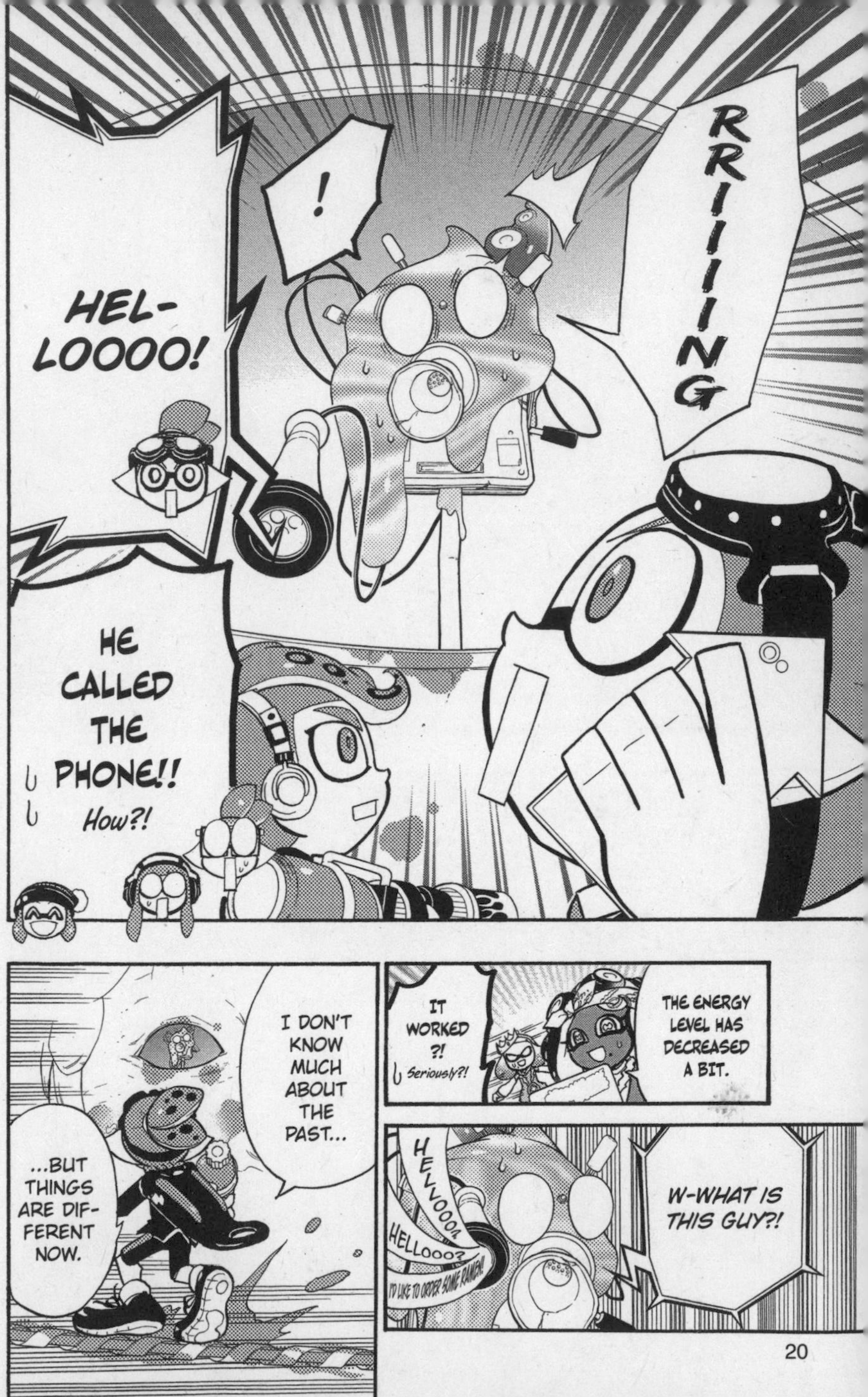
RRIIIING
!
HEL-LOOOO!
HE CALLED THE PHONE!!
How?!
THE ENERGY LEVEL HAS DECREASED A BIT.
IT WORKED?!
Seriously?!
W-WHAT IS THIS GUY?!
HELLOOOO
HELLOOO?
I'D LIKE TO ORDER SOME RAMEN!
I DON'T KNOW MUCH ABOUT THE PAST...
...BUT THINGS ARE DIFFERENT NOW.

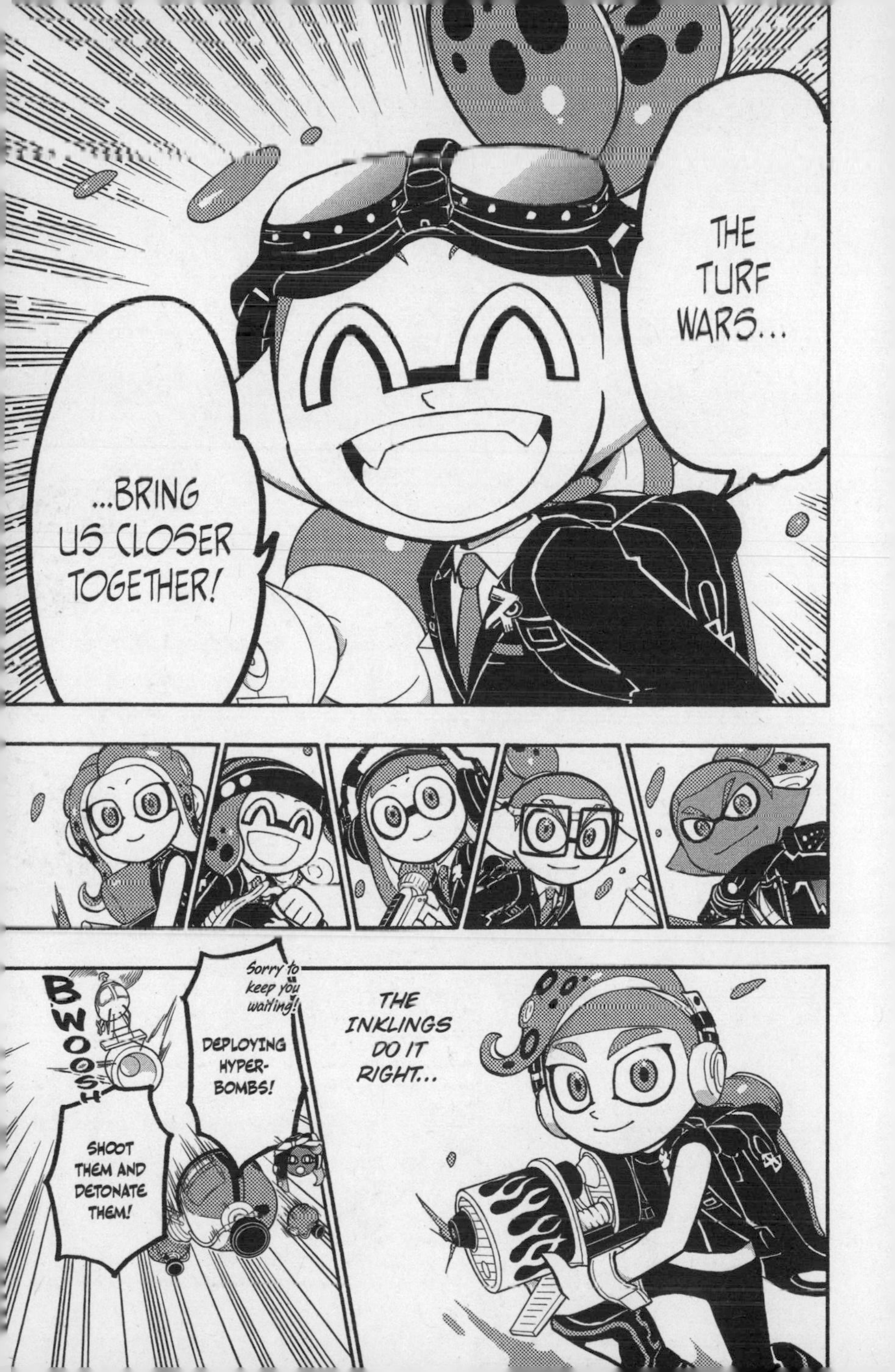
THE TURF WARS...
...BRING US CLOSER TOGETHER!
THE INKLINGS DO IT RIGHT...
Sorry to keep you waiting!
DEPLOYING HYPER-BOMBS!
BWOOSH
SHOOT THEM AND DETONATE THEM!

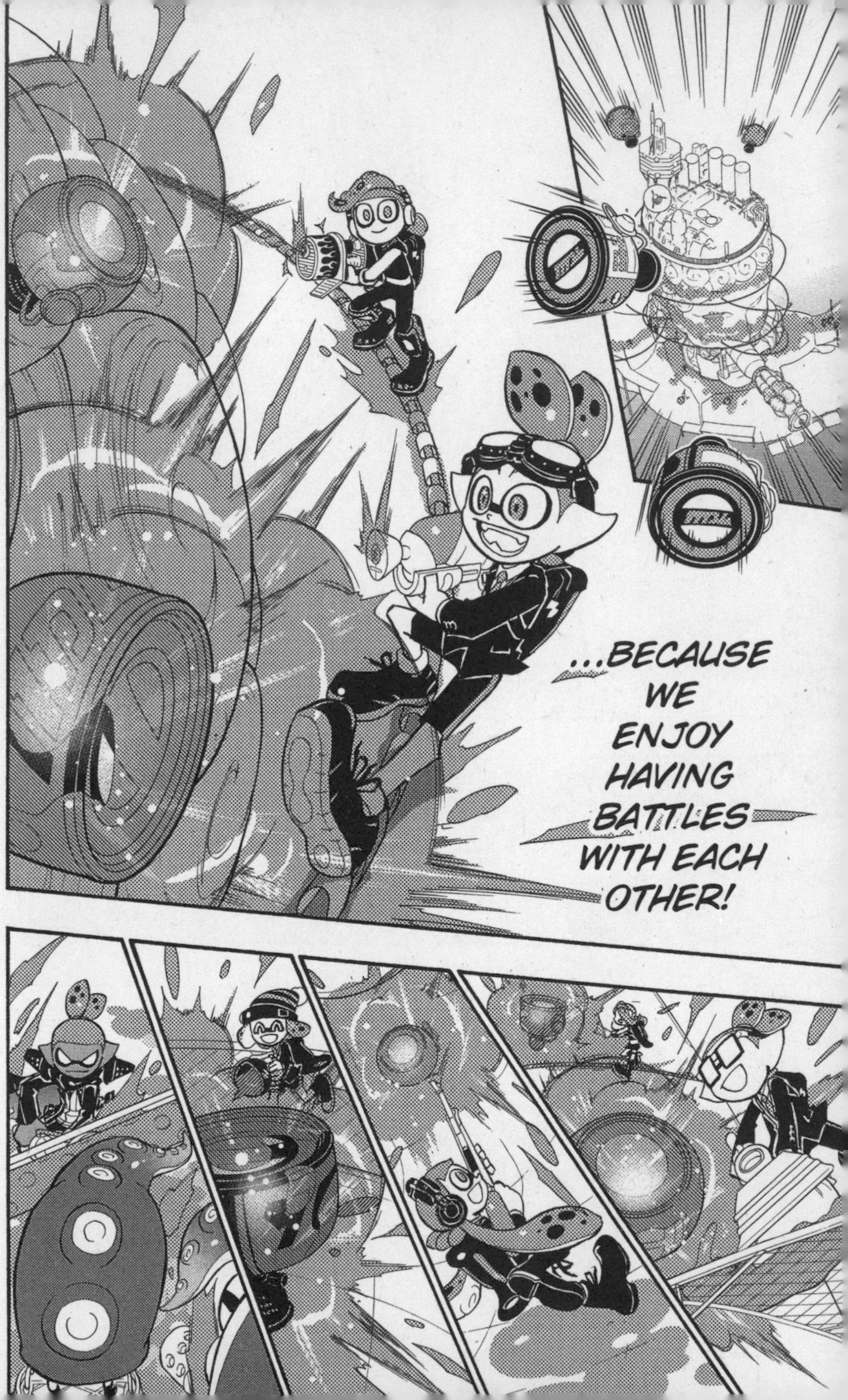
...BECAUSE WE ENJOY HAVING BATTLES WITH EACH OTHER!

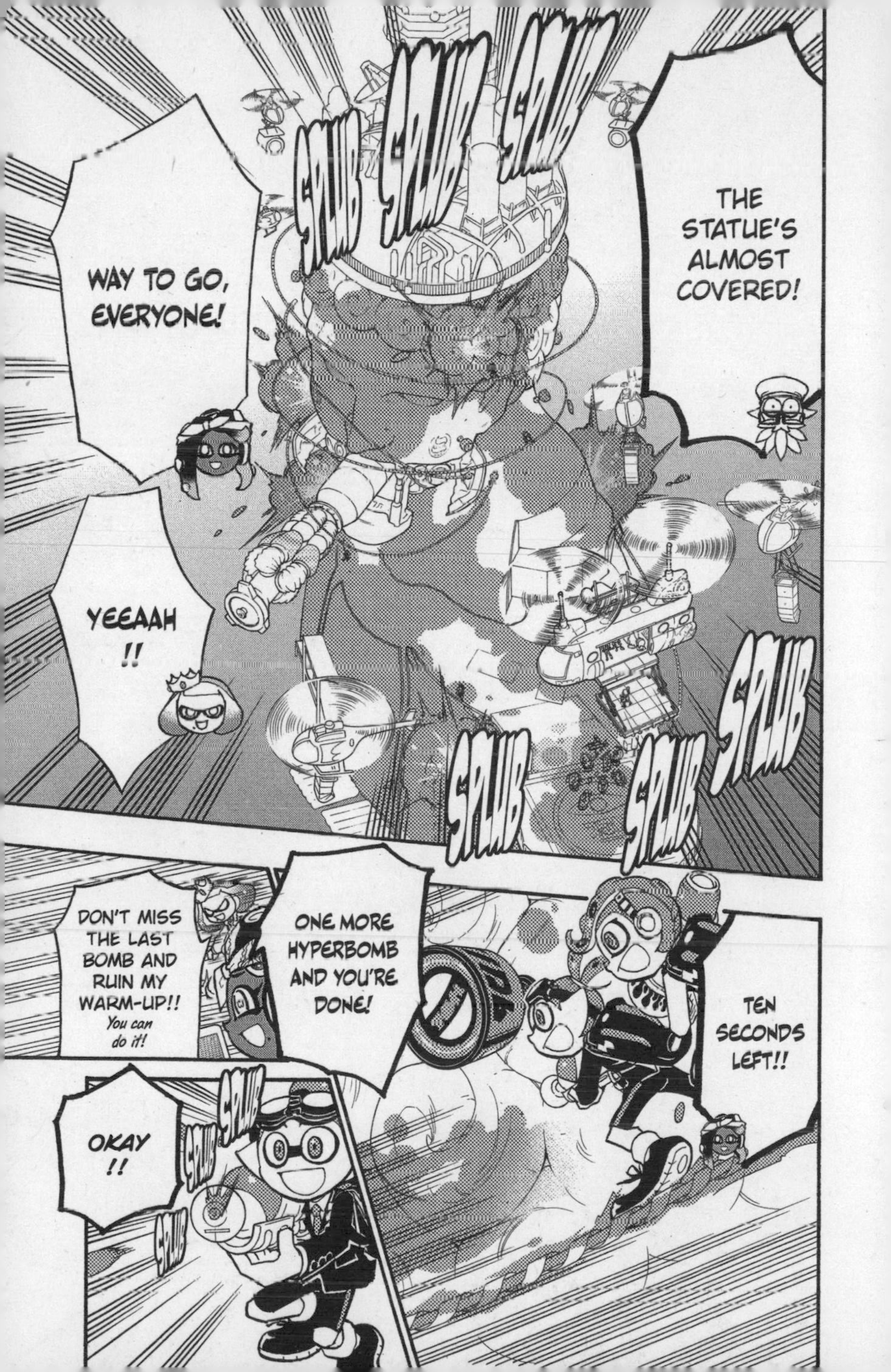
THE STATUE'S ALMOST COVERED!
SPLUB SPLUB SPLUB
WAY TO GO, EVERYONE!
YEEAAH !!
SPLUB SPLUB SPLUB
TEN SECONDS LEFT!!
ONE MORE HYPERBOMB AND YOU'RE DONE!
DON'T MISS THE LAST BOMB AND RUIN MY WARM-UP!!
You can do it!
OKAY !!
SPLUB SPLUB SPLUB

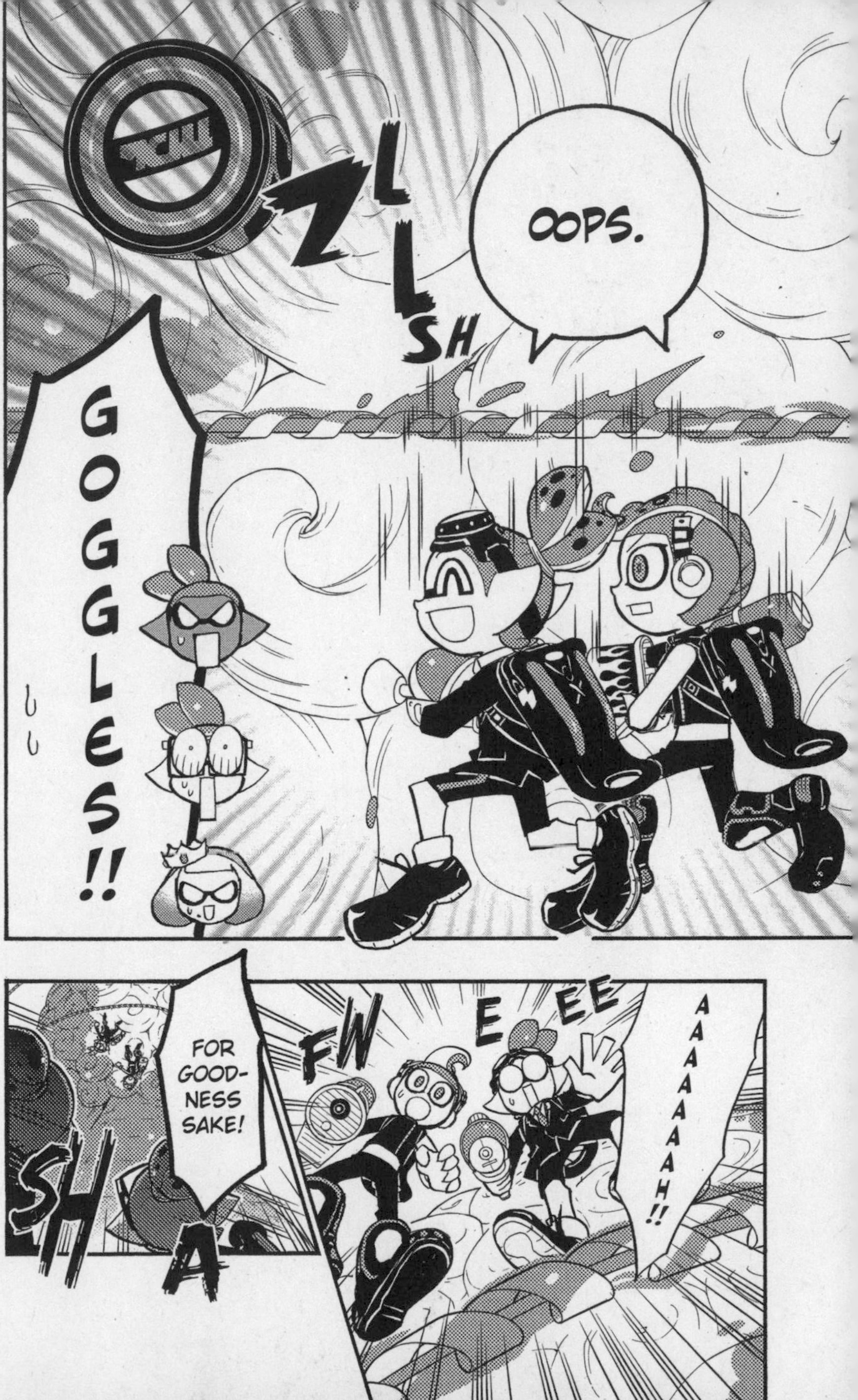

OOPS.
ZLLSH
GOGGLES!!
AAAAAAAAH!!
FWEEE
FOR GOOD-NESS SAKE!
SHA

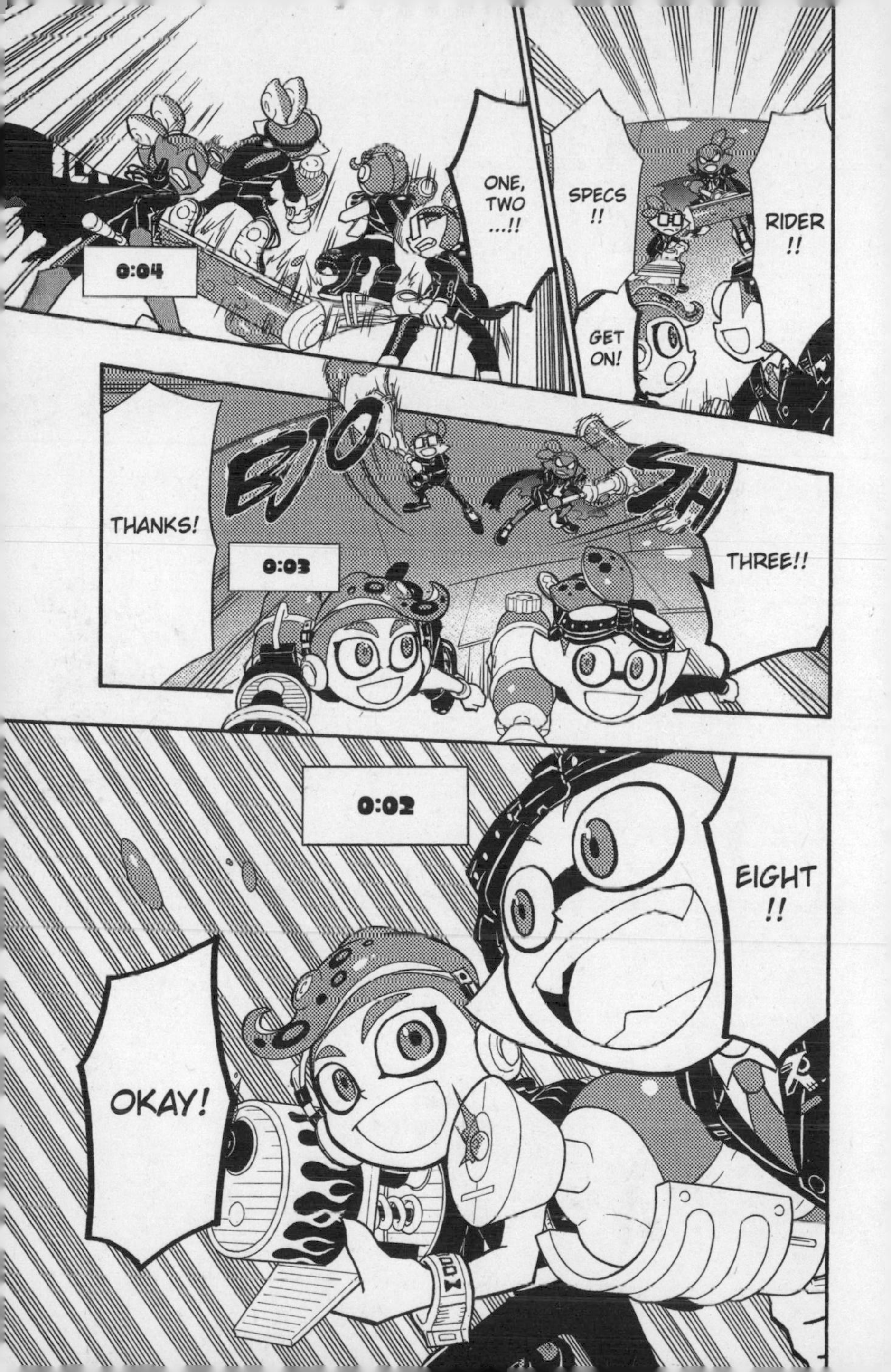
RIDER !!
SPECS !!
GET ON!
ONE, TWO ....!!
0:04
THREE!!
0:03
THANKS!
0:02
EIGHT !!
OKAY!

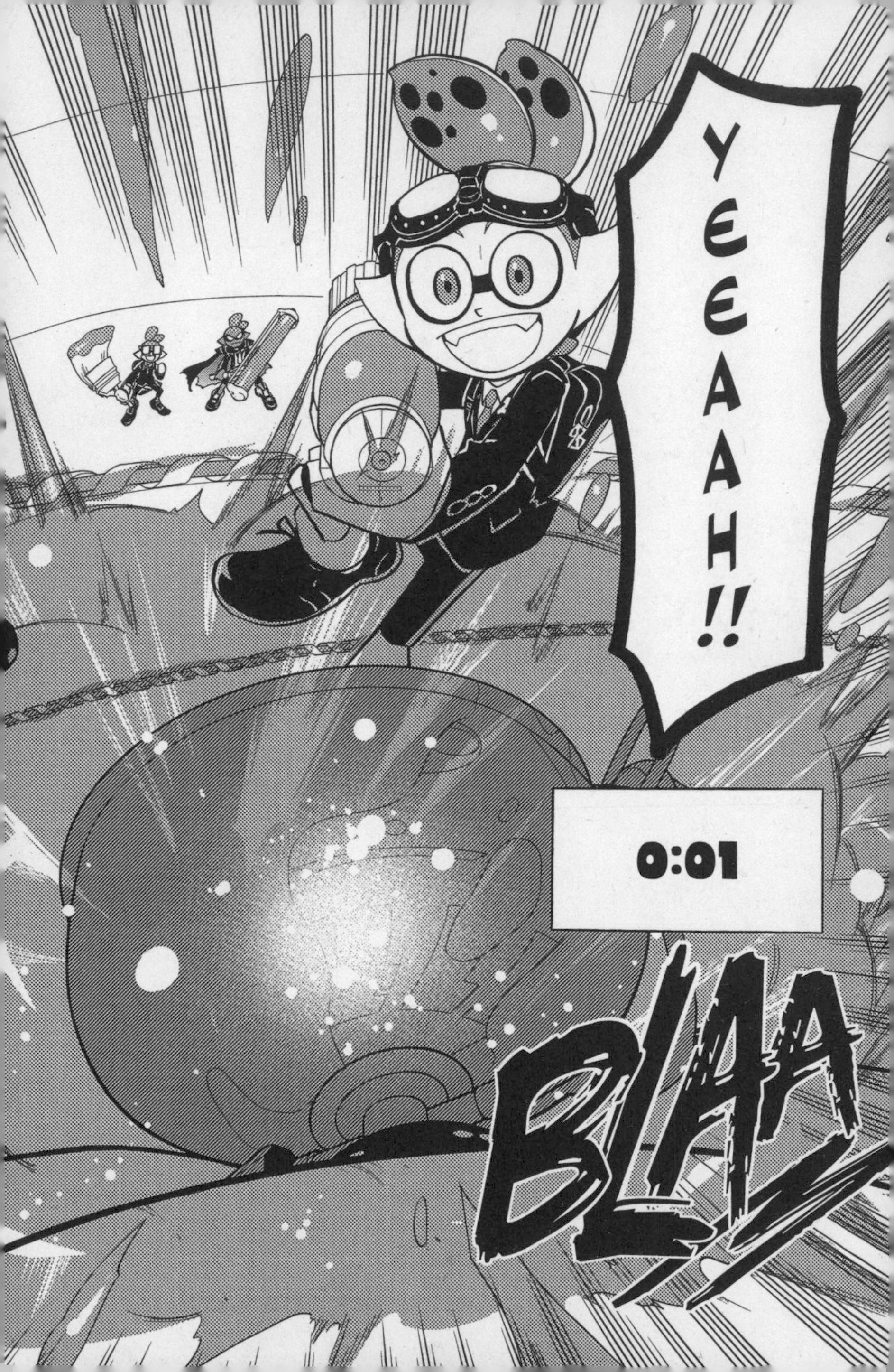
YEEAAH!!
0:01
BLAM

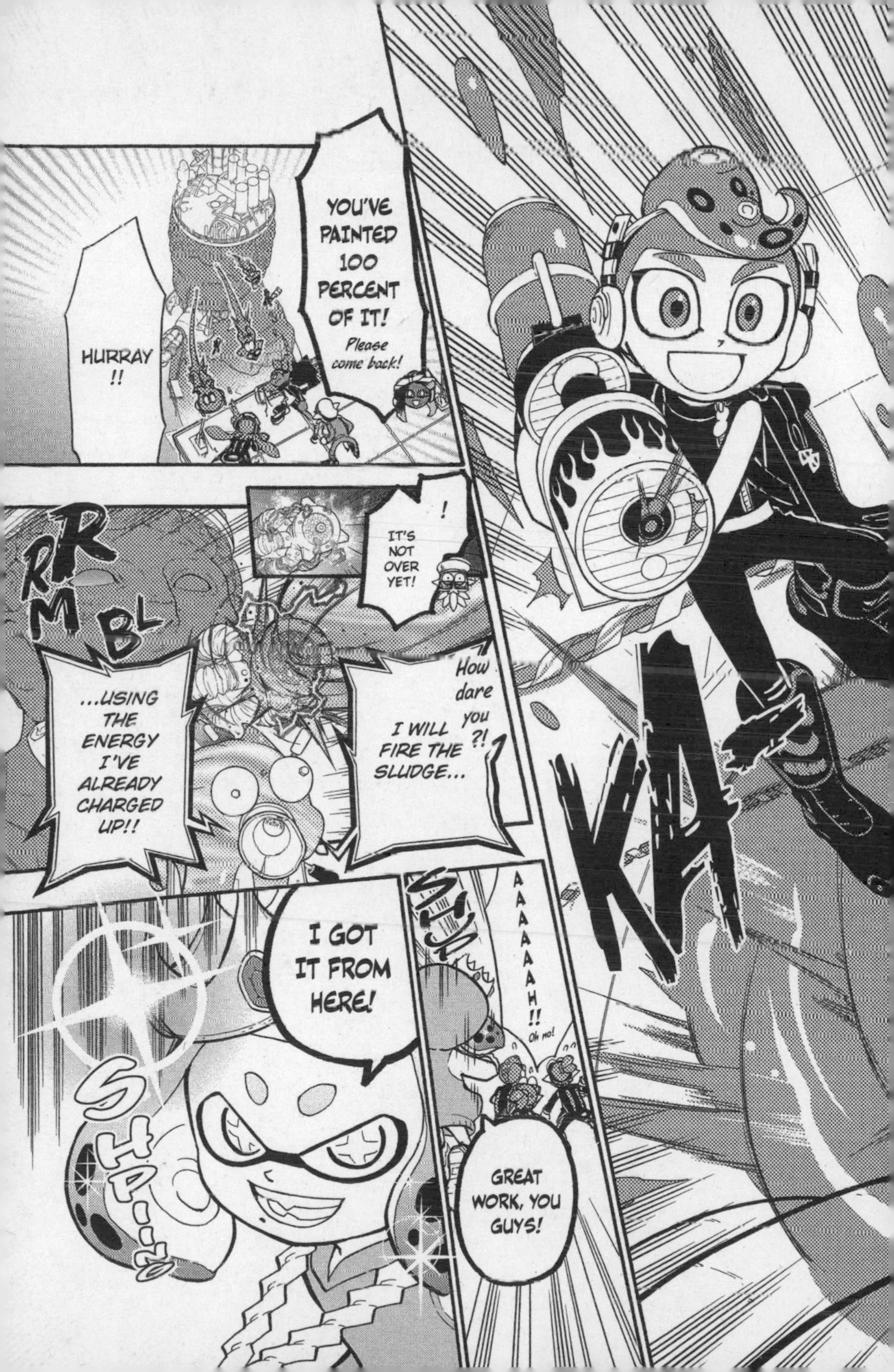
KA
YOU'VE PAINTED 100 PERCENT OF IT!
Please come back!
HURRAY!!
!
IT'S NOT OVER YET!
RRMBL
How dare you?!
I WILL FIRE THE SLUDGE...
...USING THE ENERGY I'VE ALREADY CHARGED UP!!
SHUN
I GOT IT FROM HERE!
SHHP...
AAAAAAAH!!
Oh no!
GREAT WORK, YOU GUYS!

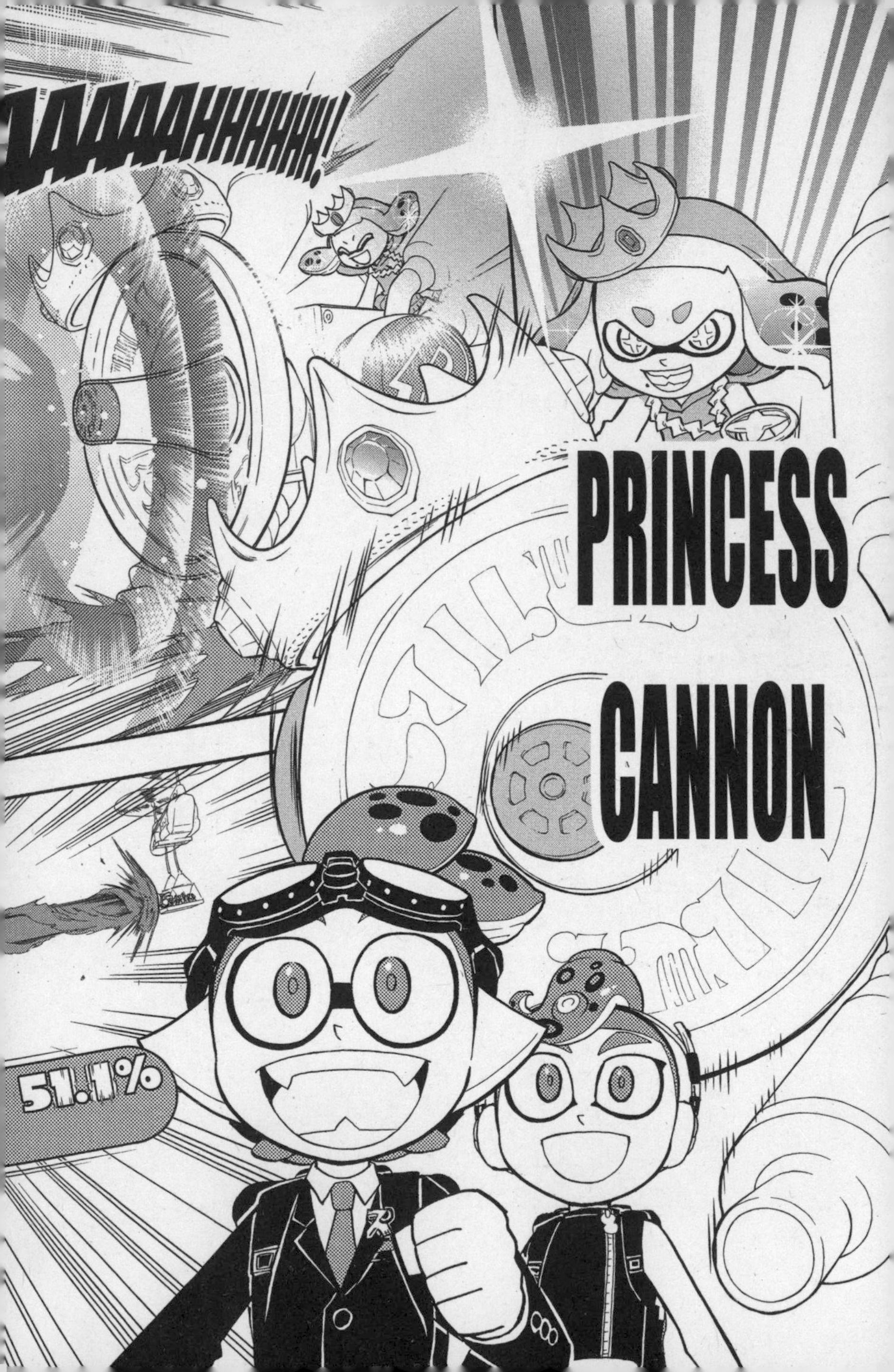
AAAAAHHHHH!!
PRINCESS CANNON
51.1%

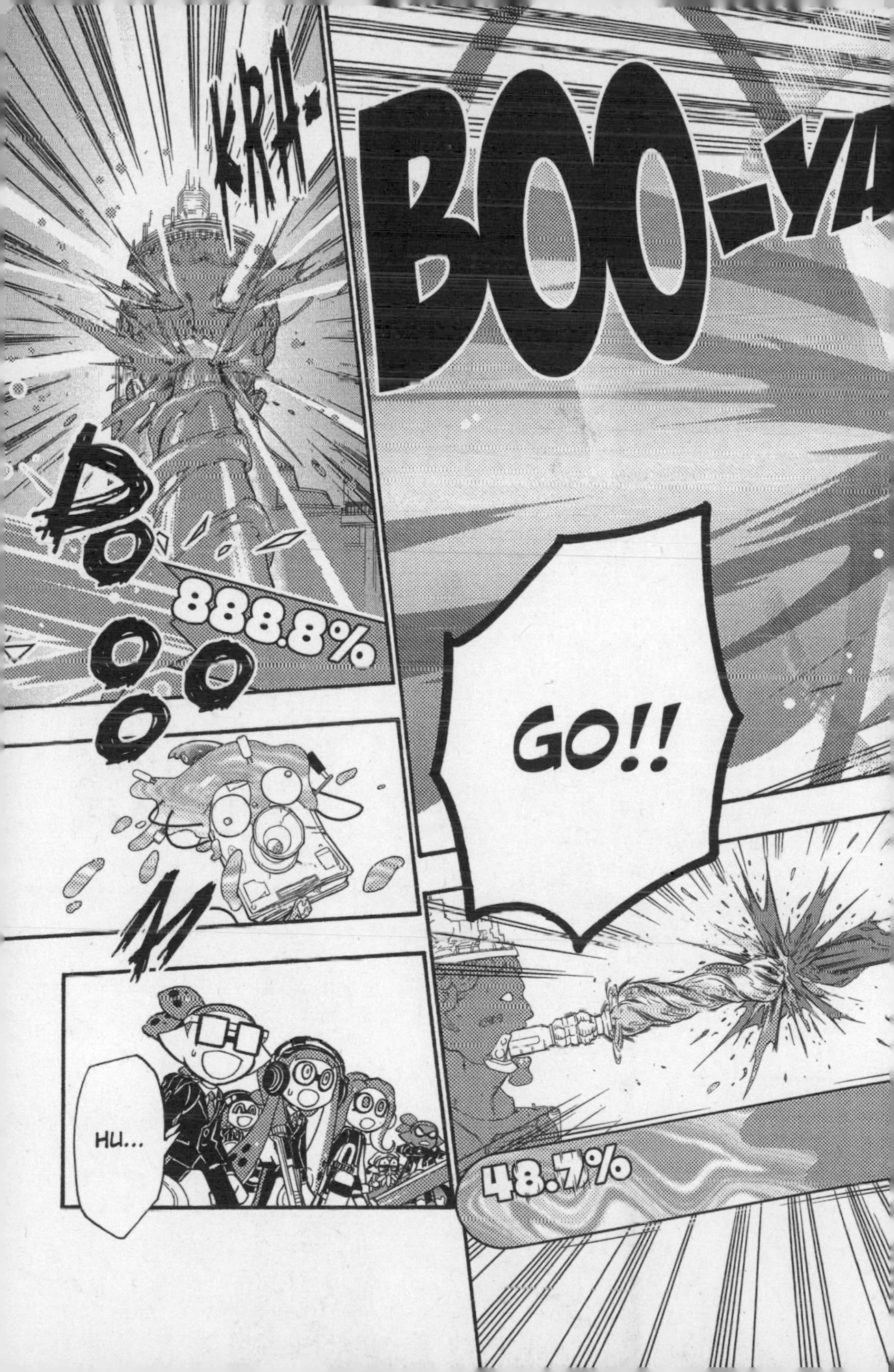

BOO-YA
GO!!
48.7%
KRA-
DOOOOM
888.8%
HU...

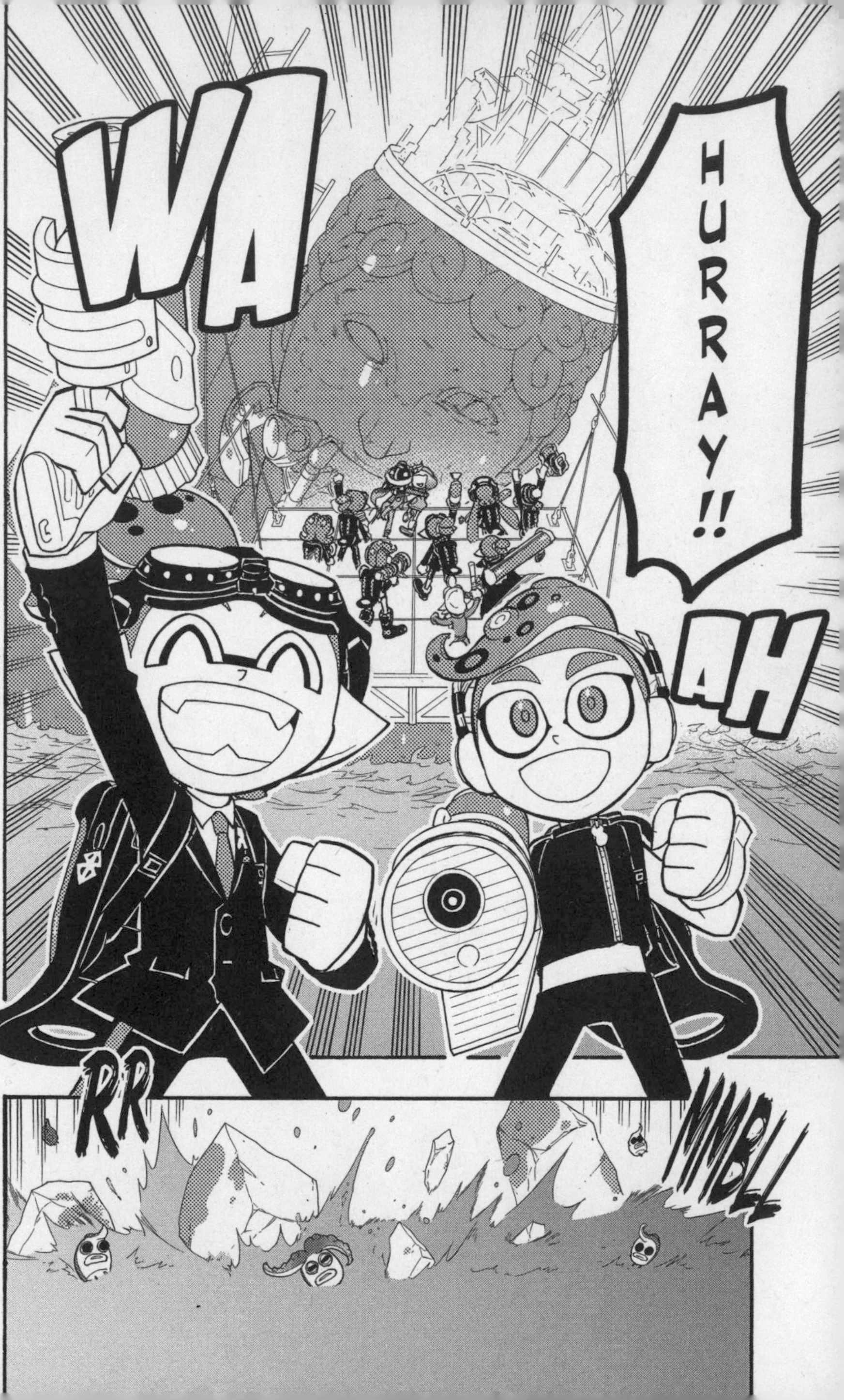
HURRAY!!
WA
AH
RR
MMBLE!

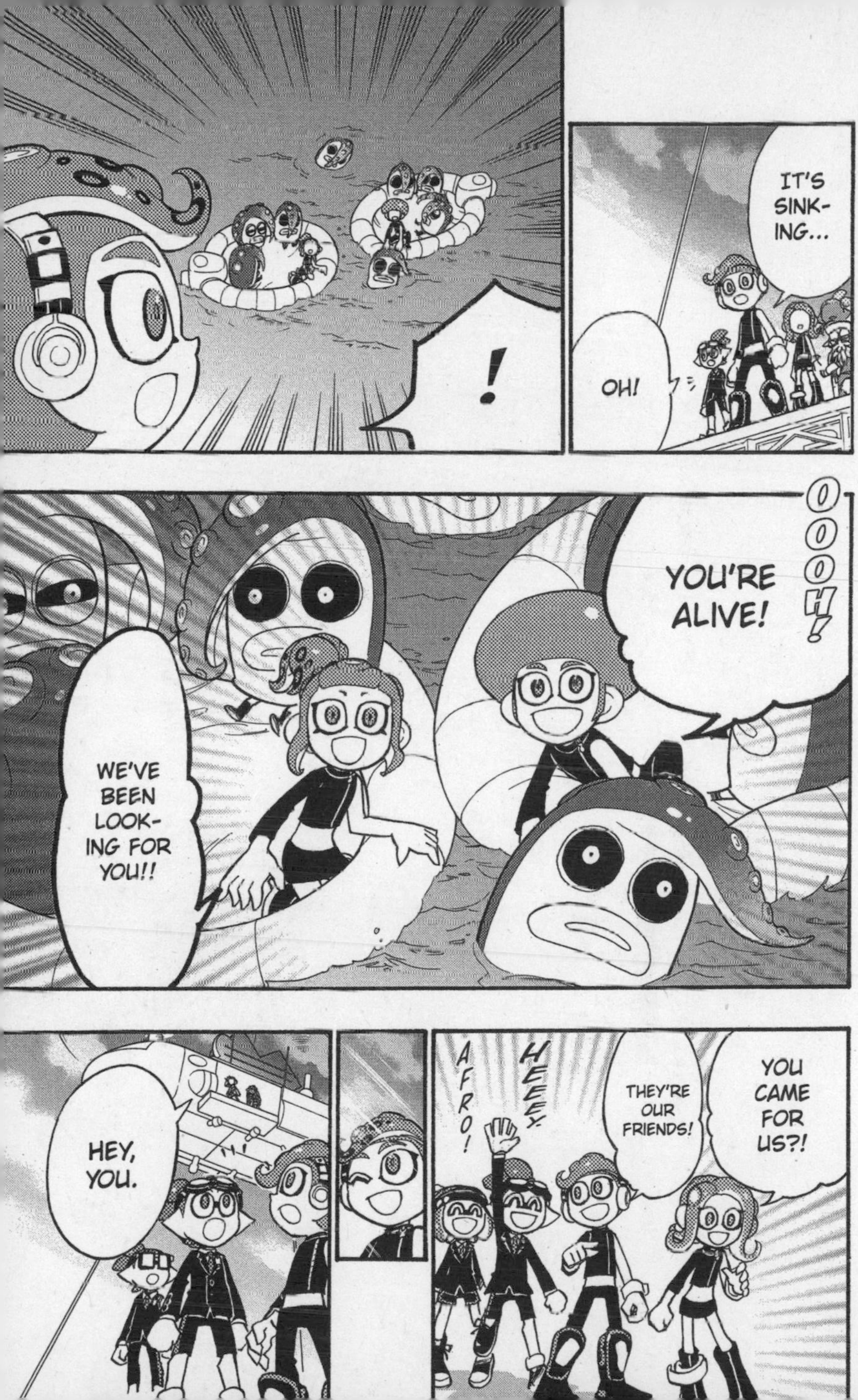
IT'S SINK-ING...
OH!
!
OOOOH!
YOU'RE ALIVE!
WE'VE BEEN LOOKING FOR YOU!!
YOU CAME FOR US?!
THEY'RE OUR FRIENDS!
HEEEY.
AFRO!
HEY, YOU.

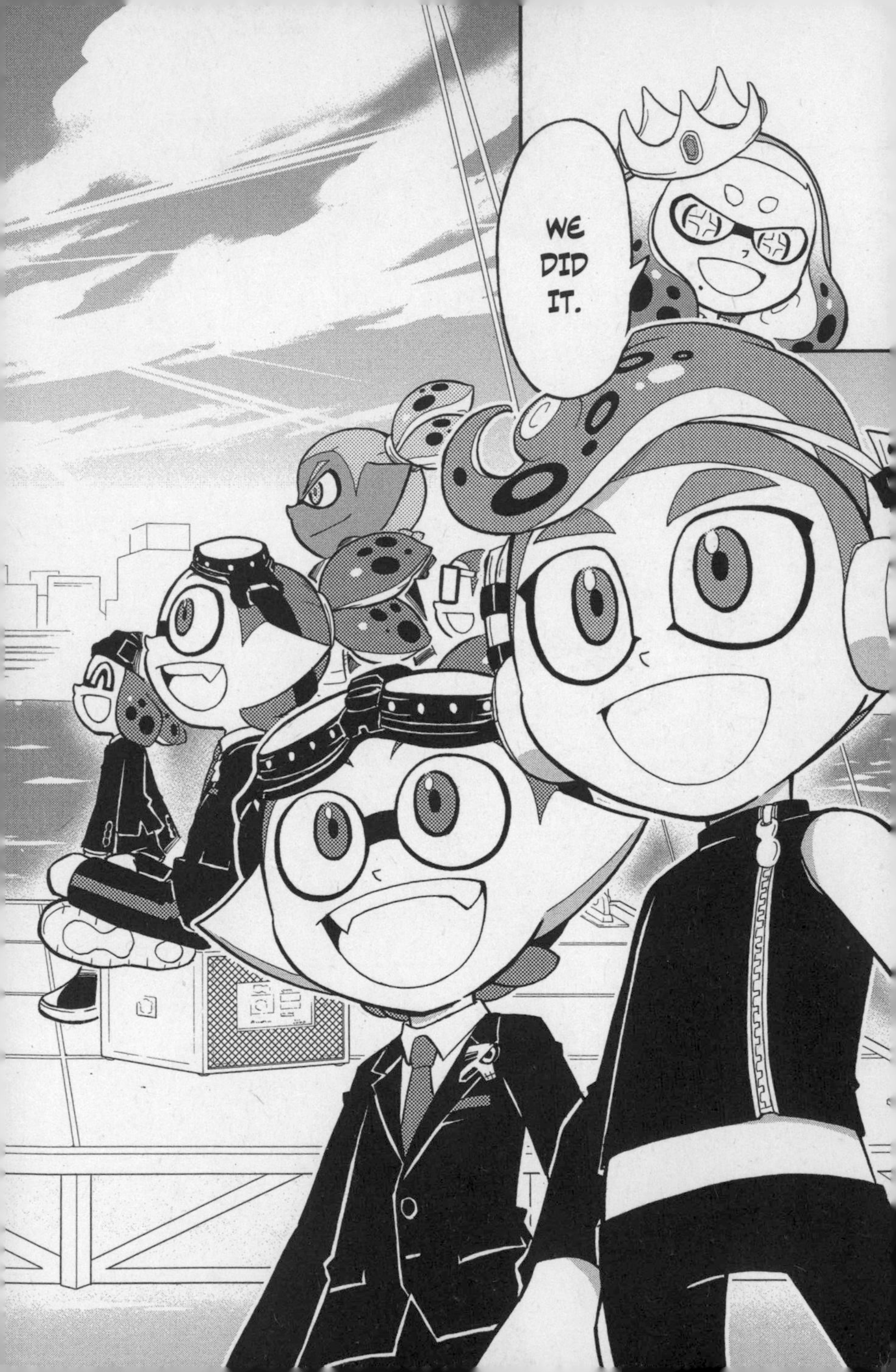
WE DID IT.

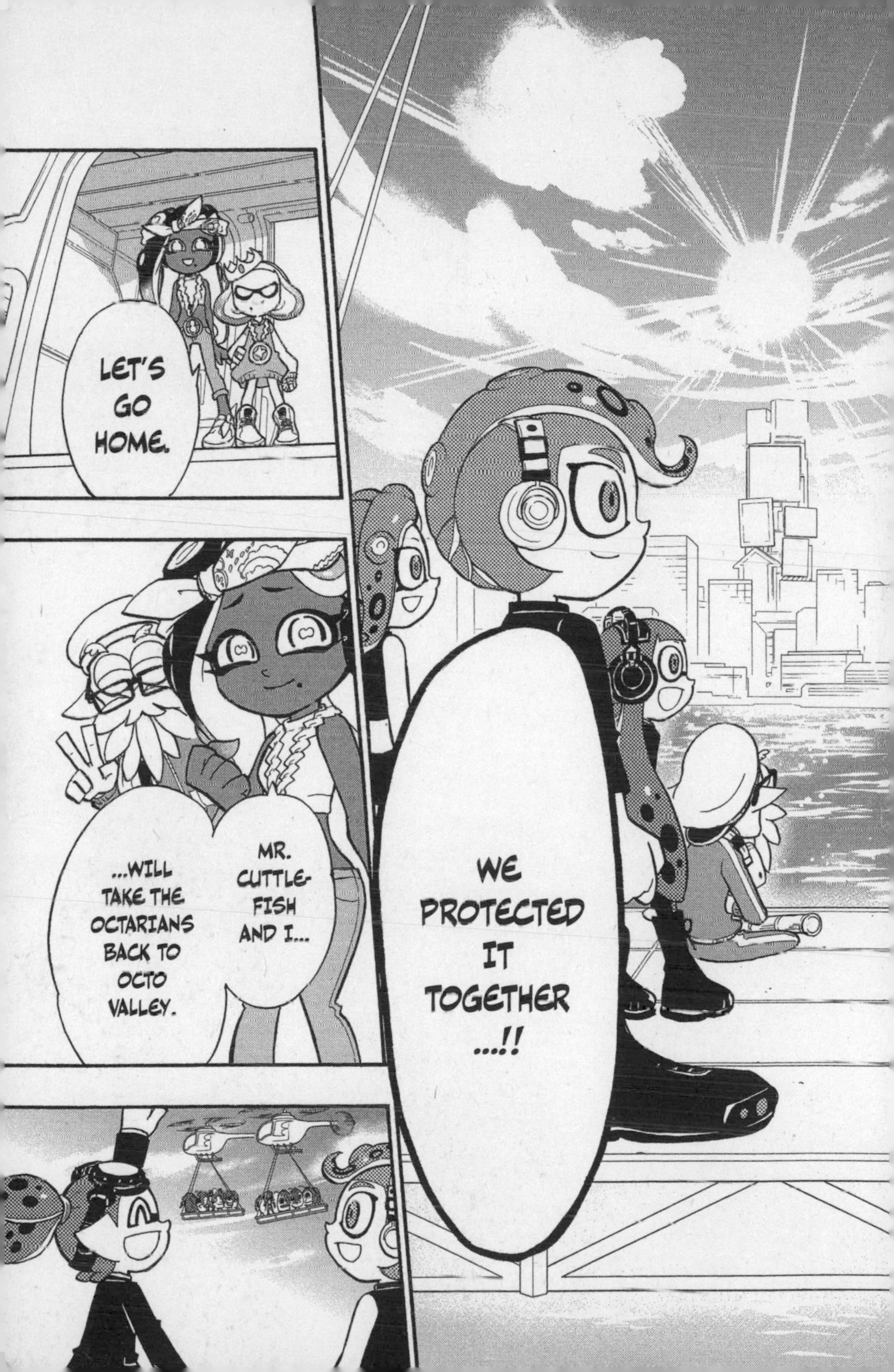
WE PROTECTED IT TOGETHER ...!!
LET'S GO HOME.
MR. CUTTLE-FISH AND I...
...WILL TAKE THE OCTARIANS BACK TO OCTO VALLEY.

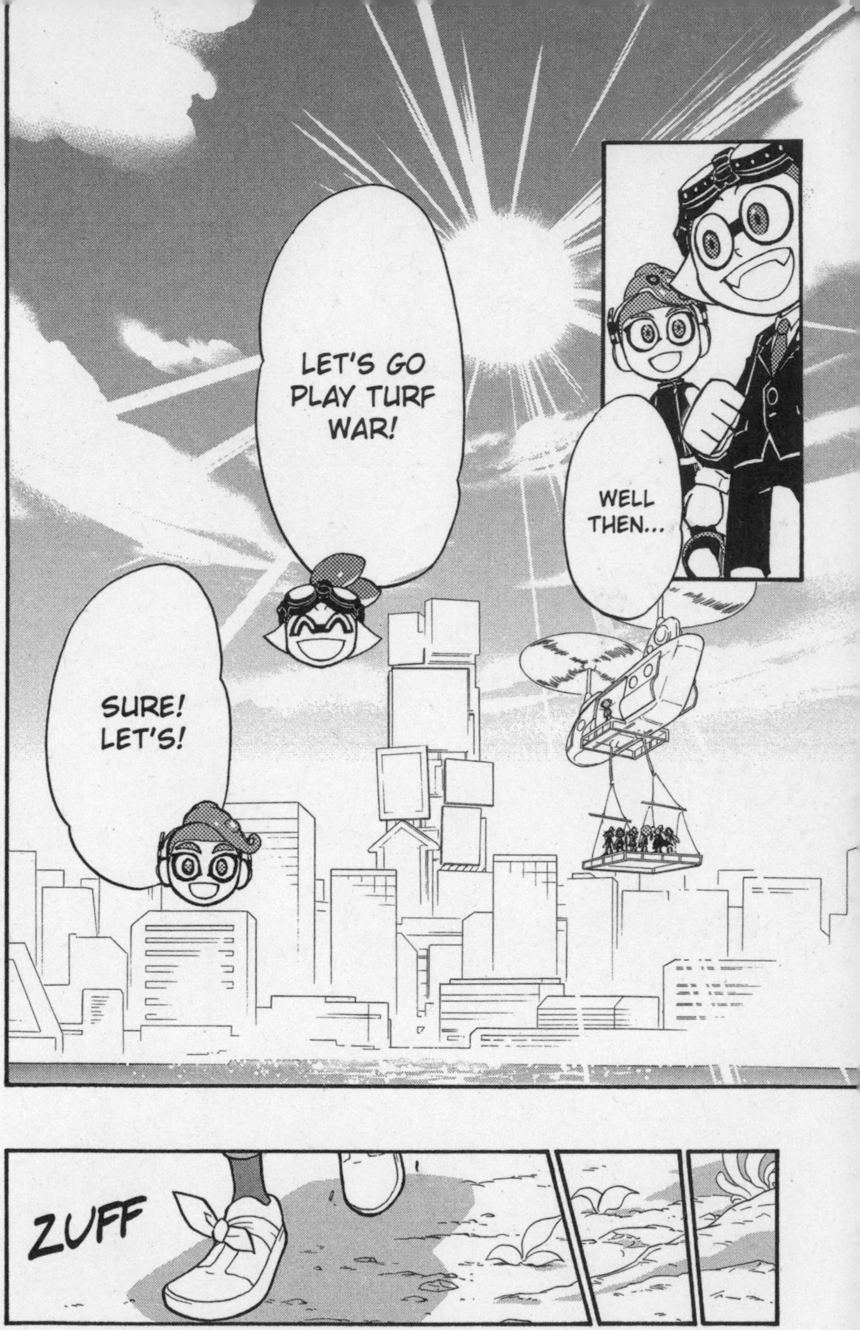
WELL THEN...
LET'S GO PLAY TURF WAR!
SURE! LET'S!
ZUFF

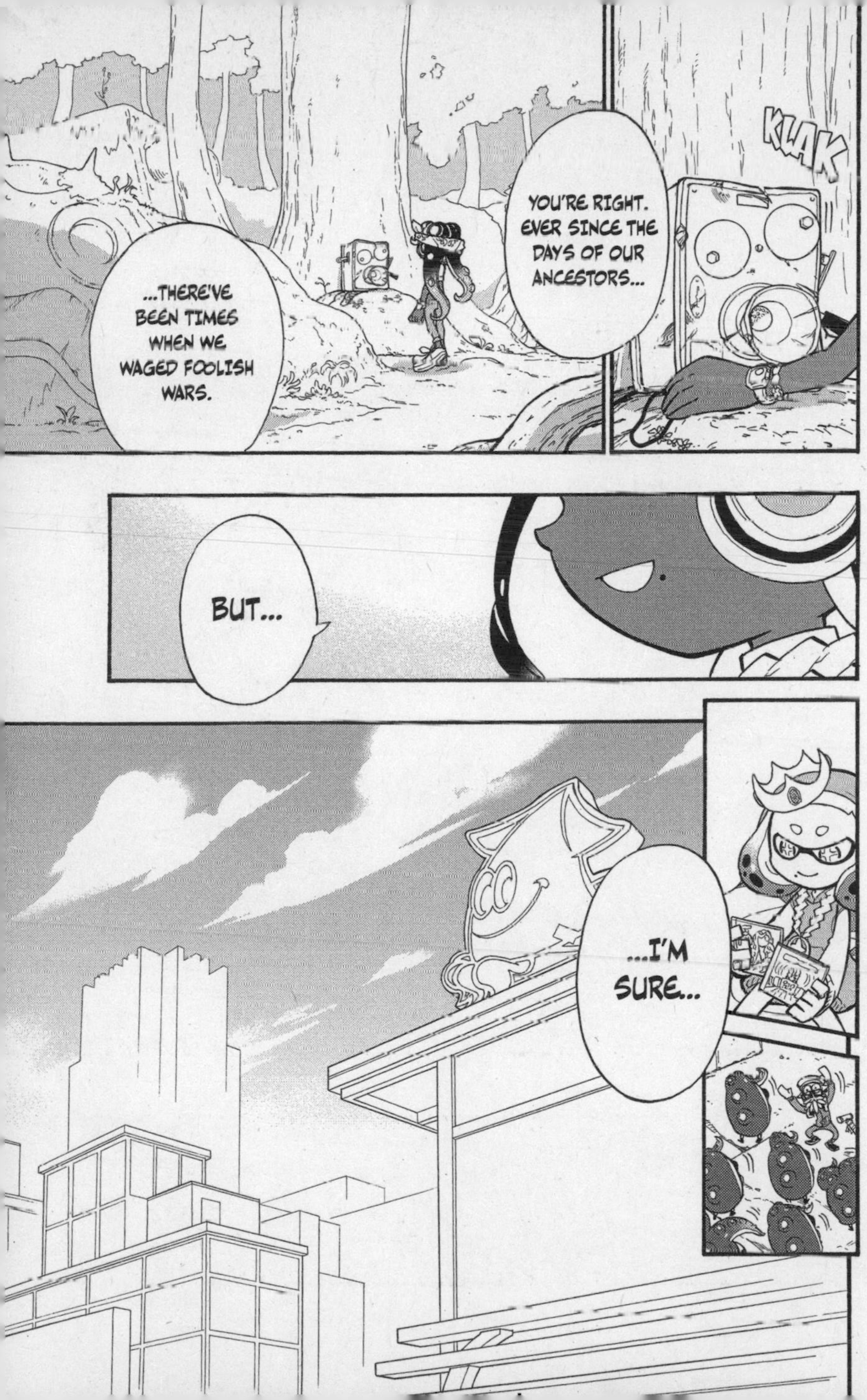
KLAK
YOU'RE RIGHT. EVER SINCE THE DAYS OF OUR ANCESTORS...
...THERE'VE BEEN TIMES WHEN WE WAGED FOOLISH WARS.
BUT...
...I'M SURE...

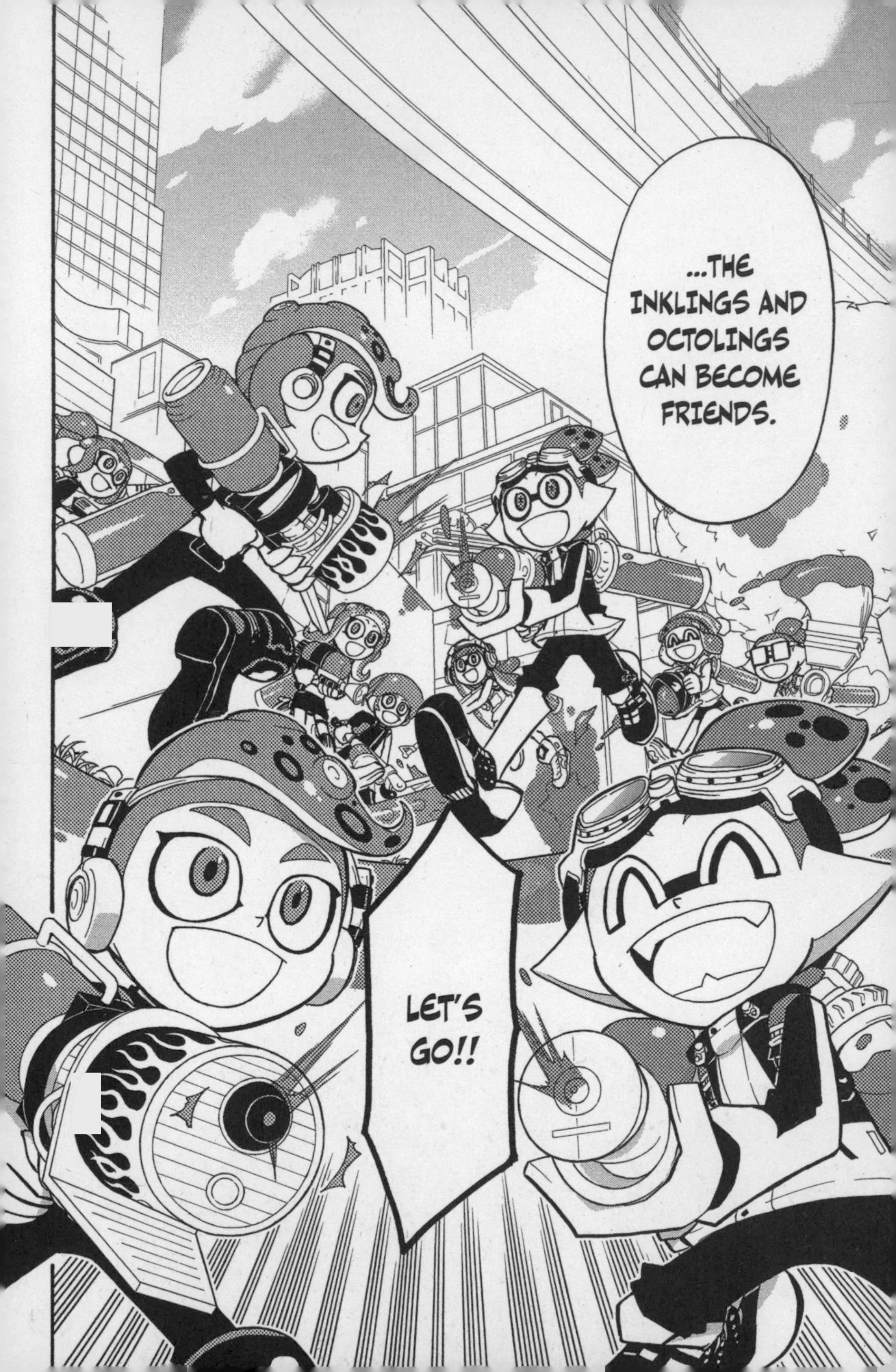
...THE INKLINGS AND OCTOLINGS CAN BECOME FRIENDS.
LET'S GO!!

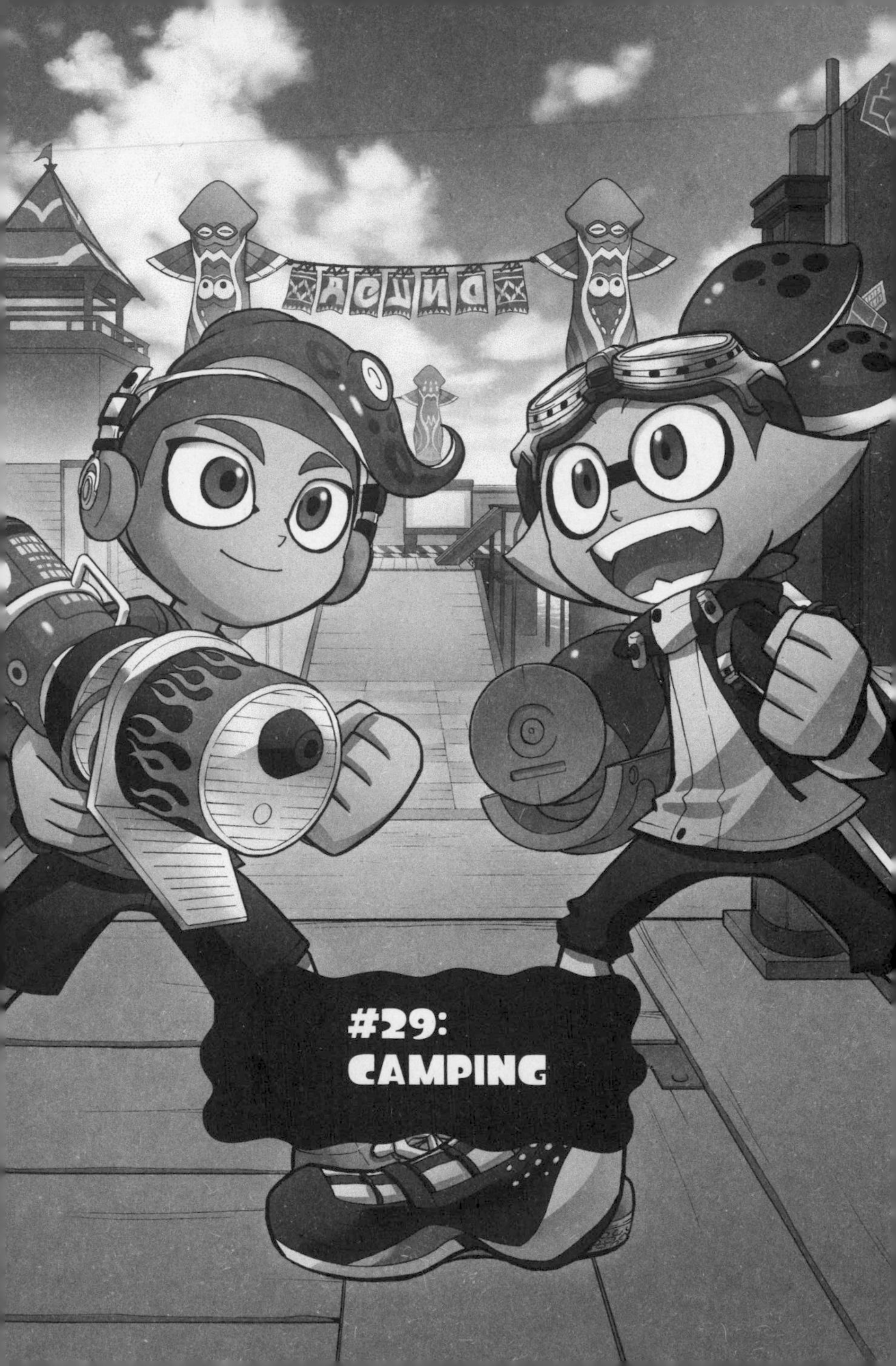
#29:
CAMPING

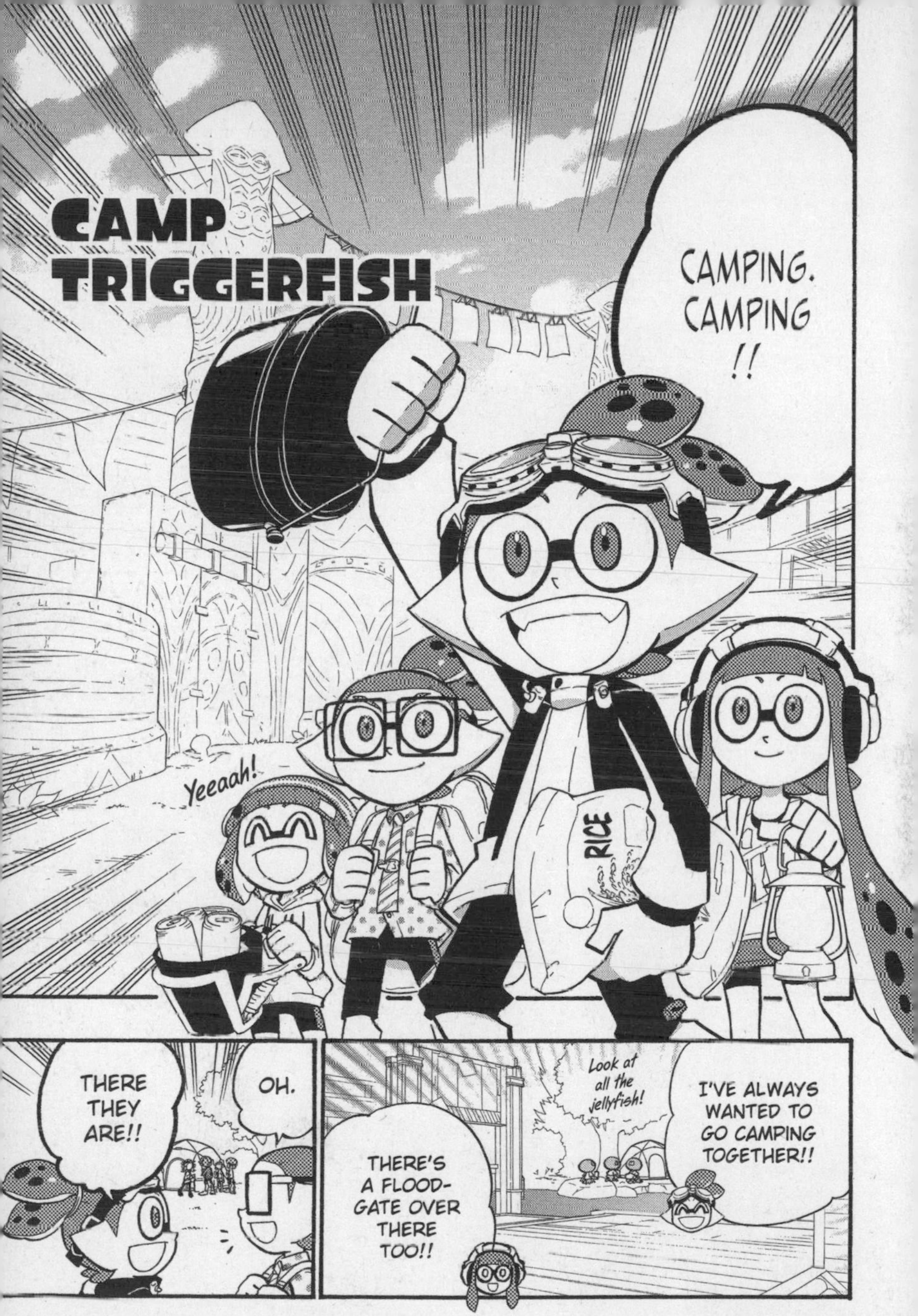
CAMPING. CAMPING !!
CAMP TRIGGERFISH
Yeeaah!
RICE
I'VE ALWAYS WANTED TO GO CAMPING TOGETHER!!
Look at all the jellyfish!
THERE'S A FLOOD-GATE OVER THERE TOO!!
OH.
THERE THEY ARE!!

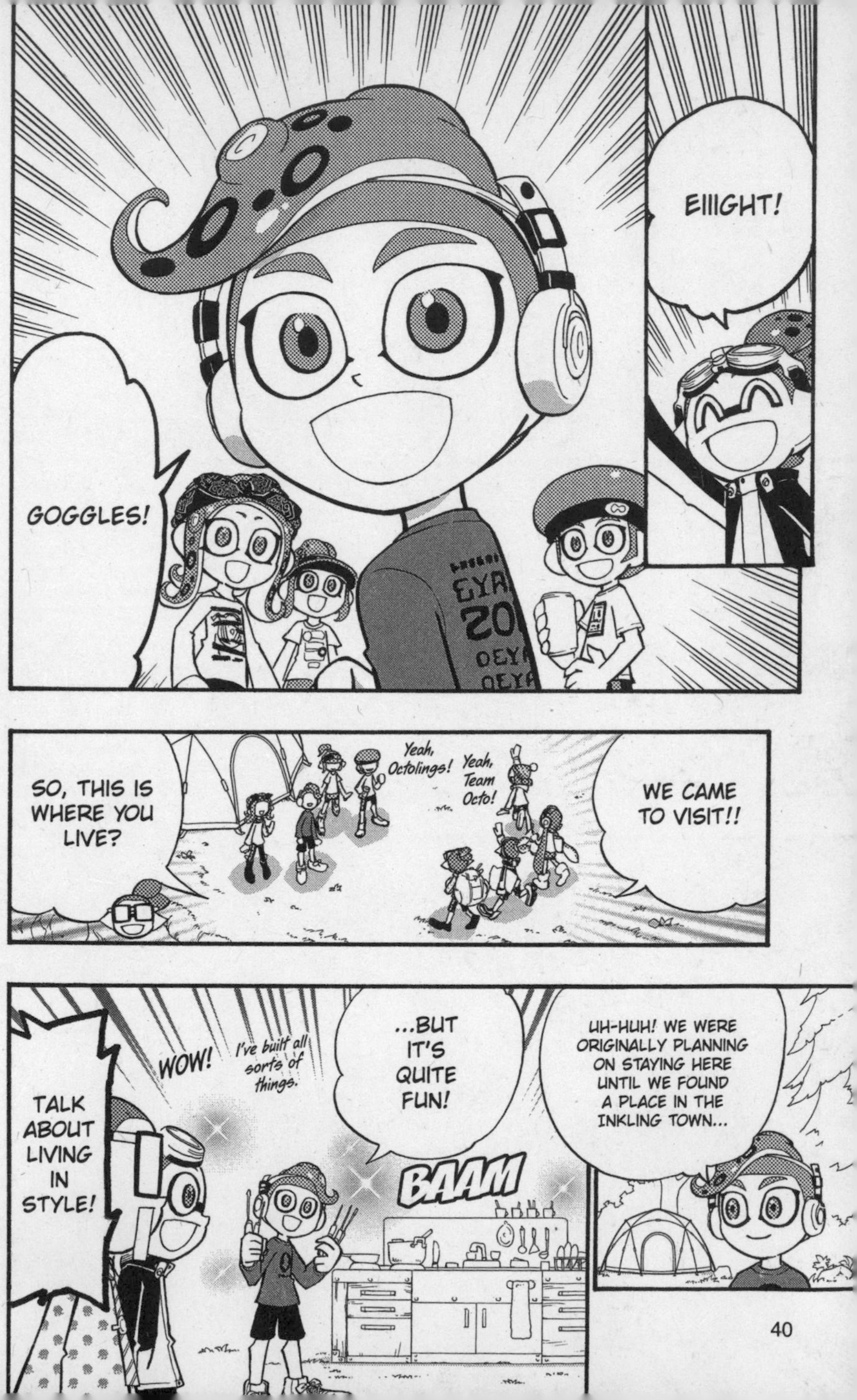
EIIIGHT!
GOGGLES!
WE CAME TO VISIT!!
Yeah, Team Octo!
Yeah, Octolings!
SO, THIS IS WHERE YOU LIVE?
UH-HUH! WE WERE ORIGINALLY PLANNING ON STAYING HERE UNTIL WE FOUND A PLACE IN THE INKLING TOWN...
...BUT IT'S QUITE FUN!
BAAM
I've built all sorts of things.
WOW!
TALK ABOUT LIVING IN STYLE!

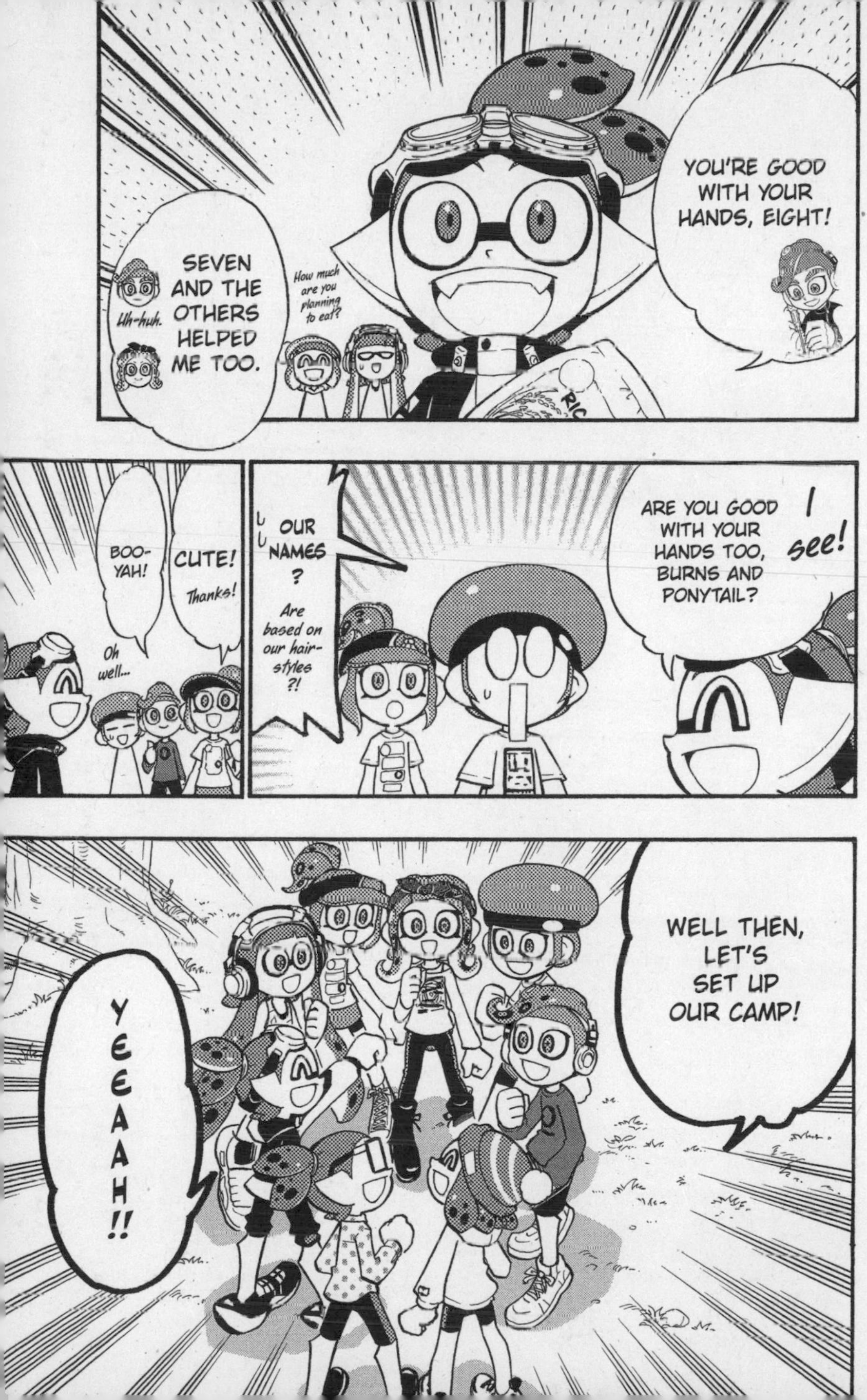
YOU'RE GOOD WITH YOUR HANDS, EIGHT!
How much are you planning to eat?
SEVEN AND THE OTHERS HELPED ME TOO.
Uh-huh.
I see!
ARE YOU GOOD WITH YOUR HANDS TOO, BURNS AND PONYTAIL?
OUR NAMES?
Are based on our hair-styles ?!
CUTE!
Thanks!
BOO-YAH!
Oh well...
WELL THEN, LET'S SET UP OUR CAMP!
YEEAAH!!

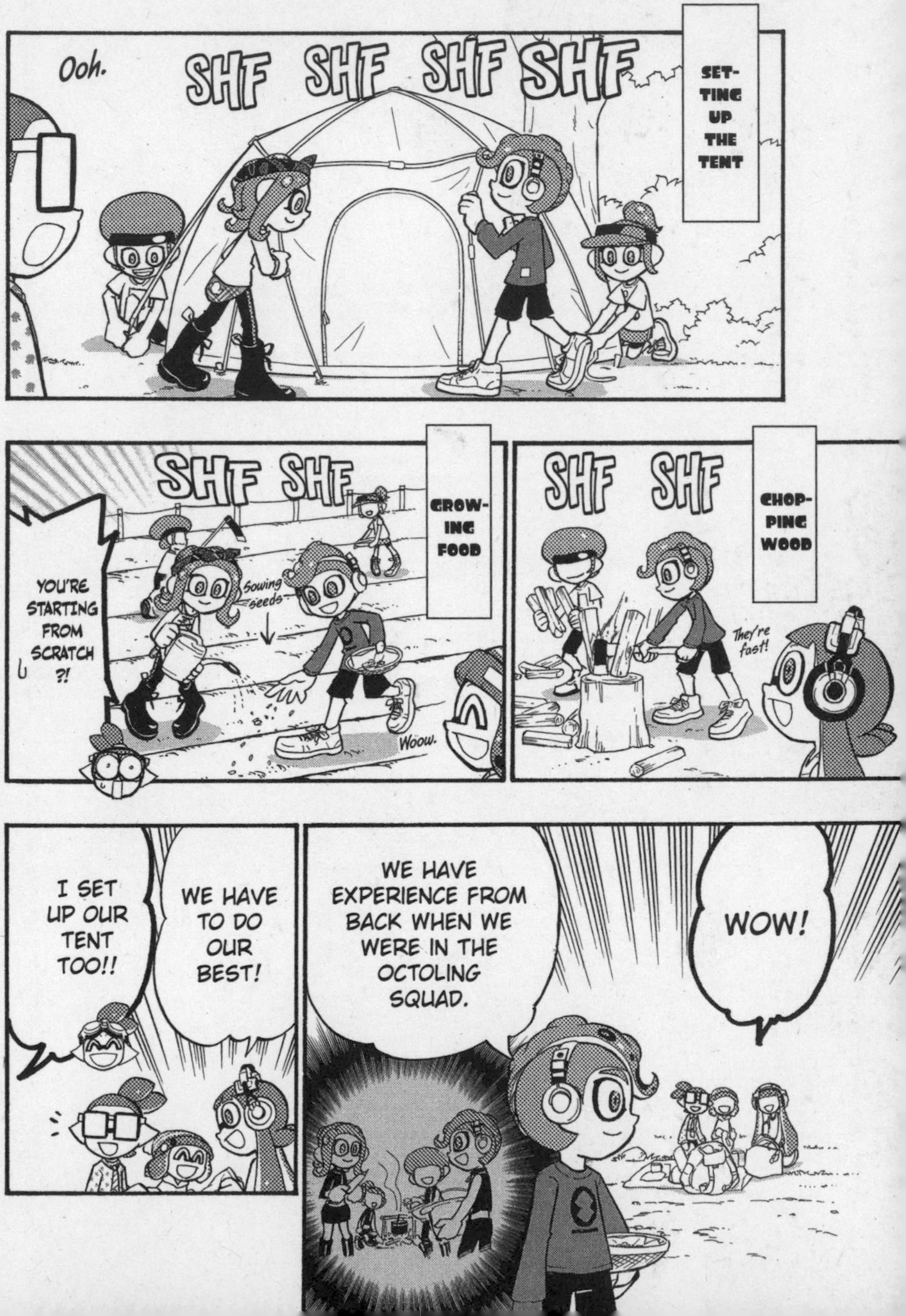
SETTING UP THE TENT
SHF SHF SHF SHF
Ooh.
CHOPPING WOOD
SHF SHF
They're fast!
GROWING FOOD
SHF SHF
Sowing seeds
Wooow.
YOU'RE STARTING FROM SCRATCH?!
WOW!
WE HAVE EXPERIENCE FROM BACK WHEN WE WERE IN THE OCTOLING SQUAD.
WE HAVE TO DO OUR BEST!
I SET UP OUR TENT TOO!!

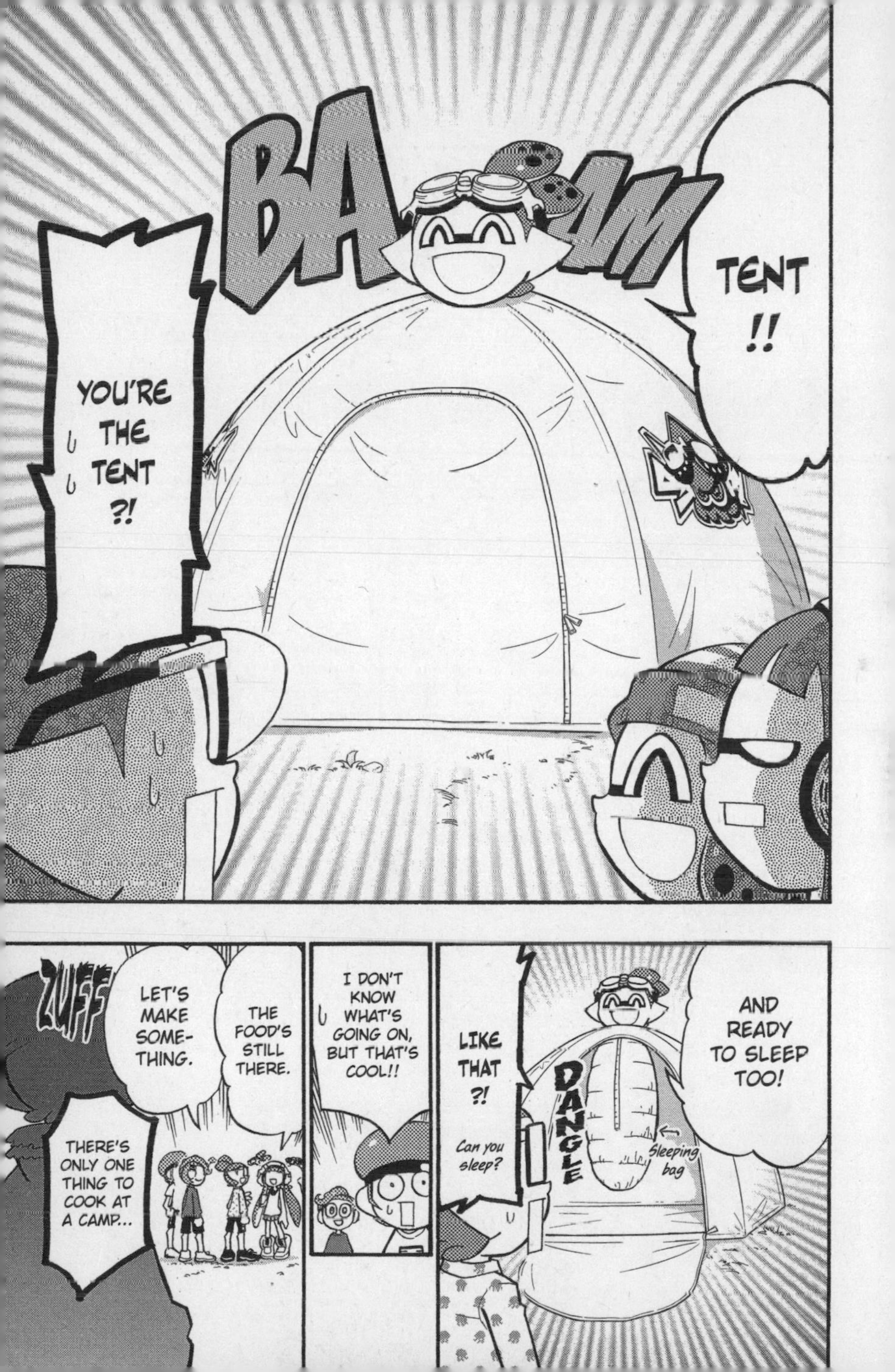

TENT !!
BAAM
YOU'RE THE TENT ?!
AND READY TO SLEEP TOO!
DANGLE
Sleeping bag
LIKE THAT ?!
Can you sleep?
I DON'T KNOW WHAT'S GOING ON, BUT THAT'S COOL!!
THE FOOD'S STILL THERE.
LET'S MAKE SOME-THING.
ZUFF
THERE'S ONLY ONE THING TO COOK AT A CAMP...

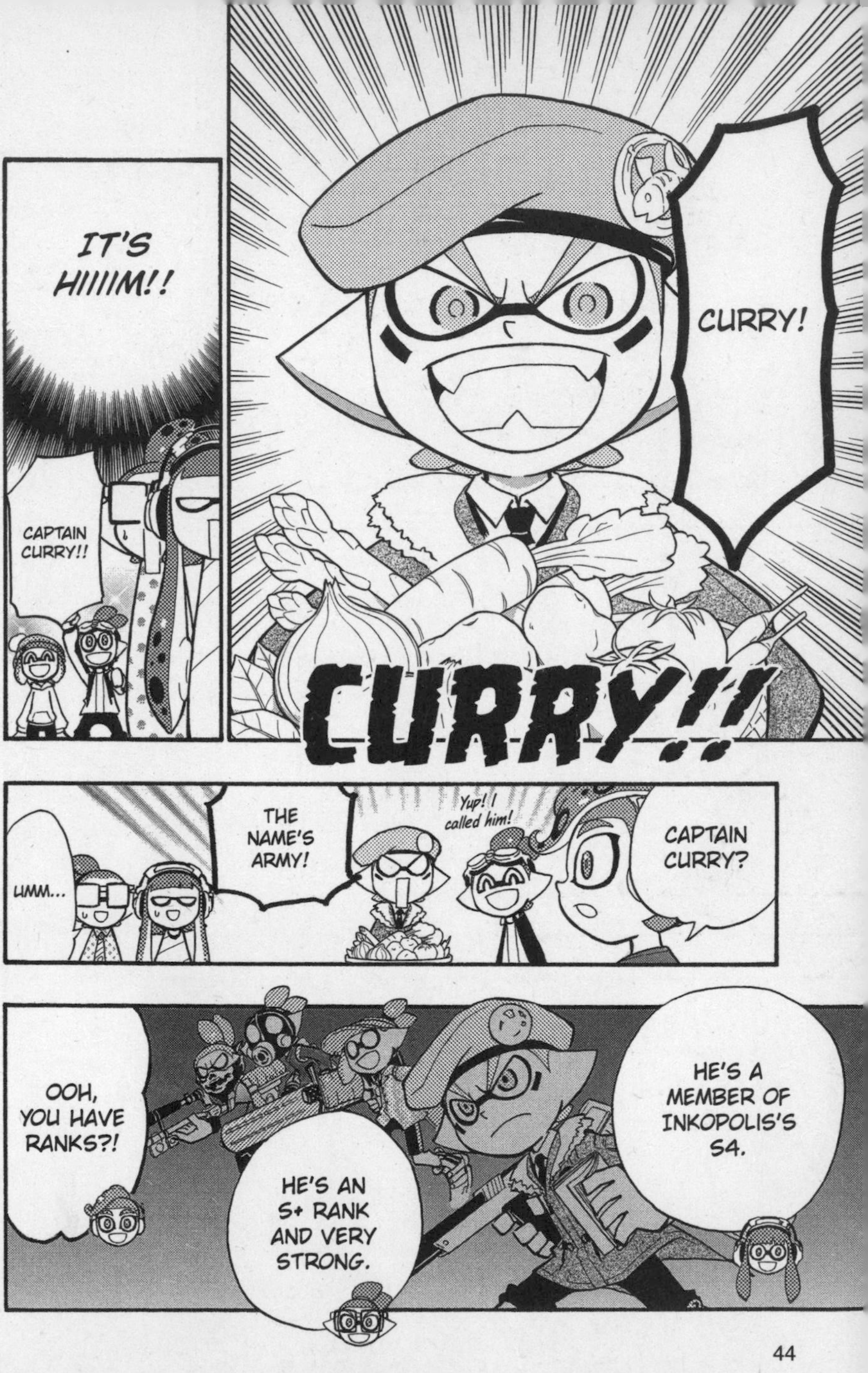

CURRY!
CURRY!!
IT'S HIIIIM!!
CAPTAIN CURRY!!
CAPTAIN CURRY?
Yup! I called him!
THE NAME'S ARMY!
UMM...
HE'S A MEMBER OF INKOPOLIS'S S4.
HE'S AN S+ RANK AND VERY STRONG.
OOH, YOU HAVE RANKS?!

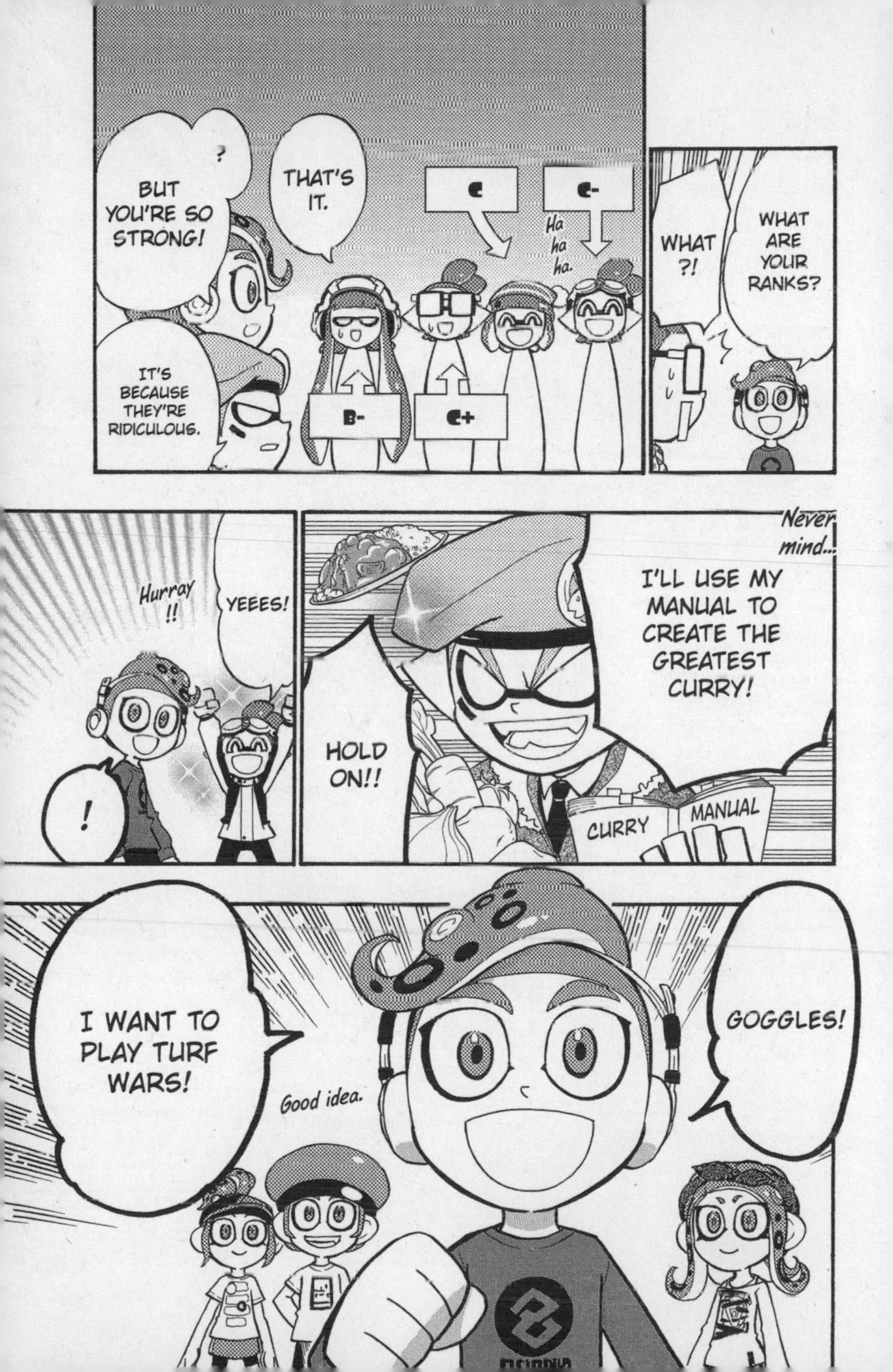
WHAT ARE YOUR RANKS?
WHAT ?!
C-
Ha ha ha.
C
THAT'S IT.
?
BUT YOU'RE SO STRONG!
C+
B-
IT'S BECAUSE THEY'RE RIDICULOUS.
Never mind...
I'LL USE MY MANUAL TO CREATE THE GREATEST CURRY!
CURRY MANUAL
HOLD ON!!
YEEES!
Hurray !!
!
GOGGLES!
Good idea.
I WANT TO PLAY TURF WARS!

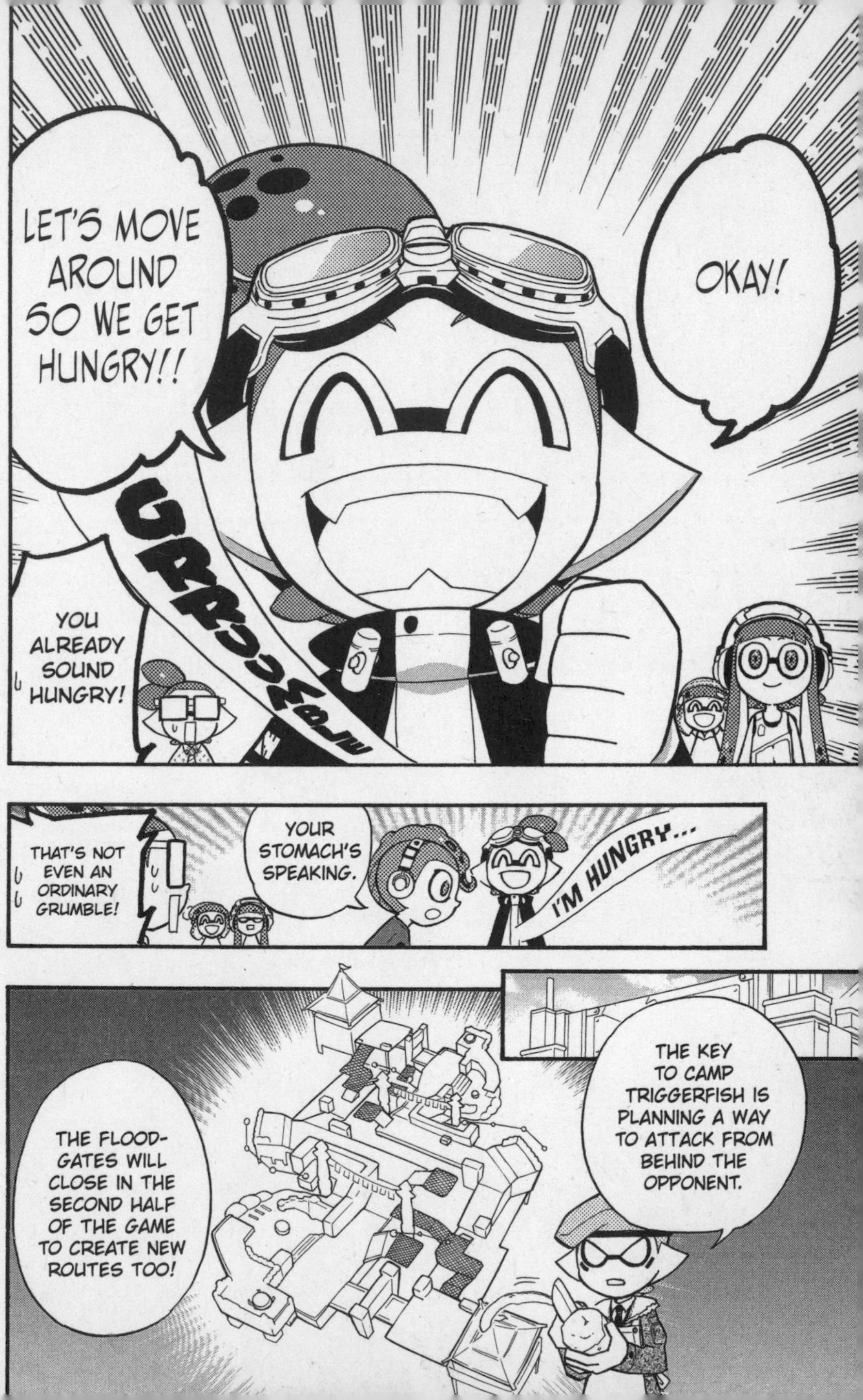
LET'S MOVE AROUND SO WE GET HUNGRY!!
OKAY!
YOU ALREADY SOUND HUNGRY!
I'M HUNGRY...
YOUR STOMACH'S SPEAKING.
THAT'S NOT EVEN AN ORDINARY GRUMBLE!
THE KEY TO CAMP TRIGGERFISH IS PLANNING A WAY TO ATTACK FROM BEHIND THE OPPONENT.
THE FLOOD-GATES WILL CLOSE IN THE SECOND HALF OF THE GAME TO CREATE NEW ROUTES TOO!

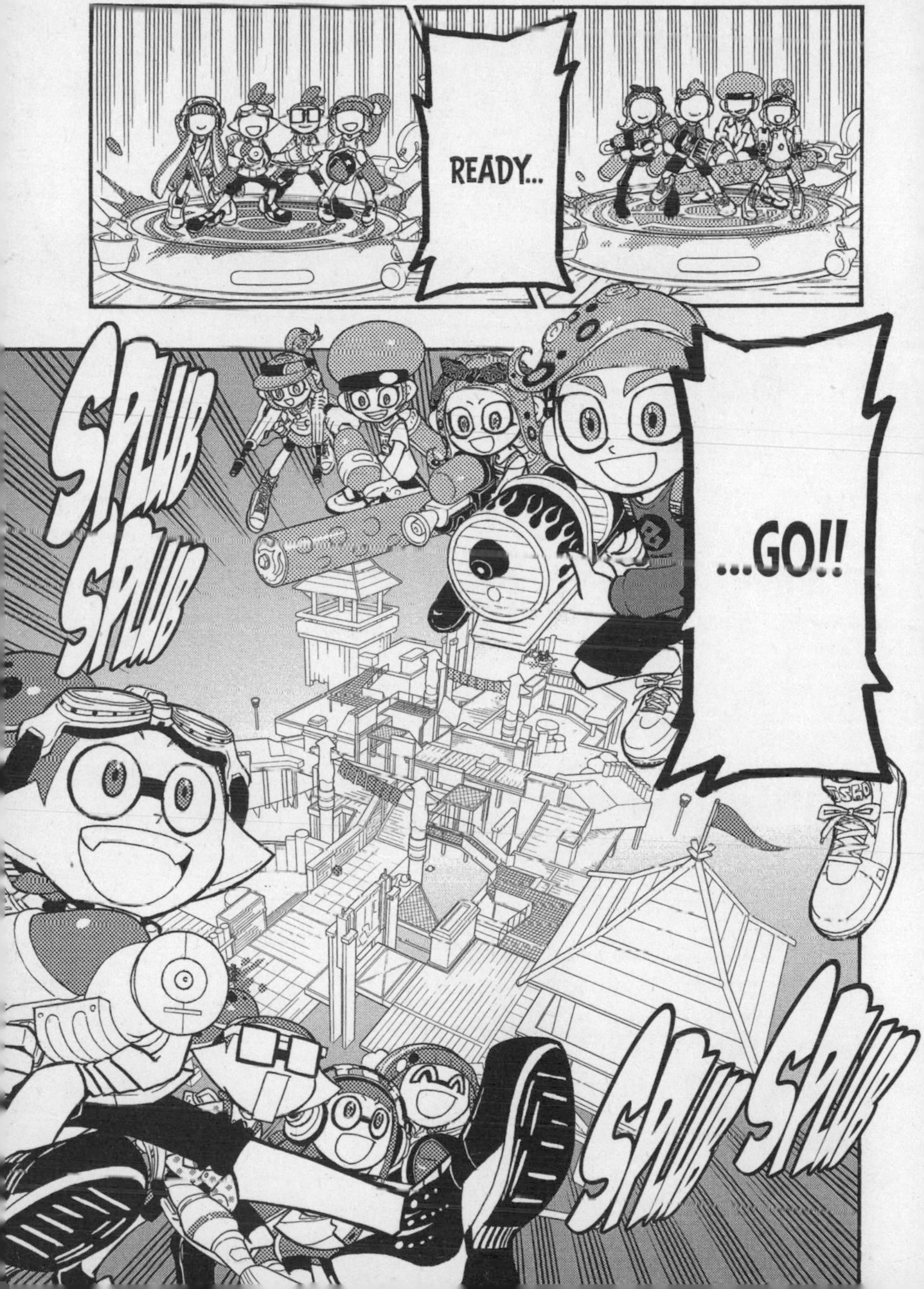
READY...
...GO!!
SPLUB SPLUB
SPLUB SPLUB

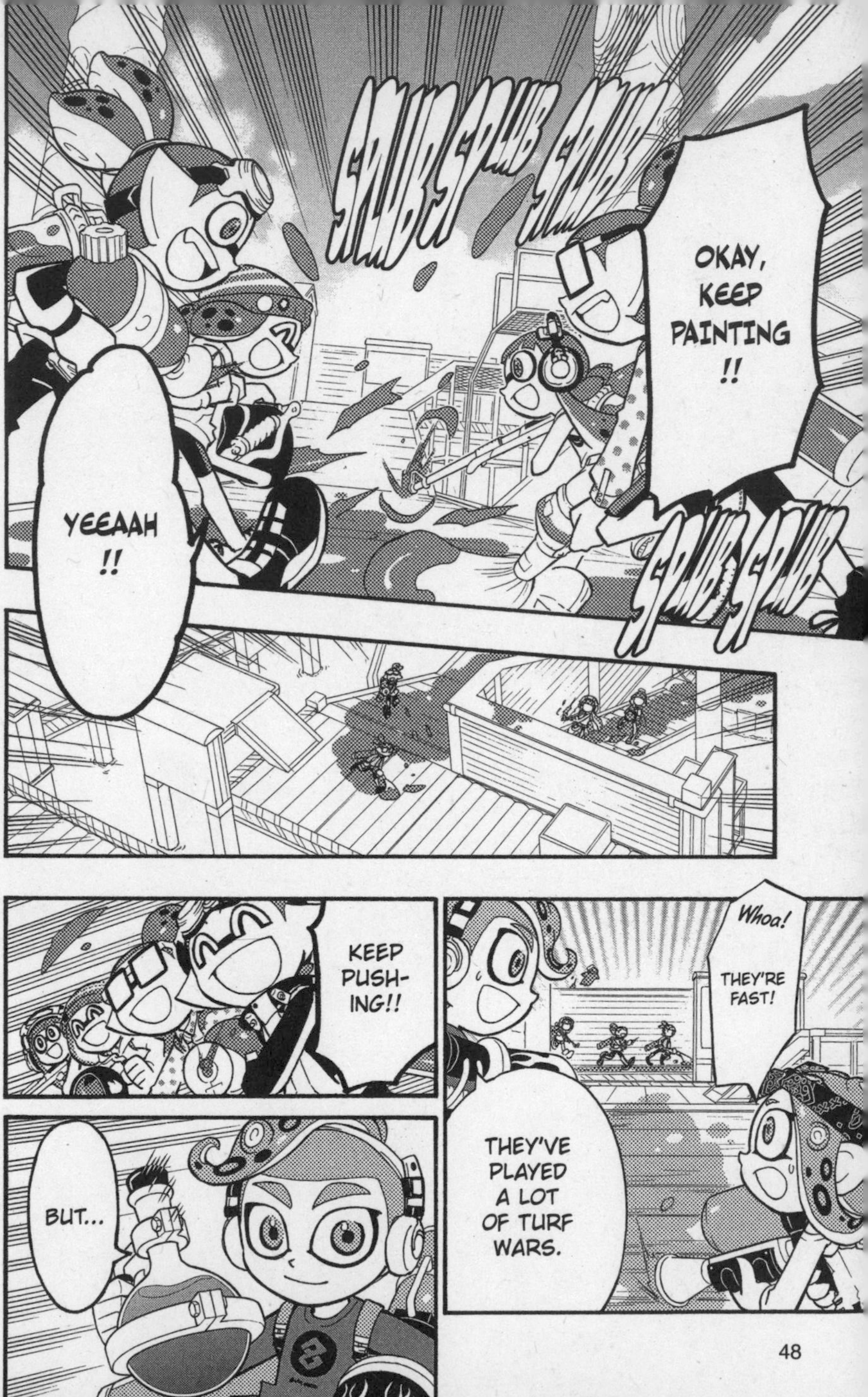
OKAY, KEEP PAINTING!!
YEEAAH!!
Whoa!
THEY'RE FAST!
THEY'VE PLAYED A LOT OF TURF WARS.
KEEP PUSH-ING!!
BUT...

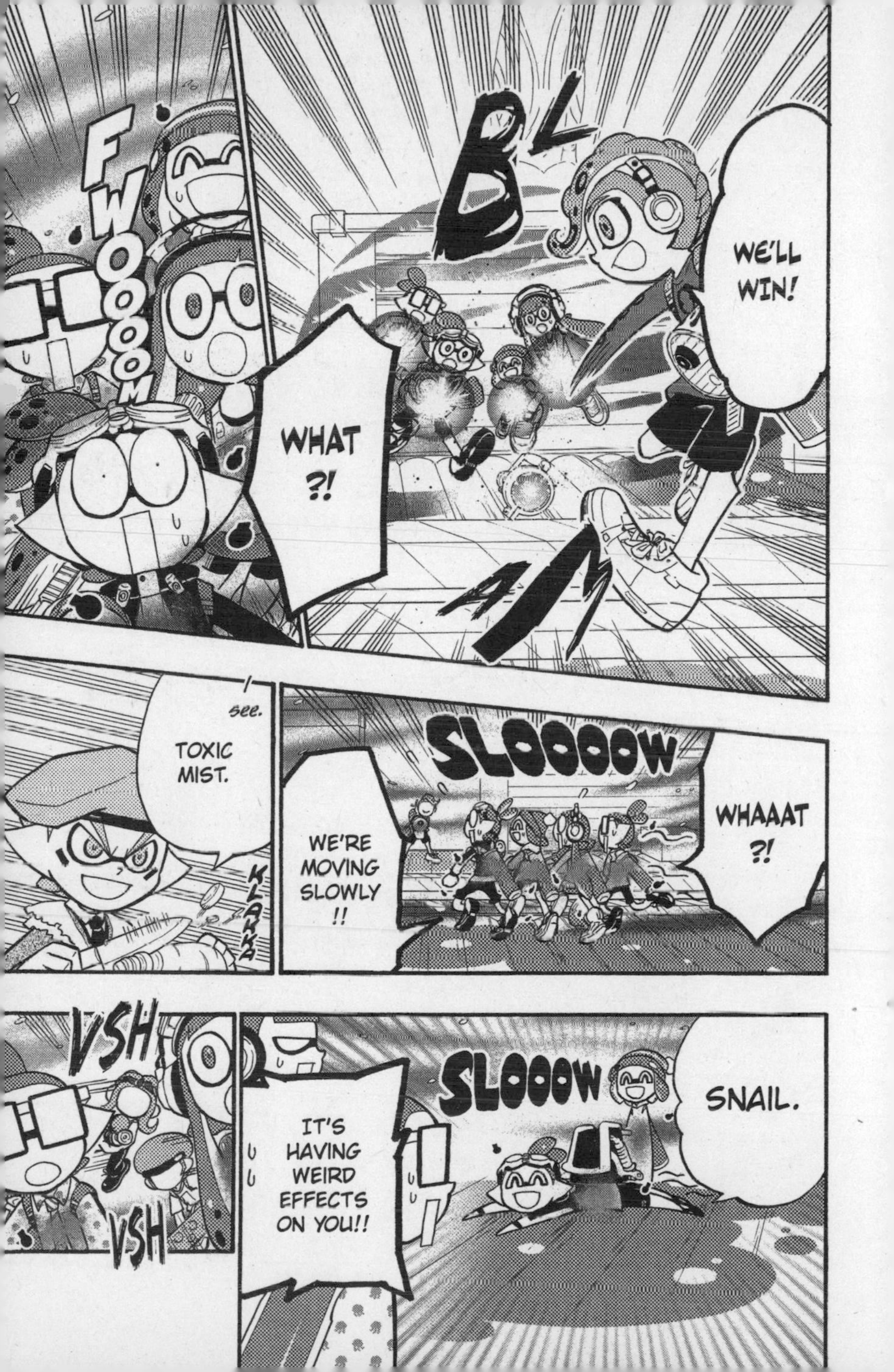
WE'LL WIN!
BL
AM
WHAT ?!
FWOOOOM
SLOOOOW
WHAAAT ?!
WE'RE MOVING SLOWLY !!
I see.
TOXIC MIST.
KLAKKA
SNAIL.
SLOOOW
IT'S HAVING WEIRD EFFECTS ON YOU!!
VSH
VSH

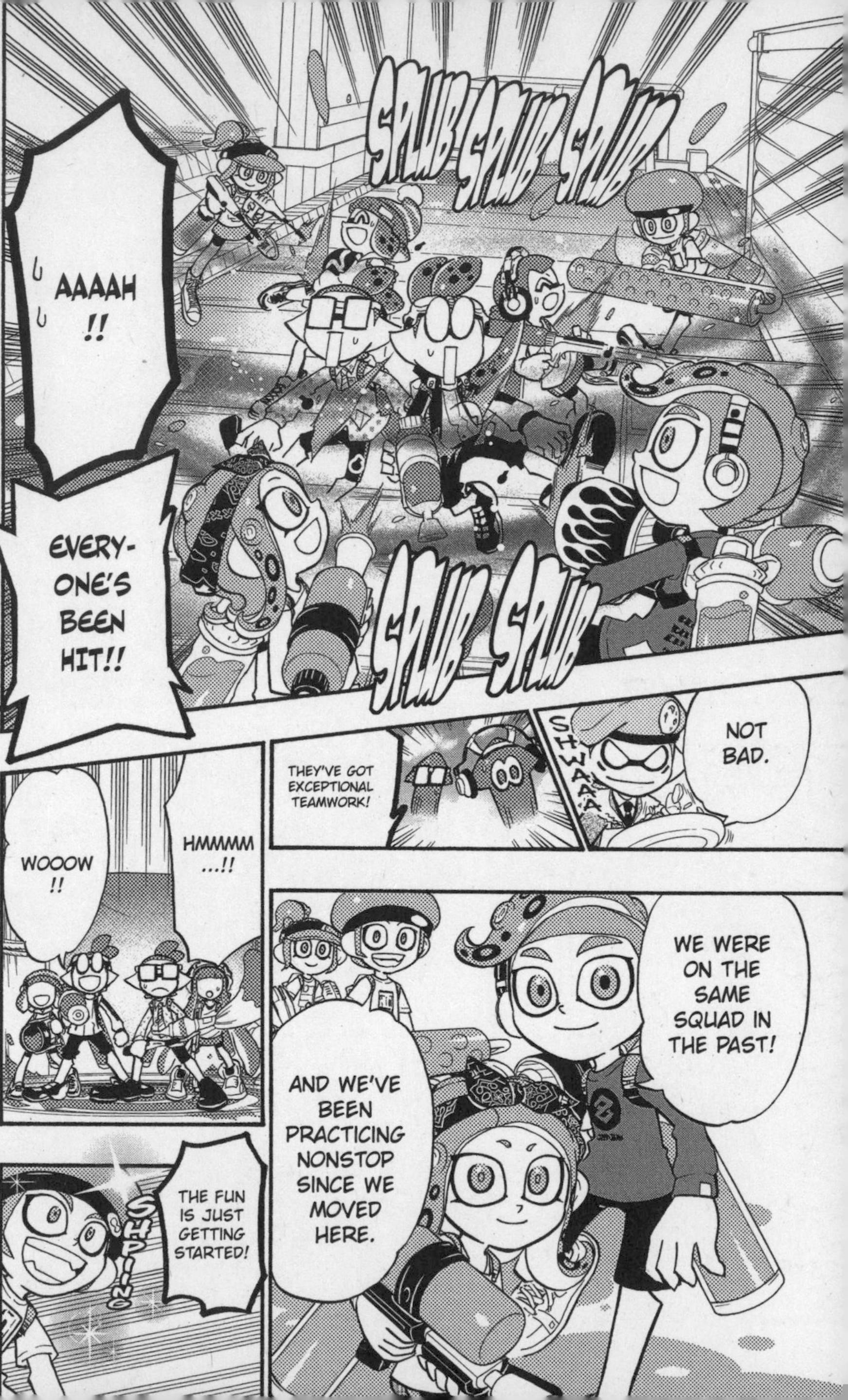
SPLUB SPLUB SPLUB
AAAAH!!
SPLUB SPLUB
EVERY-ONE'S BEEN HIT!!
SHWAAA
NOT BAD.
THEY'VE GOT EXCEPTIONAL TEAMWORK!
WE WERE ON THE SAME SQUAD IN THE PAST!
AND WE'VE BEEN PRACTICING NONSTOP SINCE WE MOVED HERE.
HMMMM...!!
WOOOW!!
SHPING
THE FUN IS JUST GETTING STARTED!

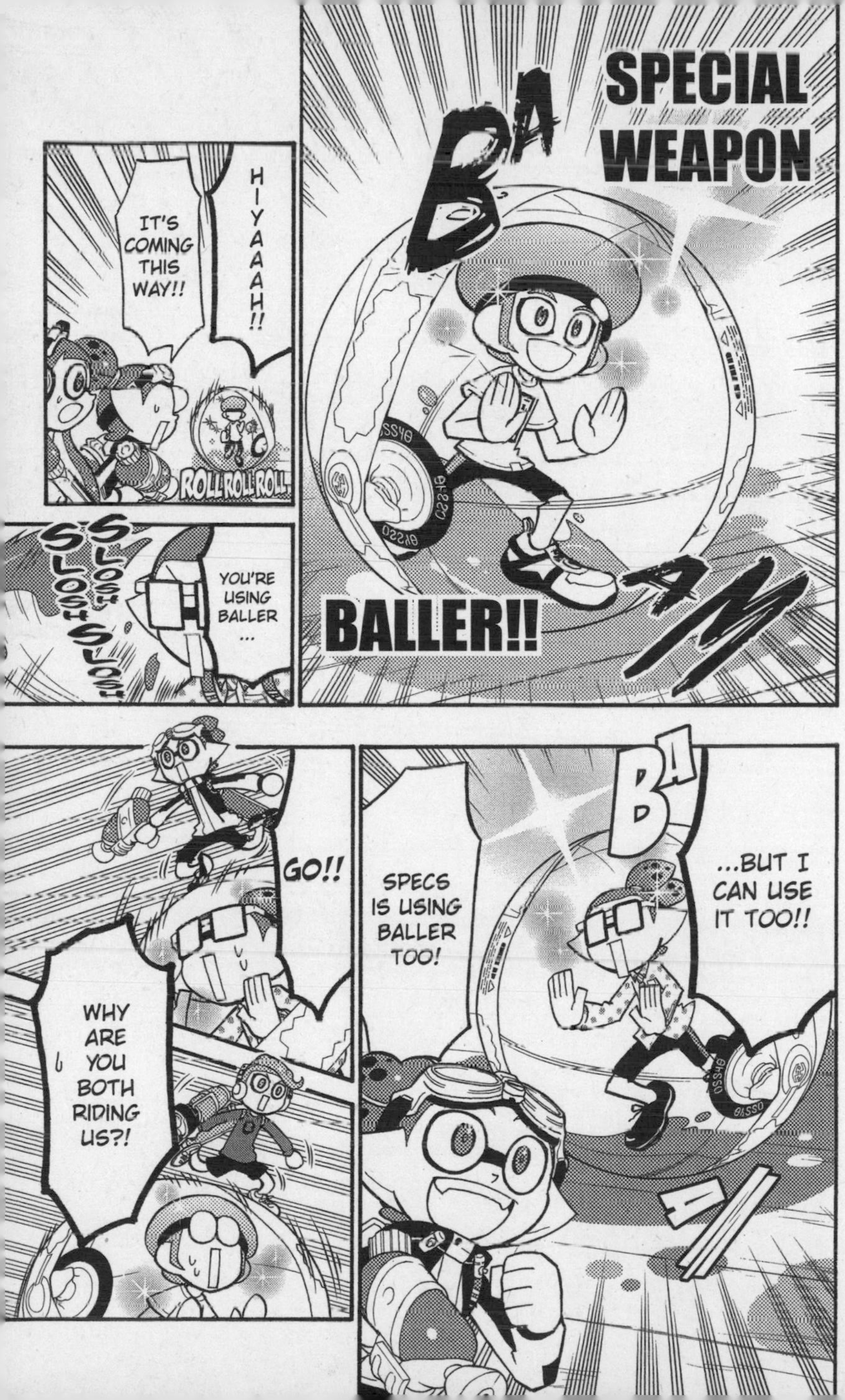
SPECIAL WEAPON
BA
BALLER!!
AM
HIYAAAAH!!
IT'S COMING THIS WAY!!
ROLL ROLL ROLL
SLOSH SLOSH
YOU'RE USING BALLER ...
SLOSH SLOSH
BA
...BUT I CAN USE IT TOO!!
SPECS IS USING BALLER TOO!
A
GO!!
WHY ARE YOU BOTH RIDING US?!

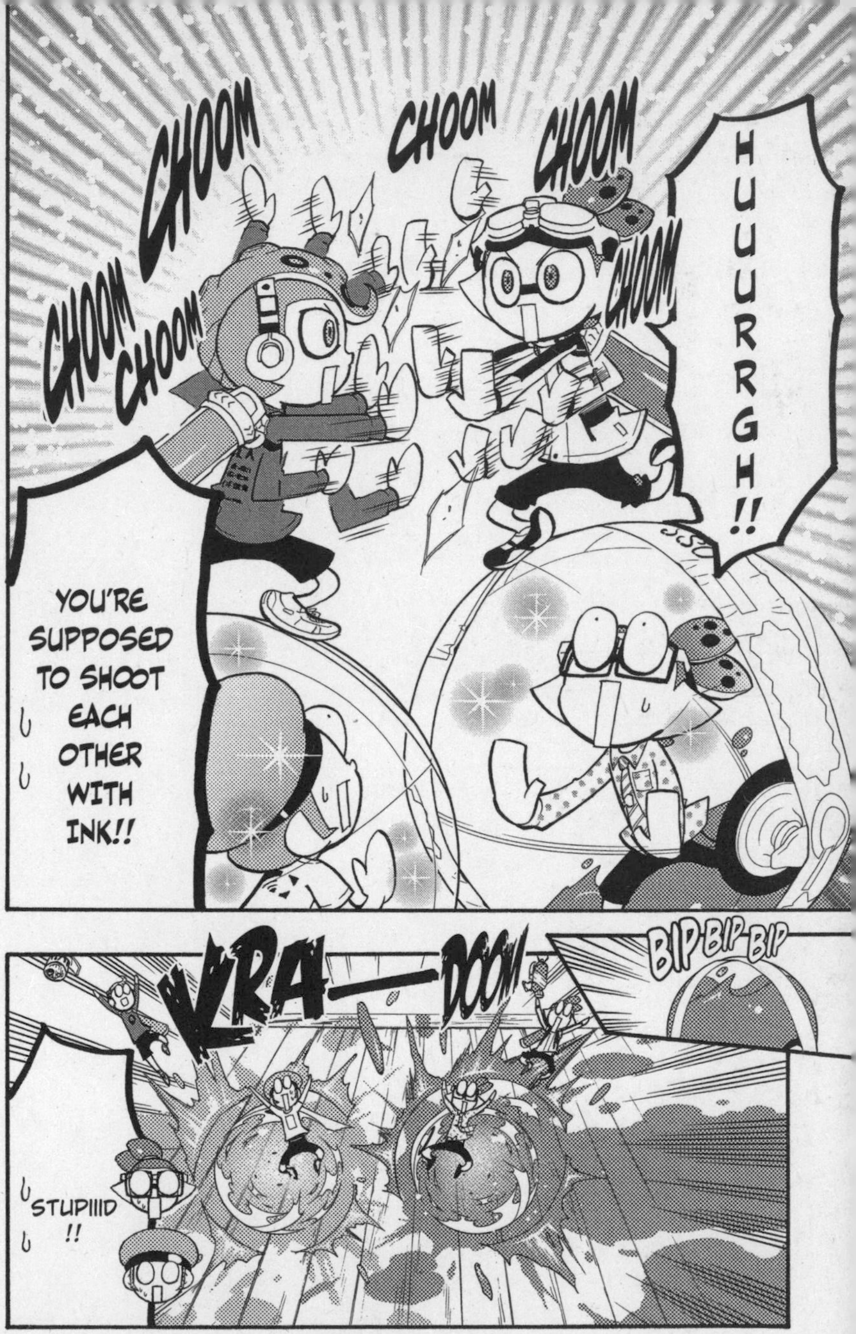
HUUURRGH!!
CHOOM
CHOOM
CHOOM
CHOOM
CHOOM
CHOOM
YOU'RE SUPPOSED TO SHOOT EACH OTHER WITH INK!!
BIP-BIP-BIP
KRA—DOOM
STUPIIID!!

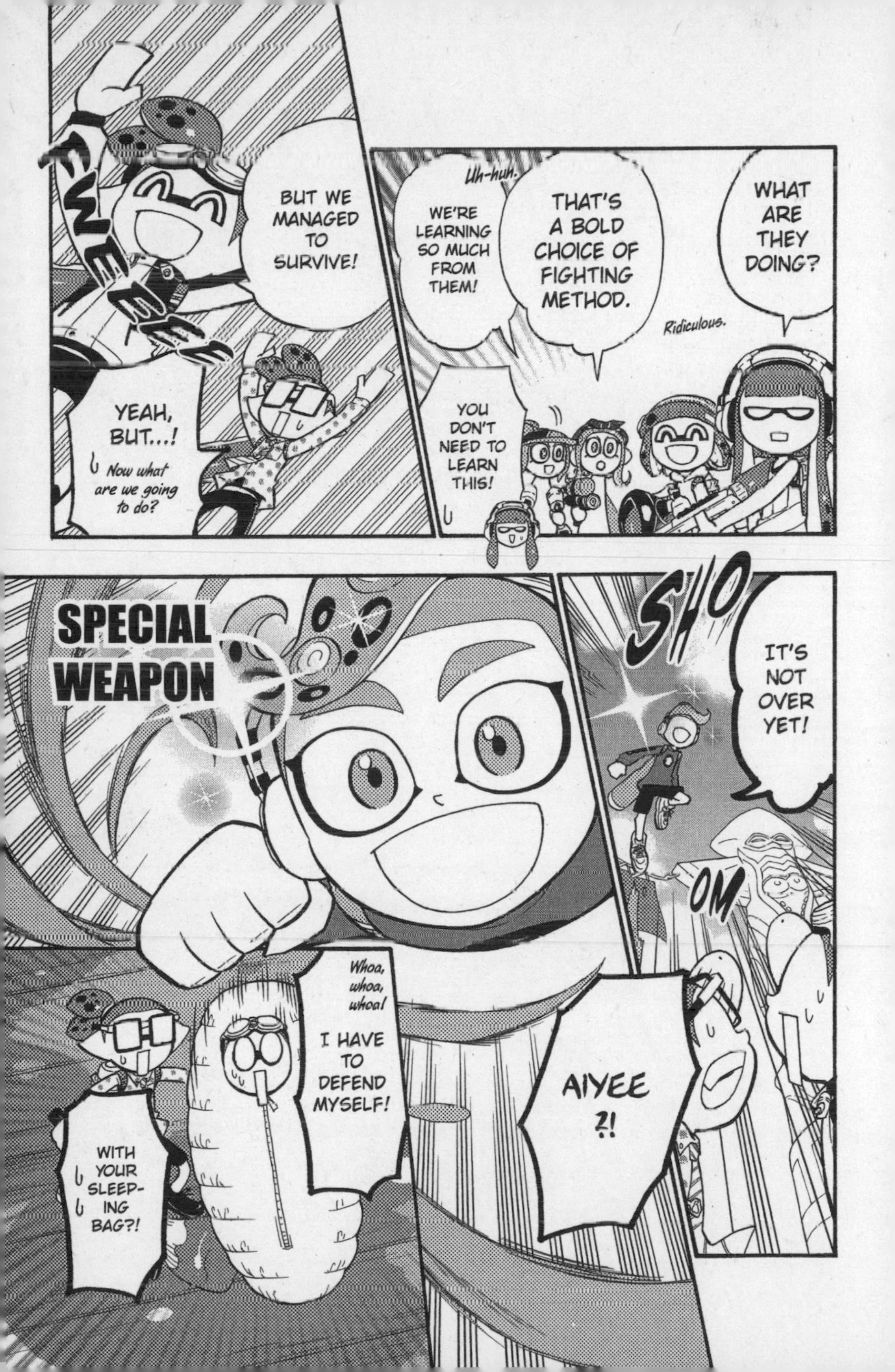
WHAT ARE THEY DOING?
Ridiculous.
THAT'S A BOLD CHOICE OF FIGHTING METHOD.
Uh-huh.
WE'RE LEARNING SO MUCH FROM THEM!
YOU DON'T NEED TO LEARN THIS!
BUT WE MANAGED TO SURVIVE!
YEAH, BUT...!
Now what are we going to do?
SHOOM
IT'S NOT OVER YET!
AIYEE ?!
SPECIAL WEAPON
Whoa, whoa, whoa!
I HAVE TO DEFEND MYSELF!
WITH YOUR SLEEPING-BAG?!

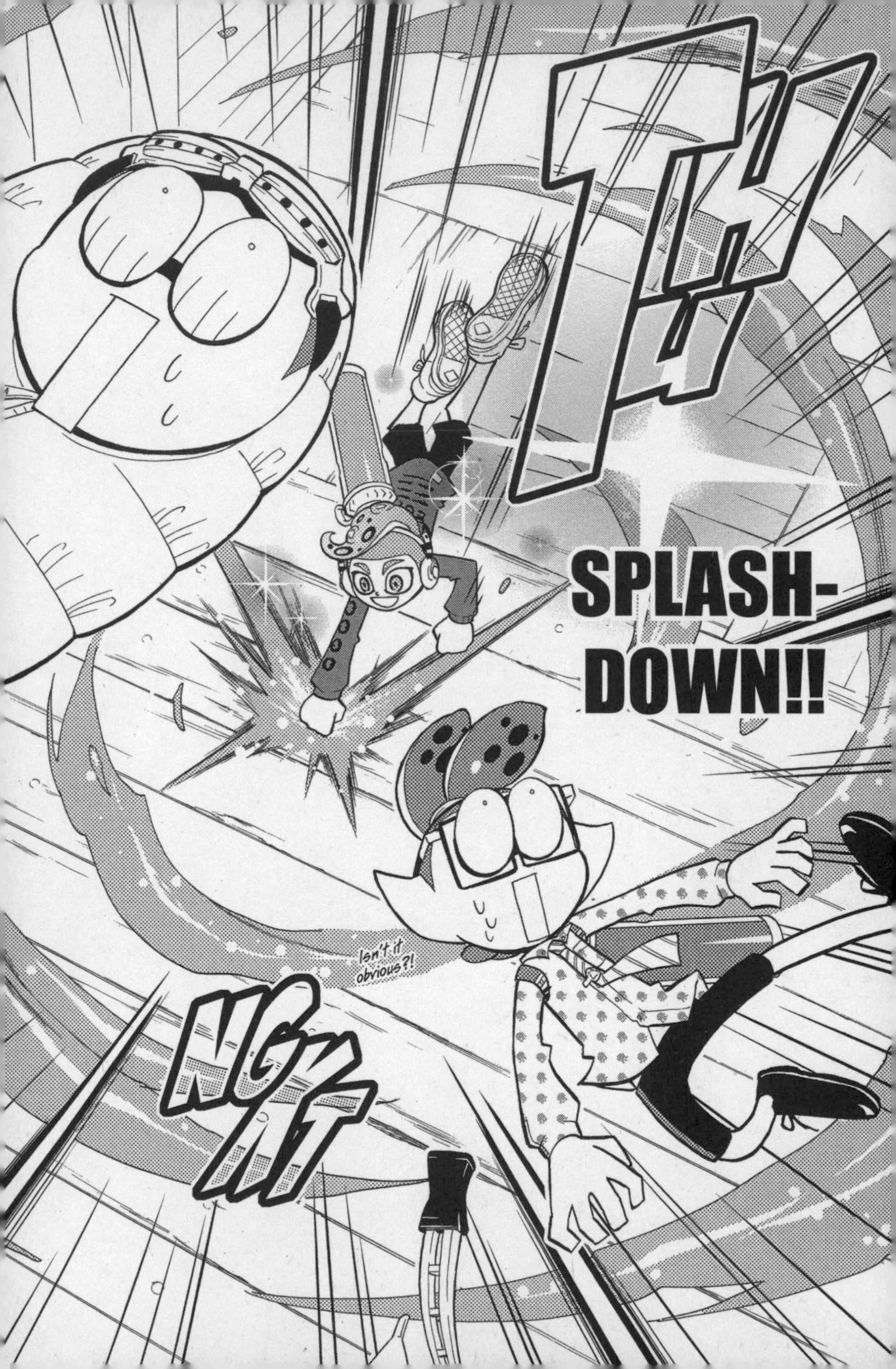
SPLASH-
DOWN!!
Isn't it obvious?!

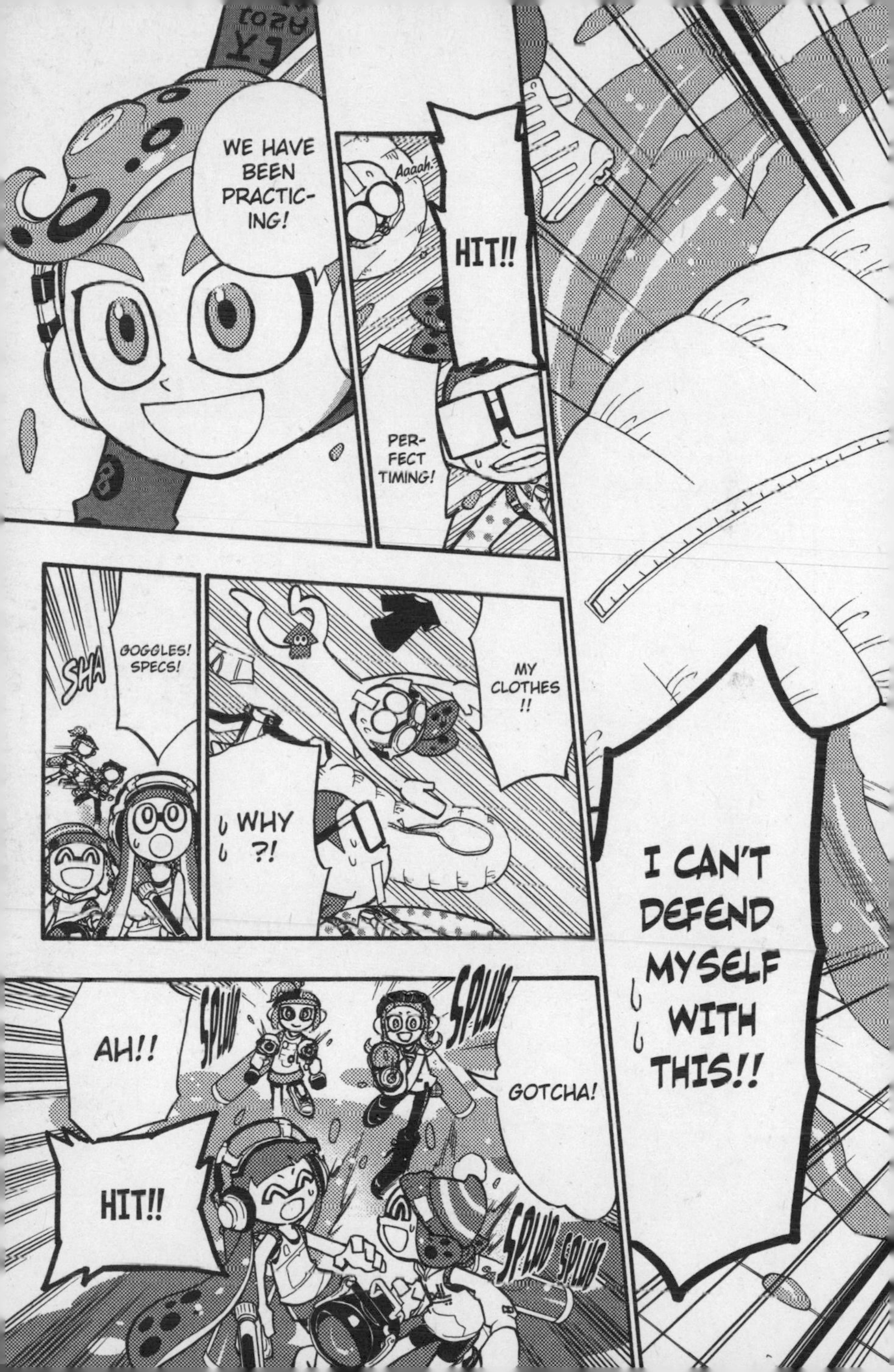
I CAN'T DEFEND MYSELF WITH THIS!!
HIT!!
PER-FECT TIMING!
WE HAVE BEEN PRACTIC-ING!
MY CLOTHES!!
WHY?!
GOGGLES! SPECS!
SHA
SPLUB
GOTCHA!
SPLUB
AH!!
HIT!!
SPLUB SPLUB

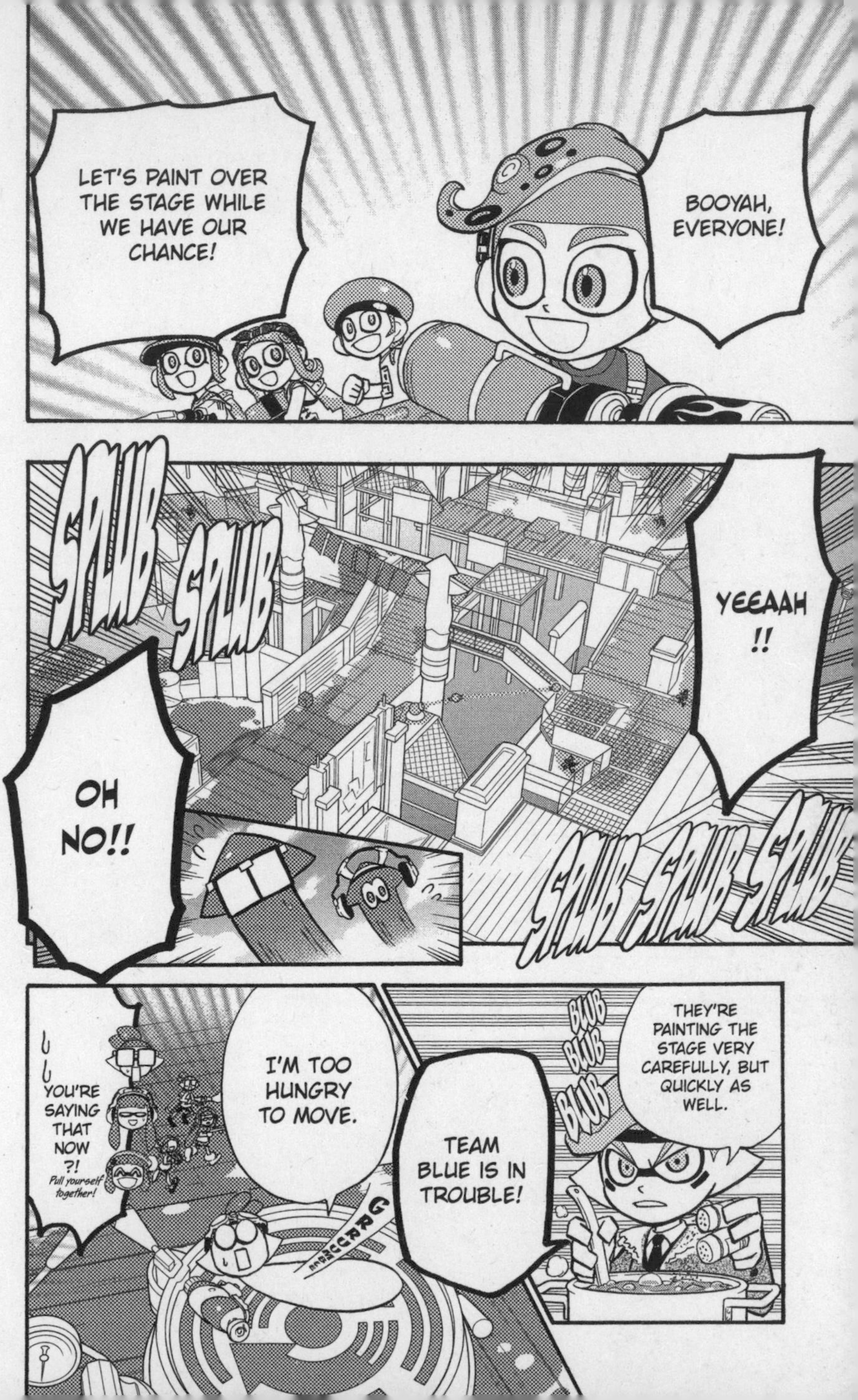
BOOYAH, EVERYONE!
LET'S PAINT OVER THE STAGE WHILE WE HAVE OUR CHANCE!
YEEAAH!!
SPLUB SPLUB
OH NO!!
SPLUB SPLUB SPLUB
BLUB BLUB BLUB
THEY'RE PAINTING THE STAGE VERY CAREFULLY, BUT QUICKLY AS WELL.
TEAM BLUE IS IN TROUBLE!
I'M TOO HUNGRY TO MOVE.
YOU'RE SAYING THAT NOW ?!
Pull yourself together!

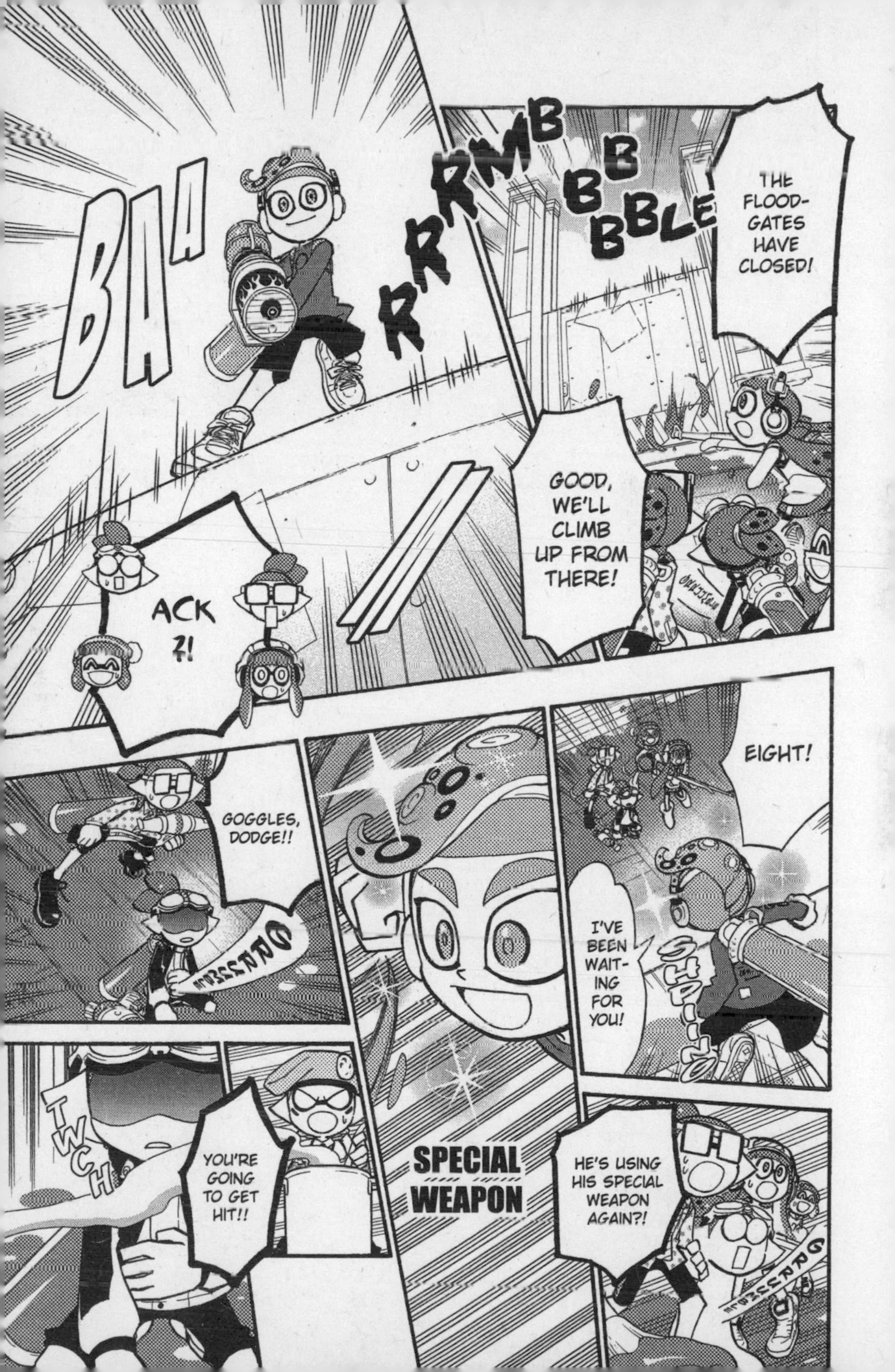
RRRMB BBBBLE
THE FLOODGATES HAVE CLOSED!
GOOD, WE'LL CLIMB UP FROM THERE!
BAA
ACK ?!
EIGHT!
I'VE BEEN WAITING FOR YOU!
HE'S USING HIS SPECIAL WEAPON AGAIN?!
SPECIAL WEAPON
GOGGLES, DODGE!!
YOU'RE GOING TO GET HIT!!
TWCH

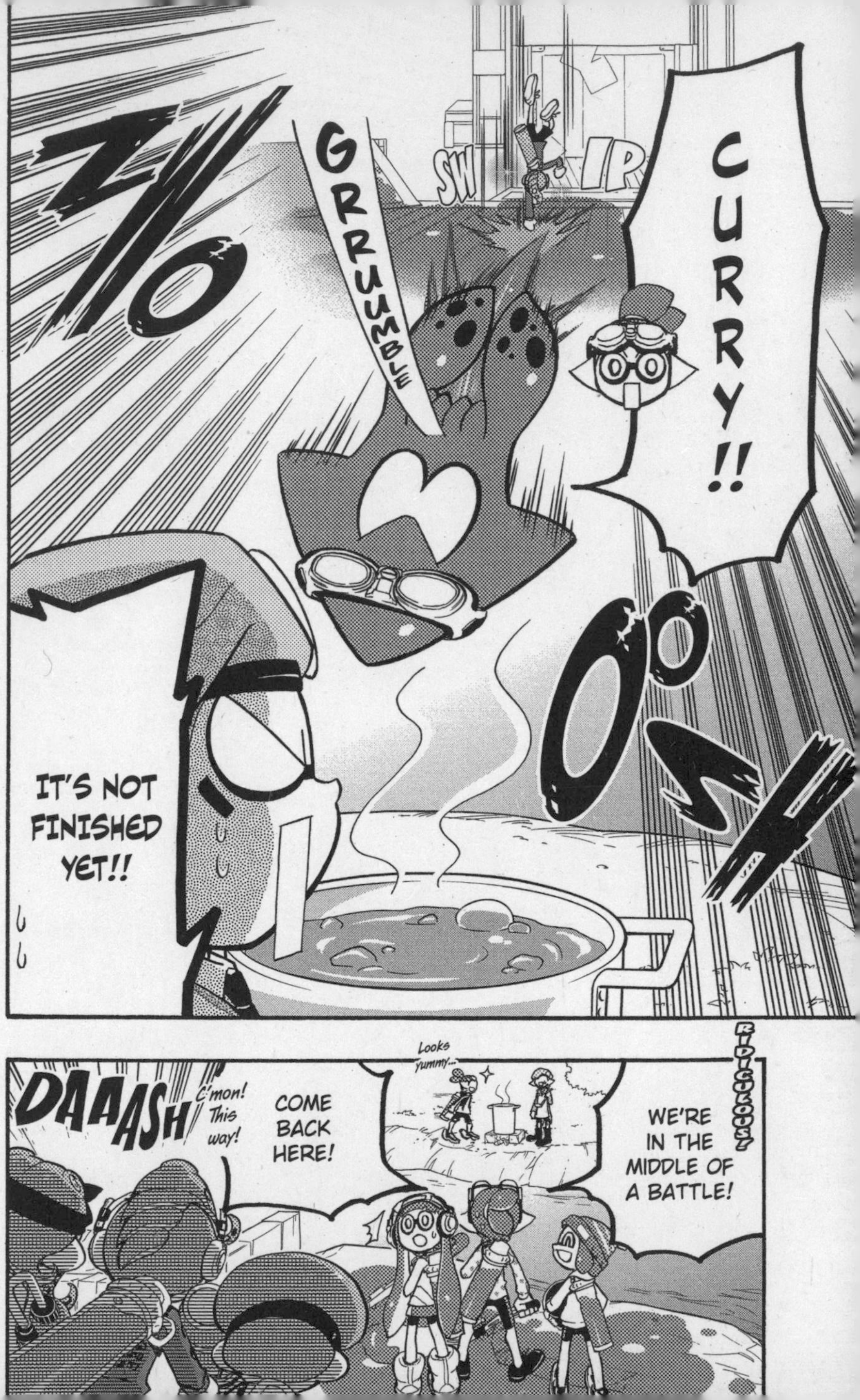
CURRY!!
SWIP
GRRUUMBLE
IT'S NOT FINISHED YET!!
RIDICULOUS!
WE'RE IN THE MIDDLE OF A BATTLE!
Looks yummy...
COME BACK HERE!
C'mon! This way!
DAAAASH

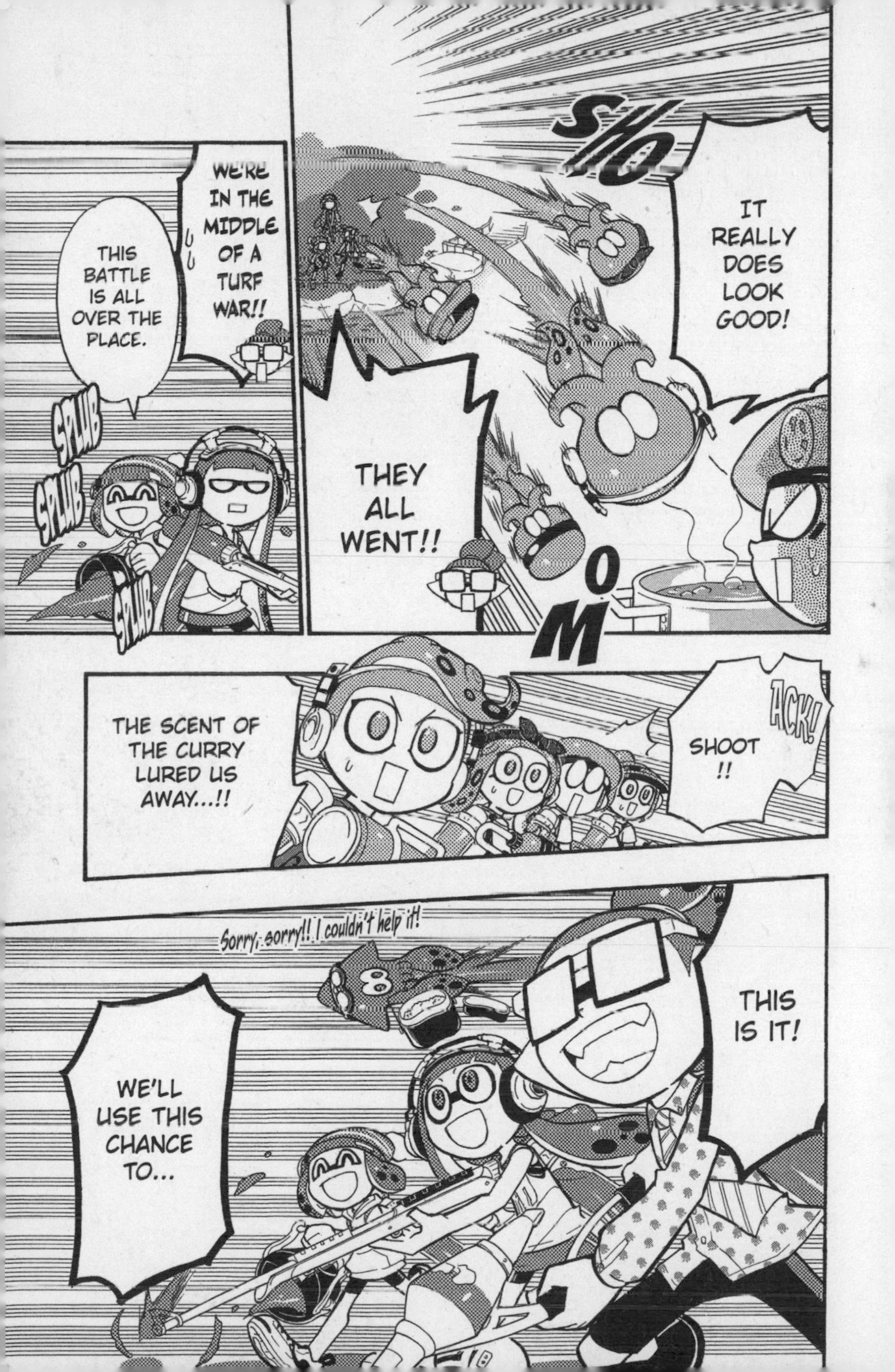
SHO
IT REALLY DOES LOOK GOOD!
OM
THEY ALL WENT!!
WE'RE IN THE MIDDLE OF A TURF WAR!!
THIS BATTLE IS ALL OVER THE PLACE.
SPLUB
SPLUB
SPLUB
ACK!
SHOOT!!
THE SCENT OF THE CURRY LURED US AWAY...!!
THIS IS IT!
Sorry, sorry!! I couldn't help it!
WE'LL USE THIS CHANCE TO...

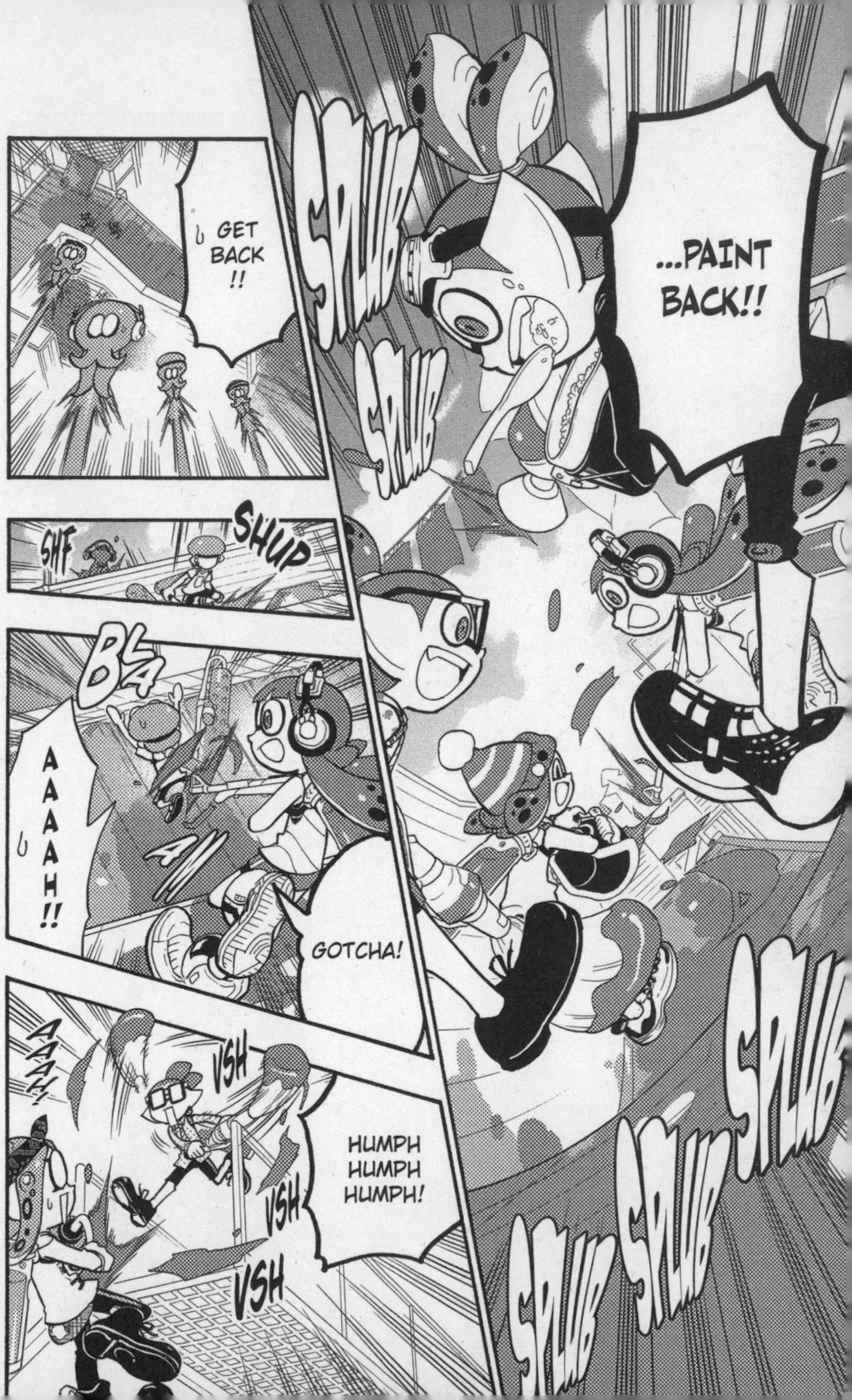
SPLUB
...PAINT BACK!!
SPLUB
SPLUB
SPLUB
SPLUB
GET BACK!!
SHUP
SHF
BLA
AAAAAH!!
A
GOTCHA!
VSH
AAAAH!
HUMPH HUMPH HUMPH!
VSH
VSH

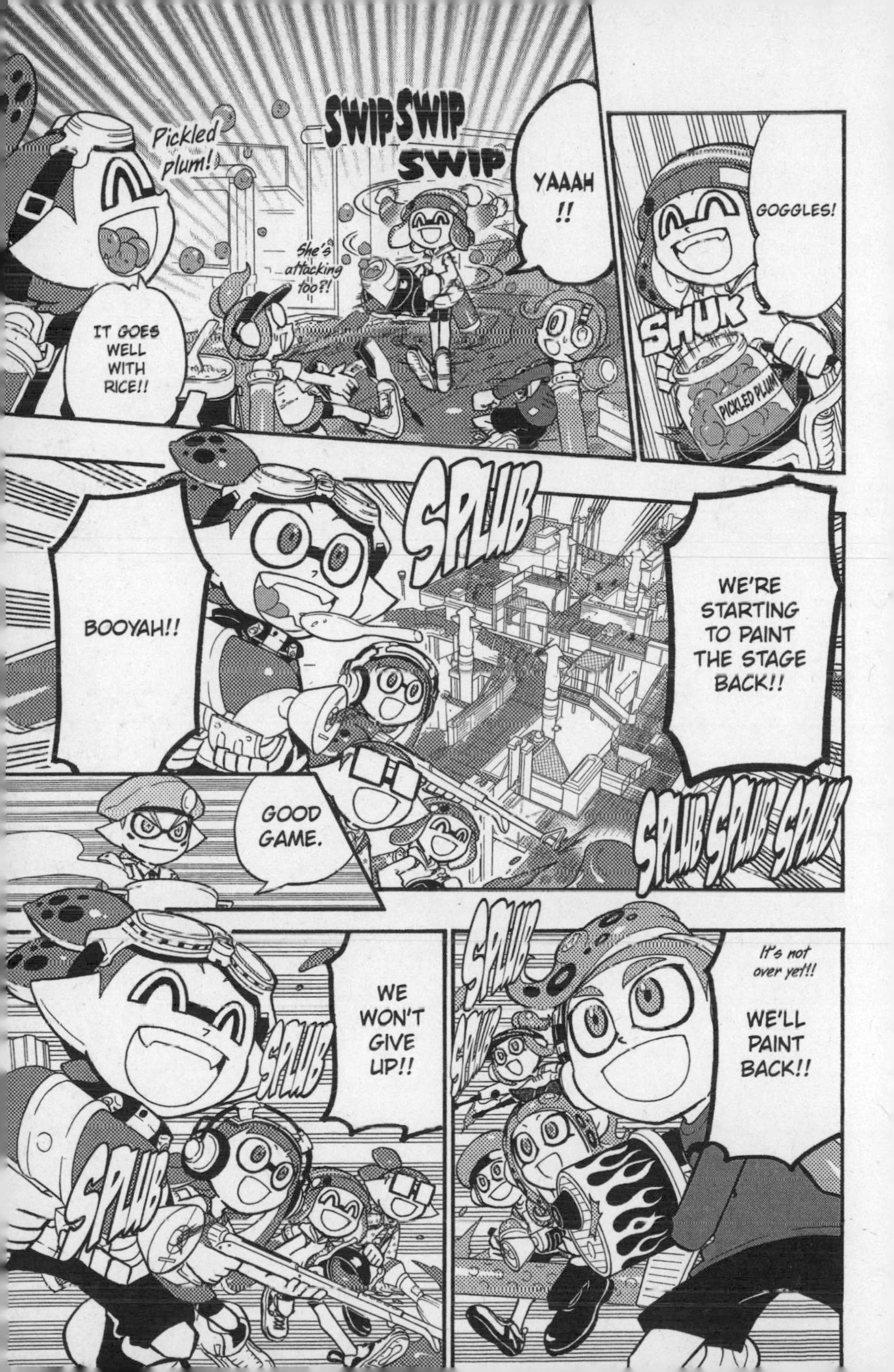
GOGGLES!
SHUK
PICKLED PLUM
YAAAH!!
SWIP SWIP
SWIP
She's attacking too?!
Pickled plum!
IT GOES WELL WITH RICE!!
WE'RE STARTING TO PAINT THE STAGE BACK!!
SPLUB
BOOYAH!!
SPLUB SPLUB SPLUB
GOOD GAME.
It's not over yet!!
WE'LL PAINT BACK!!
SPLUB
WE WON'T GIVE UP!!
SPLUB
SPLUB

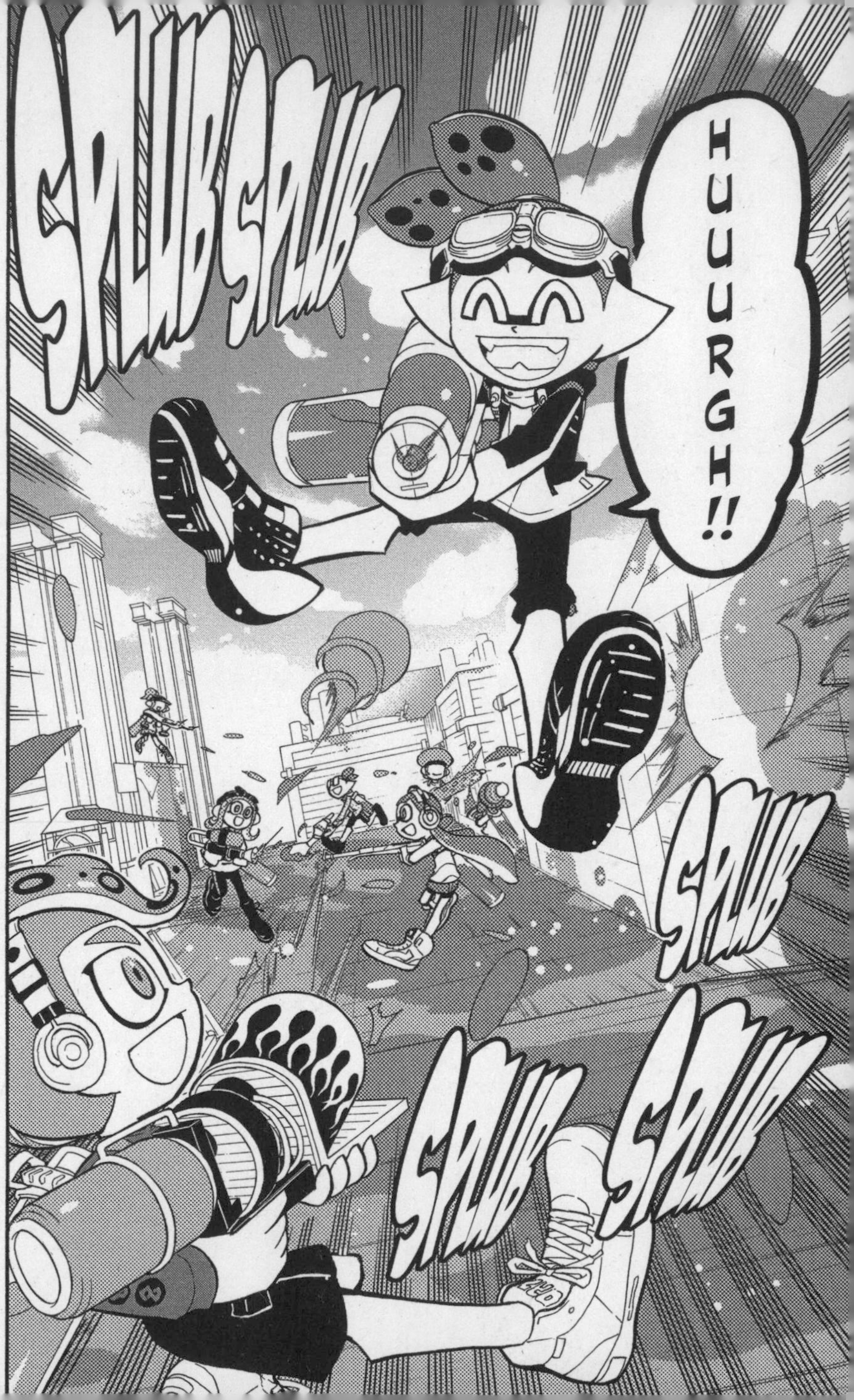

SPLUB SPLUB
HUUURGH!!
SPLUB
SPLUB SPLUB

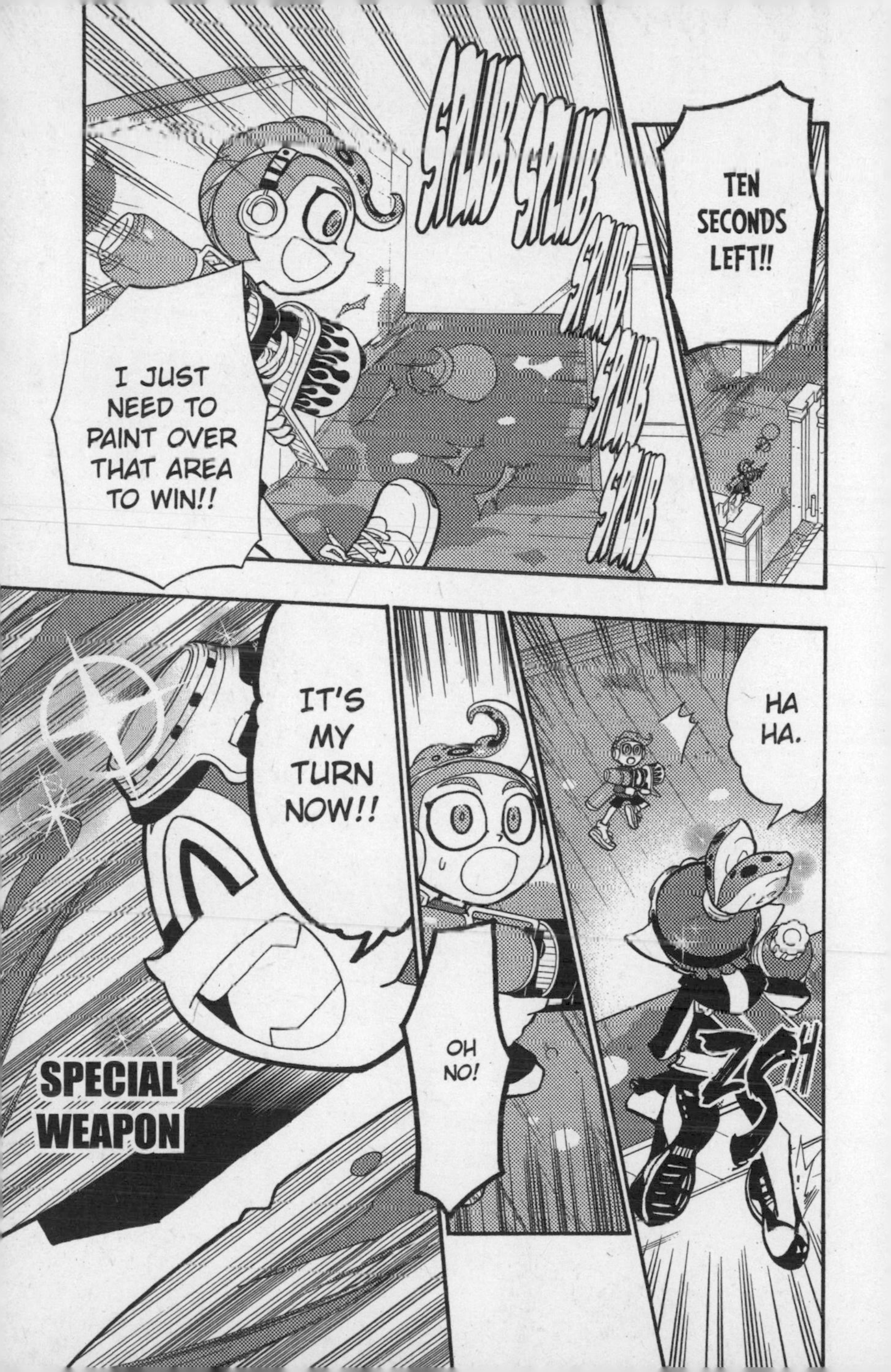
TEN SECONDS LEFT!!
SPLUB SPLUB SPLUB SPLUB SPLUB
I JUST NEED TO PAINT OVER THAT AREA TO WIN!!
HA HA.
OH NO!
IT'S MY TURN NOW!!
SPECIAL WEAPON

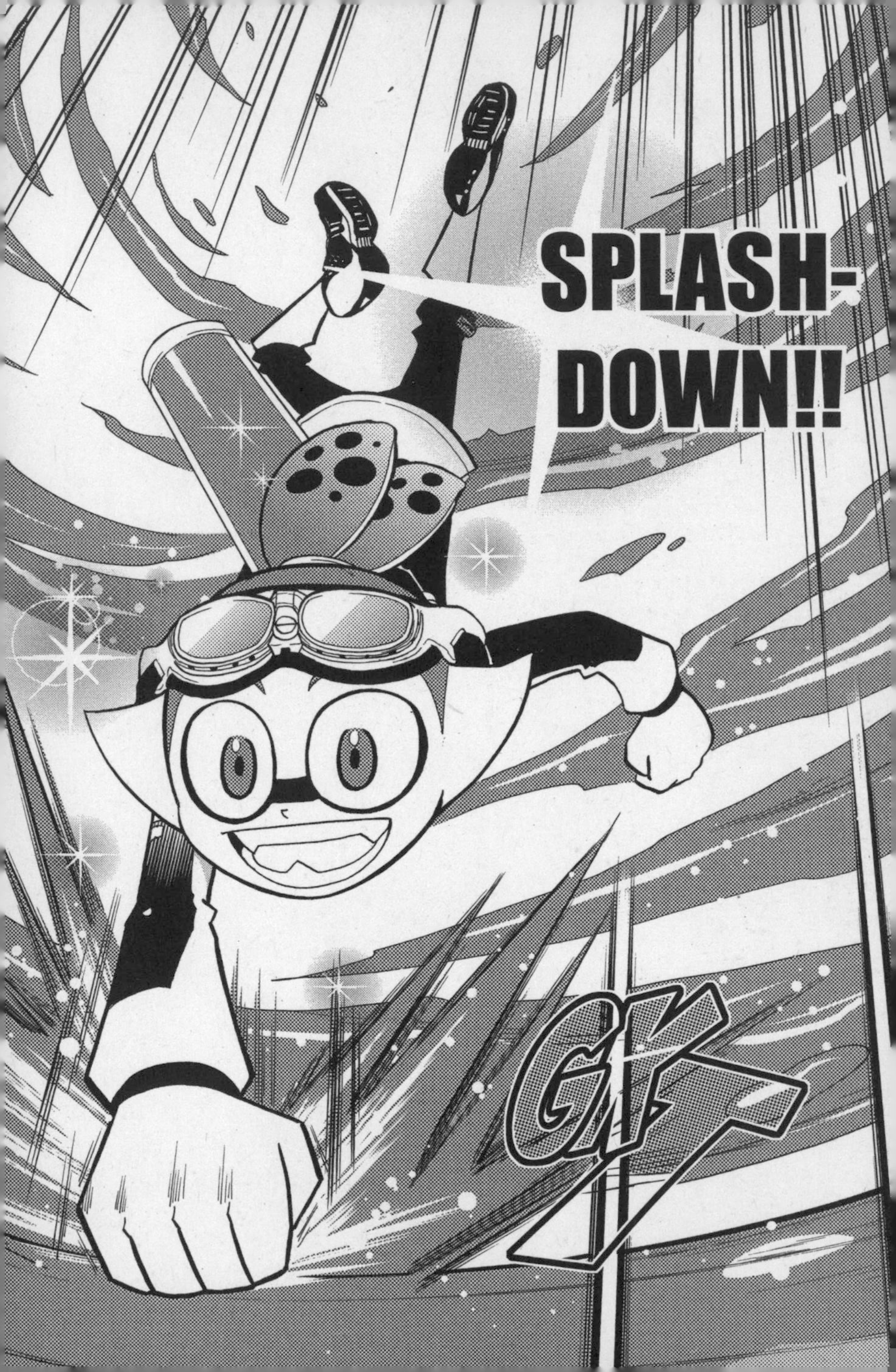
SPLASH-
DOWN!!
GK

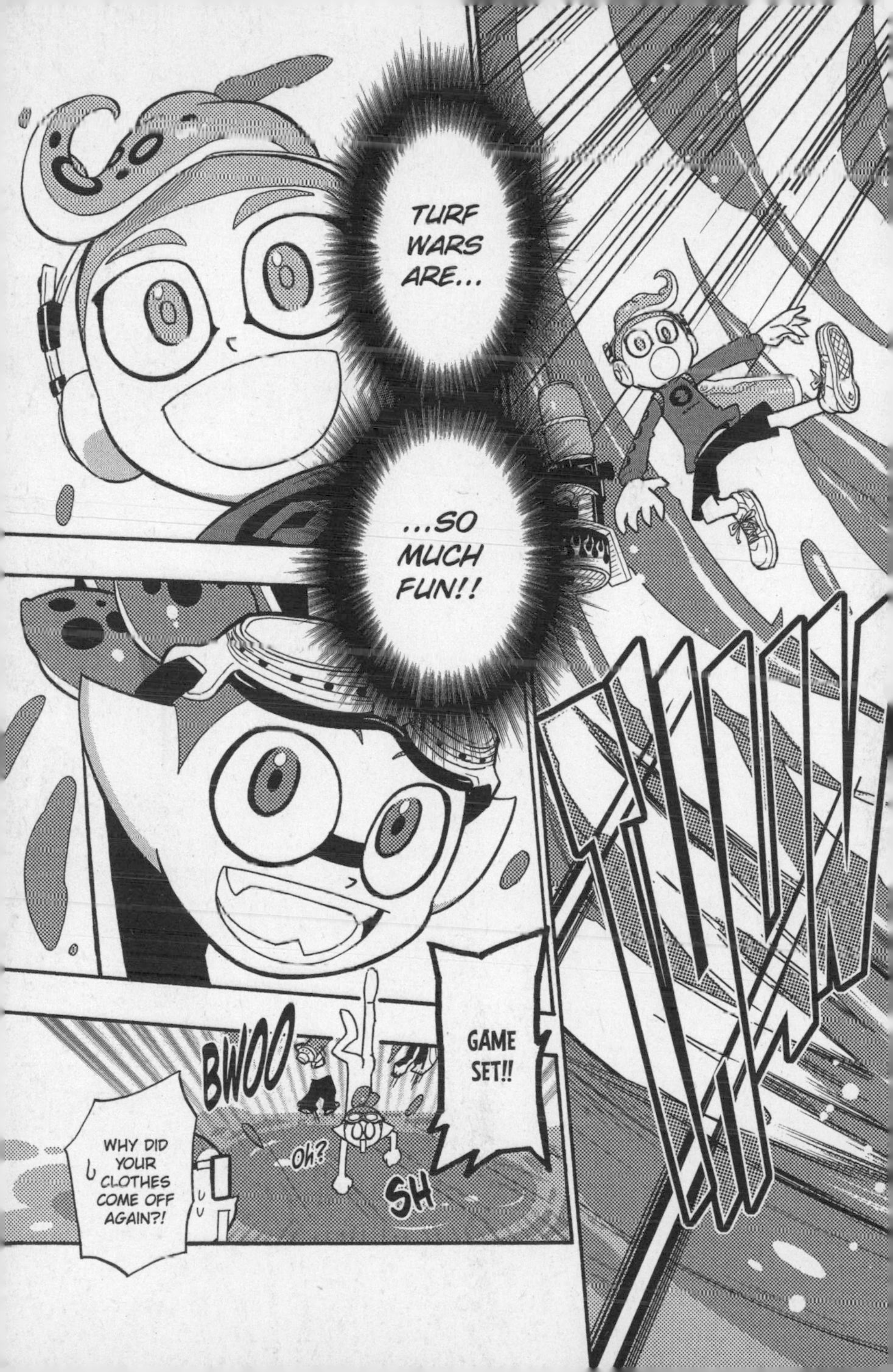
TURF WARS ARE...
...SO MUCH FUN!!
GAME SET!!
BWOO
Oh?
SH
WHY DID YOUR CLOTHES COME OFF AGAIN?!

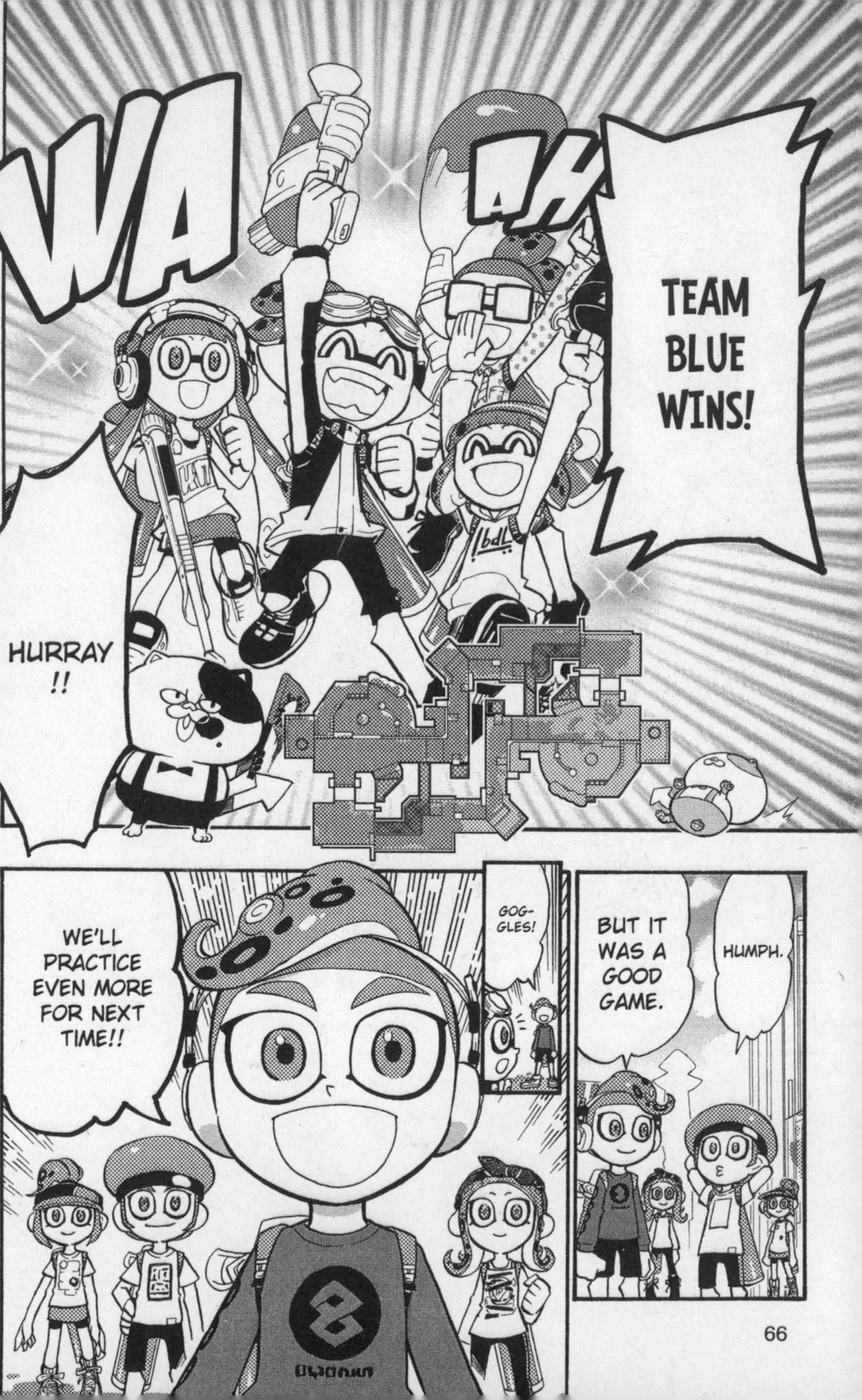
TEAM BLUE WINS!
WA AH
HURRAY!!
HUMPH.
BUT IT WAS A GOOD GAME.
GOG-GLES!
WE'LL PRACTICE EVEN MORE FOR NEXT TIME!!

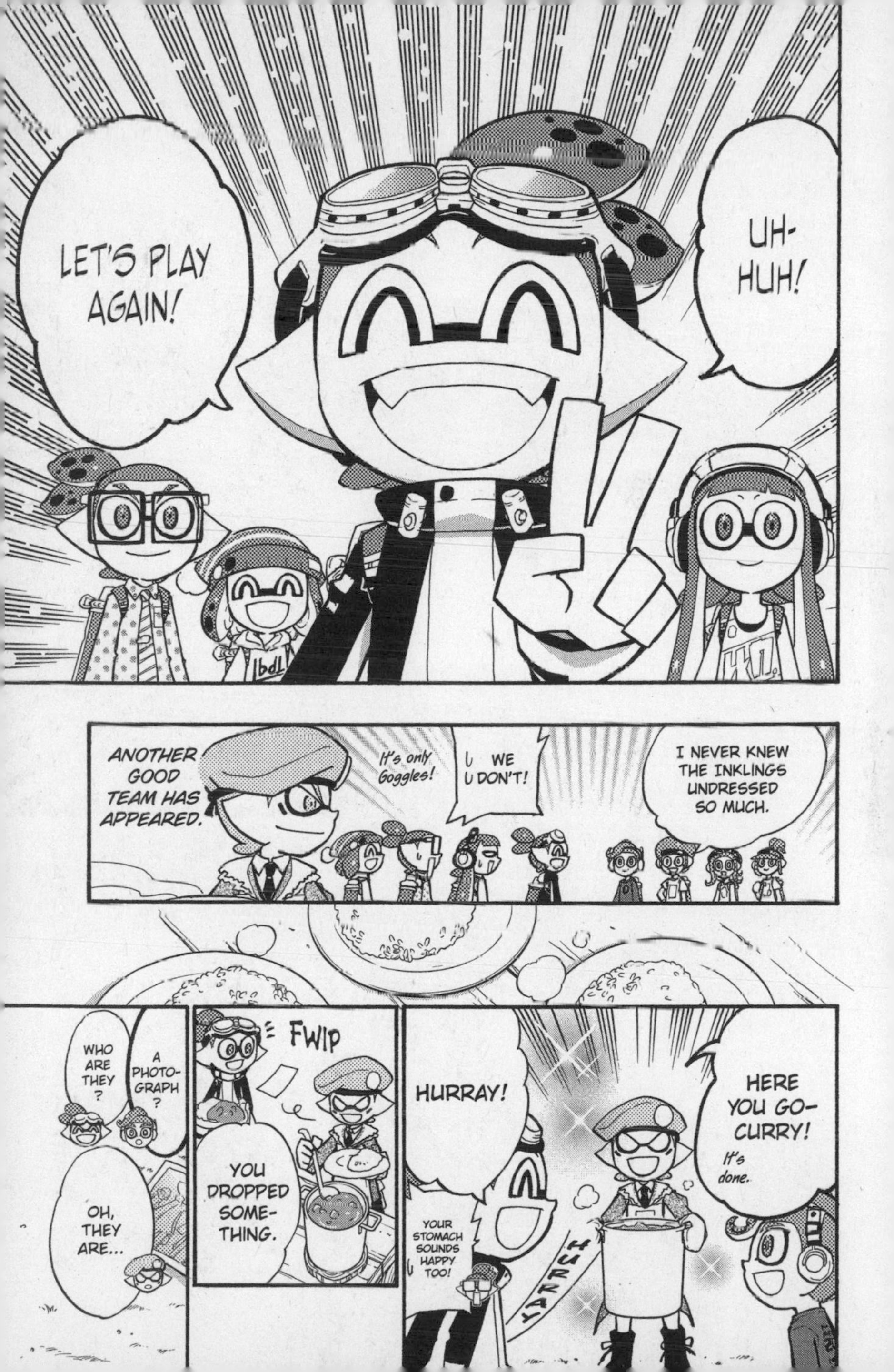
UH-HUH!
LET'S PLAY AGAIN!
I NEVER KNEW THE INKLINGS UNDRESSED SO MUCH.
WE DON'T!
It's only Goggles!
ANOTHER GOOD TEAM HAS APPEARED.
HERE YOU GO- CURRY!
It's done.
HURRAY!
HURRAY
YOUR STOMACH SOUNDS HAPPY TOO!
FWIP
YOU DROPPED SOMETHING.
A PHOTOGRAPH?
WHO ARE THEY?
OH, THEY ARE...

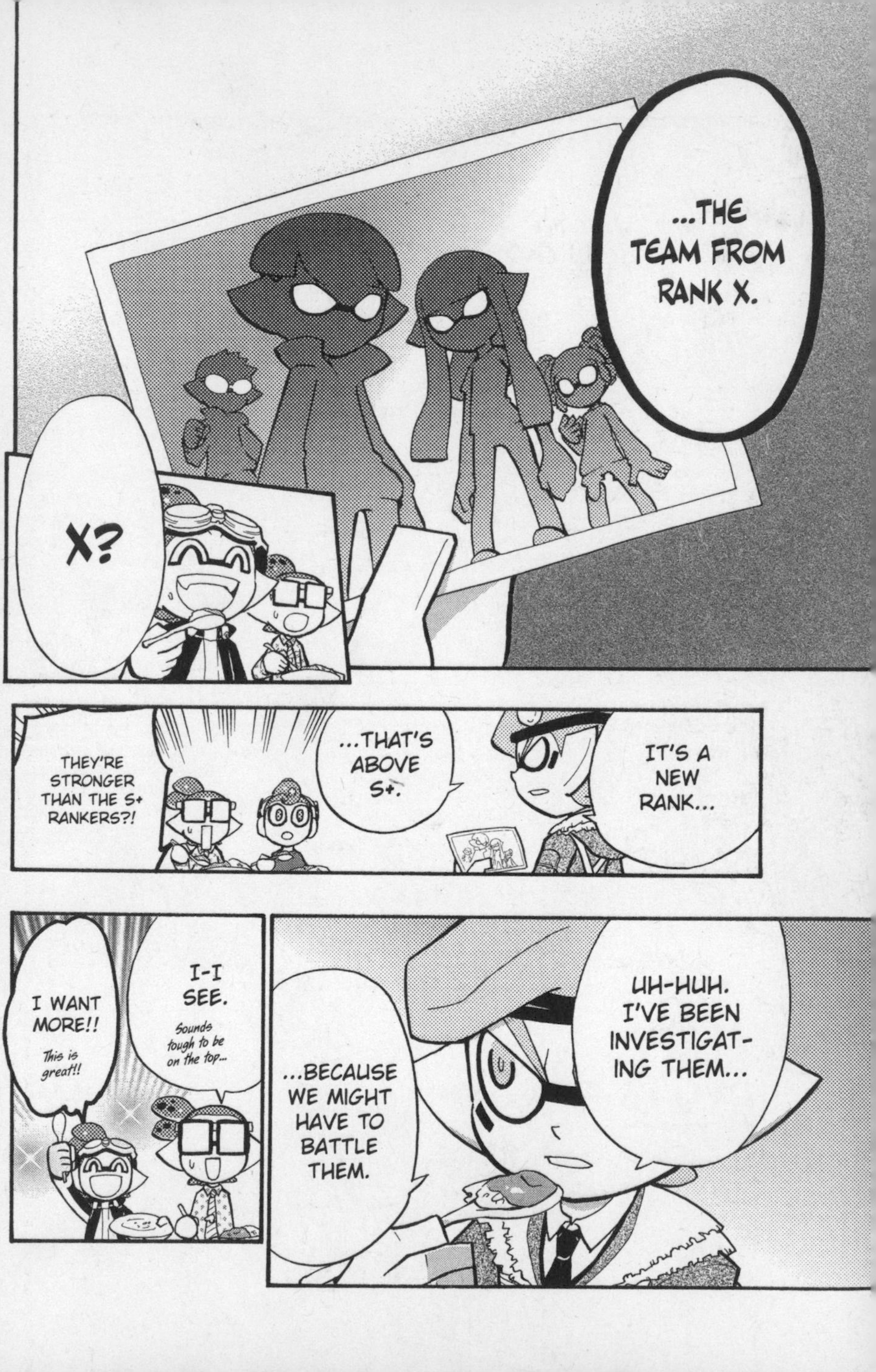
...THE TEAM FROM RANK X.
X?
IT'S A NEW RANK...
...THAT'S ABOVE S+.
THEY'RE STRONGER THAN THE S+ RANKERS?!
UH-HUH. I'VE BEEN INVESTIGAT-ING THEM...
...BECAUSE WE MIGHT HAVE TO BATTLE THEM.
I-I SEE.
Sounds tough to be on the top...
I WANT MORE!!
This is great!!

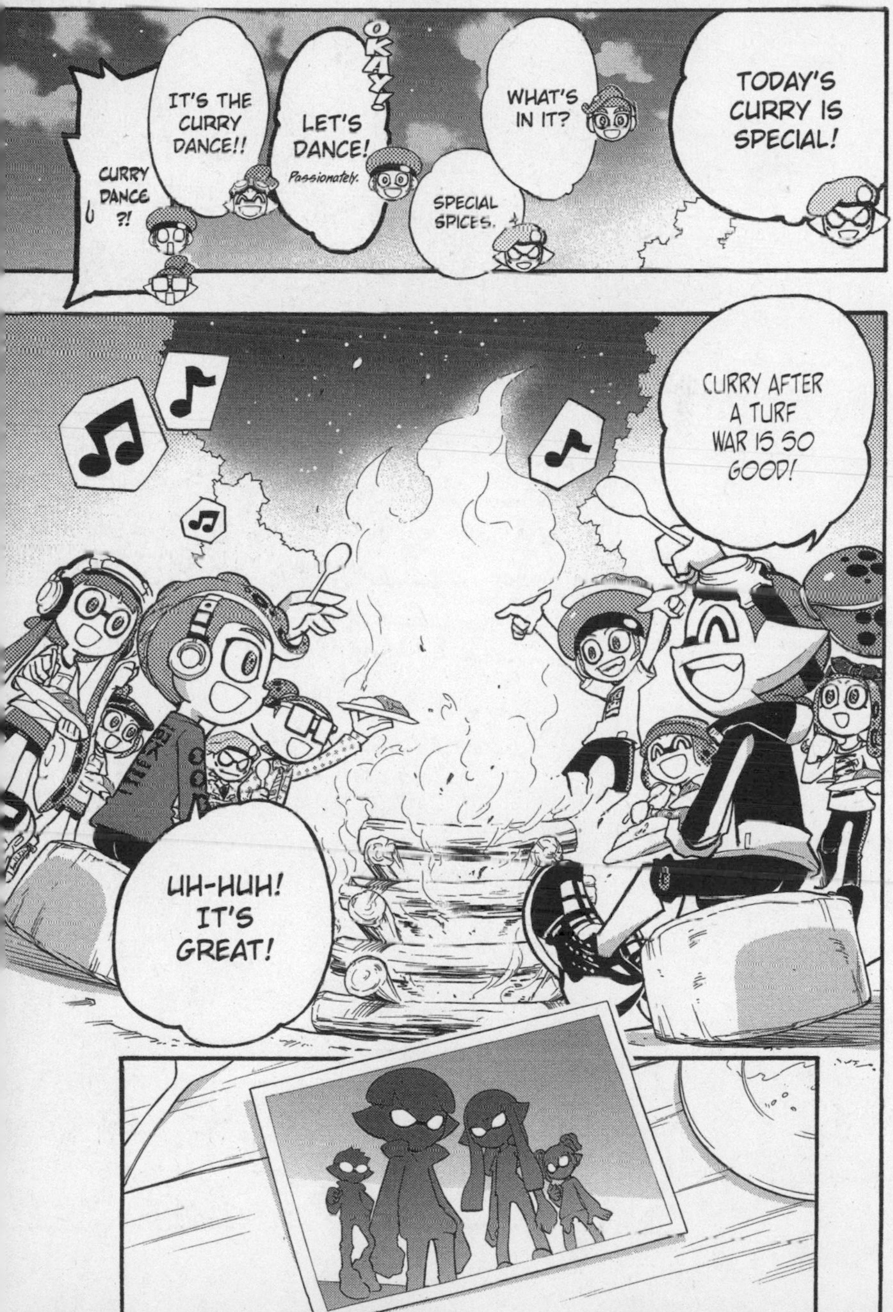
TODAY'S CURRY IS SPECIAL!
WHAT'S IN IT?
SPECIAL SPICES.
OKAY!
LET'S DANCE!
Passionately.
IT'S THE CURRY DANCE!!
CURRY DANCE ?!
CURRY AFTER A TURF WAR IS SO GOOD!
UH-HUH! IT'S GREAT!

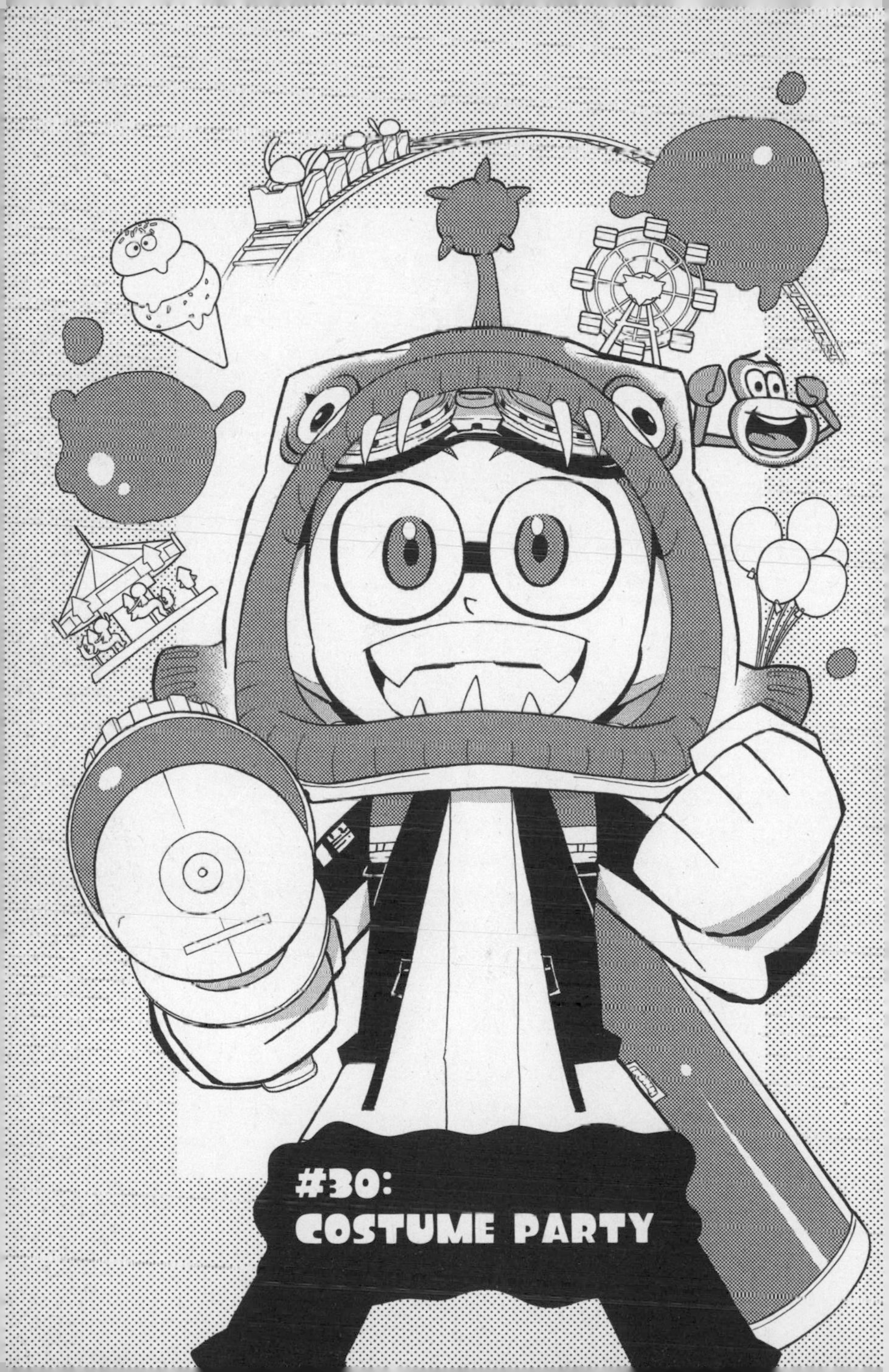
#30:
COSTUME PARTY

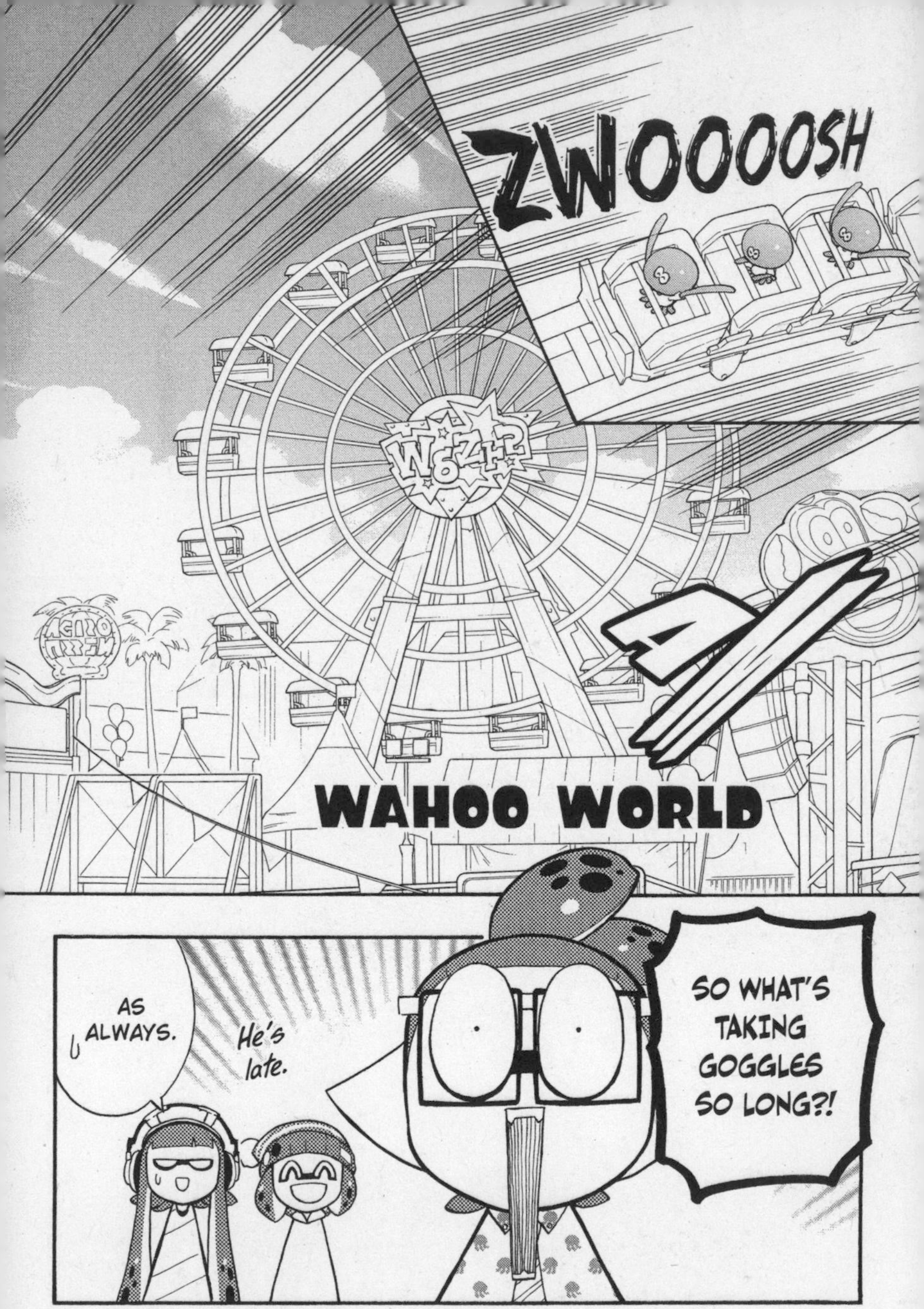
ZWOOOOSH
WAHOO WORLD
SO WHAT'S TAKING GOGGLES SO LONG?!
He's late.
AS ALWAYS.

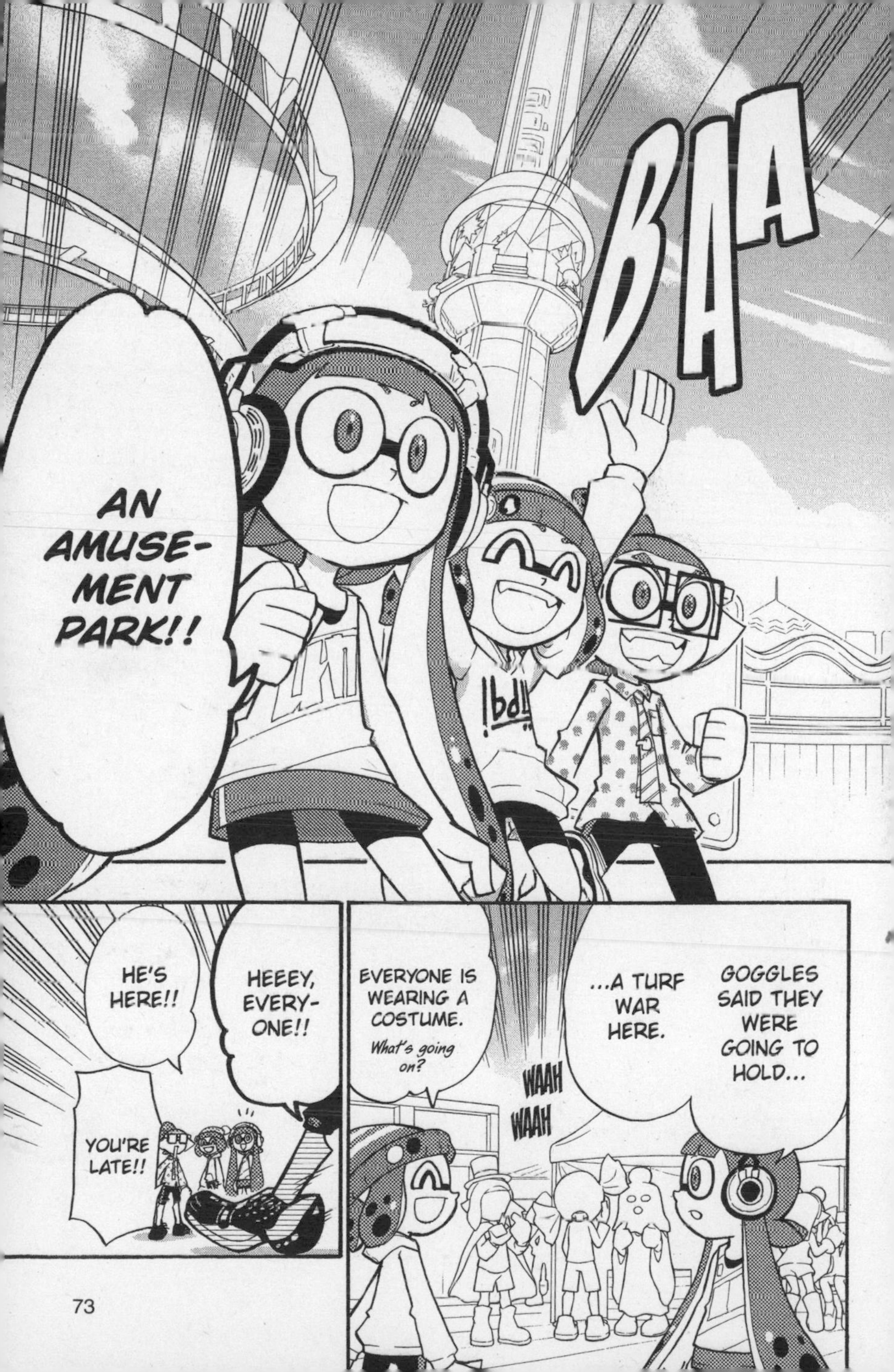
BAA
AN AMUSEMENT PARK!!
GOGGLES SAID THEY WERE GOING TO HOLD...
...A TURF WAR HERE.
WAAH WAAH
EVERYONE IS WEARING A COSTUME. What's going on?
HEEEY, EVERYONE!!
HE'S HERE!!
YOU'RE LATE!!

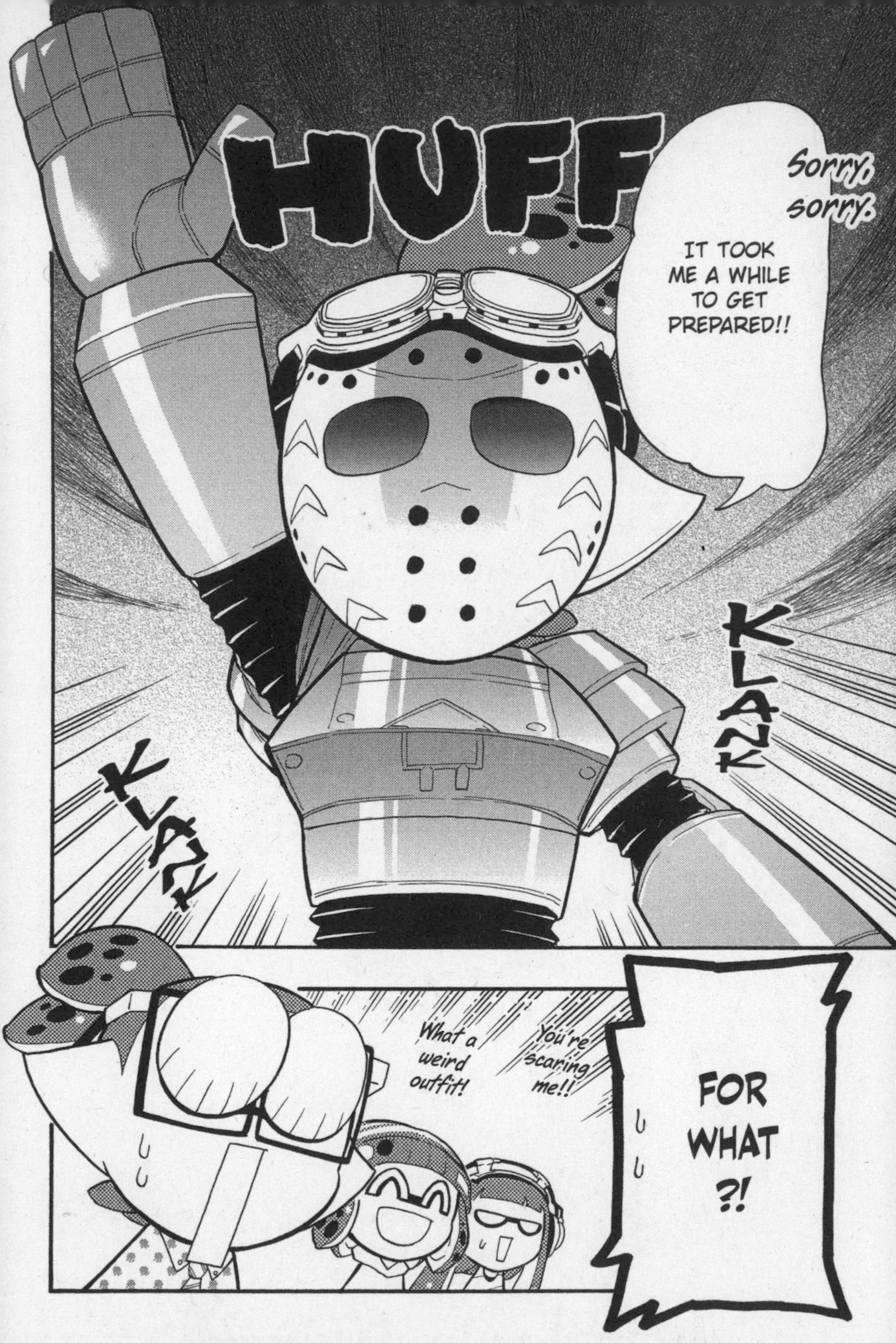
HUFF
Sorry, sorry.
IT TOOK ME A WHILE TO GET PREPARED!!
KLANK
KLANK
FOR WHAT?!
You're scaring me!!
What a weird outfit!

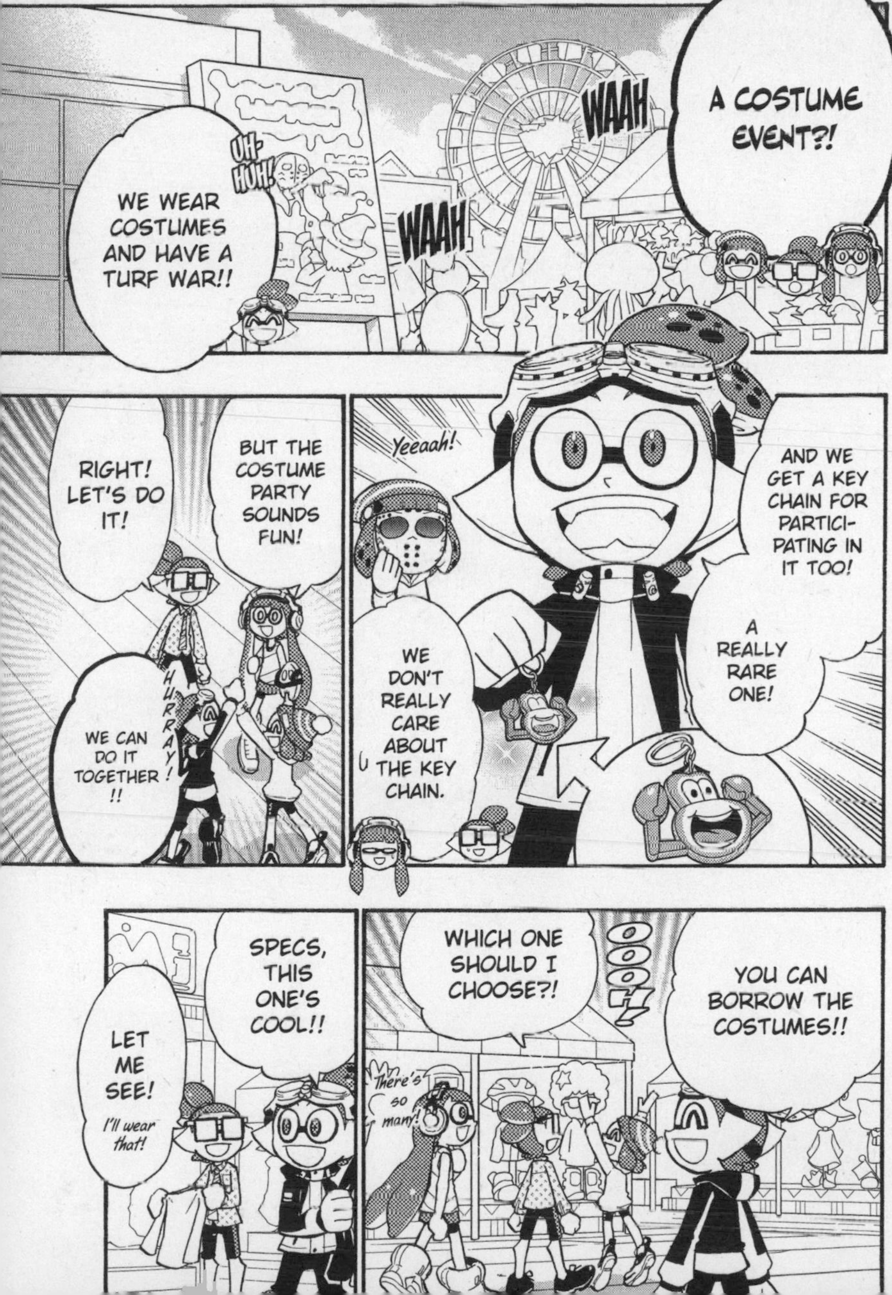
A COSTUME EVENT?!
WAAH
WAAH
UH-HUH!
WE WEAR COSTUMES AND HAVE A TURF WAR!!
AND WE GET A KEY CHAIN FOR PARTICI-PATING IN IT TOO!
A REALLY RARE ONE!
Yeeaah!
WE DON'T REALLY CARE ABOUT THE KEY CHAIN.
BUT THE COSTUME PARTY SOUNDS FUN!
RIGHT! LET'S DO IT!
HURRAY!
WE CAN DO IT TOGETHER!!
YOU CAN BORROW THE COSTUMES!!
OOOH!
WHICH ONE SHOULD I CHOOSE?!
There's so many!
SPECS, THIS ONE'S COOL!!
LET ME SEE!
I'll wear that!

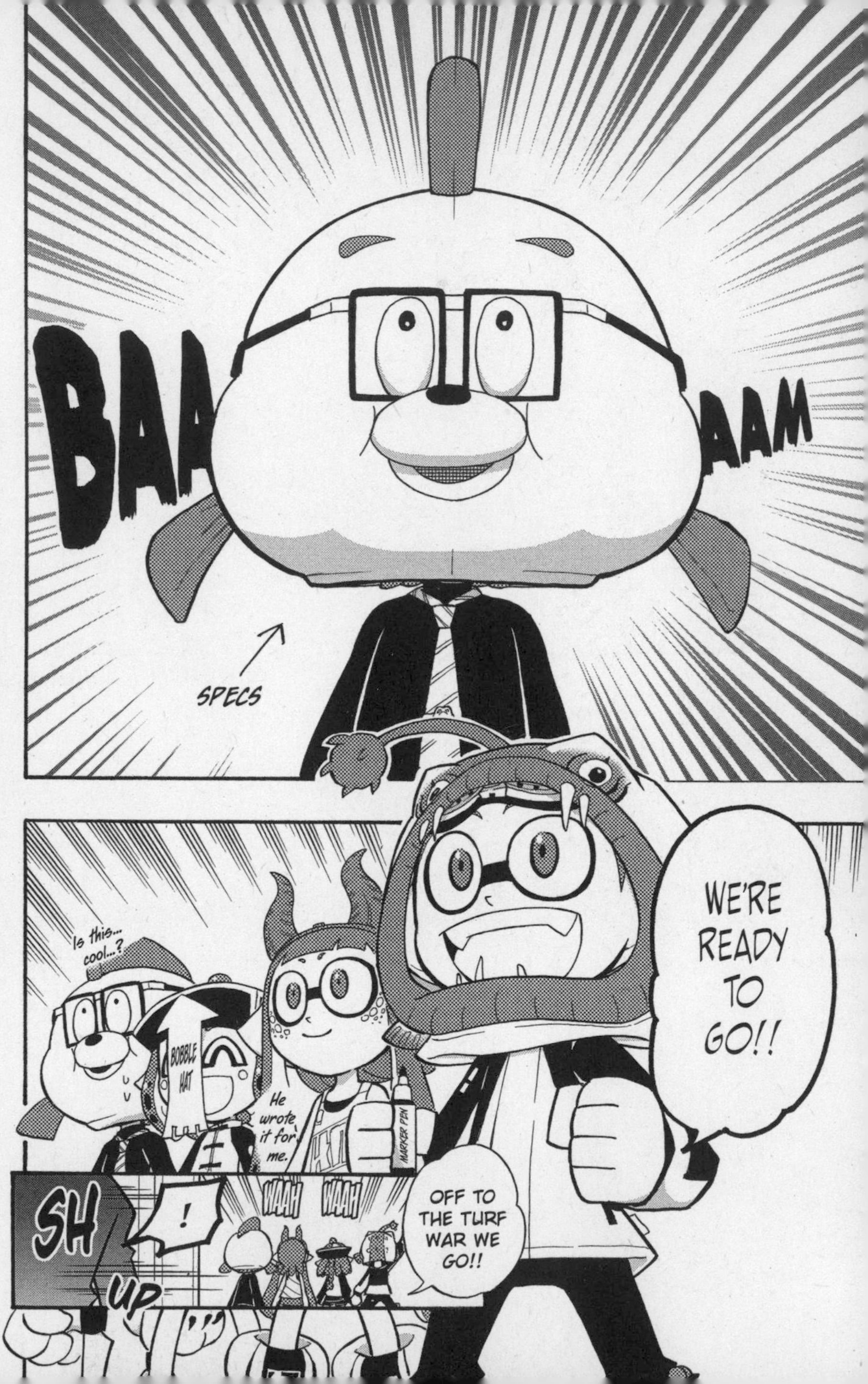
BAA
AAM
SPECS
WE'RE READY TO GO!!
MARKER PEN
He wrote it for me.
BOBBLE HAT
Is this... cool...?
OFF TO THE TURF WAR WE GO!!
WAAH
WAAH
!
SH
UP

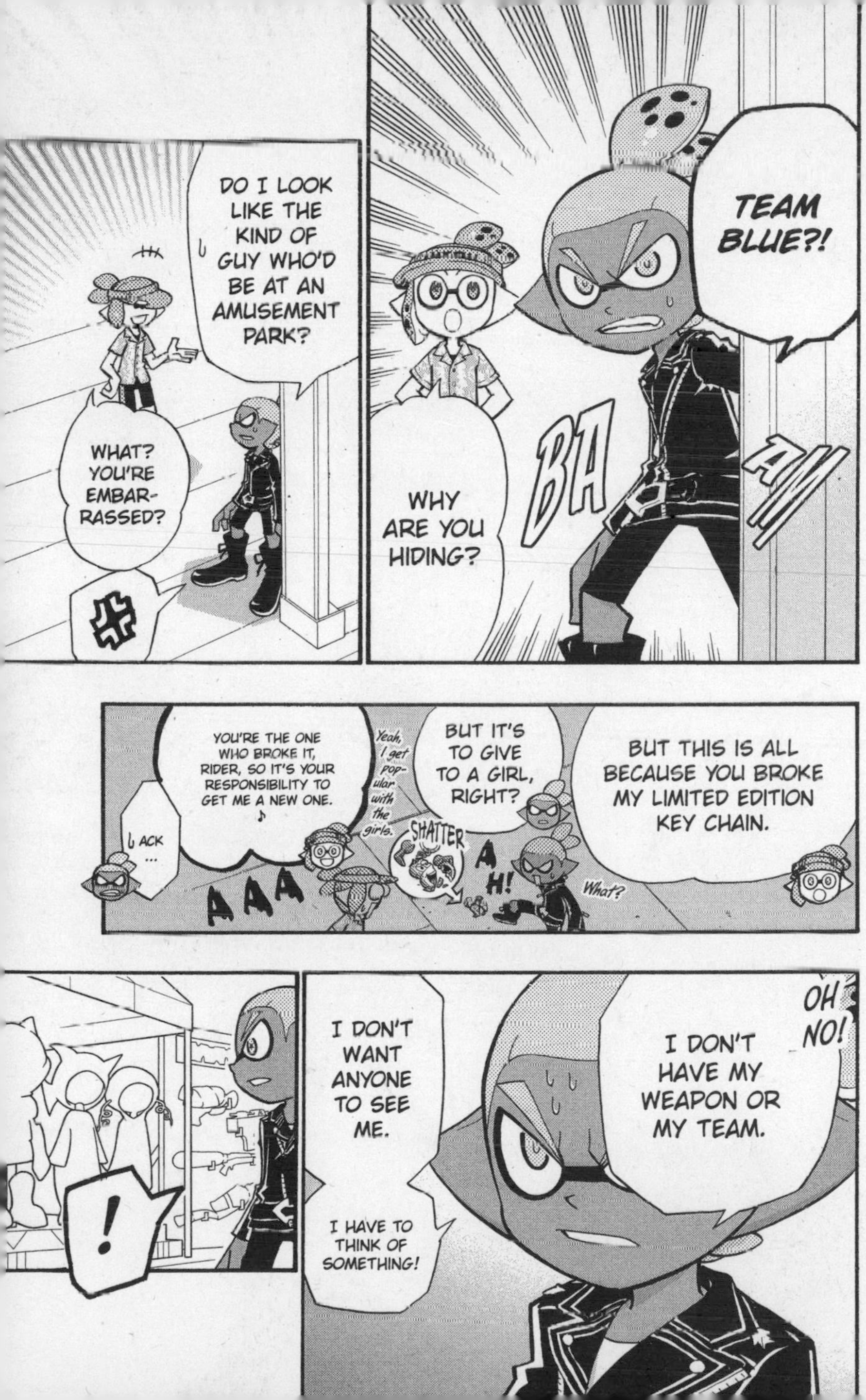
TEAM BLUE?!
BA AM
WHY ARE YOU HIDING?
DO I LOOK LIKE THE KIND OF GUY WHO'D BE AT AN AMUSEMENT PARK?
WHAT? YOU'RE EMBARRASSED?
BUT THIS IS ALL BECAUSE YOU BROKE MY LIMITED EDITION KEY CHAIN.
What?
BUT IT'S TO GIVE TO A GIRL, RIGHT?
A H!
SHATTER
Yeah, I get popular with the girls.
YOU'RE THE ONE WHO BROKE IT, RIDER, SO IT'S YOUR RESPONSIBILITY TO GET ME A NEW ONE. ♪
A A A
ACK ...
OH NO!
I DON'T HAVE MY WEAPON OR MY TEAM.
I DON'T WANT ANYONE TO SEE ME.
I HAVE TO THINK OF SOMETHING!
!

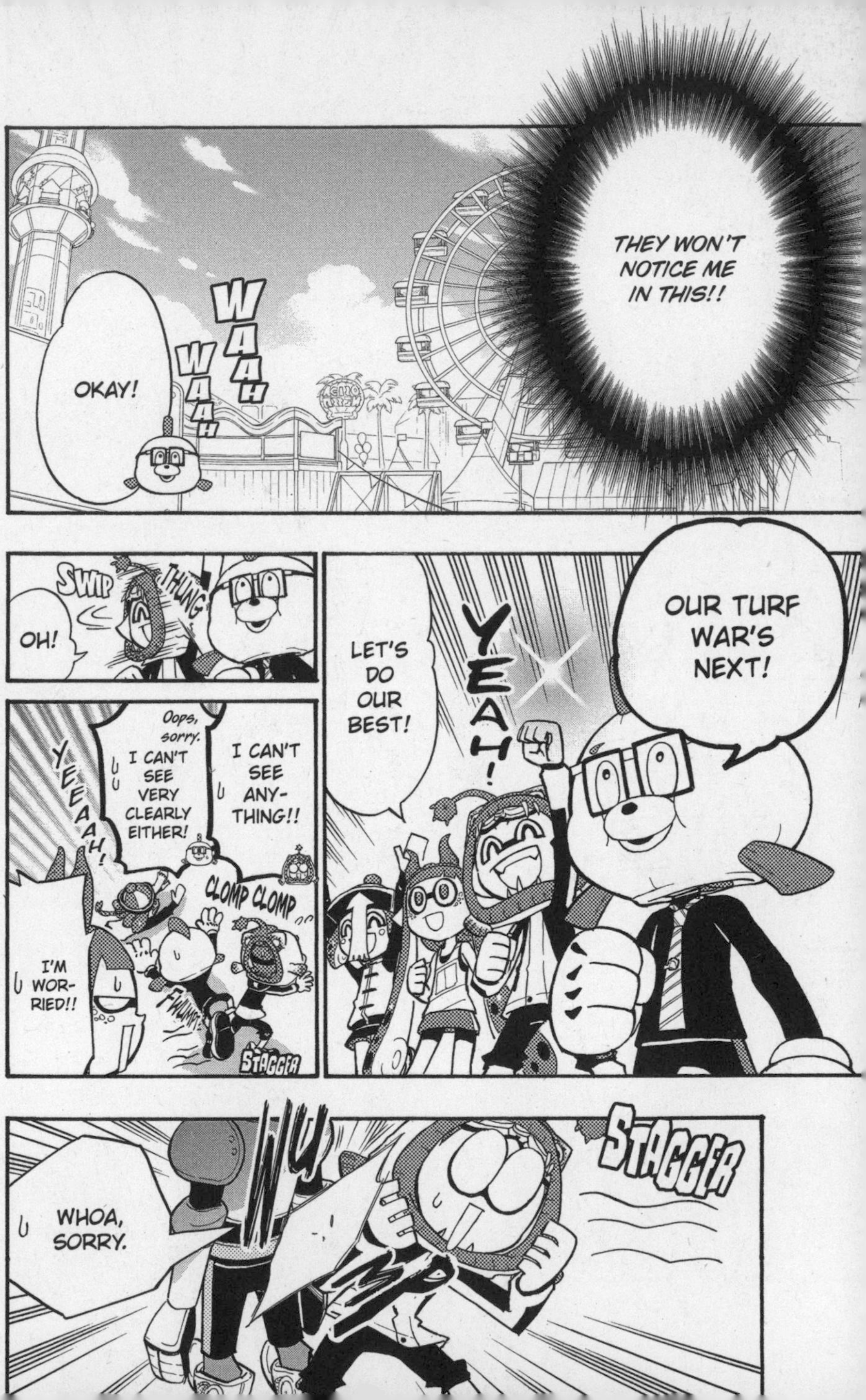
THEY WON'T NOTICE ME IN THIS!!
WAAH
WAAH
OKAY!
OUR TURF WAR'S NEXT!
YEAH!
LET'S DO OUR BEST!
THUNG
SWIP
OH!
I CAN'T SEE ANY-THING!!
Oops, sorry.
I CAN'T SEE VERY CLEARLY EITHER!
YEEAAAH!
CLOMP CLOMP
I'M WOR-RIED!!
STAGGER
STAGGER
WHOA, SORRY.

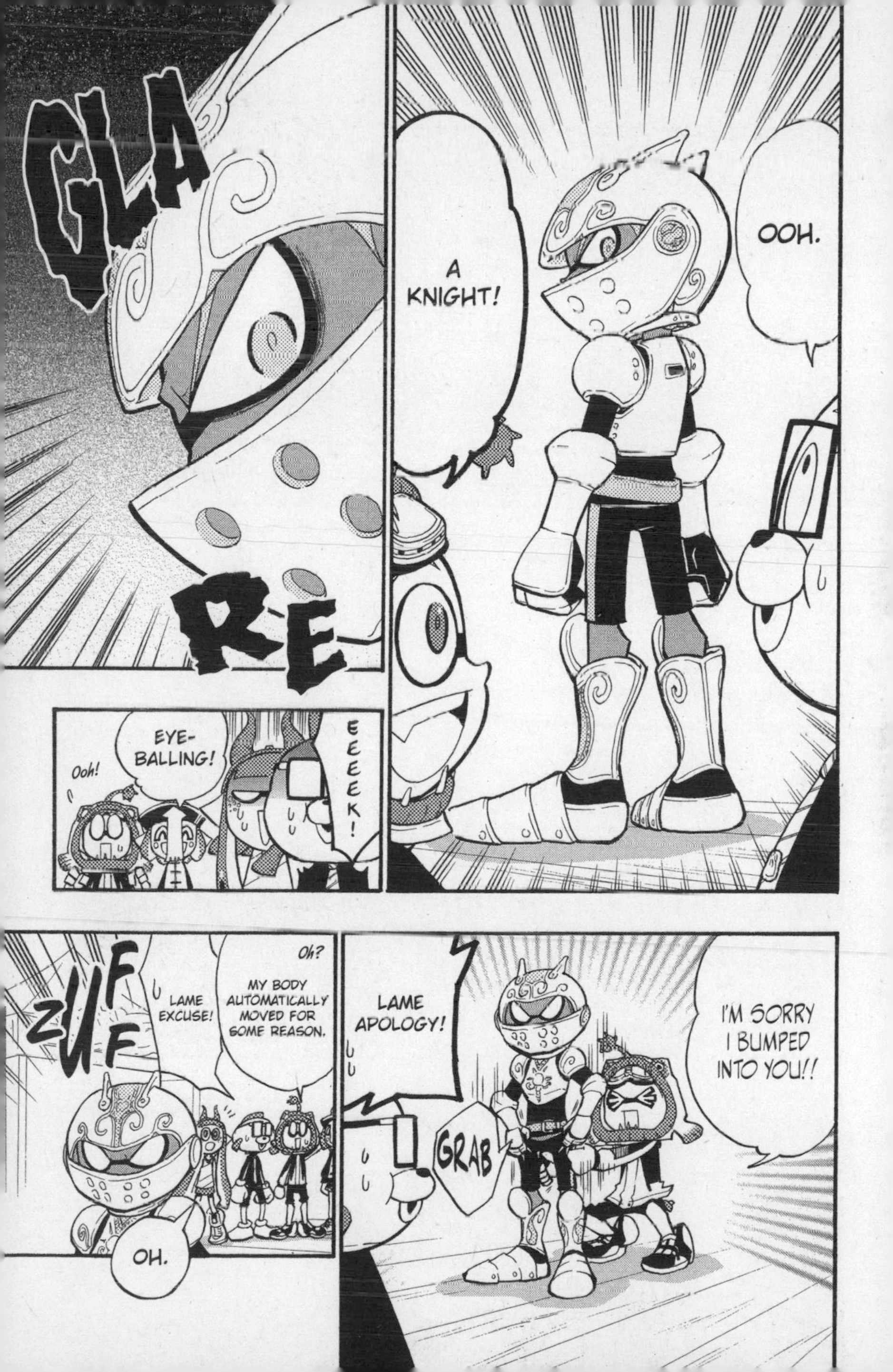
OOH.
A KNIGHT!
GLARE
EEEEK!
EYE-BALLING!
Ooh!
I'M SORRY I BUMPED INTO YOU!!
GRAB
LAME APOLOGY!
Oh?
MY BODY AUTOMATICALLY MOVED FOR SOME REASON.
LAME EXCUSE!
ZUFF
OH.

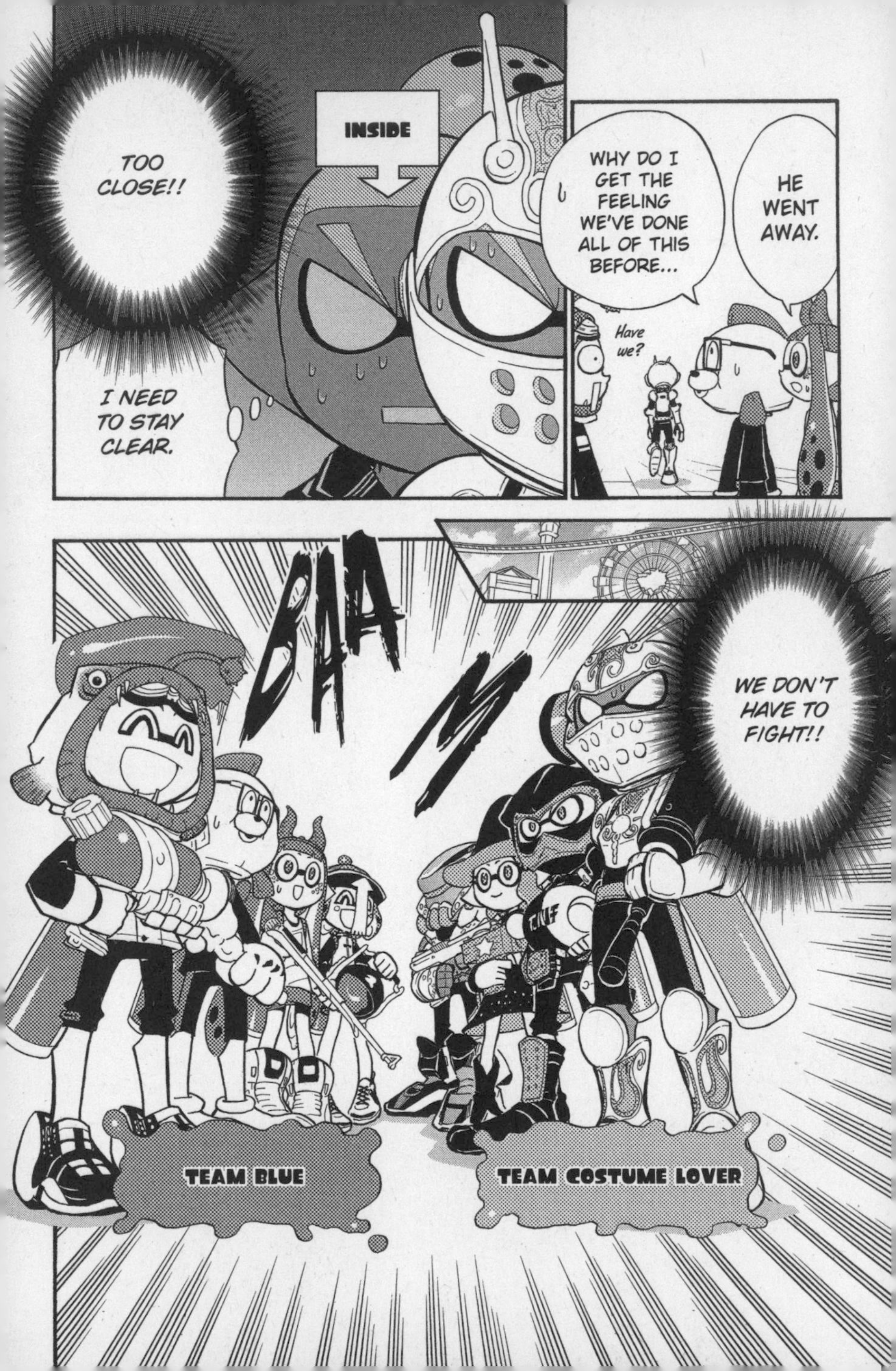
HE WENT AWAY.
WHY DO I GET THE FEELING WE'VE DONE ALL OF THIS BEFORE...
Have we?
INSIDE
TOO CLOSE!!
I NEED TO STAY CLEAR.
WE DON'T HAVE TO FIGHT!!
BAM
TEAM COSTUME LOVER
TEAM BLUE

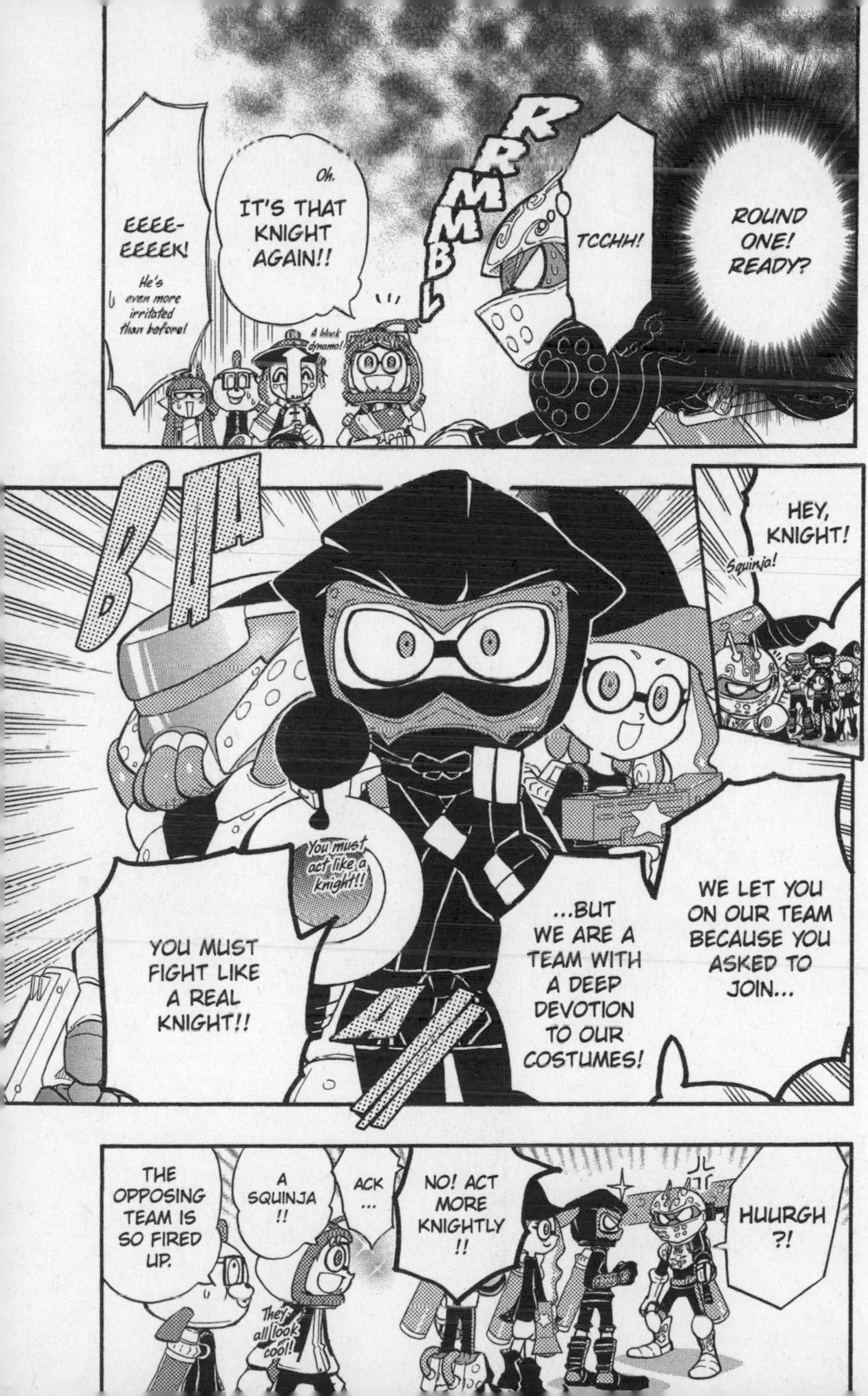
ROUND ONE! READY?
TCCHH!
RRMMBL
Oh.
IT'S THAT KNIGHT AGAIN!!
A black dynamo!
EEEE-EEEEK!
He's even more irritated than before!
HEY, KNIGHT!
Squinja!
WE LET YOU ON OUR TEAM BECAUSE YOU ASKED TO JOIN...
...BUT WE ARE A TEAM WITH A DEEP DEVOTION TO OUR COSTUMES!
You must act like a knight!!
YOU MUST FIGHT LIKE A REAL KNIGHT!!
BHA
HUURGH ?!
NO! ACT MORE KNIGHTLY !!
ACK ...
A SQUINJA !!
They all look cool!
THE OPPOSING TEAM IS SO FIRED UP.

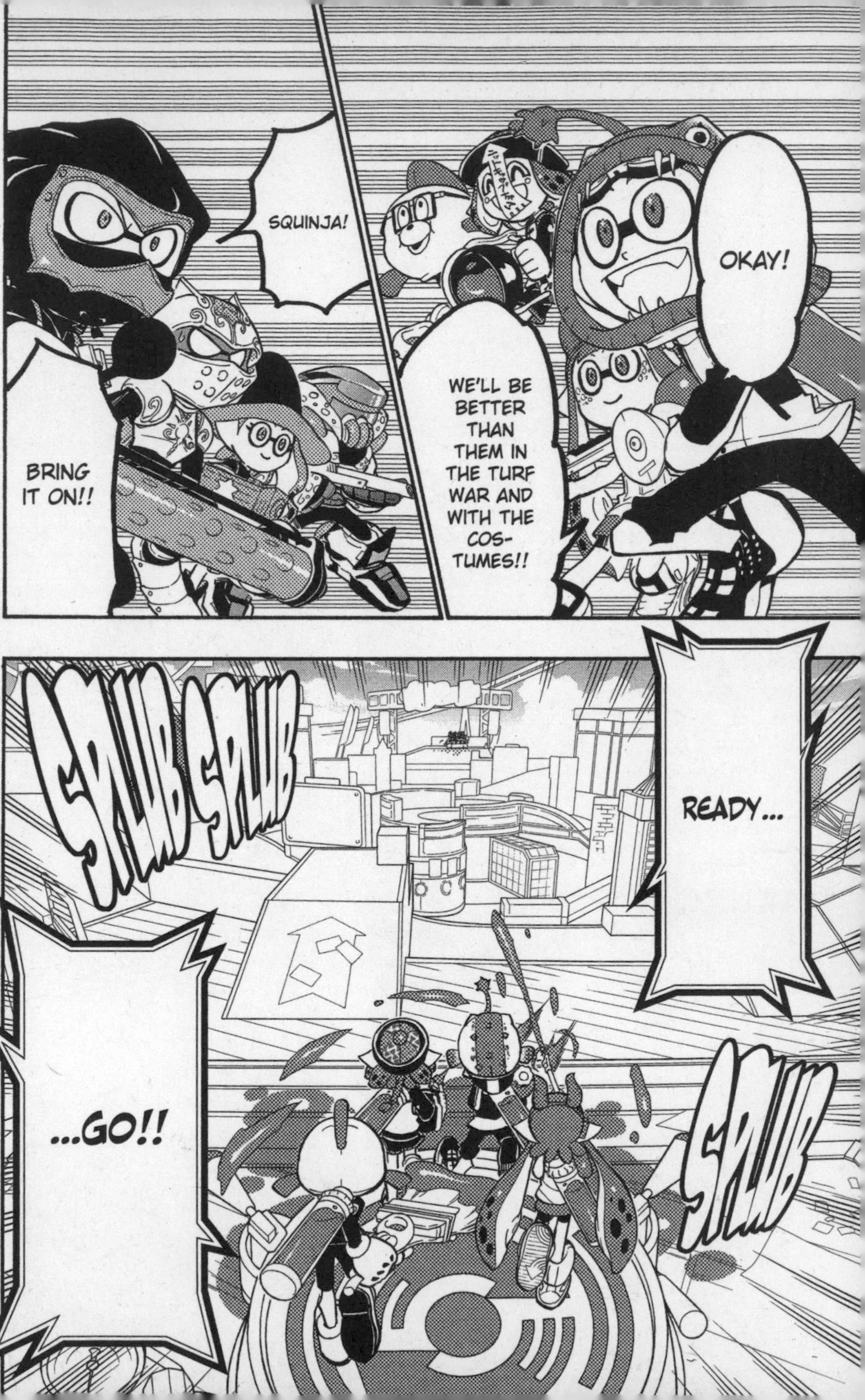
OKAY!
WE'LL BE BETTER THAN THEM IN THE TURF WAR AND WITH THE COS-TUMES!!
SQUINJA!
BRING IT ON!!
READY...
SPLUB SPLUB
...GO!!
SPLUB

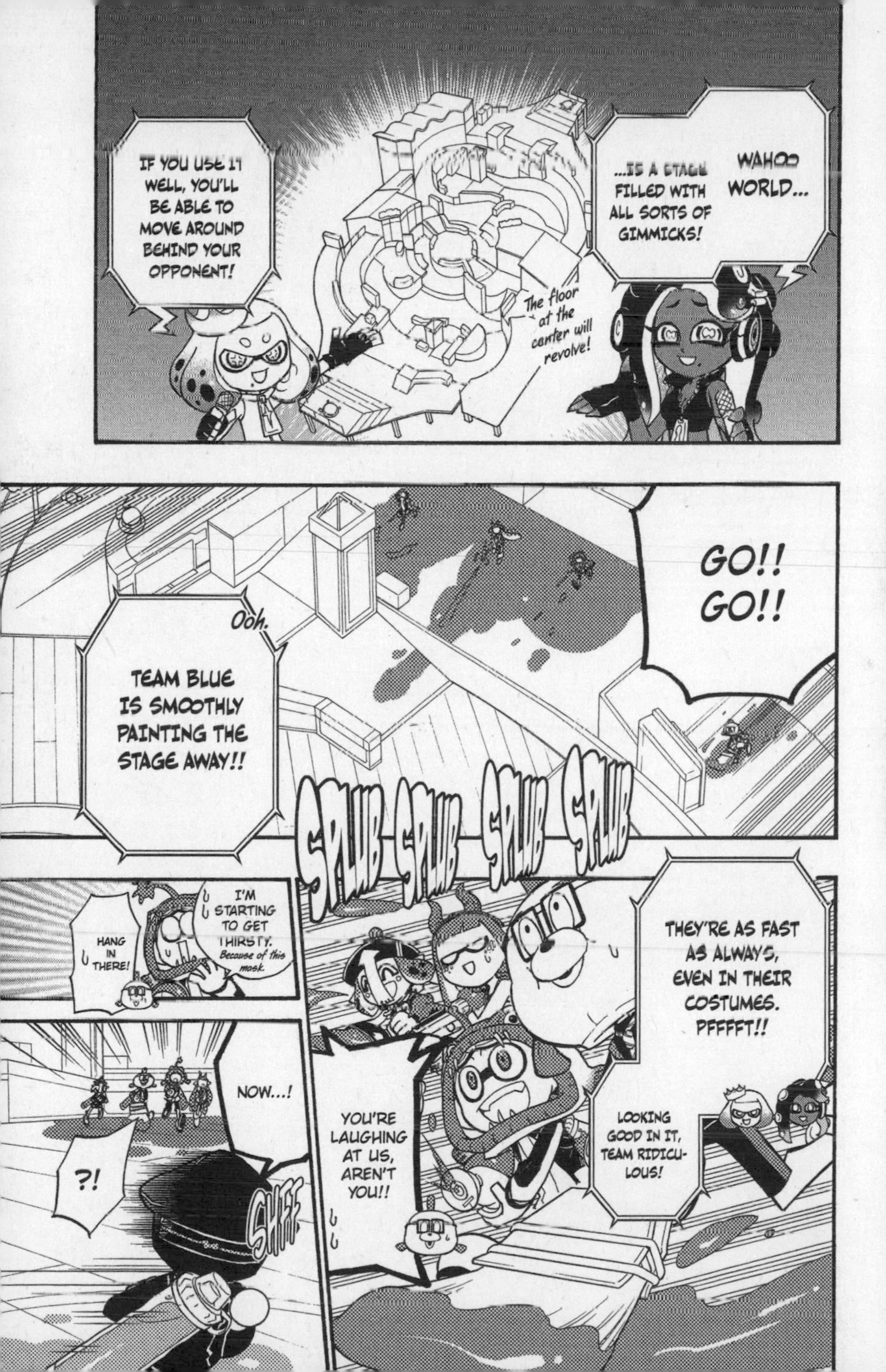
WAHOO WORLD...
...IS A STAGE FILLED WITH ALL SORTS OF GIMMICKS!
The floor at the center will revolve!
IF YOU USE IT WELL, YOU'LL BE ABLE TO MOVE AROUND BEHIND YOUR OPPONENT!
GO!! GO!!
Ooh.
TEAM BLUE IS SMOOTHLY PAINTING THE STAGE AWAY!!
SPLUB SPLUB SPLUB SPLUB
THEY'RE AS FAST AS ALWAYS, EVEN IN THEIR COSTUMES. PFFFFT!!
LOOKING GOOD IN IT, TEAM RIDICULOUS!
YOU'RE LAUGHING AT US, AREN'T YOU!!
I'M STARTING TO GET THIRSTY. Because of this mask.
HANG IN THERE!
NOW...!
?!
SHFF

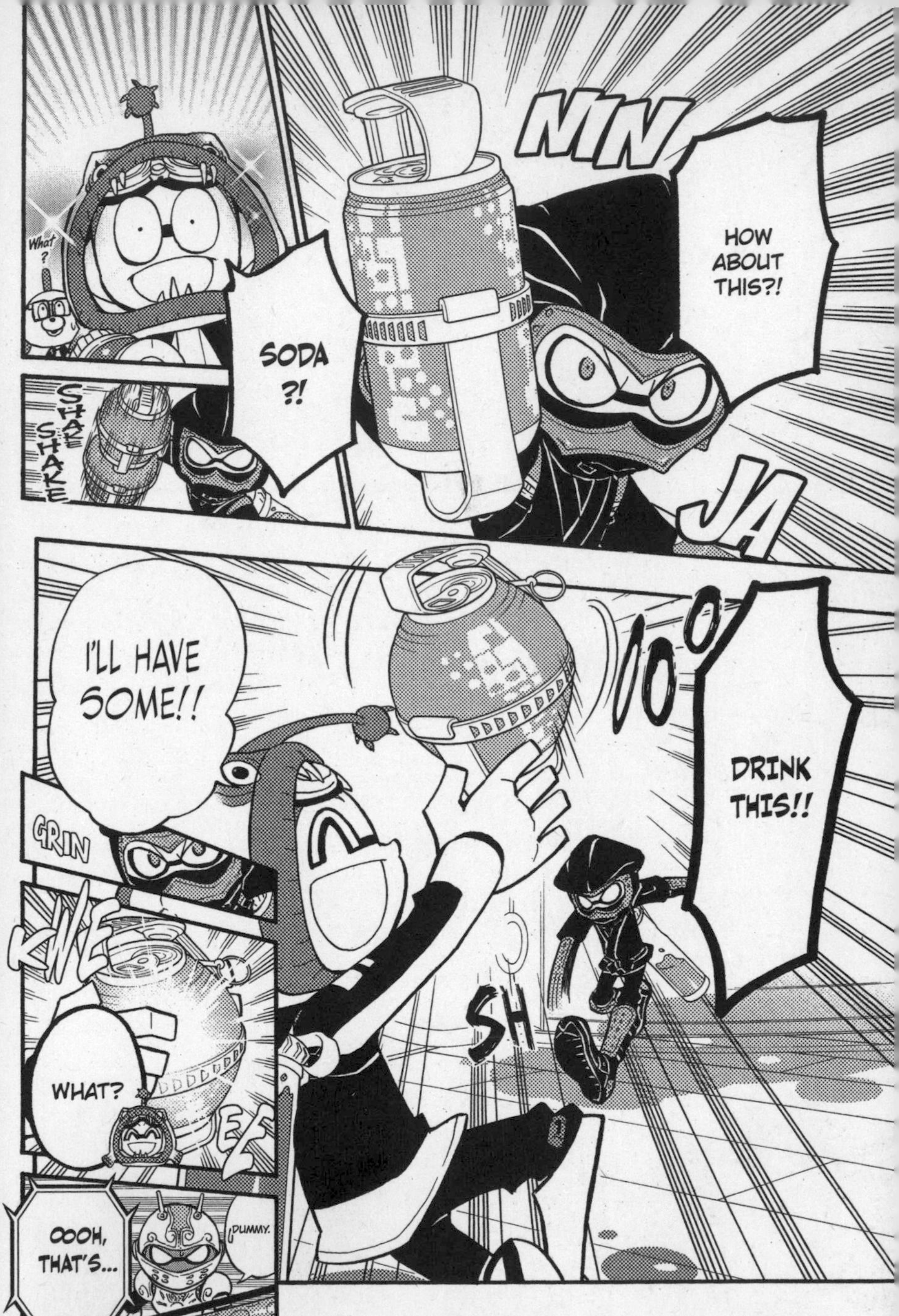
NIN
HOW ABOUT THIS?!
JA
SODA ?!
What ?
SHAKE SHAKE
DRINK THIS!!
I'LL HAVE SOME!!
SH
GRIN
WHAT?
OOOH, THAT'S...
DUMMY.

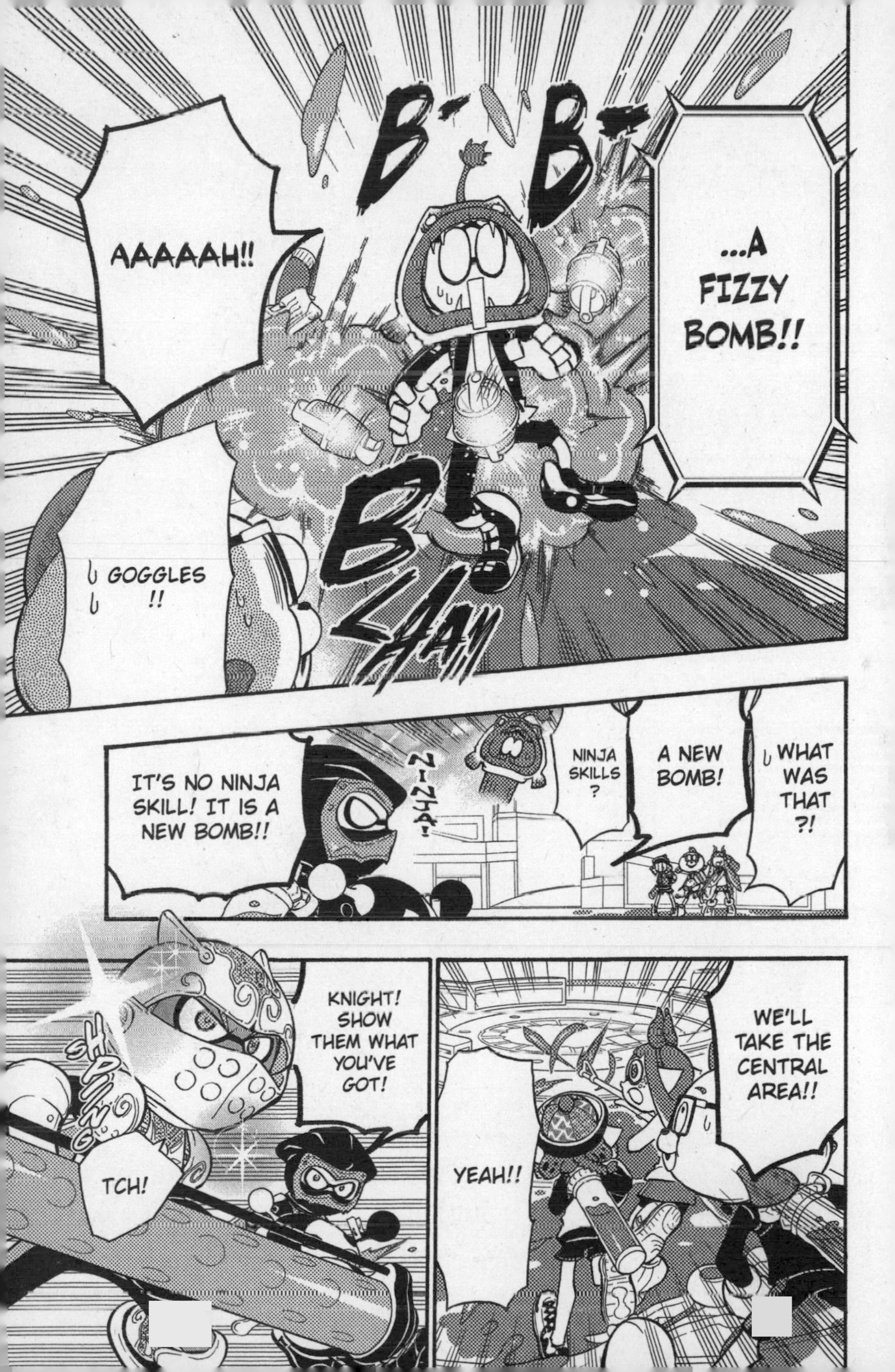
...A FIZZY BOMB!!
B-B-
AAAAAH!!
BLAM!
GOGGLES !!
WHAT WAS THAT ?!
A NEW BOMB!
NINJA SKILLS ?
NINJA!
IT'S NO NINJA SKILL! IT IS A NEW BOMB!!
WE'LL TAKE THE CENTRAL AREA!!
YEAH!!
KNIGHT! SHOW THEM WHAT YOU'VE GOT!
SHING
TCH!

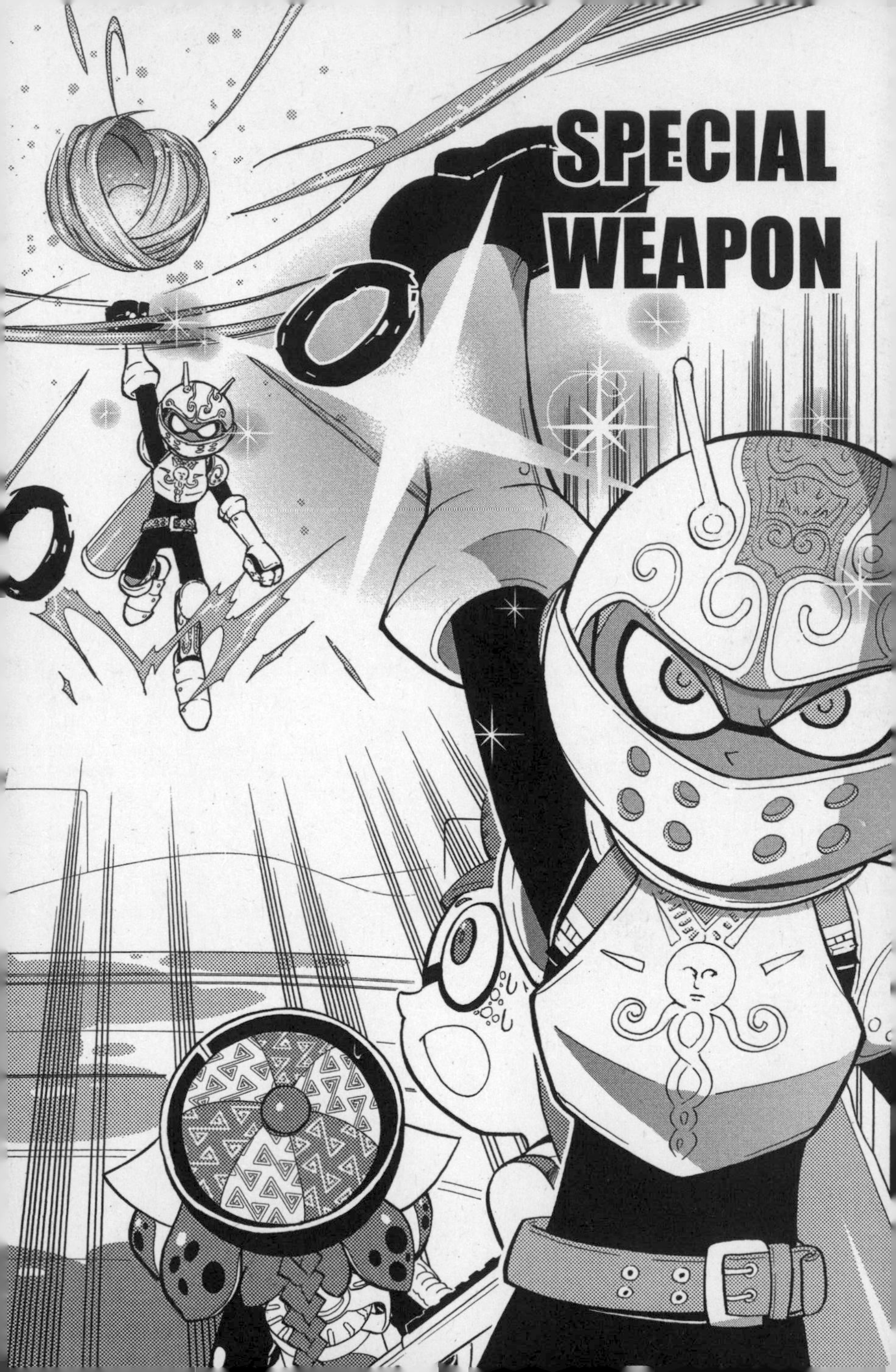
SPECIAL
WEAPON

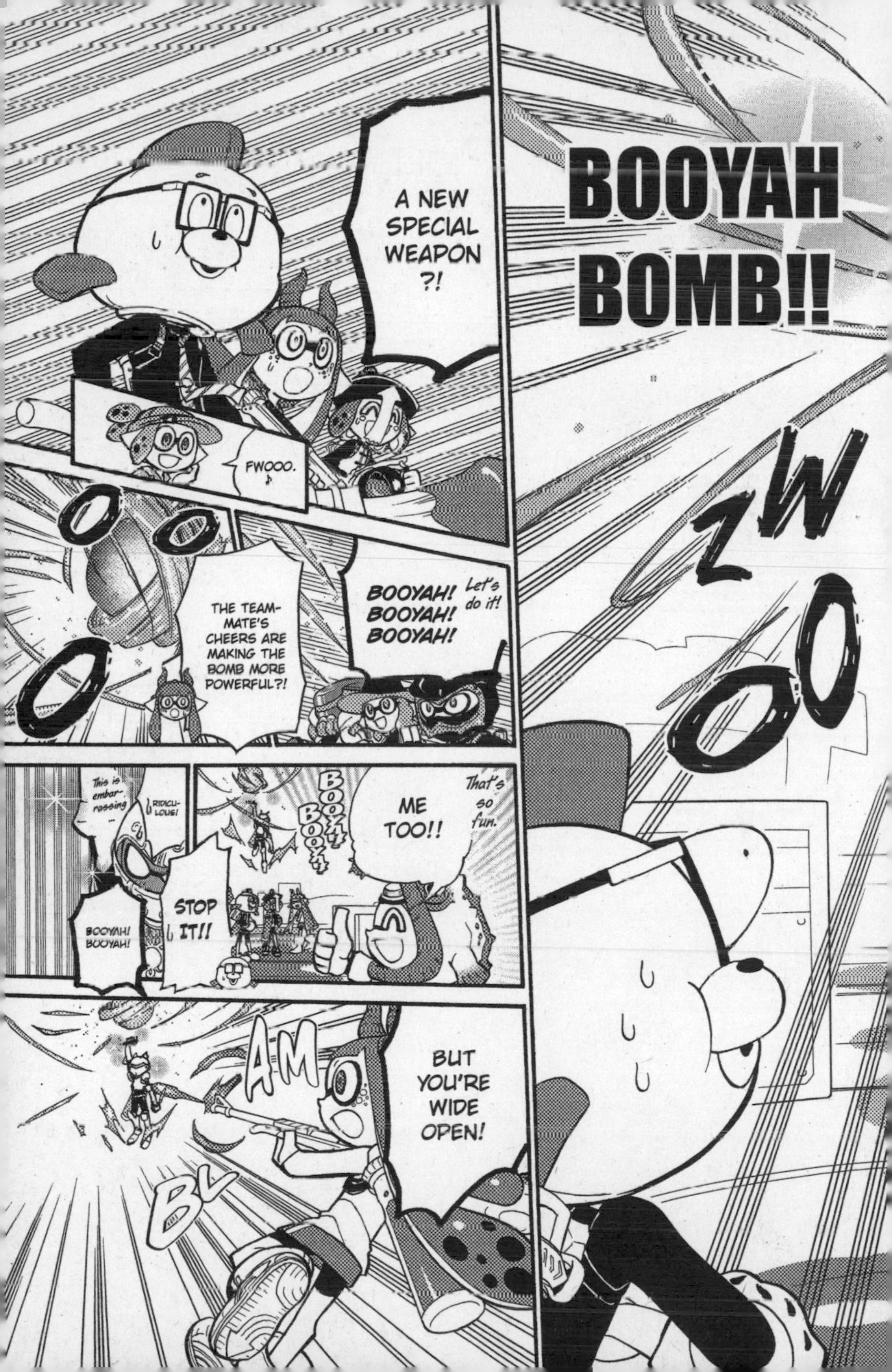

BOOYAH BOMB!!
ZWOOO
A NEW SPECIAL WEAPON ?!
FWOOO. ♪
Let's do it!
BOOYAH! BOOYAH! BOOYAH!
THE TEAM-MATE'S CHEERS ARE MAKING THE BOMB MORE POWERFUL?!
That's so fun.
ME TOO!!
STOP IT!!
RIDICULOUS!
This is embarrassing...
BOOYAH! BOOYAH!
BUT YOU'RE WIDE OPEN!

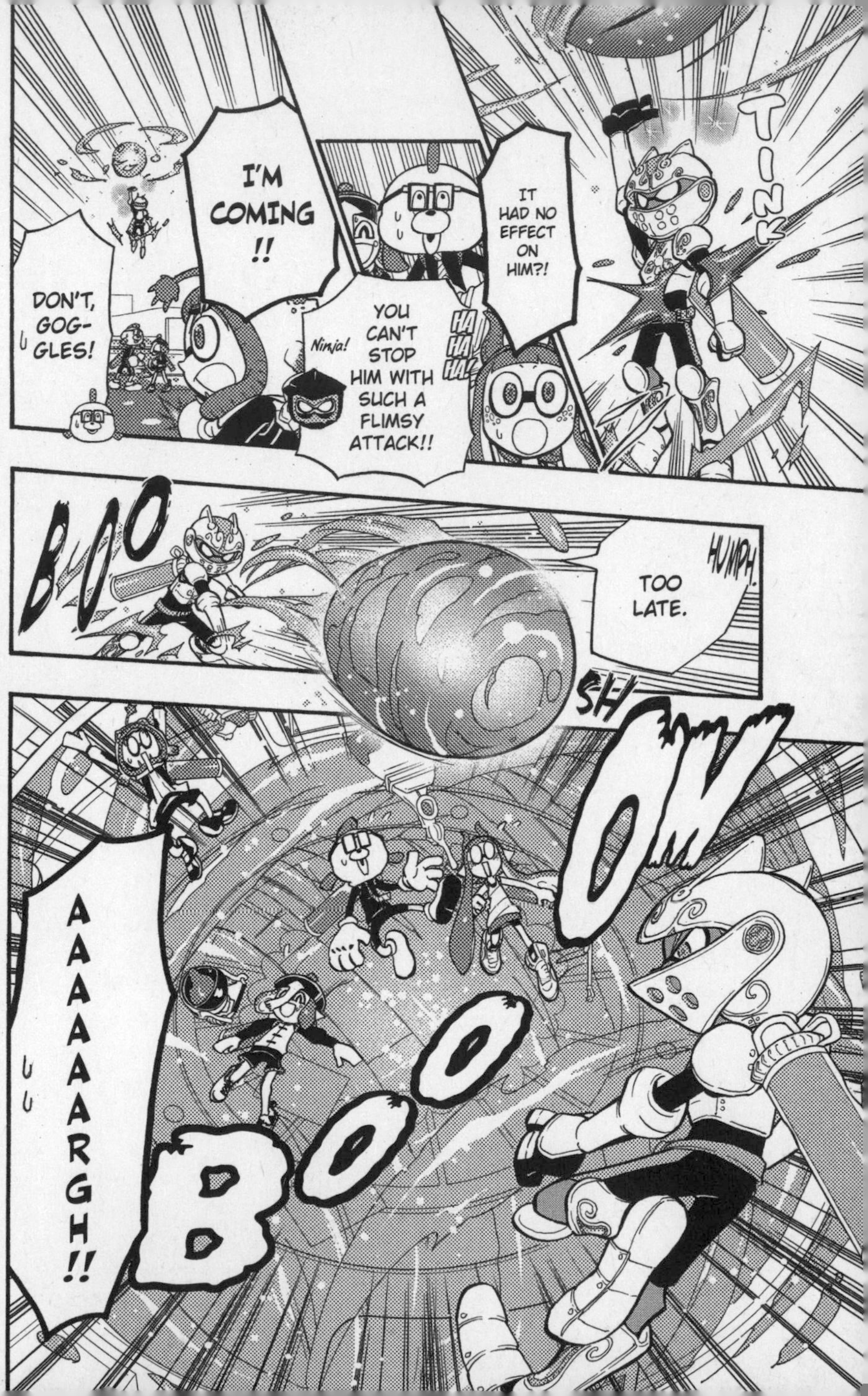

TINK
IT HAD NO EFFECT ON HIM?!
HA HA HA!
YOU CAN'T STOP HIM WITH SUCH A FLIMSY ATTACK!!
Ninja!
I'M COMING!!
DON'T, GOG-GLES!
HUMPH.
TOO LATE.
BOO
SH
ON
BOOO
AAAAAARGH!!

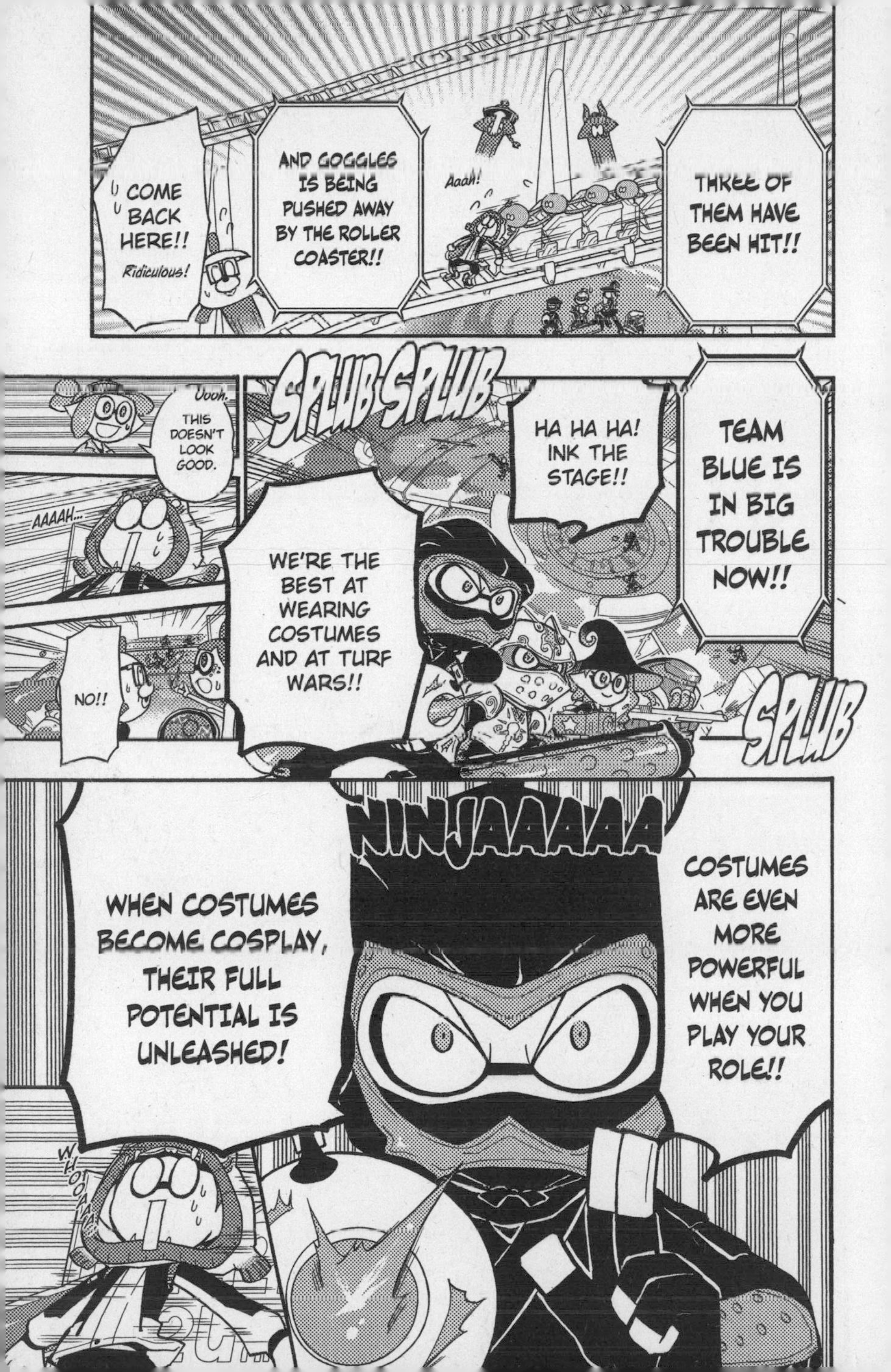
THREE OF THEM HAVE BEEN HIT!!
Aaah!
AND GOGGLES IS BEING PUSHED AWAY BY THE ROLLER COASTER!!
COME BACK HERE!!
Ridiculous!
TEAM BLUE IS IN BIG TROUBLE NOW!!
HA HA HA! INK THE STAGE!!
SPLUB SPLUB
WE'RE THE BEST AT WEARING COSTUMES AND AT TURF WARS!!
SPLUB
Oooh. THIS DOESN'T LOOK GOOD.
AAAAH...
NO!!
NINJAAAAAA
COSTUMES ARE EVEN MORE POWERFUL WHEN YOU PLAY YOUR ROLE!!
WHEN COSTUMES BECOME COSPLAY, THEIR FULL POTENTIAL IS UNLEASHED!
WHOOAAA

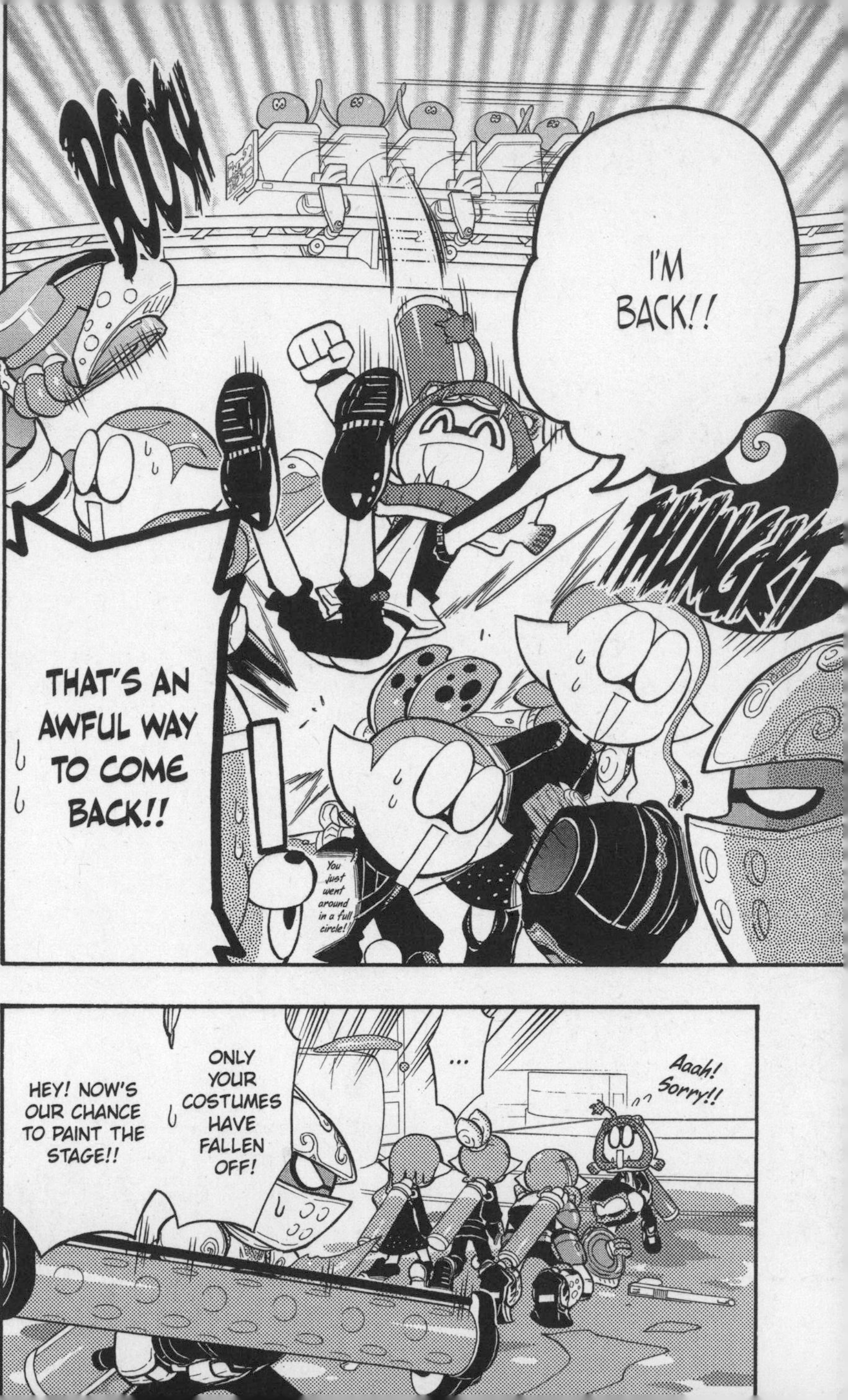
I'M BACK!!
BOOSH
THUNGK
THAT'S AN AWFUL WAY TO COME BACK!!
You just went around in a full circle!
Aaah! Sorry!!
...
ONLY YOUR COSTUMES HAVE FALLEN OFF!
HEY! NOW'S OUR CHANCE TO PAINT THE STAGE!!

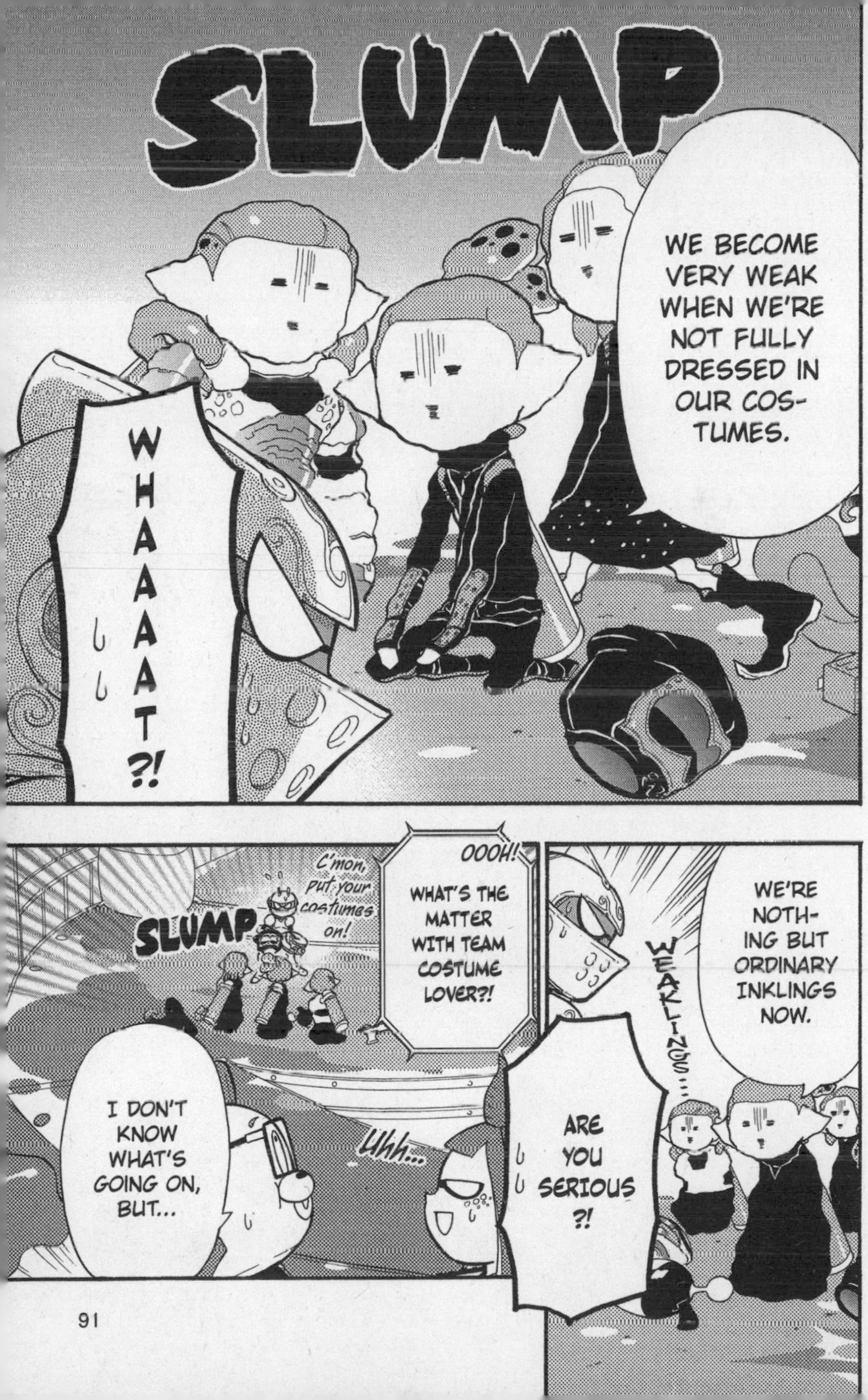
SLUMP
WE BECOME VERY WEAK WHEN WE'RE NOT FULLY DRESSED IN OUR COS-TUMES.
WHAAAAAT?!
WE'RE NOTH-ING BUT ORDINARY INKLINGS NOW.
WEAKLINGS...
OOOH!
WHAT'S THE MATTER WITH TEAM COSTUME LOVER?!
C'mon, put your costumes on!
SLUMP
ARE YOU SERIOUS?!
Uhh...
I DON'T KNOW WHAT'S GOING ON, BUT...

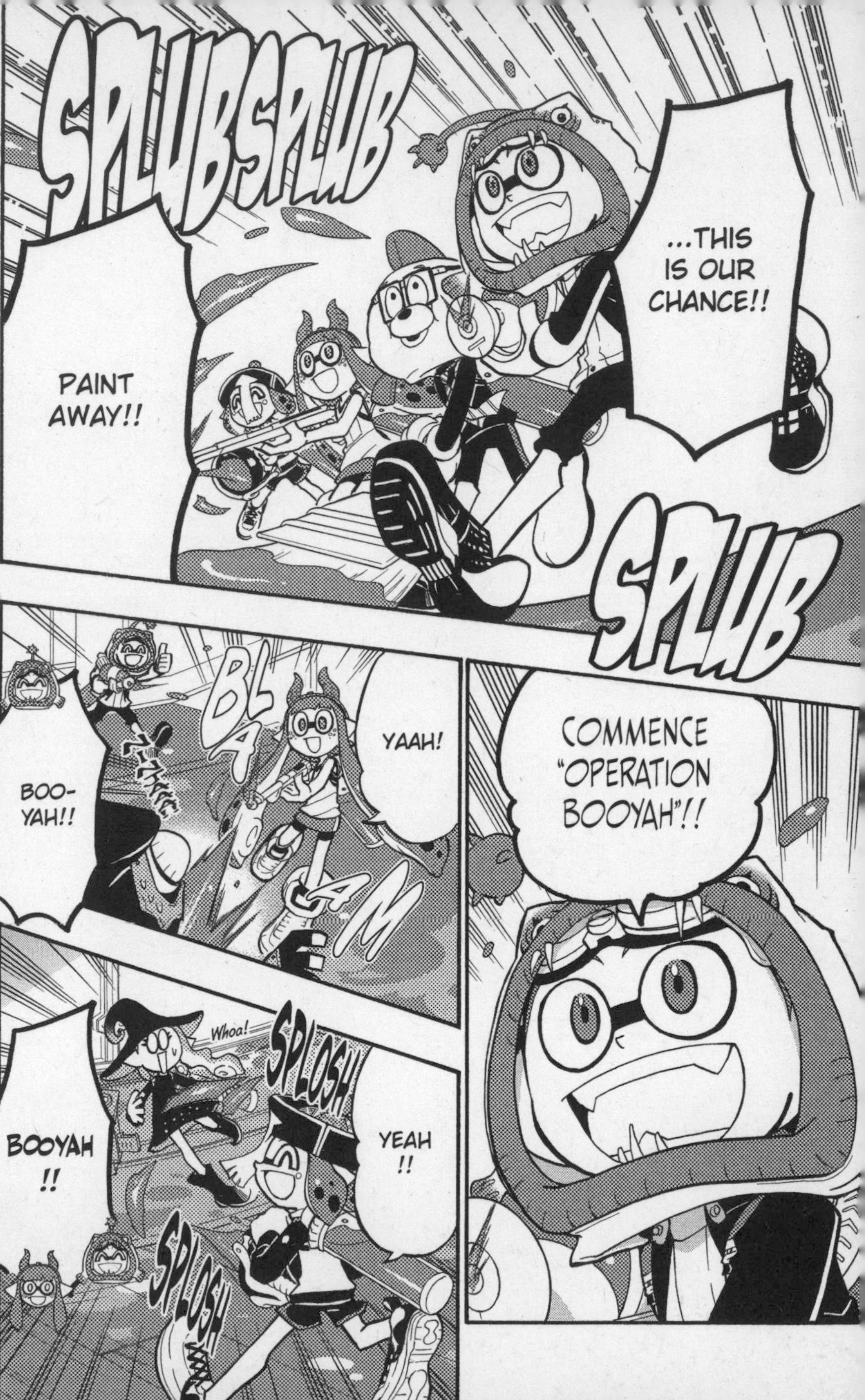
...THIS IS OUR CHANCE!!
SPLUBSPLUB
PAINT AWAY!!
SPLUB
COMMENCE "OPERATION BOOYAH"!!
YAAH!
BLAM
BOO-YAH!!
YEAH!!
SPLOSH
Whoa!
BOOYAH!!
SPLOSH

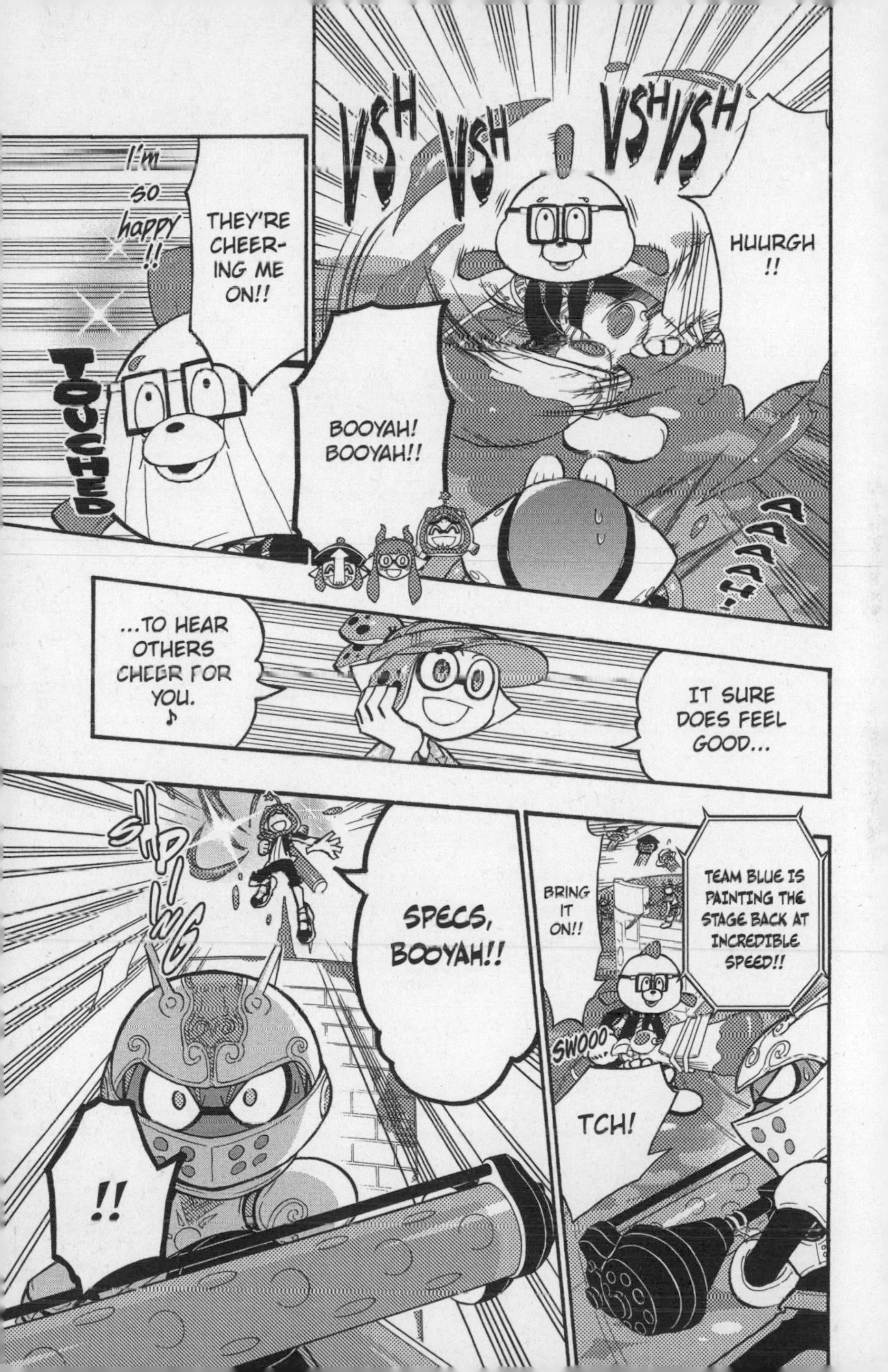
VSH VSH
VSH VSH
HUURGH!!
AAAAAH!
THEY'RE CHEER-ING ME ON!!
I'm so happy!!
TOUCHED
BOOYAH! BOOYAH!!
IT SURE DOES FEEL GOOD...
...TO HEAR OTHERS CHEER FOR YOU. ♪
TEAM BLUE IS PAINTING THE STAGE BACK AT INCREDIBLE SPEED!!
BRING IT ON!!
SWOOO
TCH!
SHPIING
SPECS, BOOYAH!!
!!

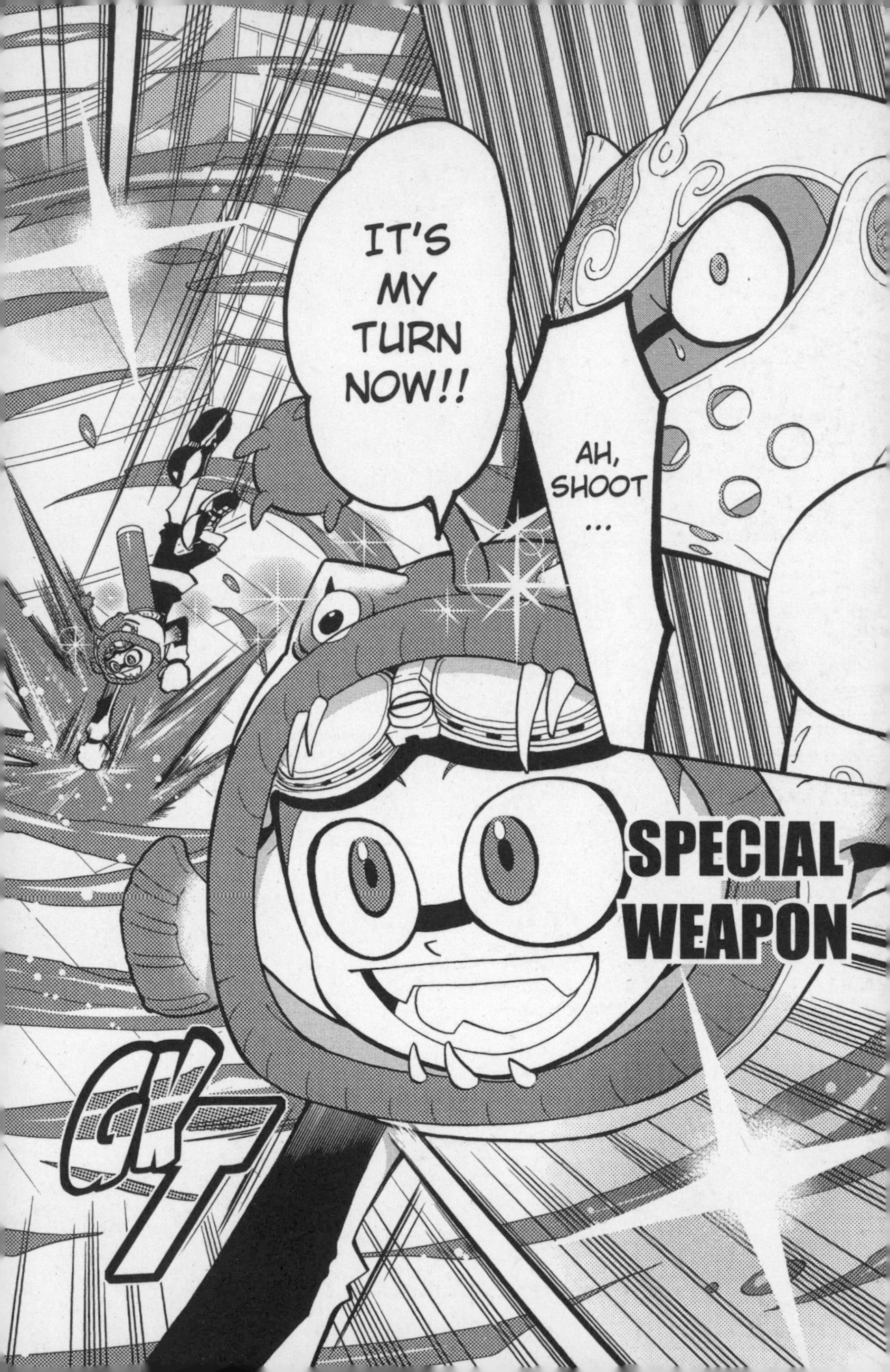
IT'S MY TURN NOW!!
AH, SHOOT ...
SPECIAL WEAPON

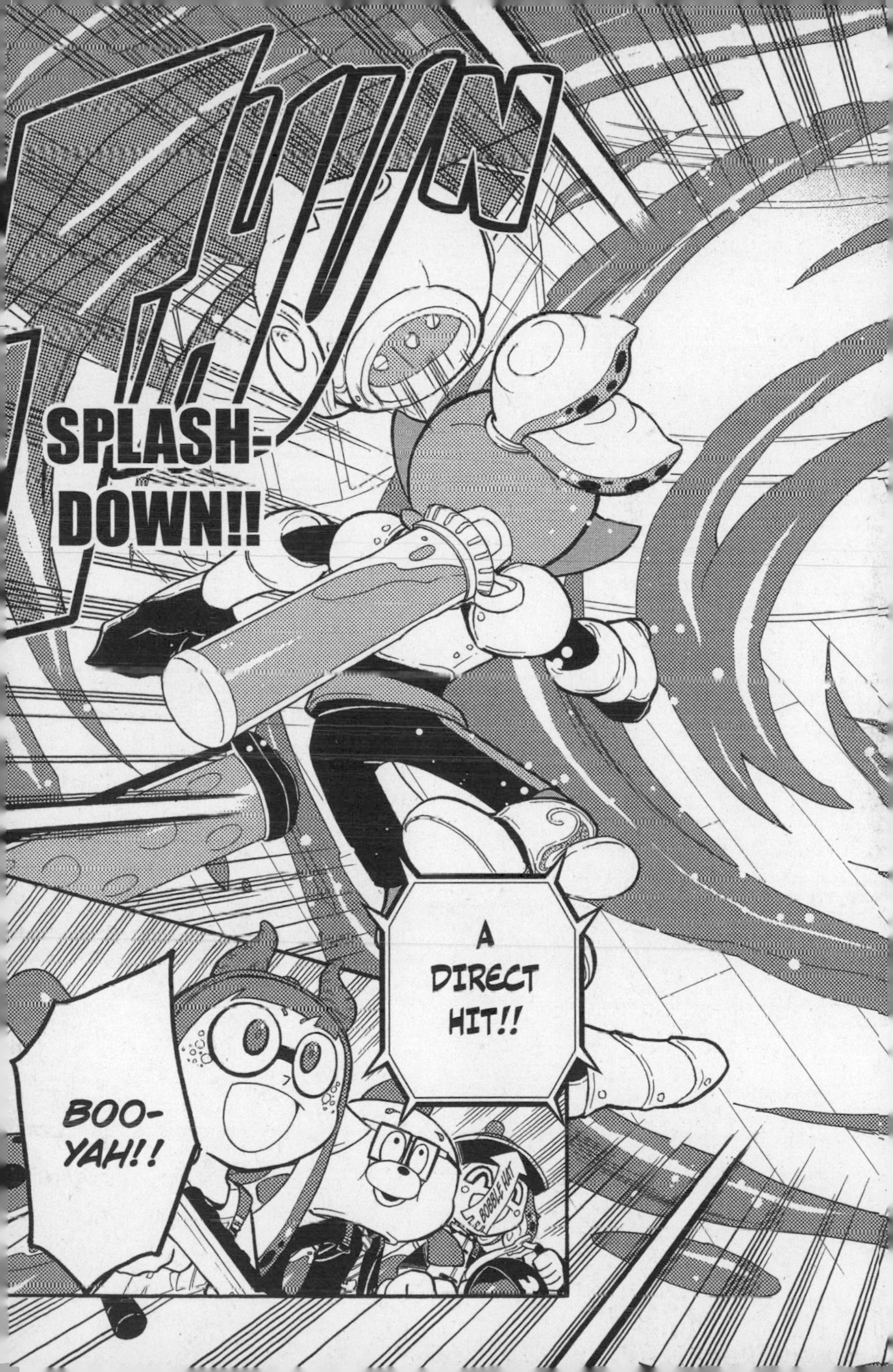
SPLASH-DOWN!!
A DIRECT HIT!!
BOBBLE HAT
BOO-YAH!!

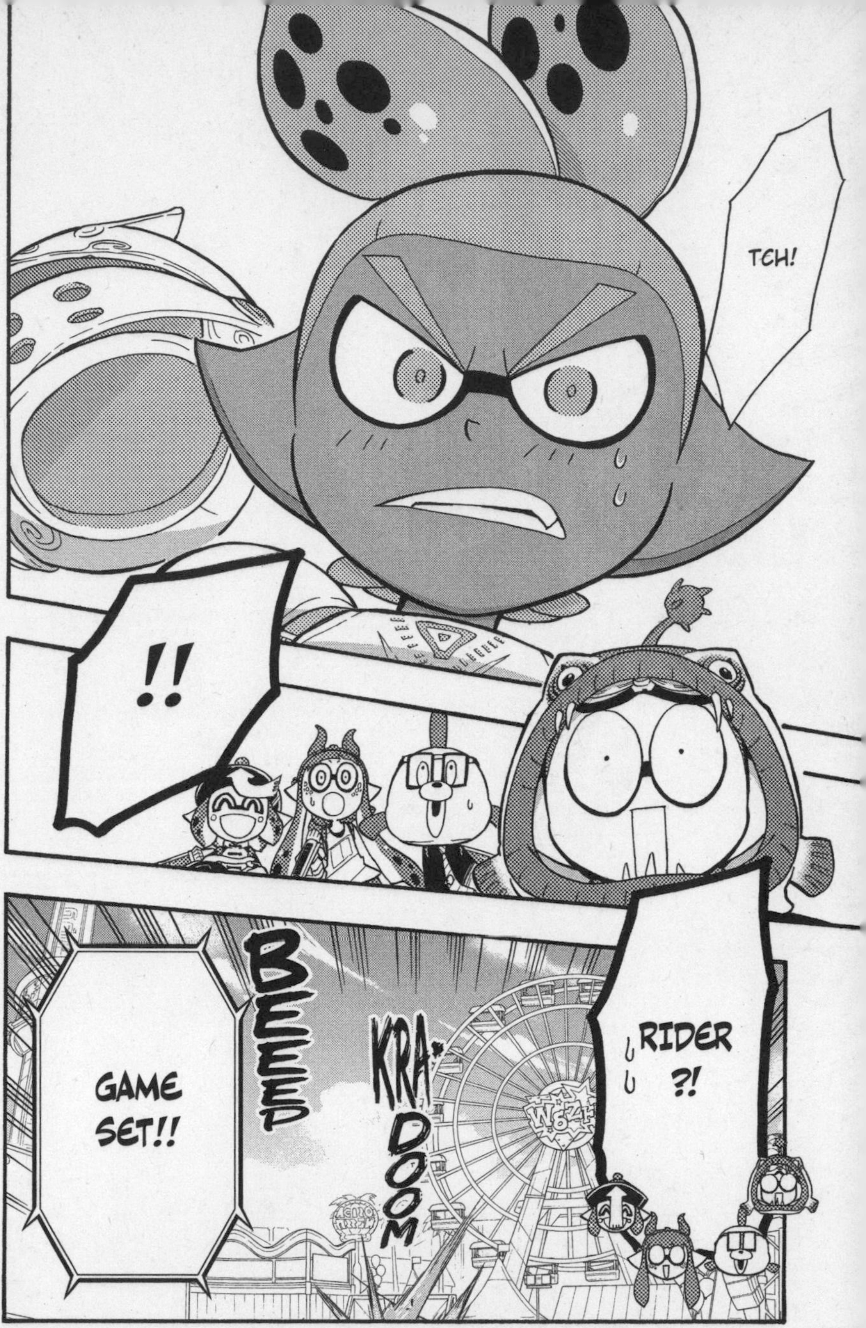
TCH!
!!
RIDER ?!
KRA DOOOM
BEEEP
GAME SET!!

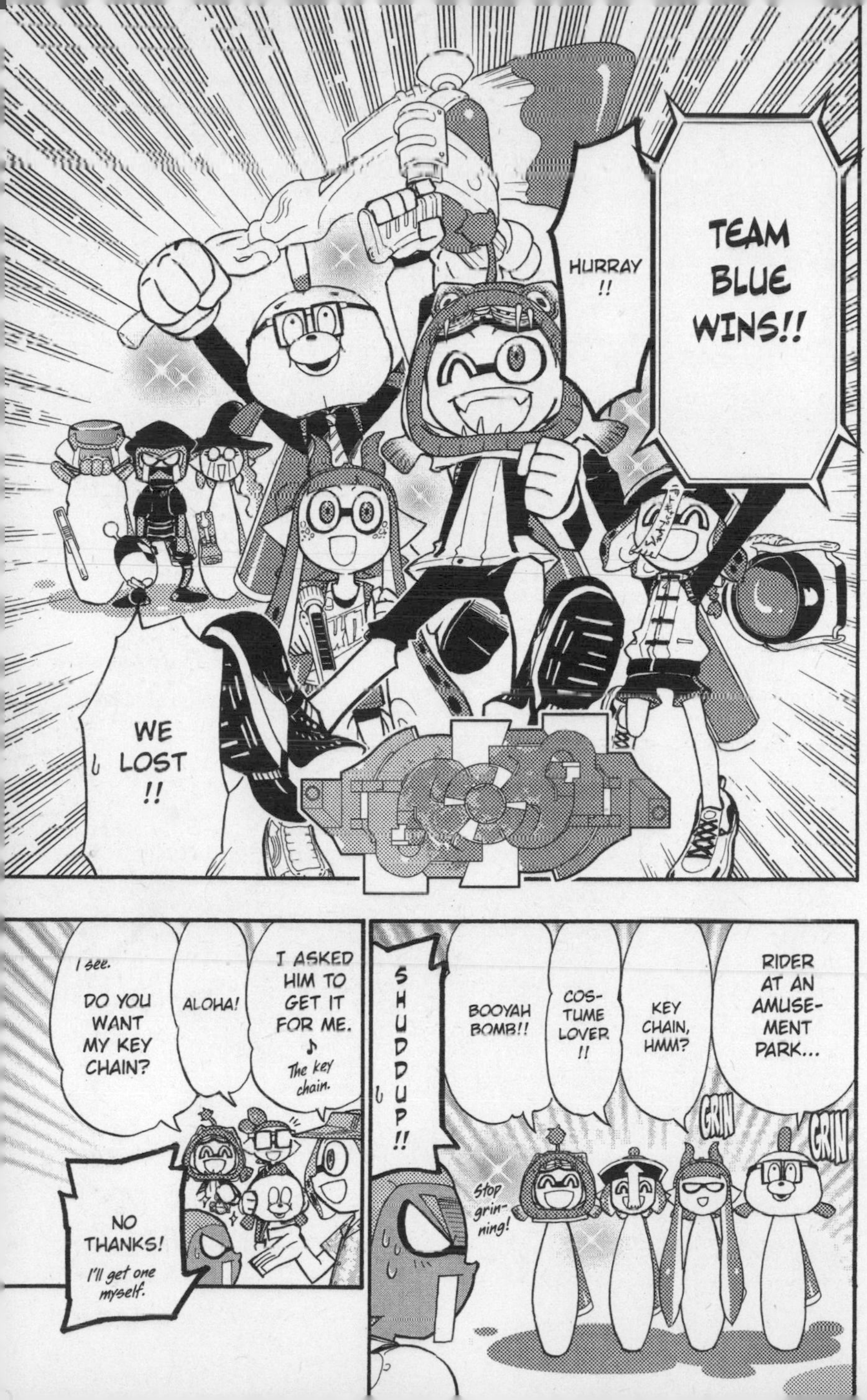
TEAM BLUE WINS!!
HURRAY!!
WE LOST!!
RIDER AT AN AMUSEMENT PARK...
KEY CHAIN, HMM?
COSTUME LOVER!!
BOOYAH BOMB!!
GRIN
GRIN
SHUDDUP!!
Stop grinning!
I ASKED HIM TO GET IT FOR ME. ♪ The key chain.
ALOHA!
I see. DO YOU WANT MY KEY CHAIN?
NO THANKS! I'll get one myself.

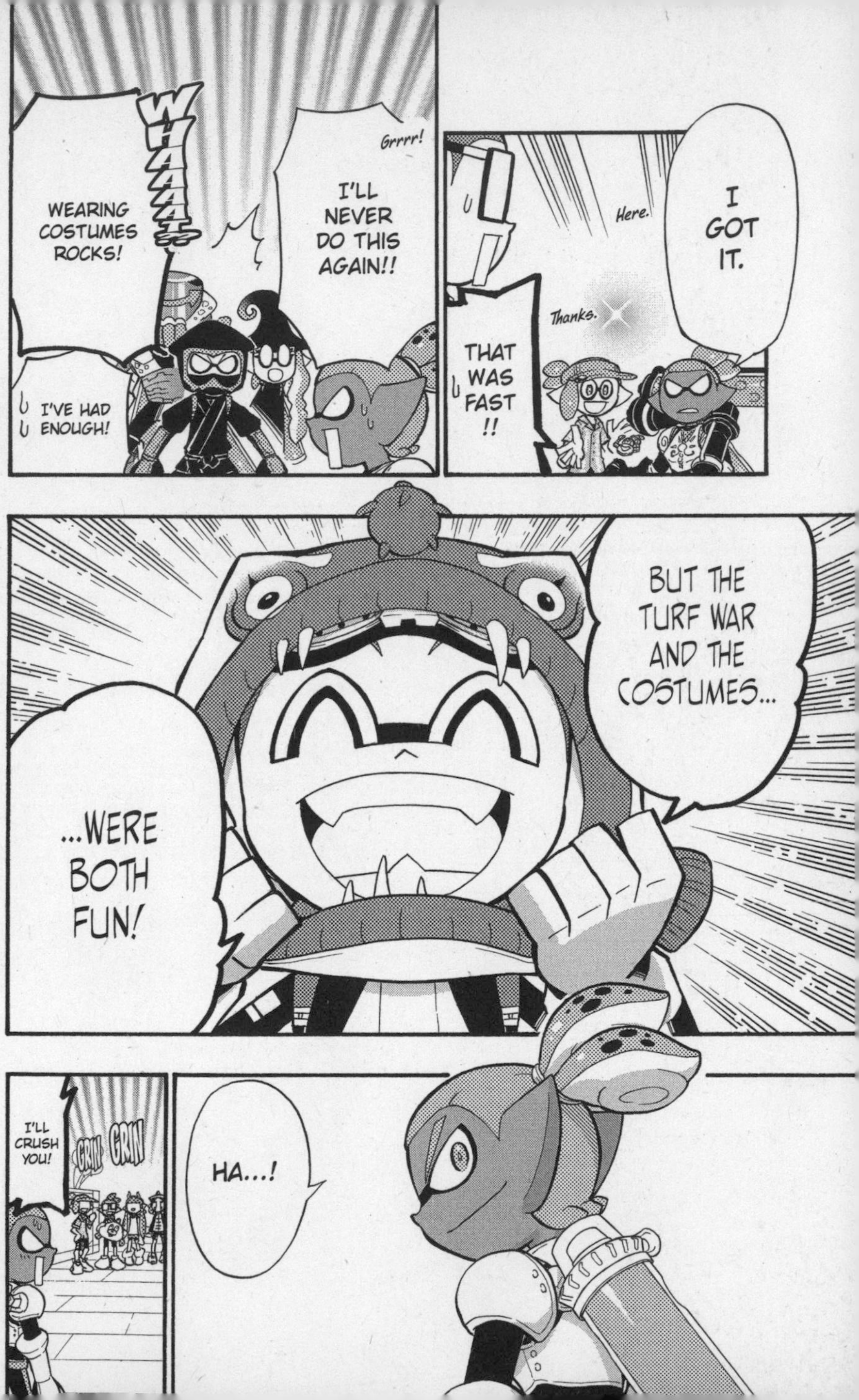
I GOT IT.
Here.
Thanks.
THAT WAS FAST!!
Grrrr!
I'LL NEVER DO THIS AGAIN!!
WHAAAAT
WEARING COSTUMES ROCKS!
I'VE HAD ENOUGH!
BUT THE TURF WAR AND THE COSTUMES...
...WERE BOTH FUN!
HA...!
GRIN GRIN
I'LL CRUSH YOU!

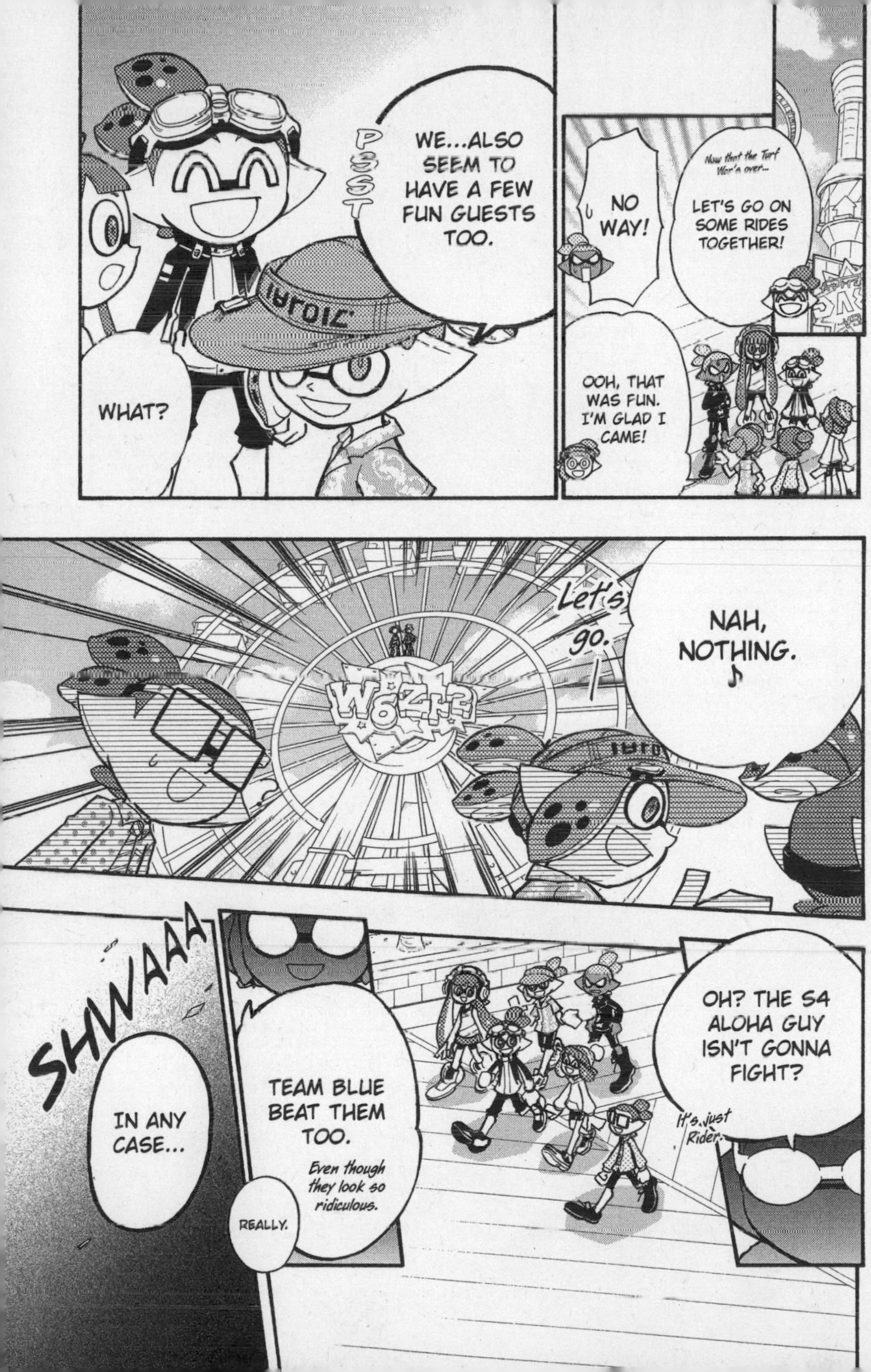
Now that the Turf War's over—
LET'S GO ON SOME RIDES TOGETHER!
NO WAY!
OOH, THAT WAS FUN. I'M GLAD I CAME!
PSST
WE...ALSO SEEM TO HAVE A FEW FUN GUESTS TOO.
WHAT?
NAH, NOTHING. ♪
Let's go.
OH? THE S4 ALOHA GUY ISN'T GONNA FIGHT?
It's just Rider.
TEAM BLUE BEAT THEM TOO.
Even though they look so ridiculous.
REALLY.
IN ANY CASE...
SHWAAA

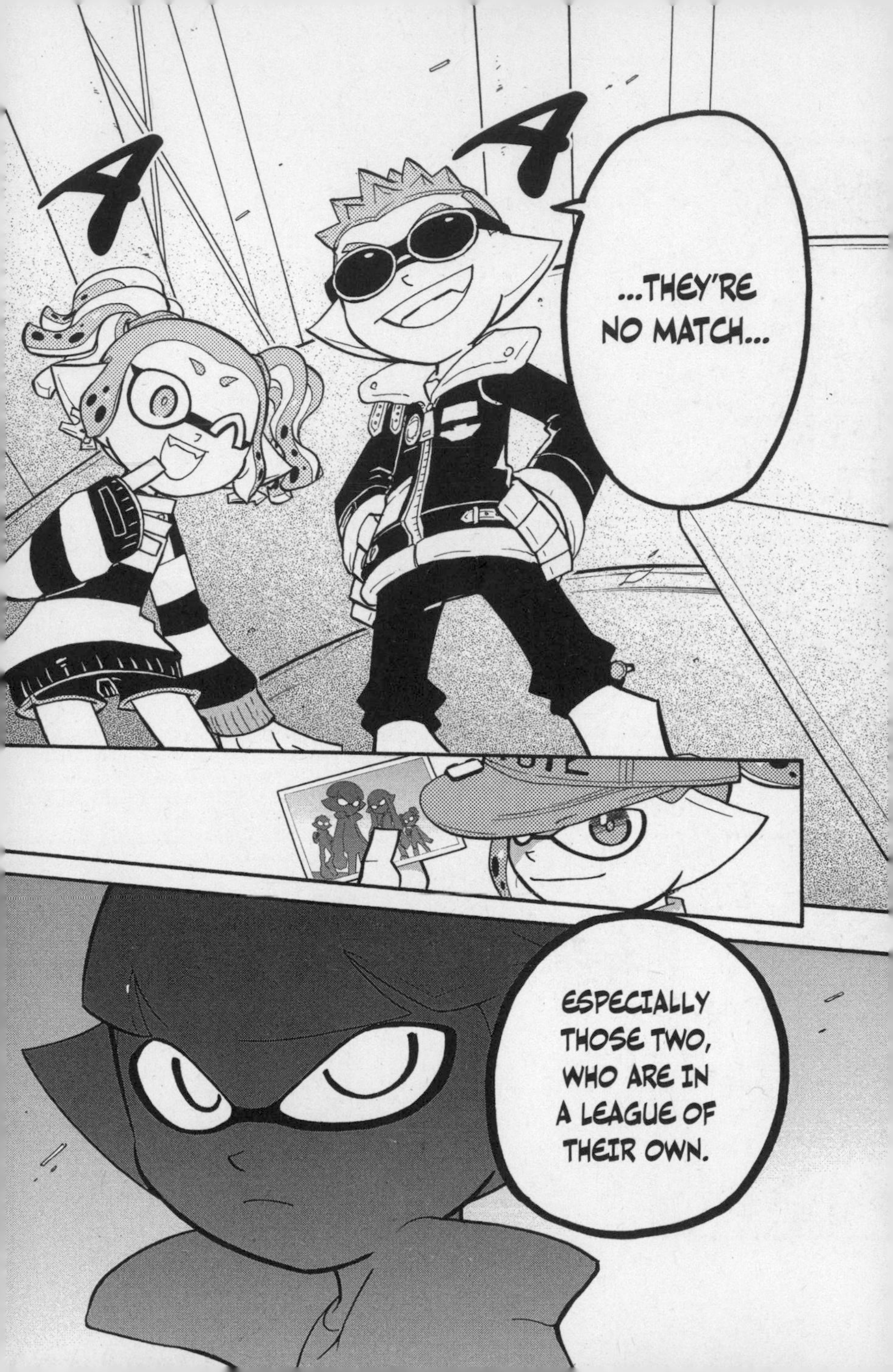
...THEY'RE NO MATCH...
ESPECIALLY THOSE TWO, WHO ARE IN A LEAGUE OF THEIR OWN.

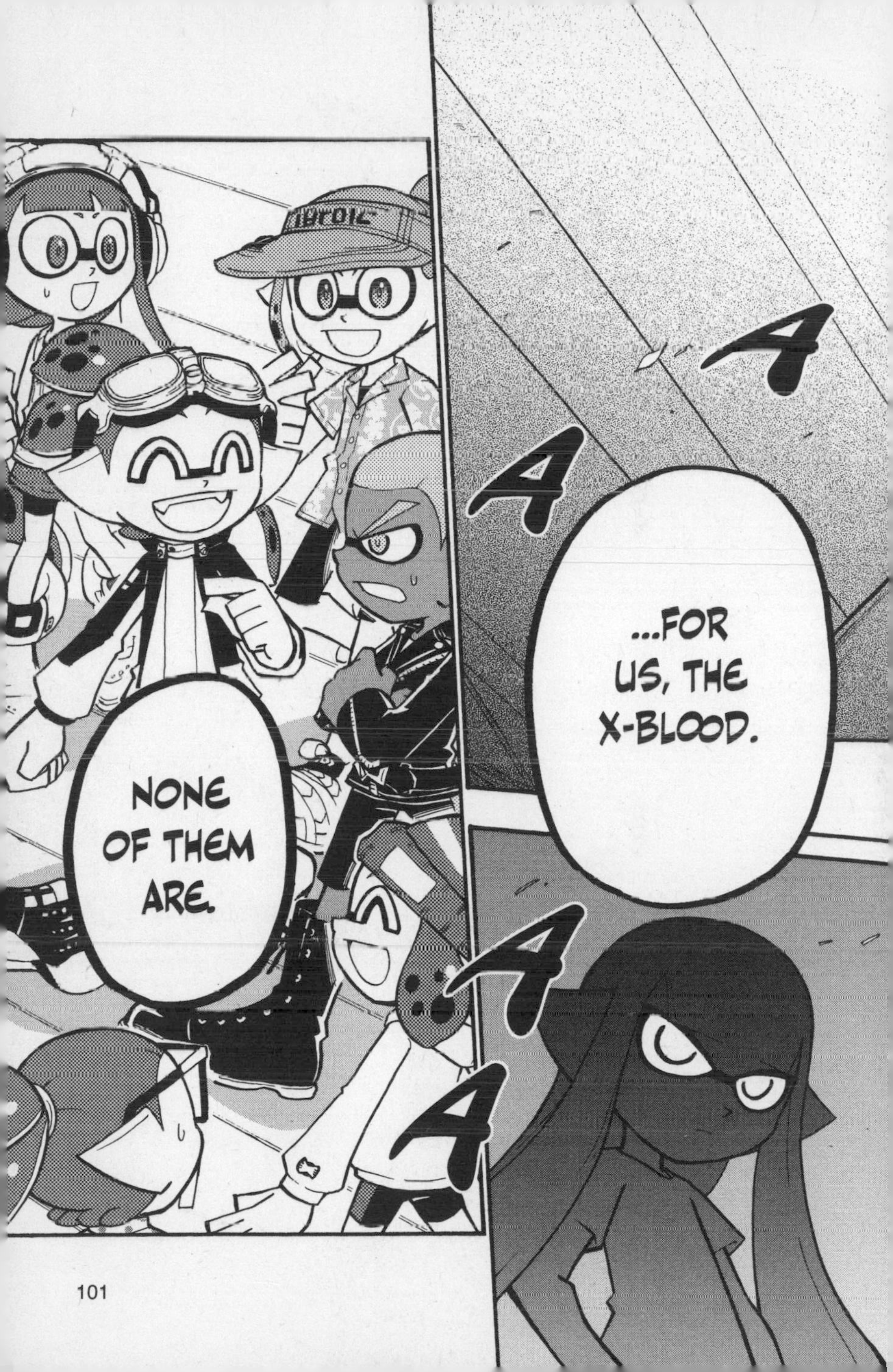
...FOR US, THE X-BLOOD.
NONE OF THEM ARE.

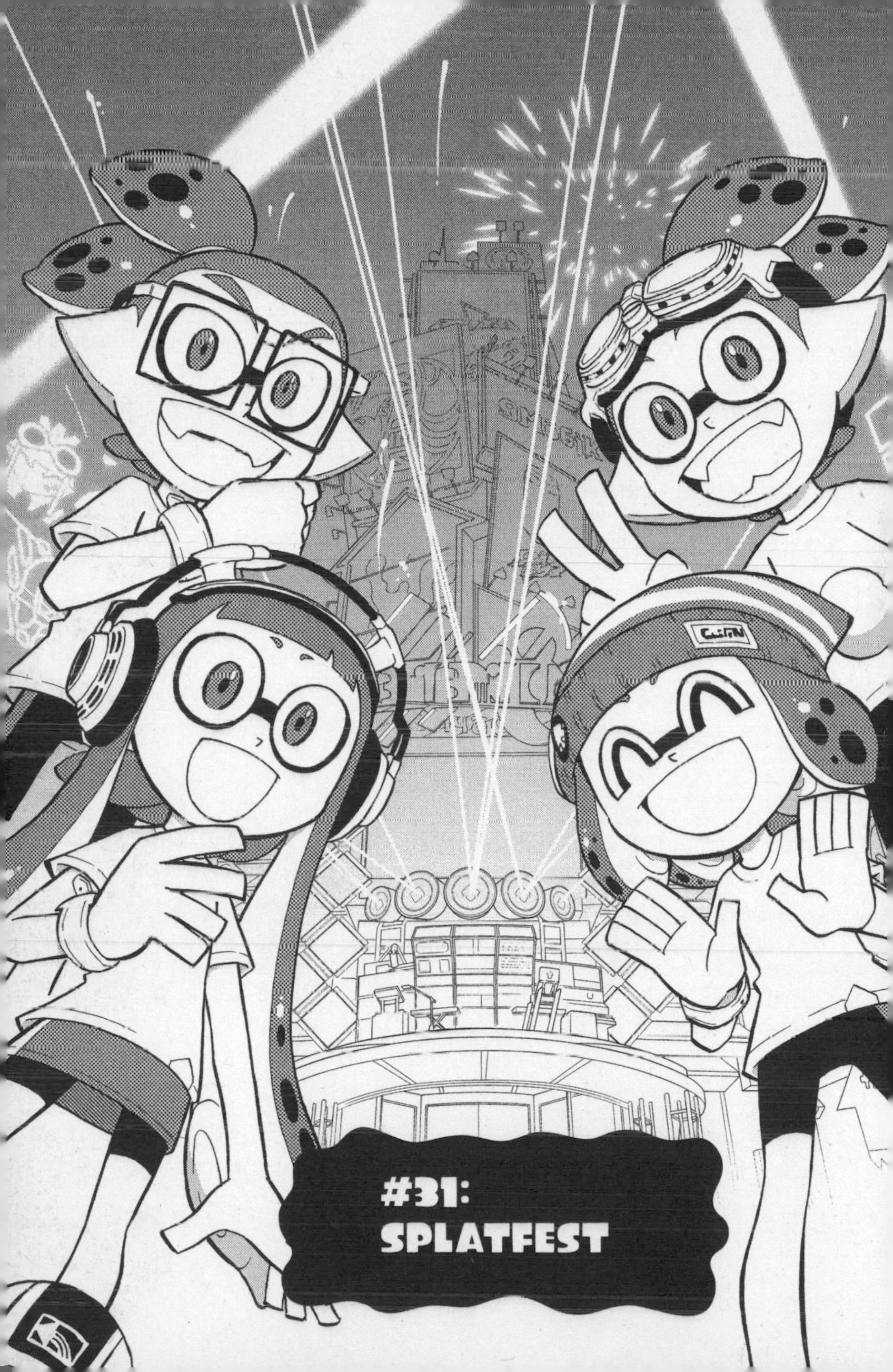
#31:
SPLATFEST

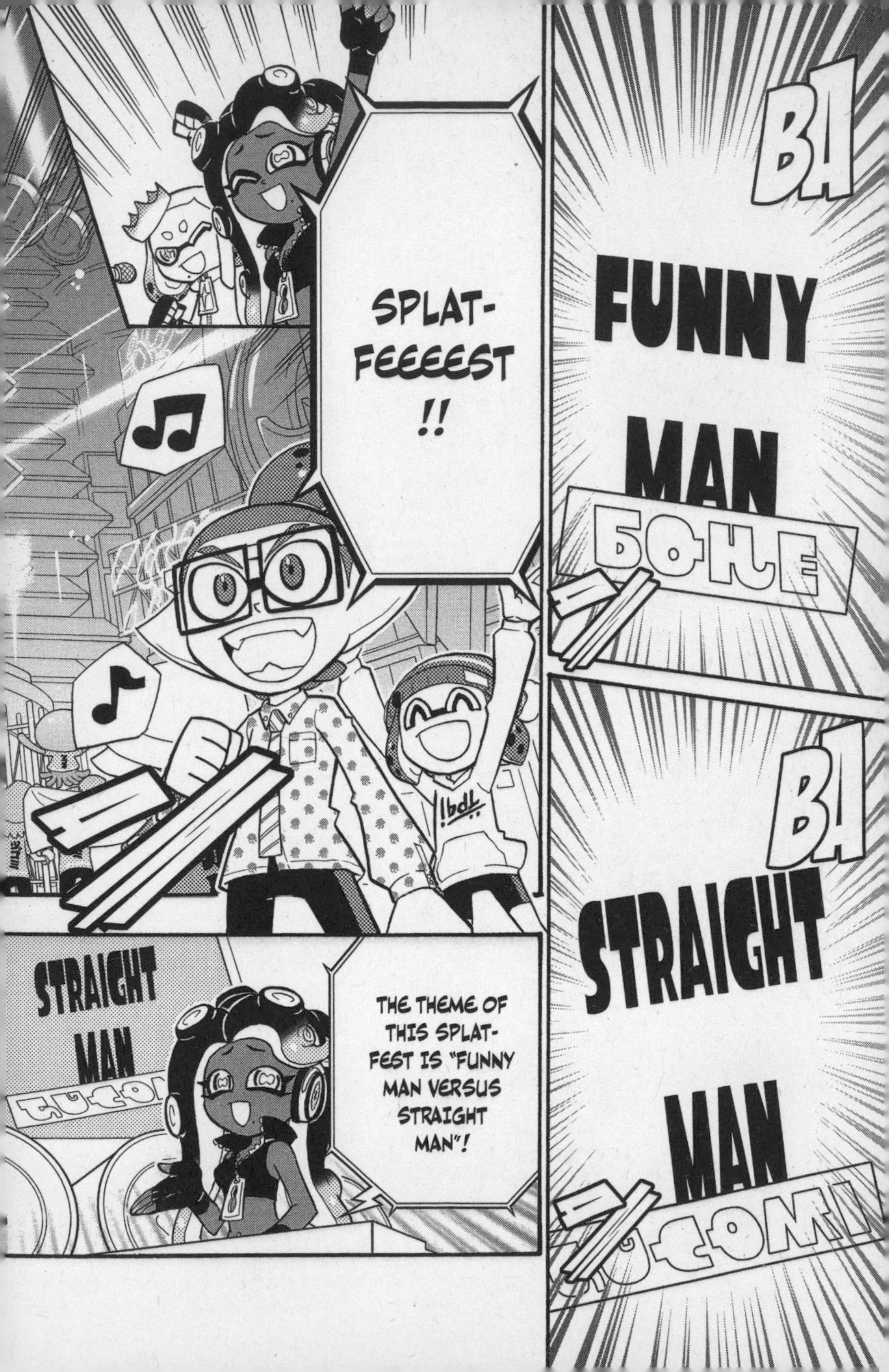
BA
FUNNY MAN
BA
STRAIGHT MAN
SPLAT-FEEEEEST!!
STRAIGHT MAN
THE THEME OF THIS SPLATFEST IS "FUNNY MAN VERSUS STRAIGHT MAN"!

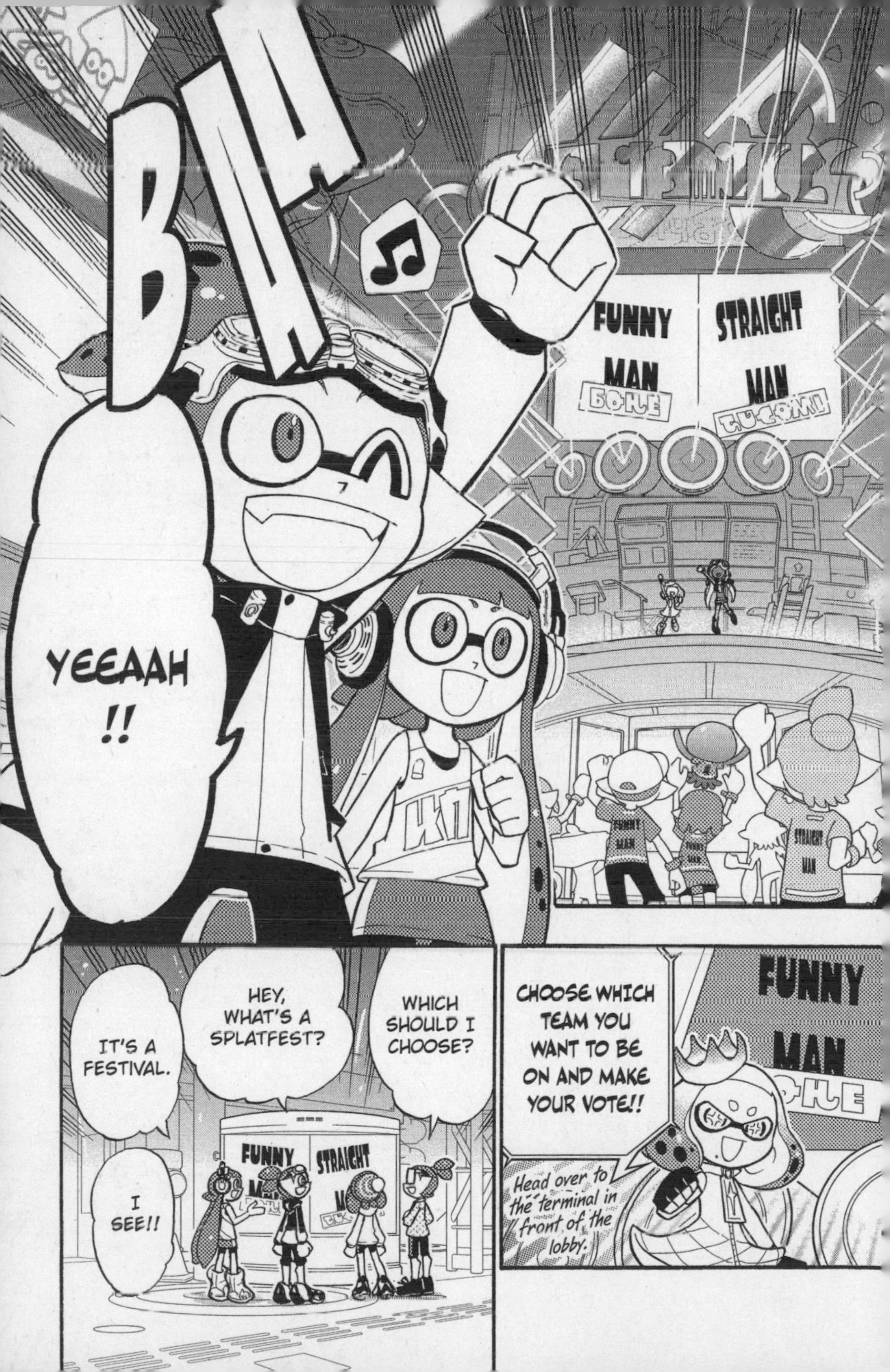
BWAH
FUNNY MAN
STRAIGHT MAN
YEEAAH!!
FUNNY MAN
STRAIGHT MAN
CHOOSE WHICH TEAM YOU WANT TO BE ON AND MAKE YOUR VOTE!!
Head over to the terminal in front of the lobby.
FUNNY MAN
WHICH SHOULD I CHOOSE?
HEY, WHAT'S A SPLATFEST?
IT'S A FESTIVAL.
FUNNY
STRAIGHT
I SEE!!

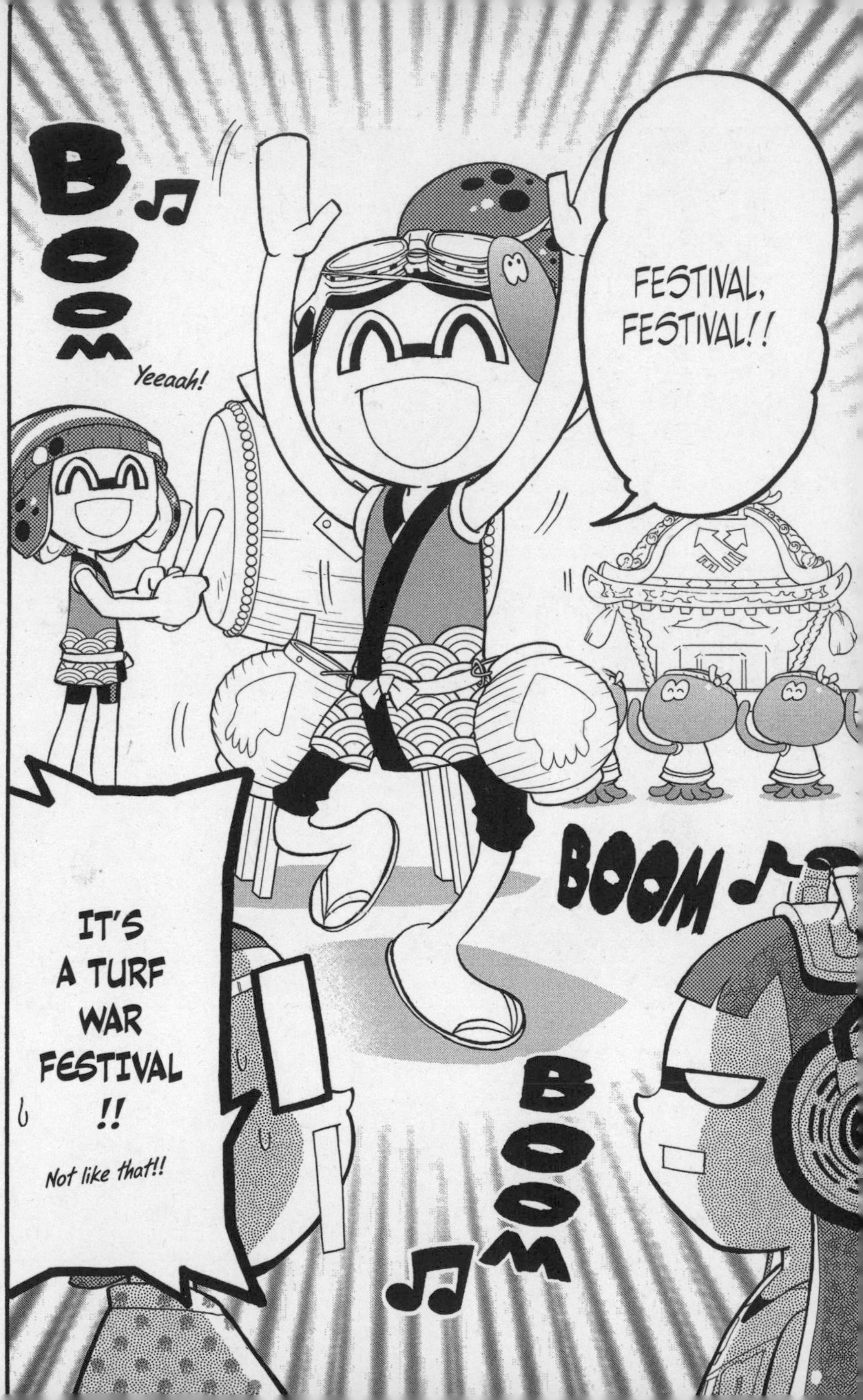
FESTIVAL, FESTIVAL!!
BOOM ♪
Yeeaah!
BOOM ♪
BOOM ♪
IT'S A TURF WAR FESTIVAL!!
Not like that!!

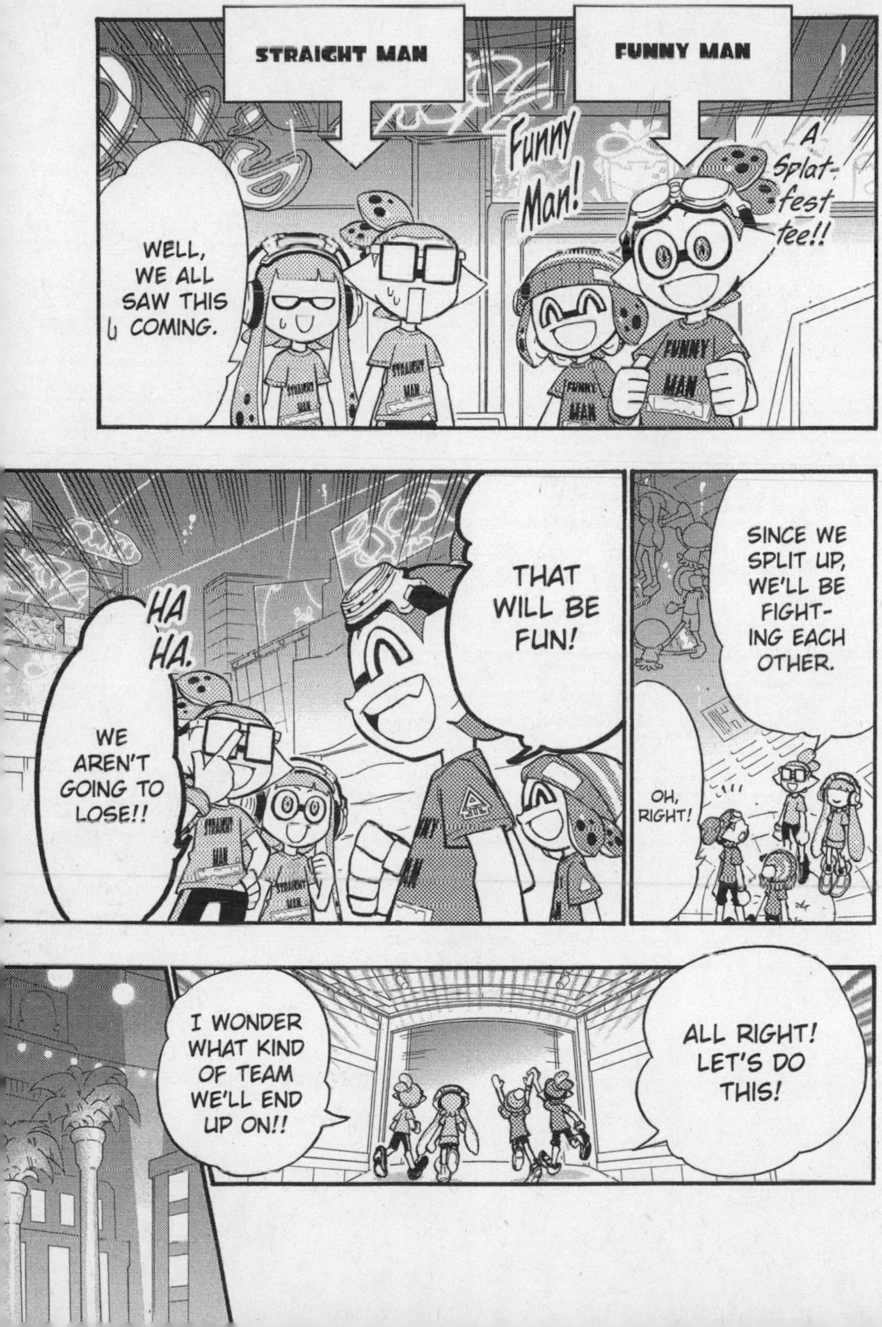
FUNNY MAN
A Splat-fest tee!!
Funny Man!
STRAIGHT MAN
WELL, WE ALL SAW THIS COMING.
SINCE WE SPLIT UP, WE'LL BE FIGHT-ING EACH OTHER.
OH, RIGHT!
THAT WILL BE FUN!
HA HA.
WE AREN'T GOING TO LOSE!!
ALL RIGHT! LET'S DO THIS!
I WONDER WHAT KIND OF TEAM WE'LL END UP ON!!

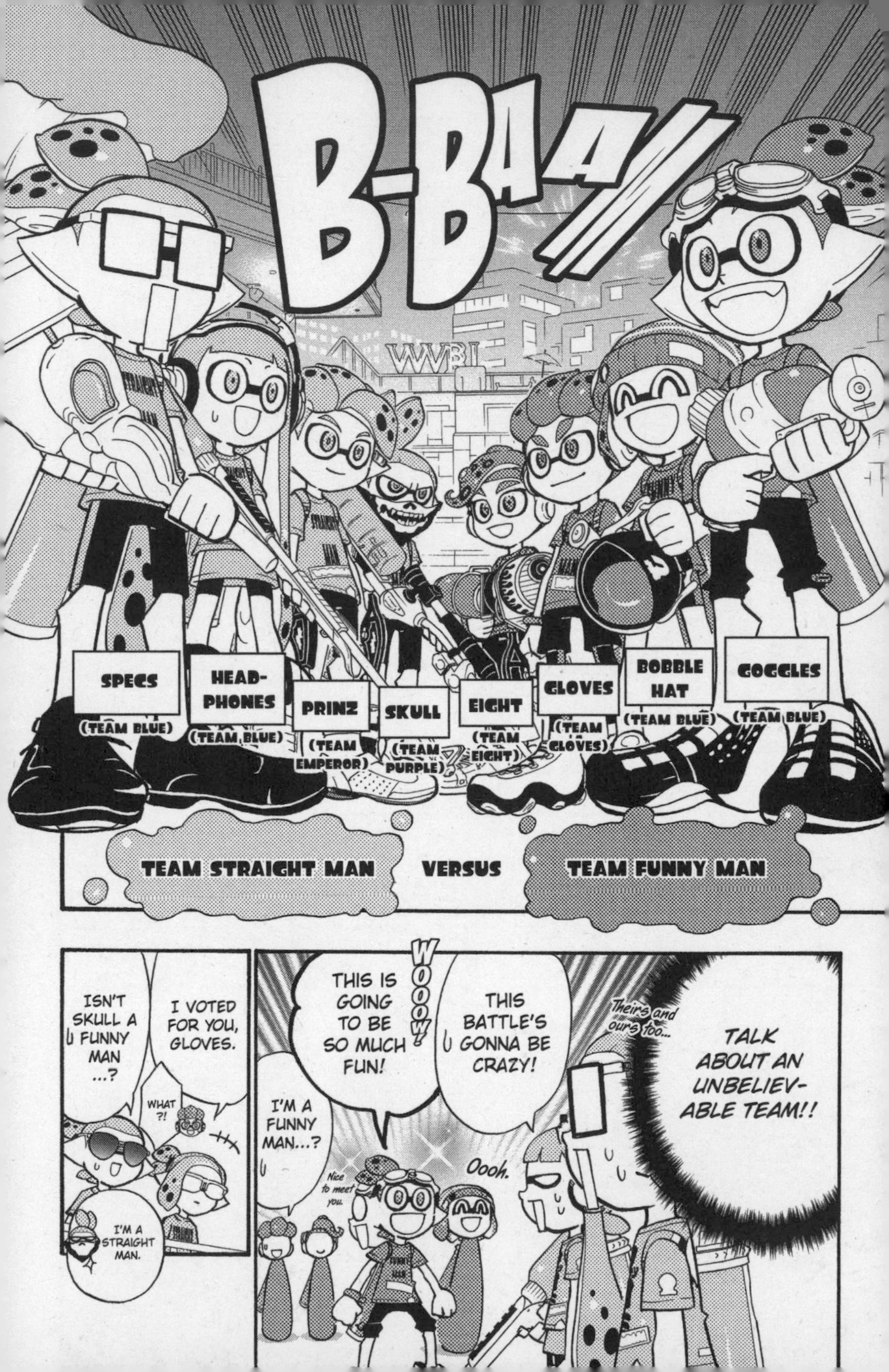
B-BAA
SPECS
(TEAM BLUE)
HEAD-PHONES
(TEAM BLUE)
PRINZ
(TEAM EMPEROR)
SKULL
(TEAM PURPLE)
EIGHT
(TEAM EIGHT)
GLOVES
(TEAM GLOVES)
BOBBLE HAT
(TEAM BLUE)
GOGGLES
(TEAM BLUE)
TEAM STRAIGHT MAN
VERSUS
TEAM FUNNY MAN
TALK ABOUT AN UNBELIEV-ABLE TEAM!!
Theirs and ours too...
THIS BATTLE'S GONNA BE CRAZY!
WOOOOW!
THIS IS GOING TO BE SO MUCH FUN!
Oooh.
I'M A FUNNY MAN...?
Nice to meet you.
I VOTED FOR YOU, GLOVES.
ISN'T SKULL A FUNNY MAN ...?
WHAT ?!
I'M A STRAIGHT MAN.

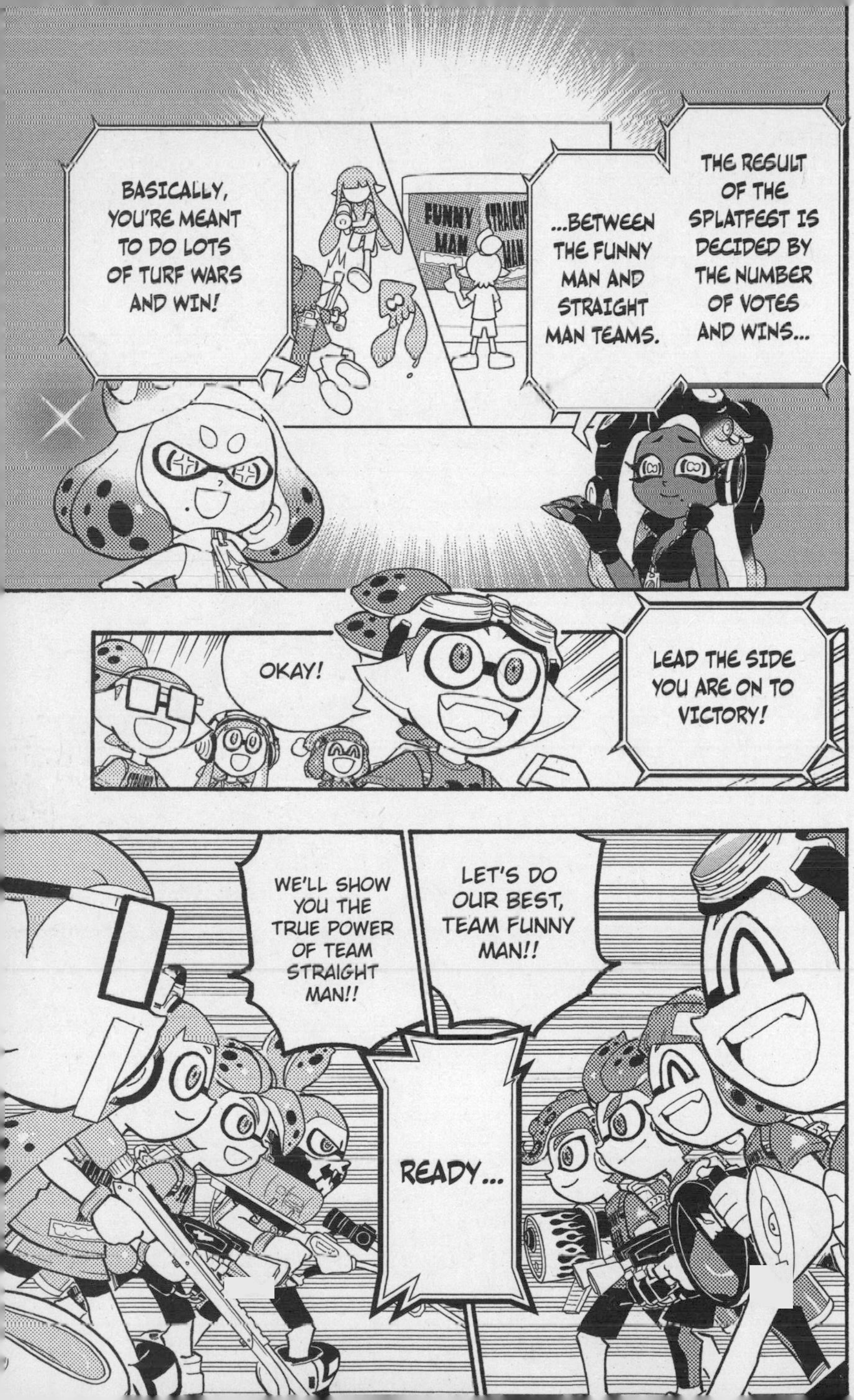
THE RESULT OF THE SPLATFEST IS DECIDED BY THE NUMBER OF VOTES AND WINS...
...BETWEEN THE FUNNY MAN AND STRAIGHT MAN TEAMS.
FUNNY MAN
STRAIGHT MAN
BASICALLY, YOU'RE MEANT TO DO LOTS OF TURF WARS AND WIN!
LEAD THE SIDE YOU ARE ON TO VICTORY!
OKAY!
LET'S DO OUR BEST, TEAM FUNNY MAN!!
WE'LL SHOW YOU THE TRUE POWER OF TEAM STRAIGHT MAN!!
READY...

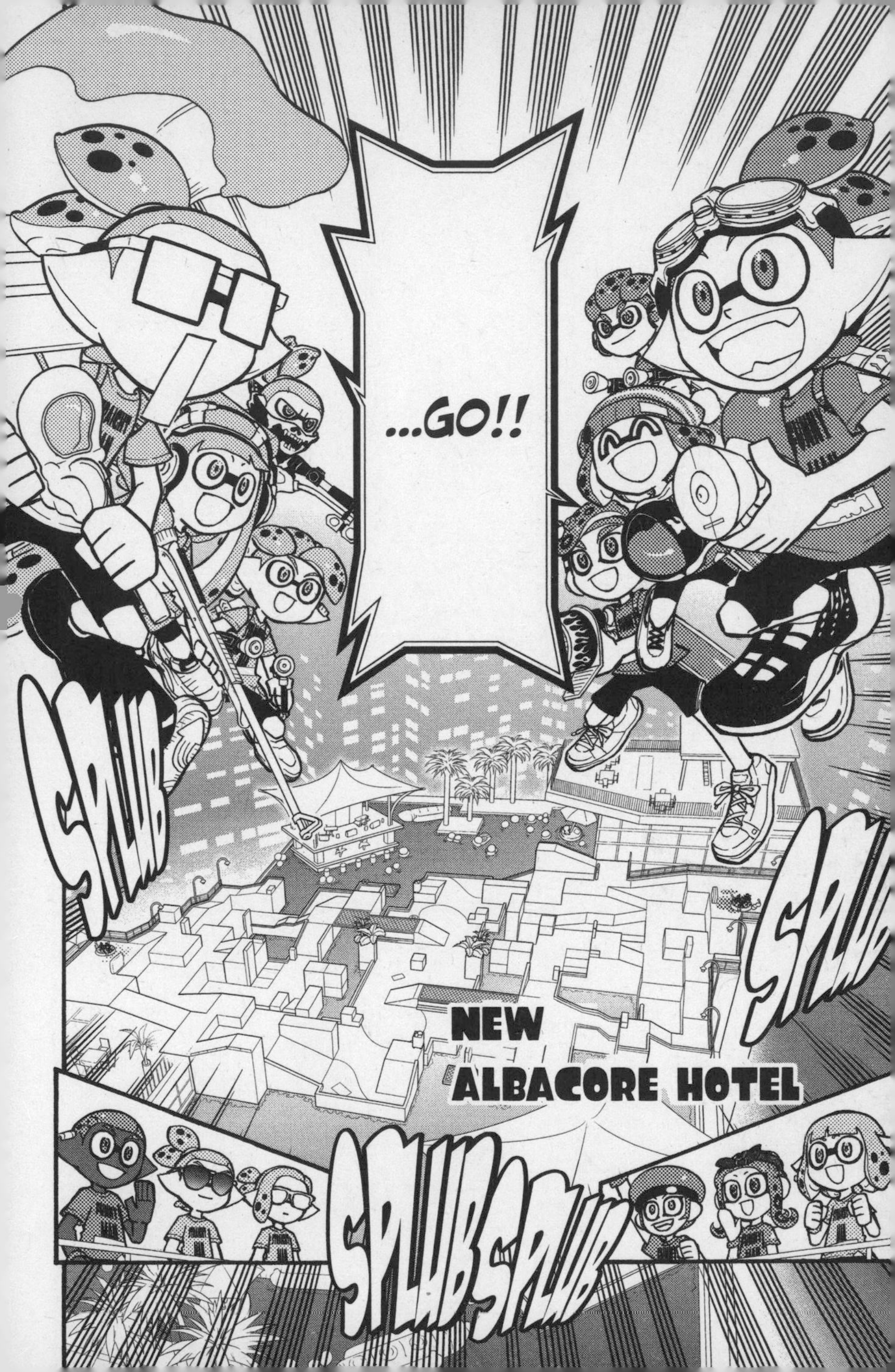
...GO!!
SPLU
SPLUB
NEW ALBACORE HOTEL
SPLUB SPLUB

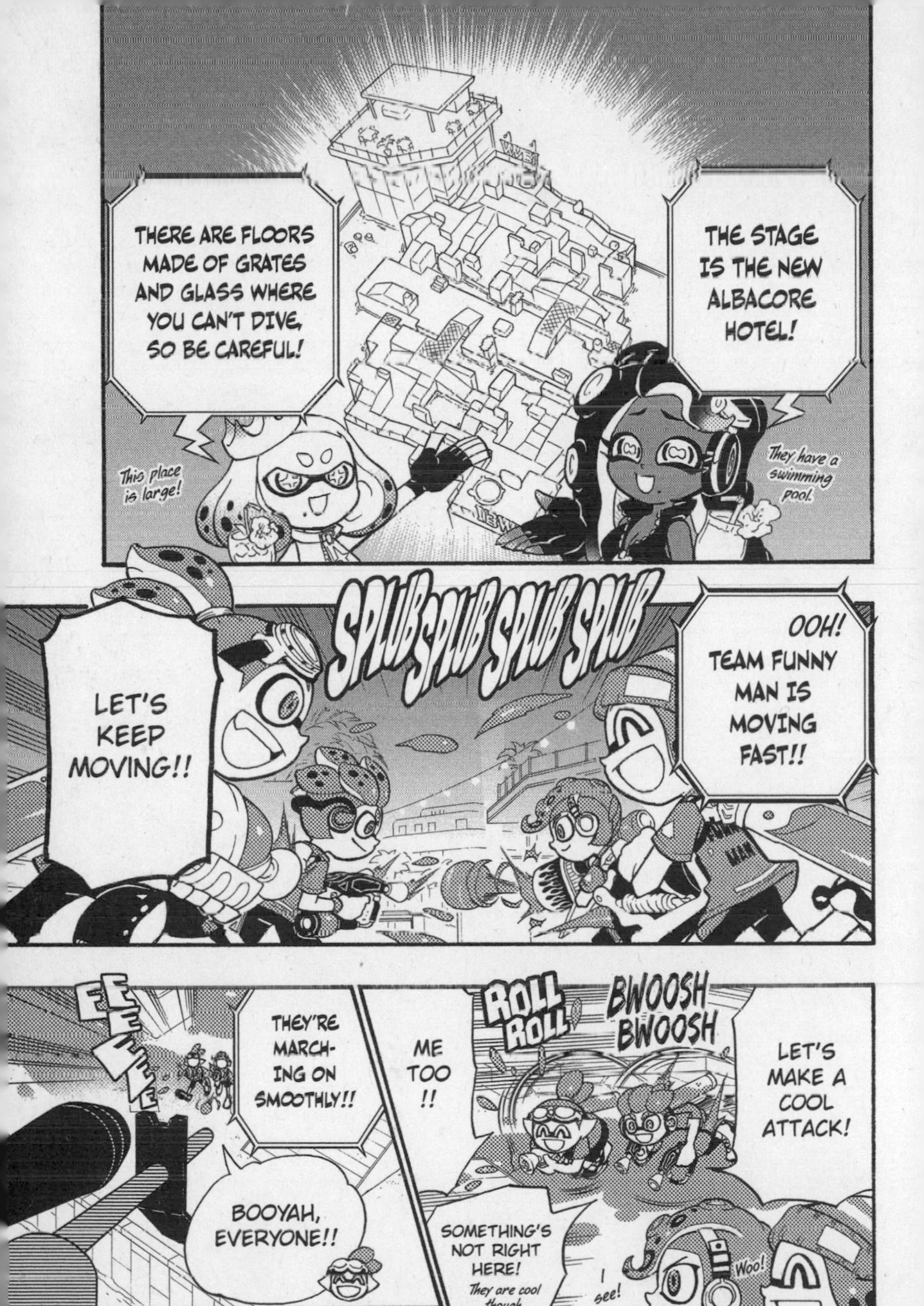

THE STAGE IS THE NEW ALBACORE HOTEL!
They have a swimming pool.
THERE ARE FLOORS MADE OF GRATES AND GLASS WHERE YOU CAN'T DIVE, SO BE CAREFUL!
This place is large!
OOH! TEAM FUNNY MAN IS MOVING FAST!!
SPLUB SPLUB SPLUB SPLUB
LET'S KEEP MOVING!!
BWOOSH BWOOSH
ROLL ROLL
LET'S MAKE A COOL ATTACK!
ME TOO!!
Woo!
I see!
SOMETHING'S NOT RIGHT HERE!
They are cool though.
THEY'RE MARCHING ON SMOOTHLY!!
BOOYAH, EVERYONE!!

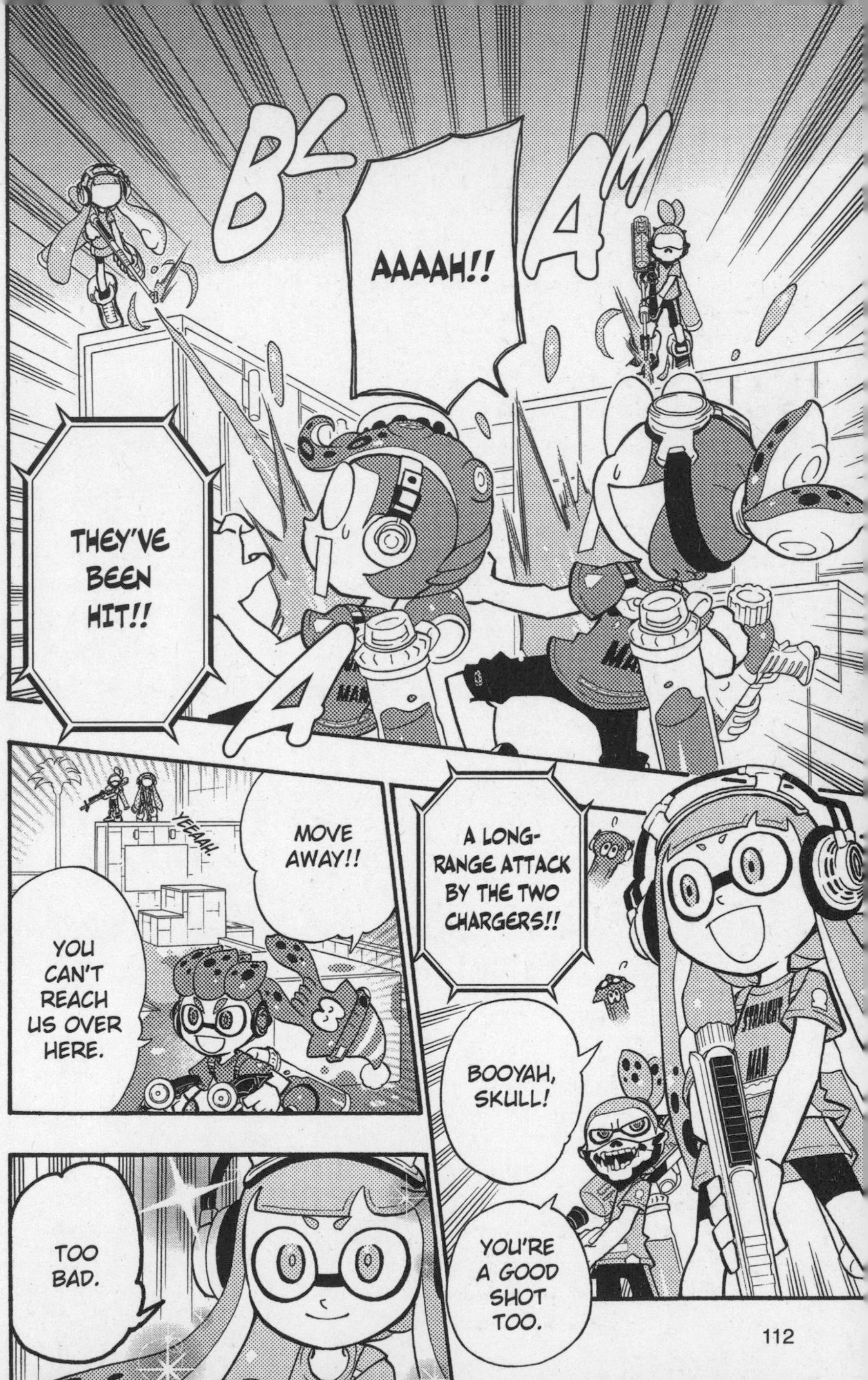
BLAAM
AAAAH!!
THEY'VE BEEN HIT!!
A LONG-RANGE ATTACK BY THE TWO CHARGERS!!
BOOYAH, SKULL!
YOU'RE A GOOD SHOT TOO.
MOVE AWAY!!
YEEAAH.
YOU CAN'T REACH US OVER HERE.
TOO BAD.

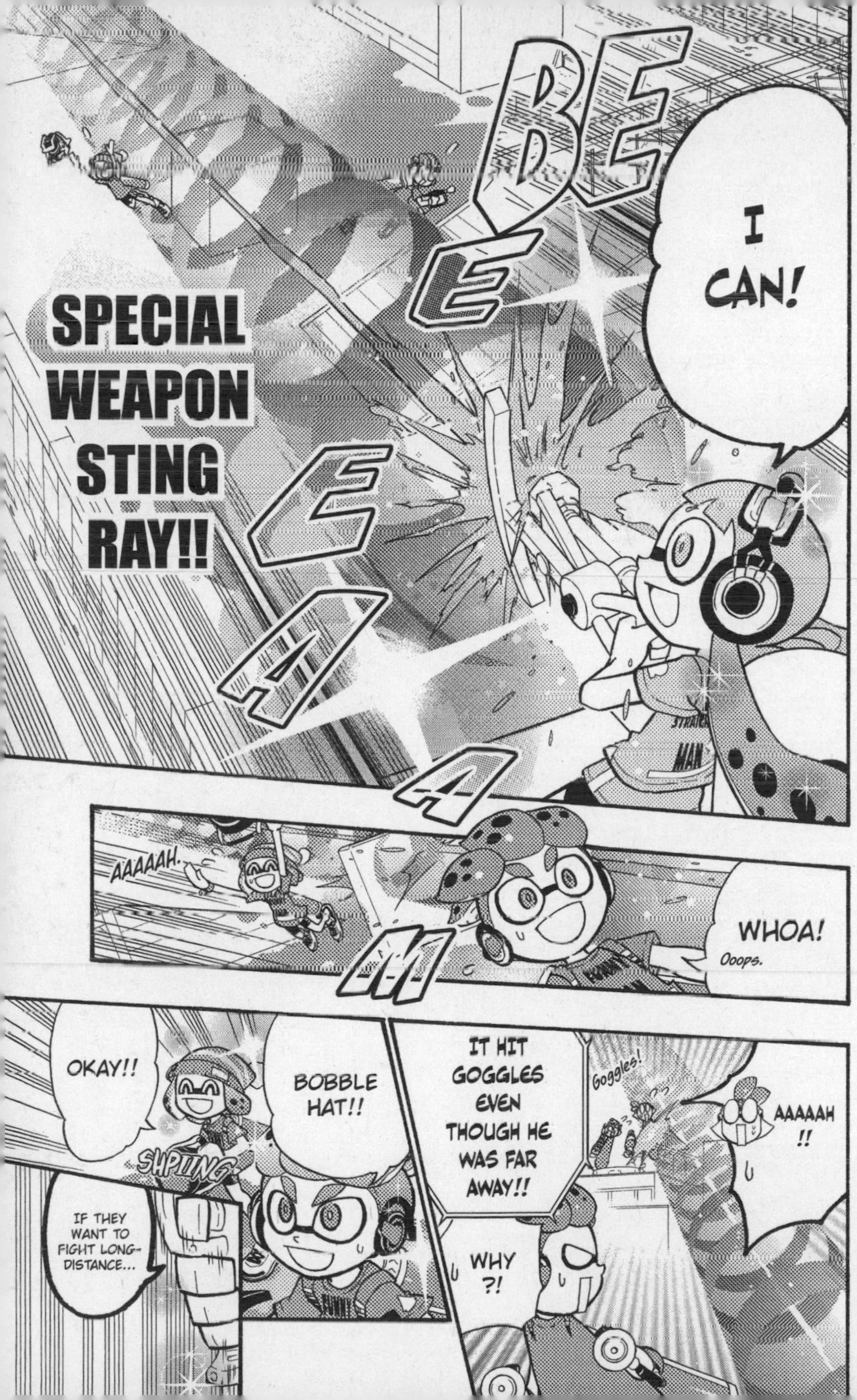
I CAN!
BEEEAAM
SPECIAL WEAPON STING RAY!!
WHOA!
Ooops.
AAAAAH.
AAAAAH!!
Goggles!
IT HIT GOGGLES EVEN THOUGH HE WAS FAR AWAY!!
WHY?!
BOBBLE HAT!!
OKAY!!
SHPING
IF THEY WANT TO FIGHT LONG-DISTANCE...

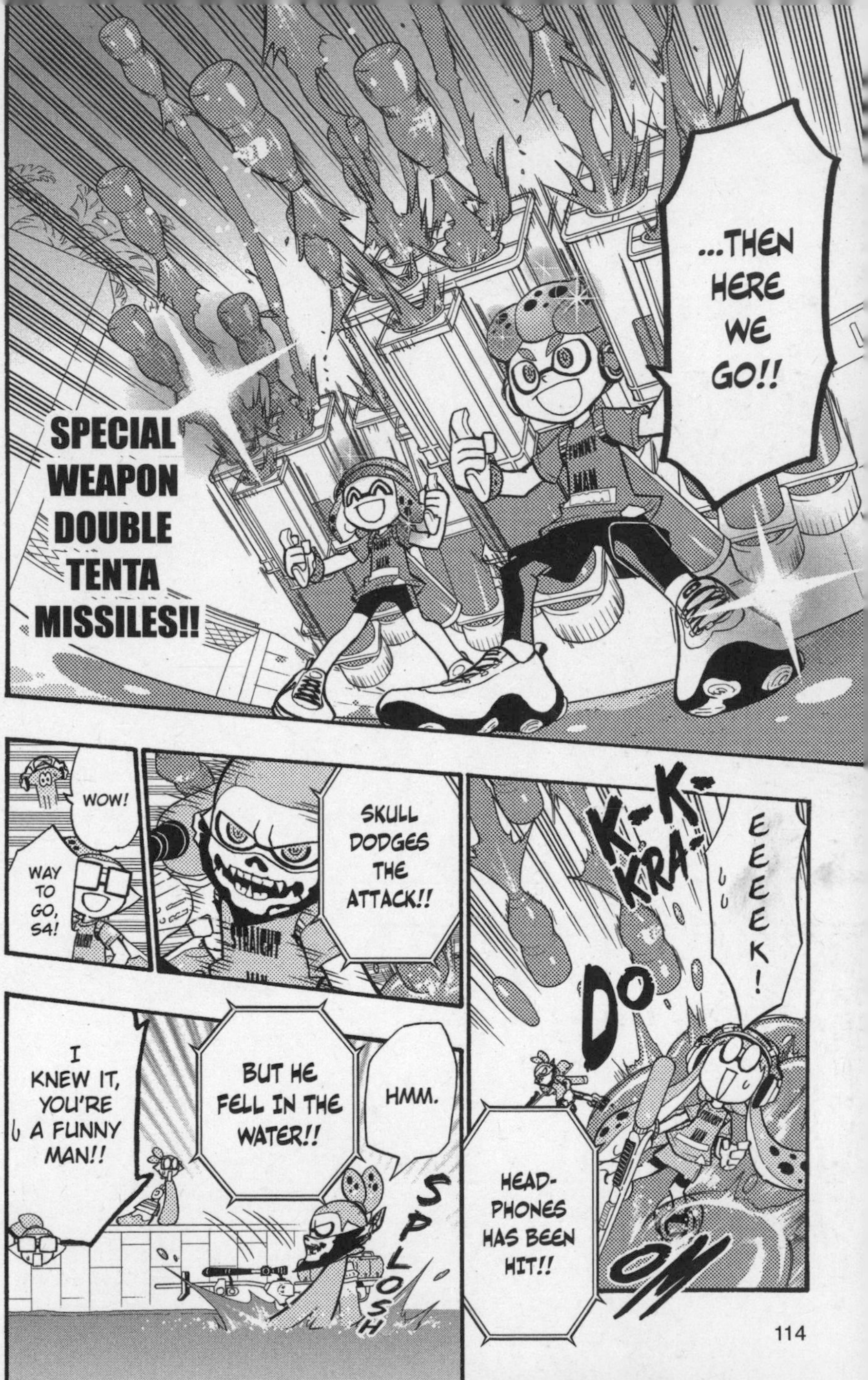
...THEN HERE WE GO!!
SPECIAL WEAPON DOUBLE TENTA MISSILES!!
K-K-KRA
EEEEEK!
DO
OM
HEAD-PHONES HAS BEEN HIT!!
SKULL DODGES THE ATTACK!!
WOW!
WAY TO GO, S4!
HMM.
BUT HE FELL IN THE WATER!!
I KNEW IT, YOU'RE A FUNNY MAN!!
SPLOSH

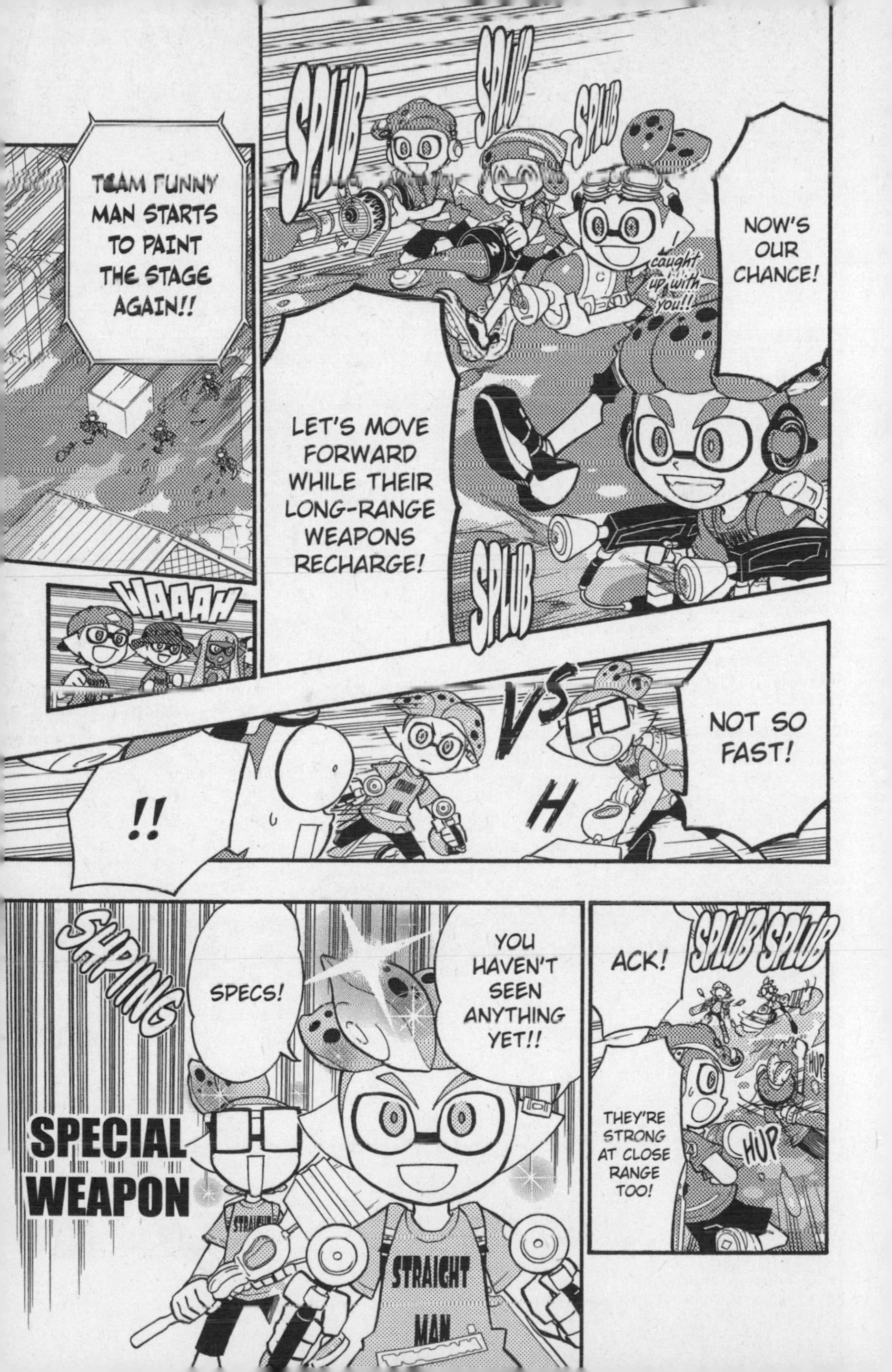
SPLUB
SPLUB
SPLUB
NOW'S OUR CHANCE!
I caught up with you!!
LET'S MOVE FORWARD WHILE THEIR LONG-RANGE WEAPONS RECHARGE!
SPLUB
TEAM FUNNY MAN STARTS TO PAINT THE STAGE AGAIN!!
WAAAH
NOT SO FAST!
VS
H
!!
SPLUB SPLUB
ACK!
HUP
HUP
THEY'RE STRONG AT CLOSE RANGE TOO!
YOU HAVEN'T SEEN ANYTHING YET!!
SPECS!
SHPING
SPECIAL WEAPON
STRAIGHT MAN

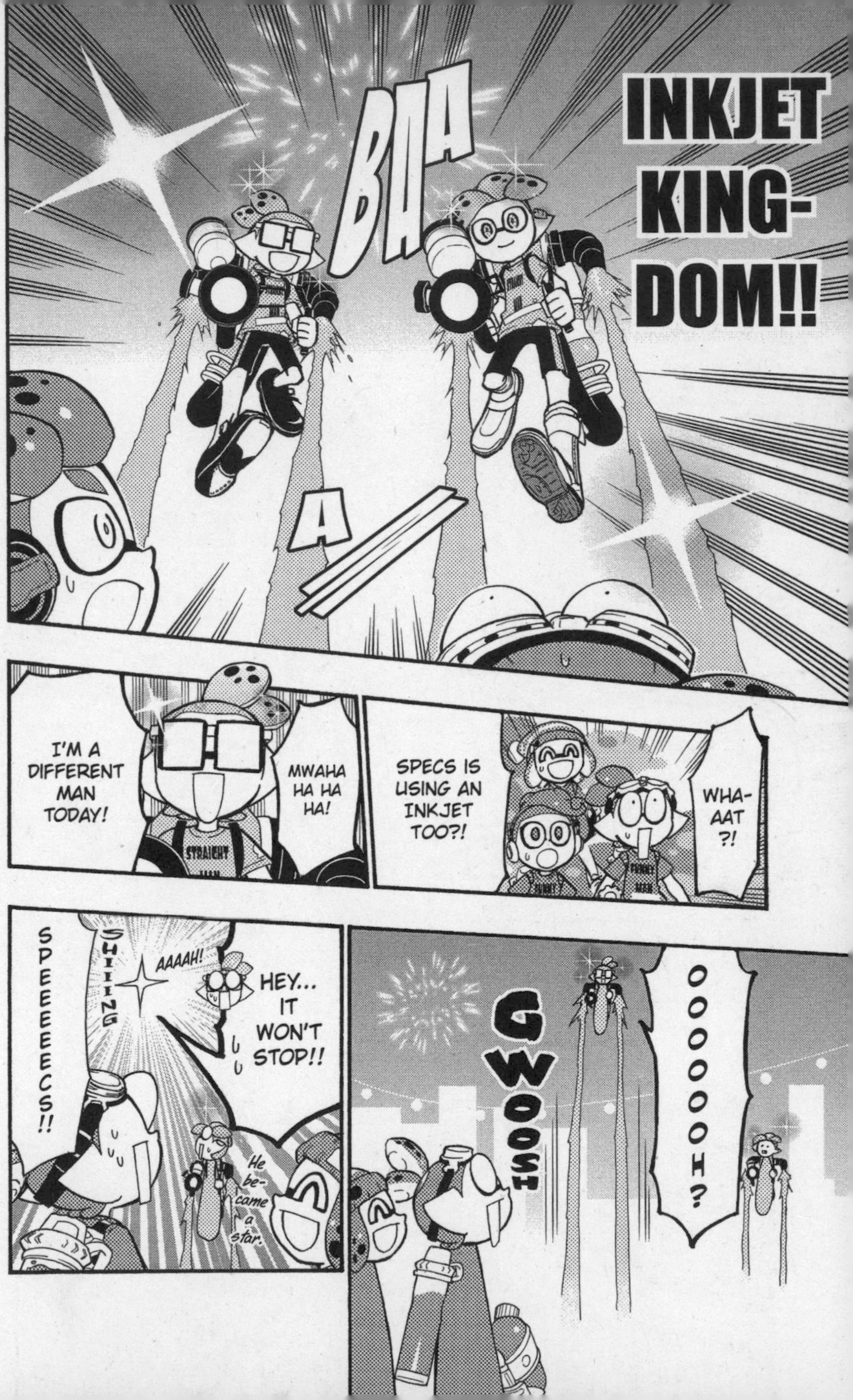
INKJET KINGDOM!!
BAA
A
WHA-AAT?!
SPECS IS USING AN INKJET TOO?!
MWAHA HA HA HA!
I'M A DIFFERENT MAN TODAY!
OOOOOOH?
GWOOSH
HEY... IT WON'T STOP!!
AAAAH!
SHIIING
SPEEEEEECS!!
He became a star.

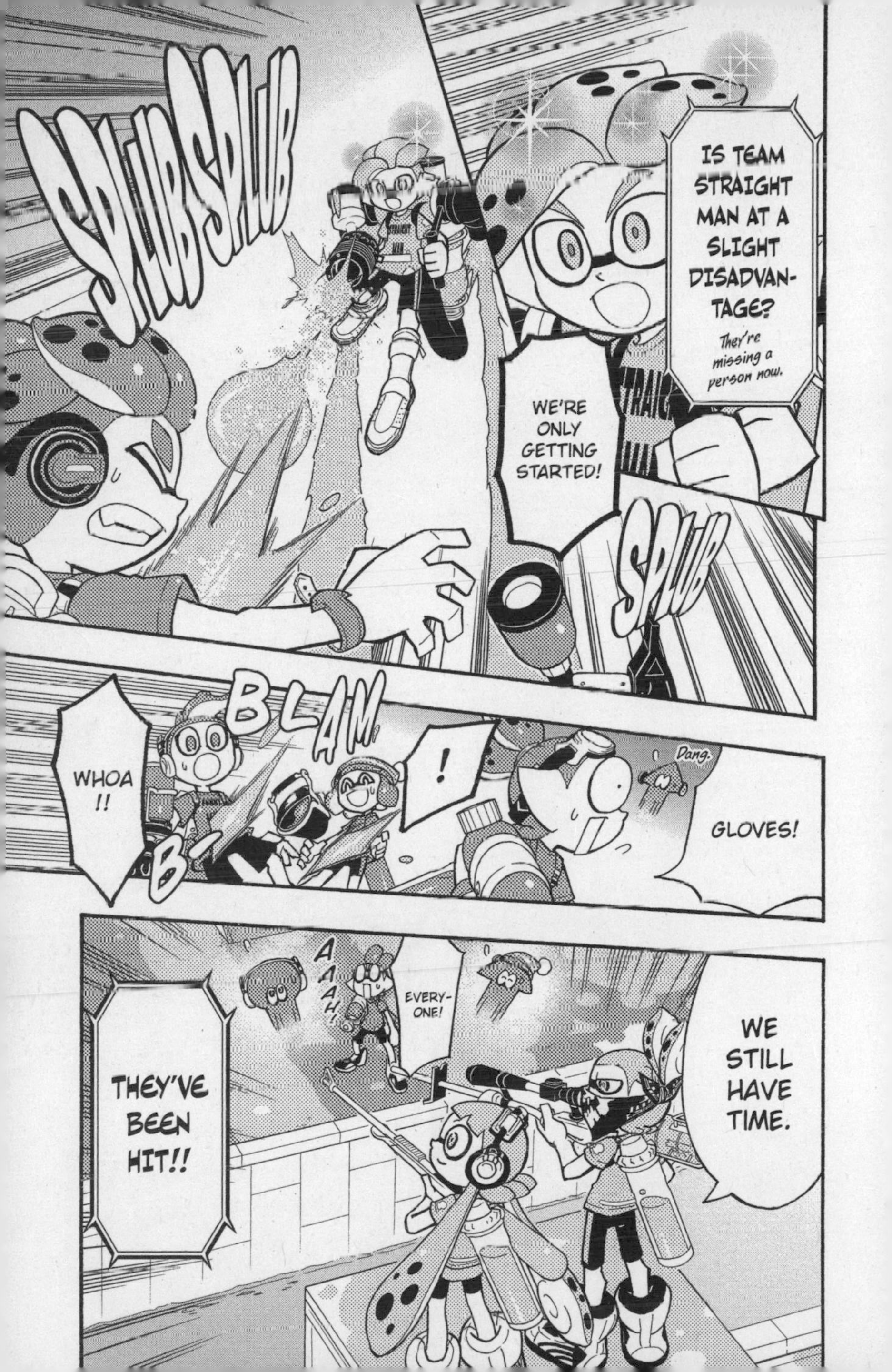
IS TEAM STRAIGHT MAN AT A SLIGHT DISADVANTAGE?
They're missing a person now.
WE'RE ONLY GETTING STARTED!
SPLUB SPLUB
SPLUB
Dang.
GLOVES!
!
BLAM
WHOA!!
WE STILL HAVE TIME.
EVERY-ONE!
AAAH!
THEY'VE BEEN HIT!!

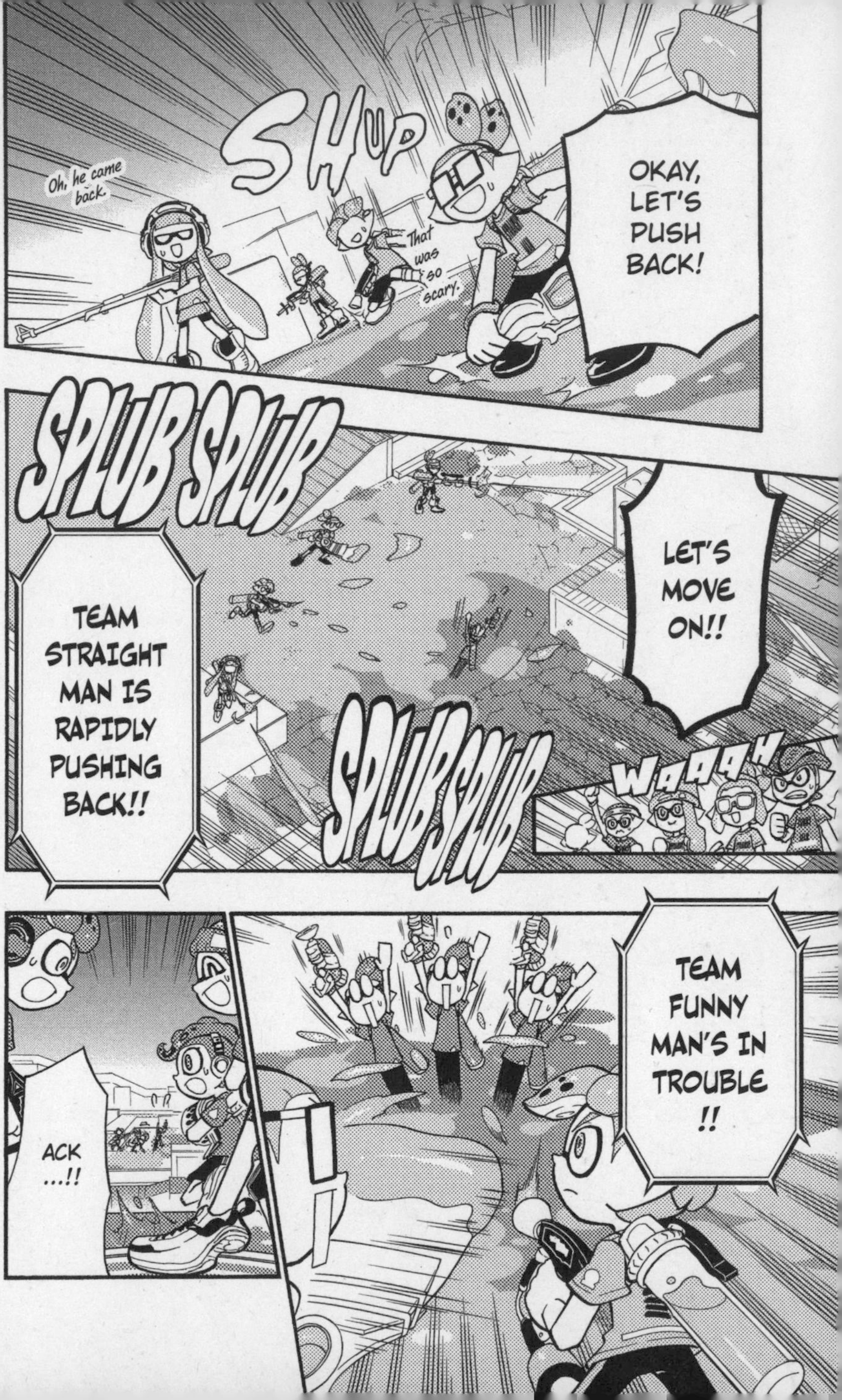
OKAY, LET'S PUSH BACK!
SHUP
That was so scary.
Oh, he came back.
LET'S MOVE ON!!
SPLUB SPLUB
TEAM STRAIGHT MAN IS RAPIDLY PUSHING BACK!!
WAAAH
SPLUB SPLUB
TEAM FUNNY MAN'S IN TROUBLE!!
ACK...!!

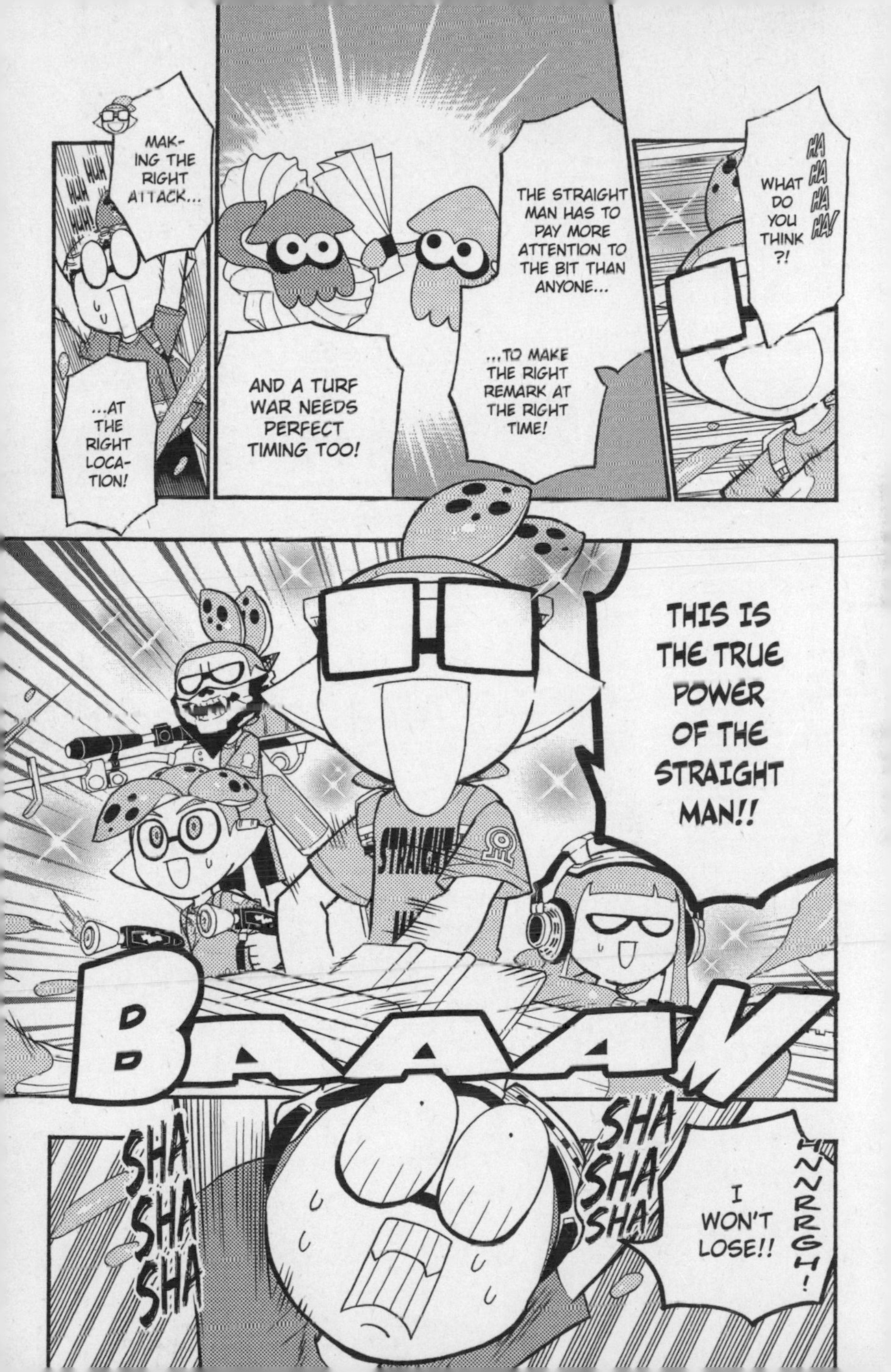
WHAT DO YOU THINK ?!
HA HA HA HA!
THE STRAIGHT MAN HAS TO PAY MORE ATTENTION TO THE BIT THAN ANYONE...
...TO MAKE THE RIGHT REMARK AT THE RIGHT TIME!
AND A TURF WAR NEEDS PERFECT TIMING TOO!
MAKING THE RIGHT ATTACK...
HUH HUH HUH!
...AT THE RIGHT LOCATION!
THIS IS THE TRUE POWER OF THE STRAIGHT MAN!!
STRAIGHT
BAAAM
HNNRRGH!
I WON'T LOSE!!
SHA SHA SHA
SHA SHA SHA

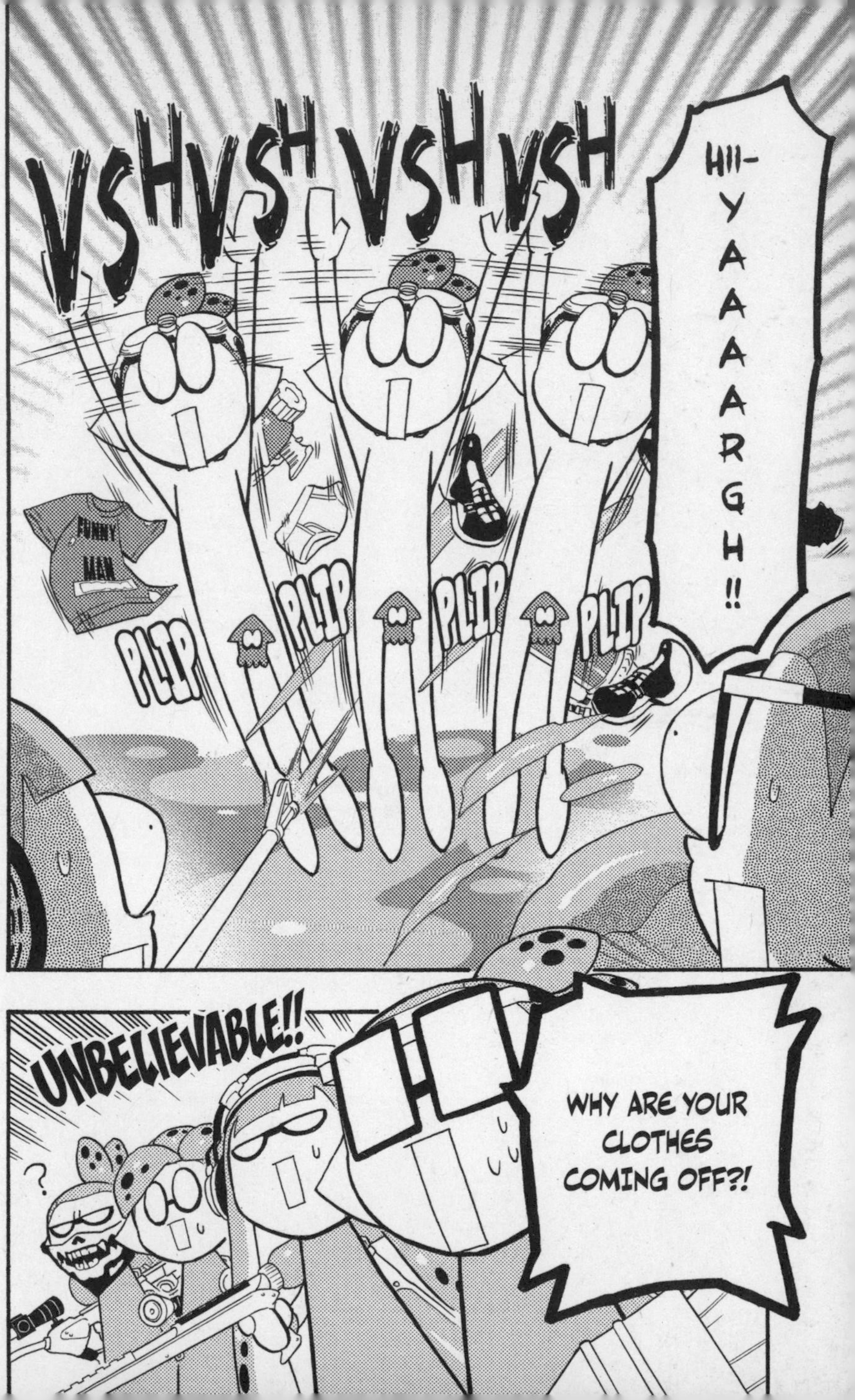
HII-YAAAAARGH!!
VSH VSH VSH VSH
PLIP PLIP PLIP PLIP
FUNNY MAN
WHY ARE YOUR CLOTHES COMING OFF?!
UNBELIEVABLE!!

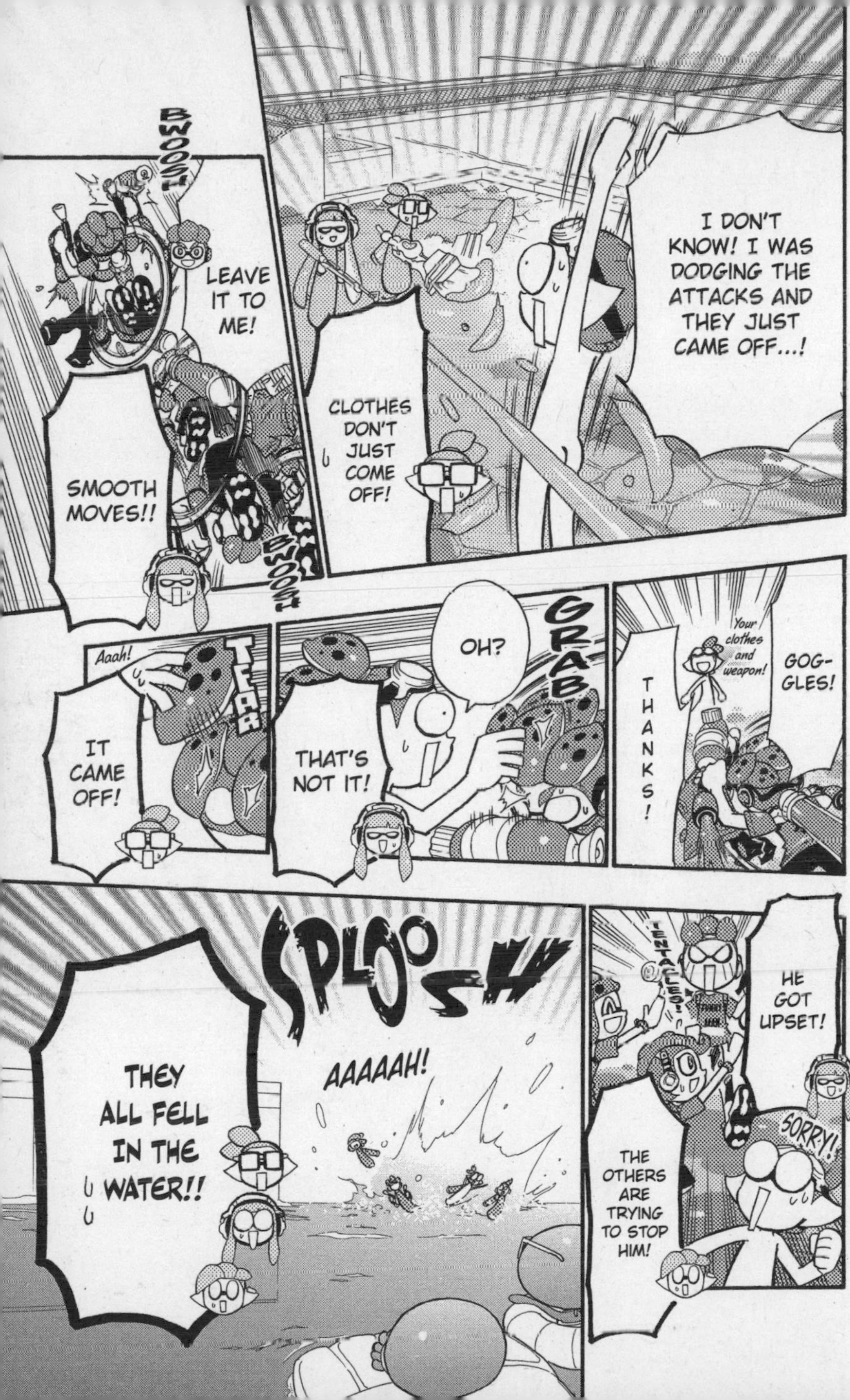
I DON'T KNOW! I WAS DODGING THE ATTACKS AND THEY JUST CAME OFF...!
CLOTHES DON'T JUST COME OFF!
BWOOSH
LEAVE IT TO ME!
SMOOTH MOVES!!
BWOOSH
GOG-GLES!
Your clothes and weapon!
THANKS!
GRAB
OH?
THAT'S NOT IT!
TEAR
Aaah!
IT CAME OFF!
TENTACLES!
HE GOT UPSET!
SORRY!
THE OTHERS ARE TRYING TO STOP HIM!
SPLOOSH
AAAAAH!
THEY ALL FELL IN THE WATER!!

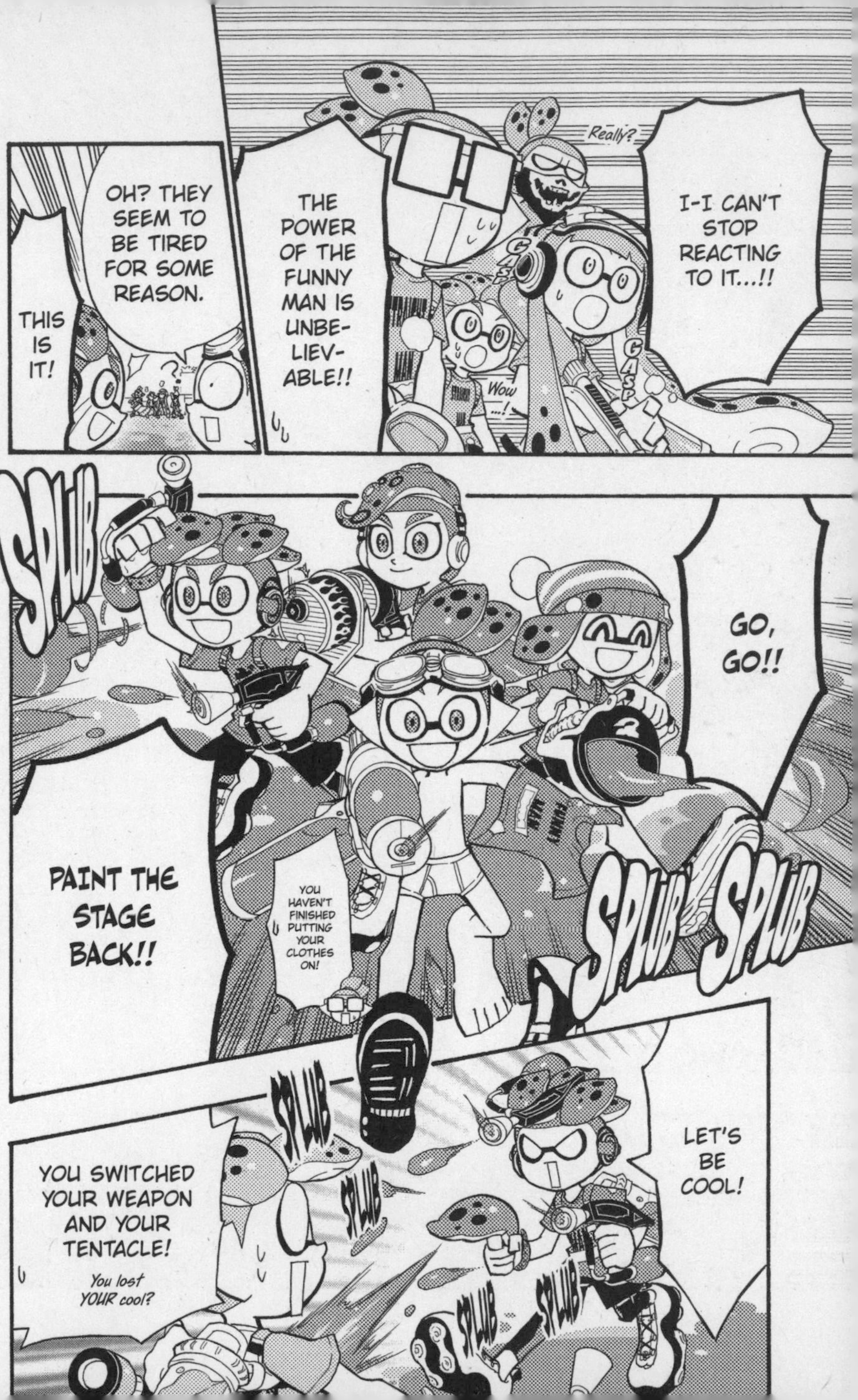

Really?
I-I CAN'T STOP REACTING TO IT...!!
GASP
GASP
THE POWER OF THE FUNNY MAN IS UNBE-LIEV-ABLE!!
Wow...!
OH? THEY SEEM TO BE TIRED FOR SOME REASON.
THIS IS IT!
SPLUB
GO, GO!!
SPLUB SPLUB
YOU HAVEN'T FINISHED PUTTING YOUR CLOTHES ON!
PAINT THE STAGE BACK!!
LET'S BE COOL!
SPLUB
SPLUB
SPLUB
SPLUB
SPLUB
YOU SWITCHED YOUR WEAPON AND YOUR TENTACLE!
You lost YOUR cool?

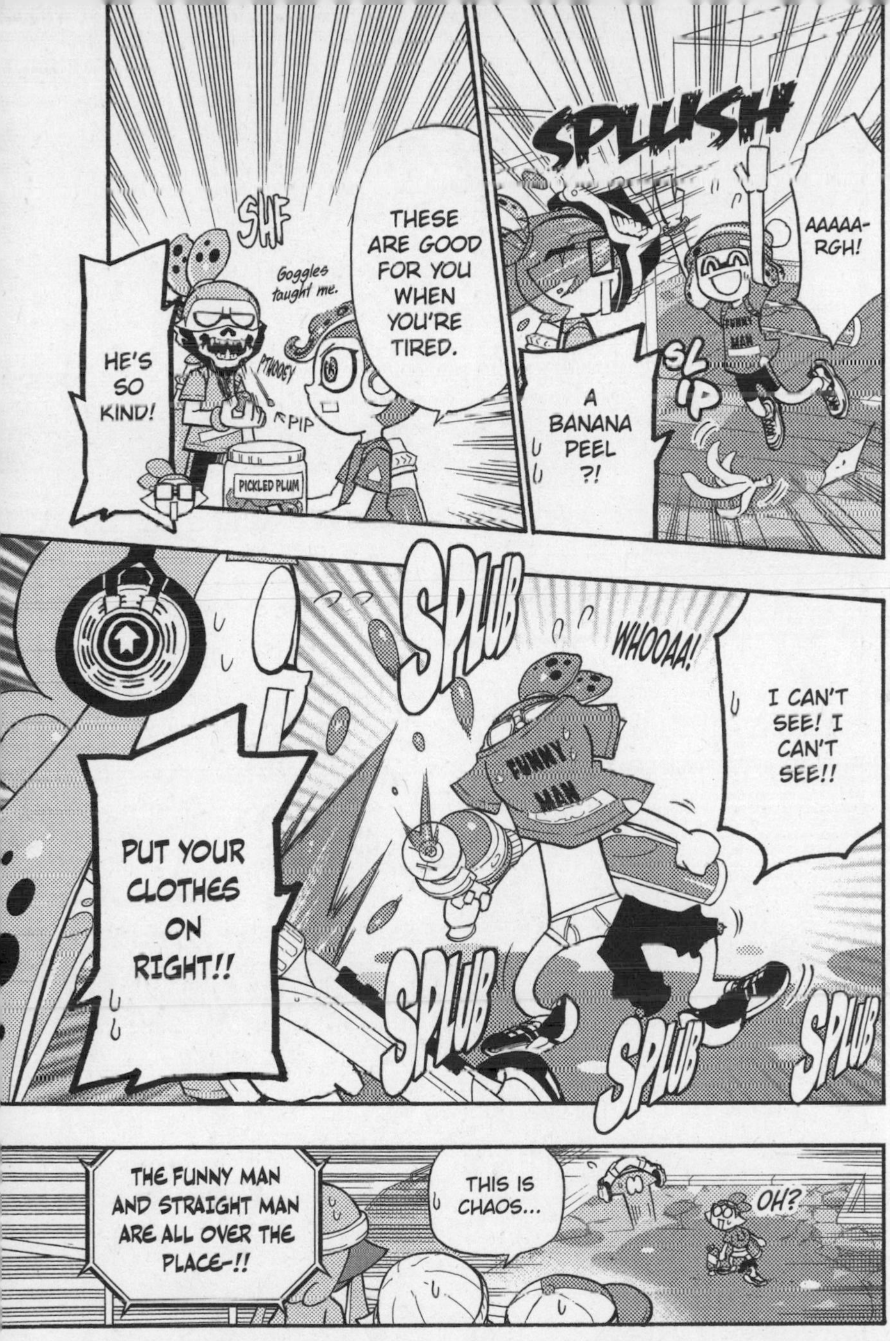
SPLUSH
AAAAA-RGH!
FUNNY MAN
SLIP
A BANANA PEEL?!
SHF
THESE ARE GOOD FOR YOU WHEN YOU'RE TIRED.
Goggles taught me.
HE'S SO KIND!
PTHOOEY
PIP
PICKLED PLUM
WHOOAA!
I CAN'T SEE! I CAN'T SEE!!
SPLUB
FUNNY MAN
PUT YOUR CLOTHES ON RIGHT!!
SPLUB
SPLUB
SPLUB
OH?
THIS IS CHAOS...
THE FUNNY MAN AND STRAIGHT MAN ARE ALL OVER THE PLACE-!!

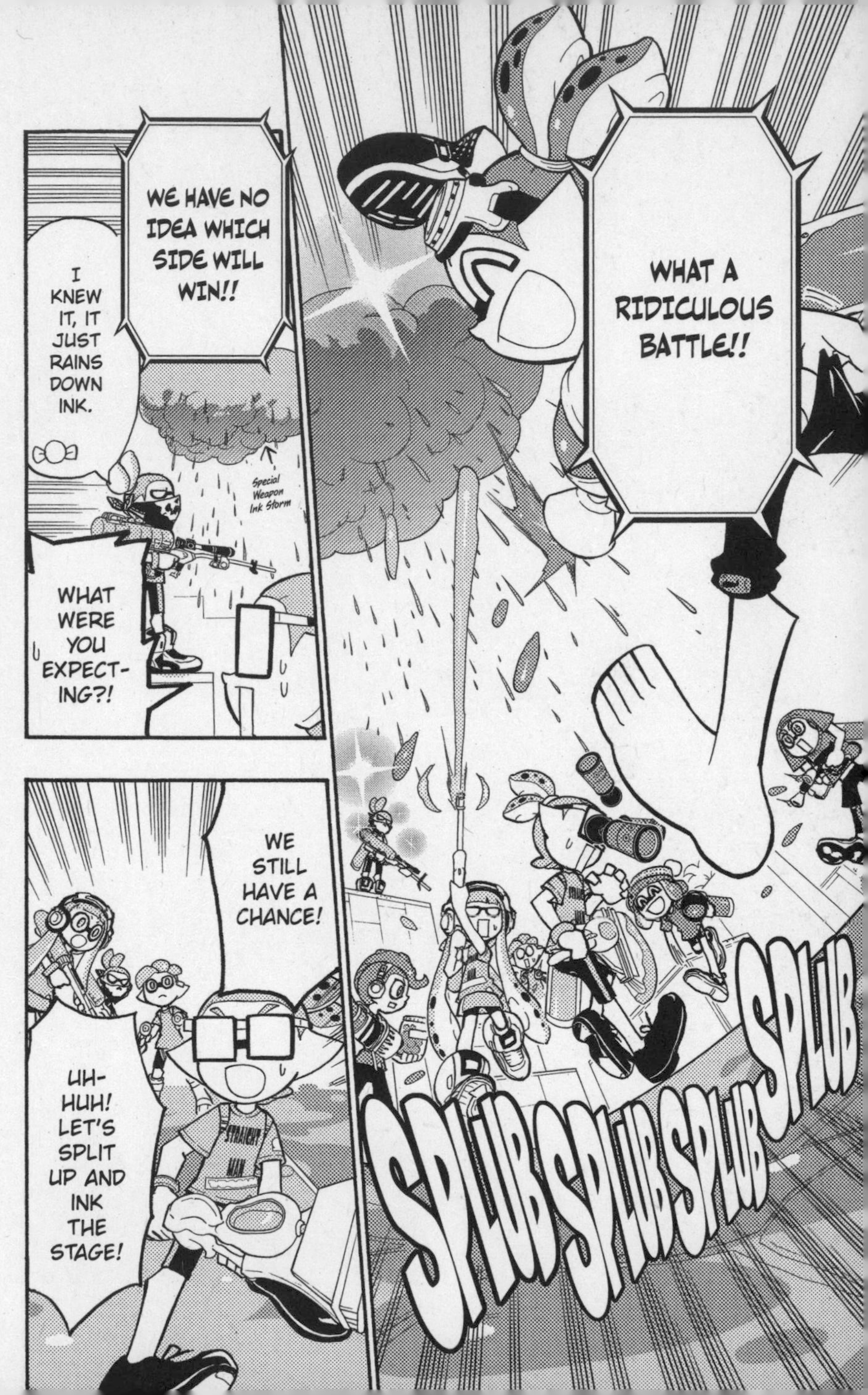
WHAT A RIDICULOUS BATTLE!!
SPLUB SPLUB SPLUB SPLUB
WE HAVE NO IDEA WHICH SIDE WILL WIN!!
I KNEW IT, IT JUST RAINS DOWN INK.
Special Weapon Ink Storm
WHAT WERE YOU EXPECT-ING?!
WE STILL HAVE A CHANCE!
UH-HUH! LET'S SPLIT UP AND INK THE STAGE!
STRAIGHT MAN

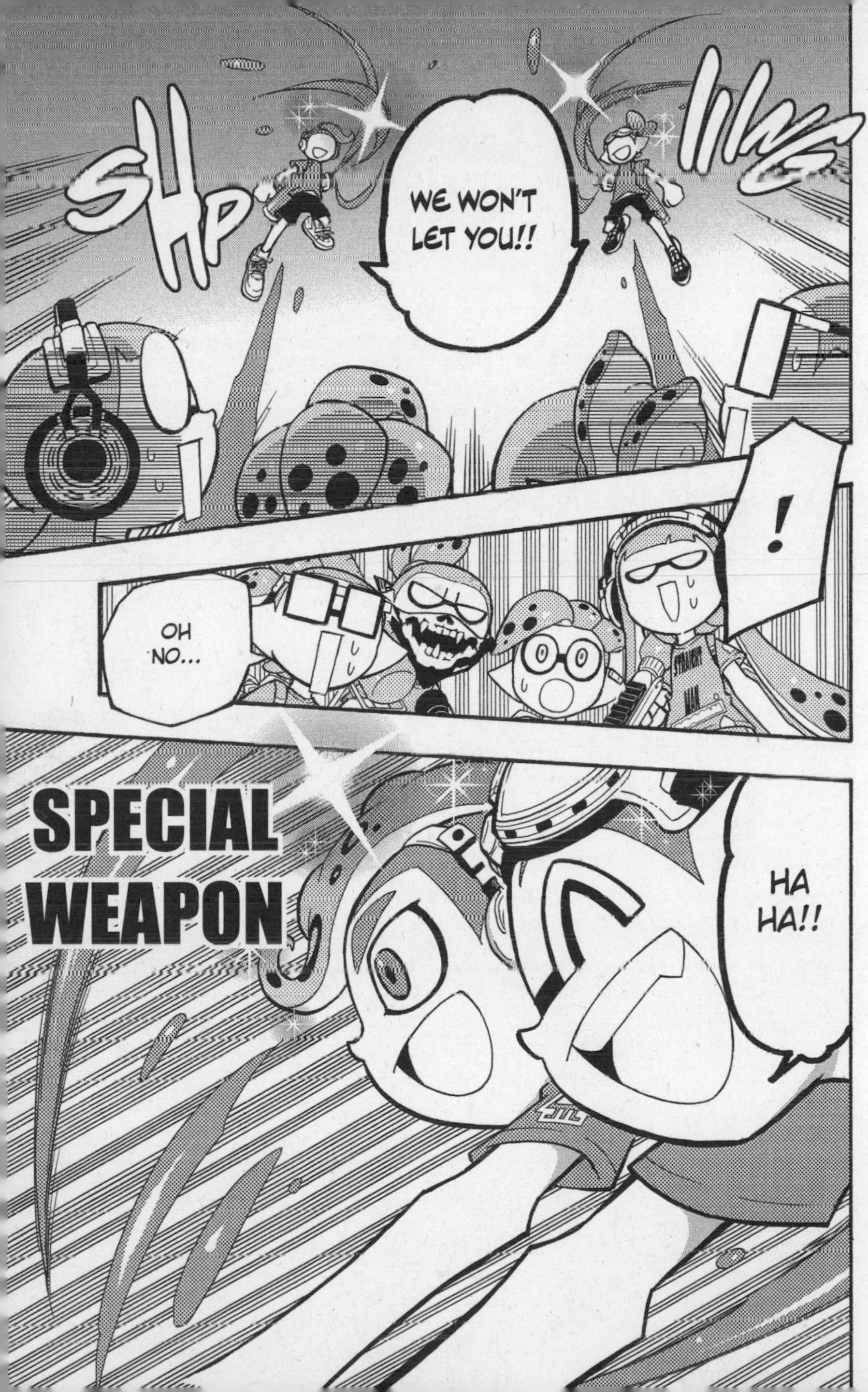
WE WON'T LET YOU!!
SHP
!
OH NO...
HA HA!!
SPECIAL WEAPON

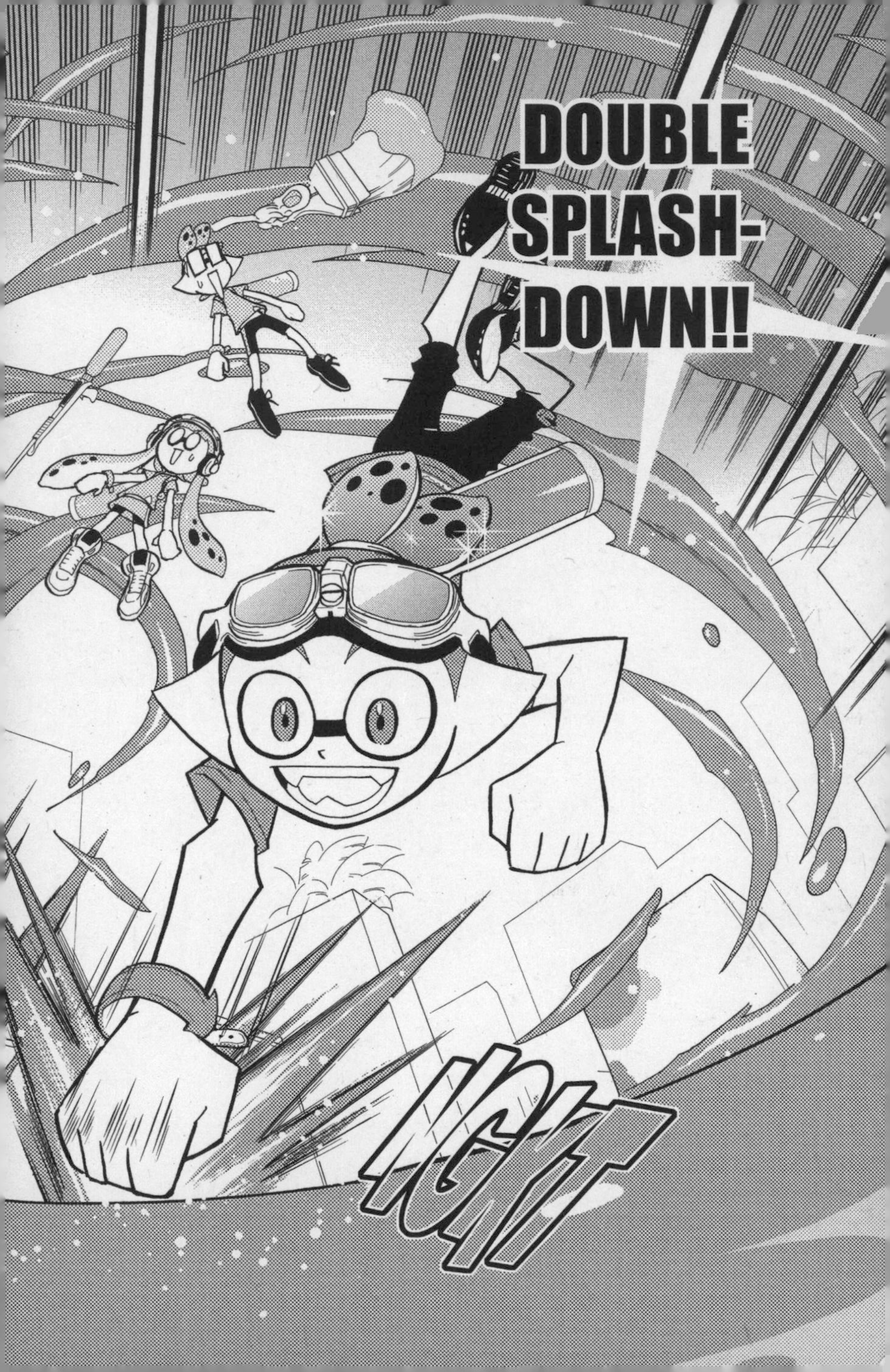
DOUBLE SPLASH-DOWN!!
KCHT

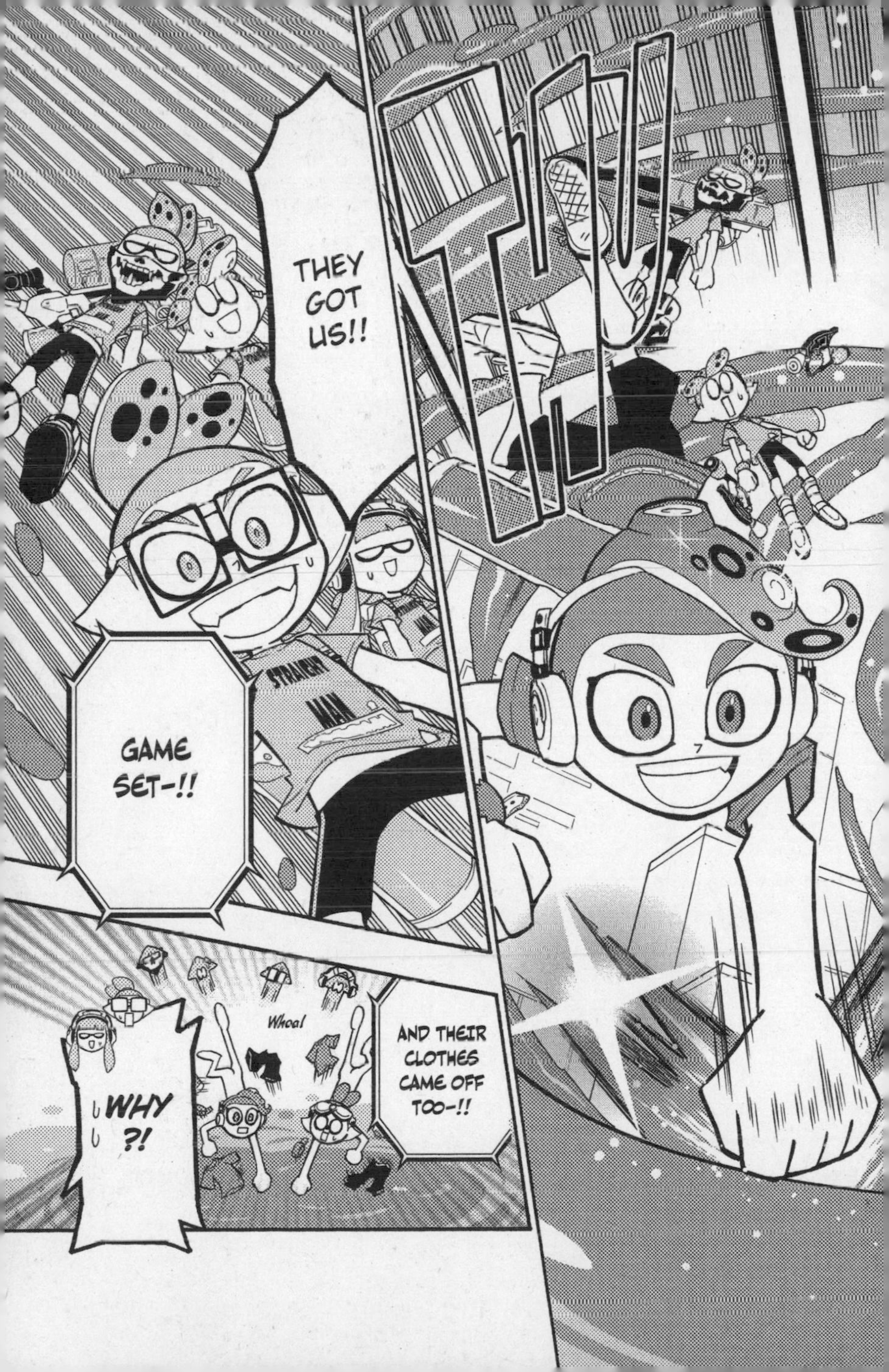
THEY GOT US!!
GAME SET-!!
AND THEIR CLOTHES CAME OFF TOO-!!
Whoa!
WHY ?!

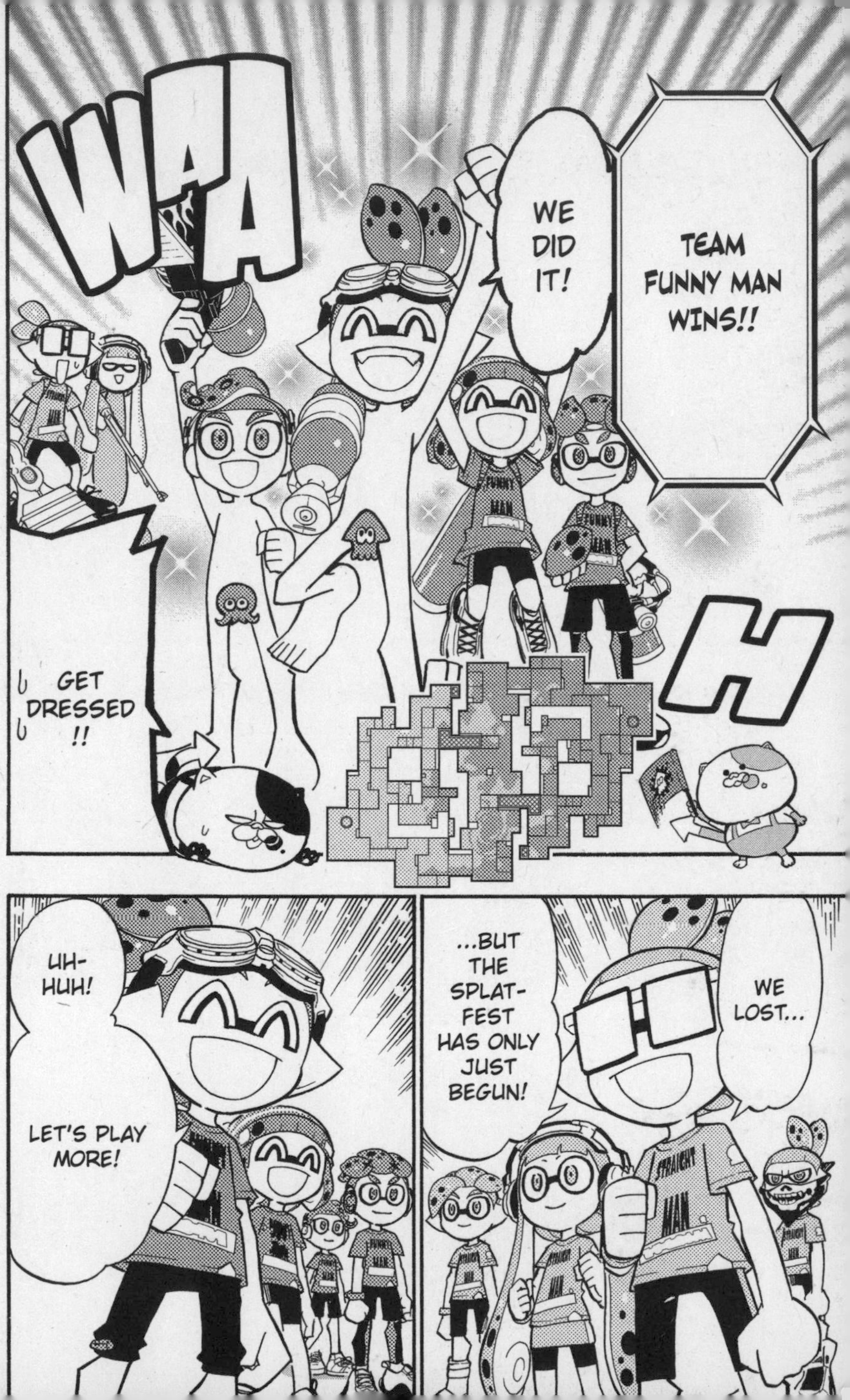
TEAM FUNNY MAN WINS!!
WE DID IT!
WAAH
GET DRESSED!!
WE LOST...
...BUT THE SPLAT-FEST HAS ONLY JUST BEGUN!
UH-HUH!
LET'S PLAY MORE!

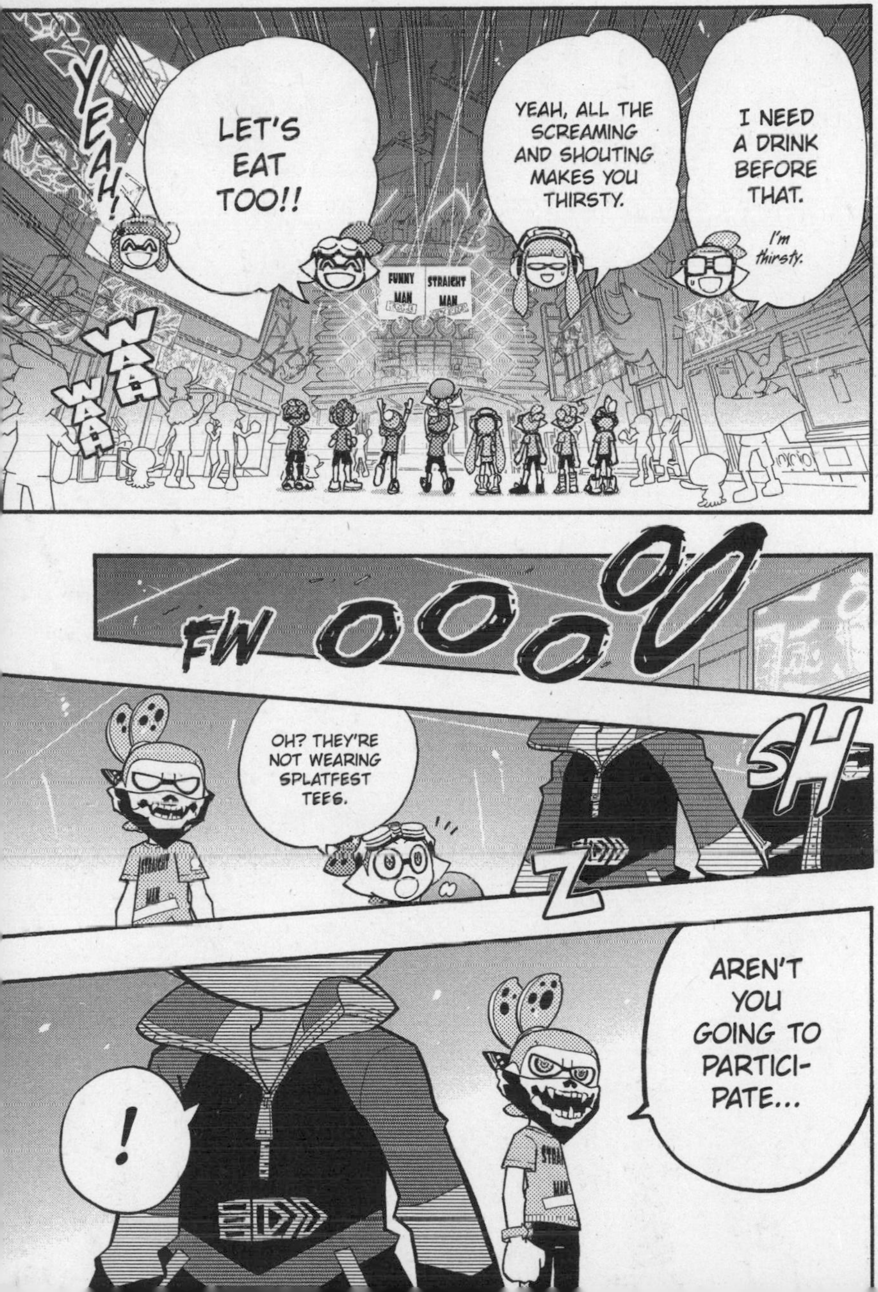
I NEED A DRINK BEFORE THAT.
I'm thirsty.
YEAH, ALL THE SCREAMING AND SHOUTING MAKES YOU THIRSTY.
STRAIGHT MAN
FUNNY MAN
LET'S EAT TOO!!
YEAH!
WAA
WAA
FWOOOOO
SH
Z
OH? THEY'RE NOT WEARING SPLATFEST TEES.
AREN'T YOU GOING TO PARTICI-PATE...
!

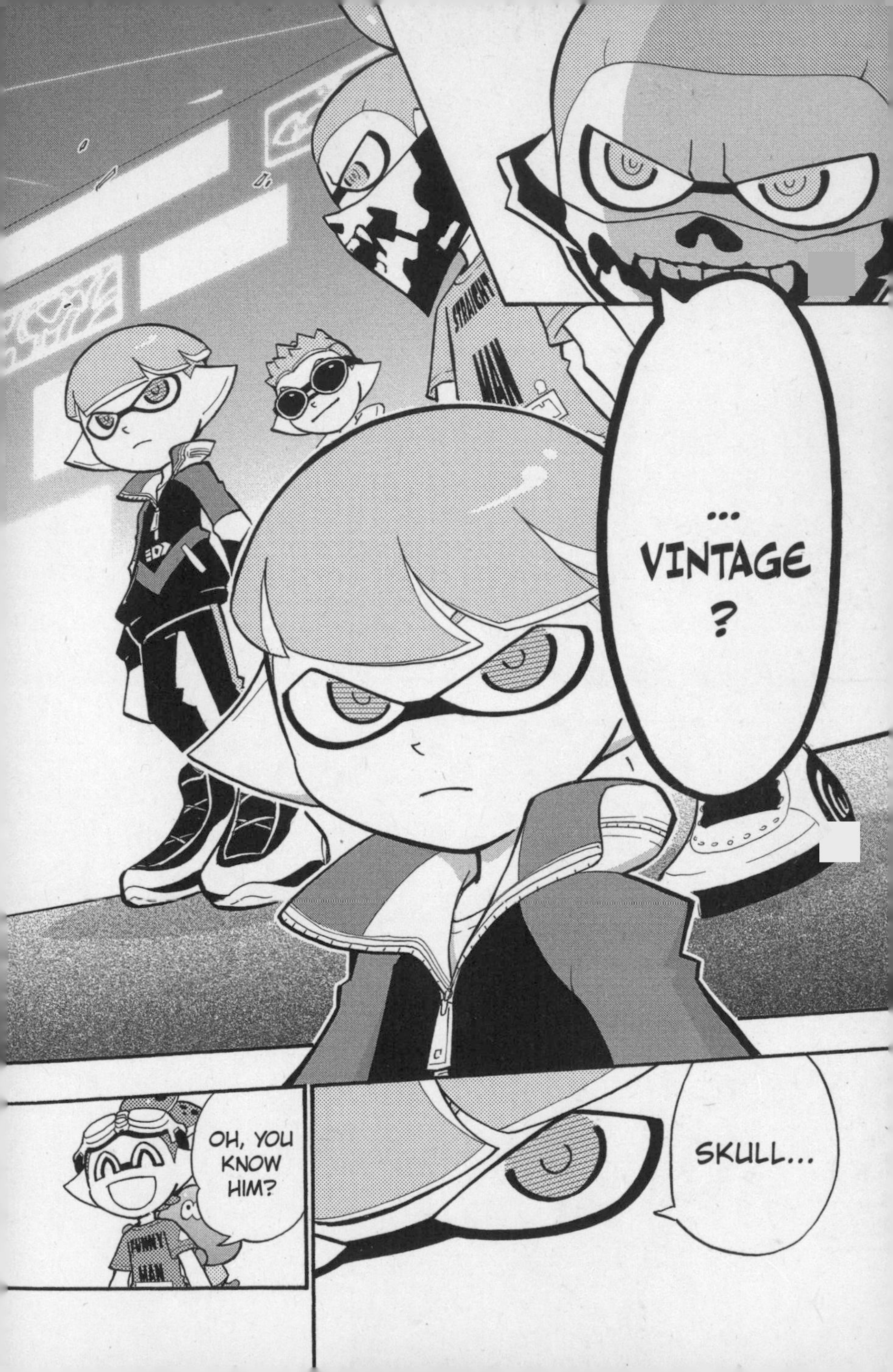
STRAIGHT MAN
...VINTAGE?
SKULL...
OH, YOU KNOW HIM?
FUNNY MAN

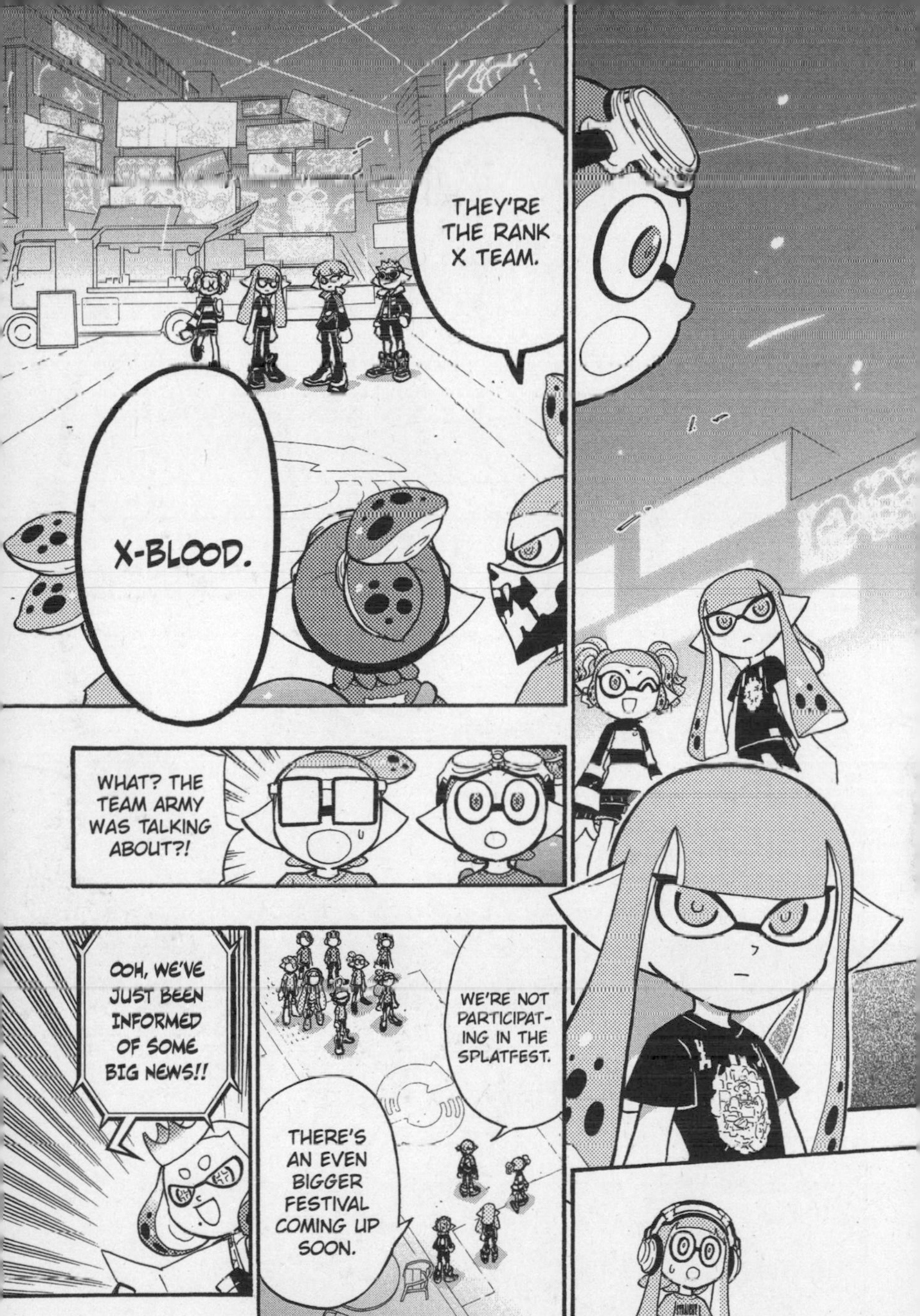
THEY'RE THE RANK X TEAM.
X-BLOOD.
WHAT? THE TEAM ARMY WAS TALKING ABOUT?!
WE'RE NOT PARTICIPAT-ING IN THE SPLATFEST.
THERE'S AN EVEN BIGGER FESTIVAL COMING UP SOON.
OOH, WE'VE JUST BEEN INFORMED OF SOME BIG NEWS!!

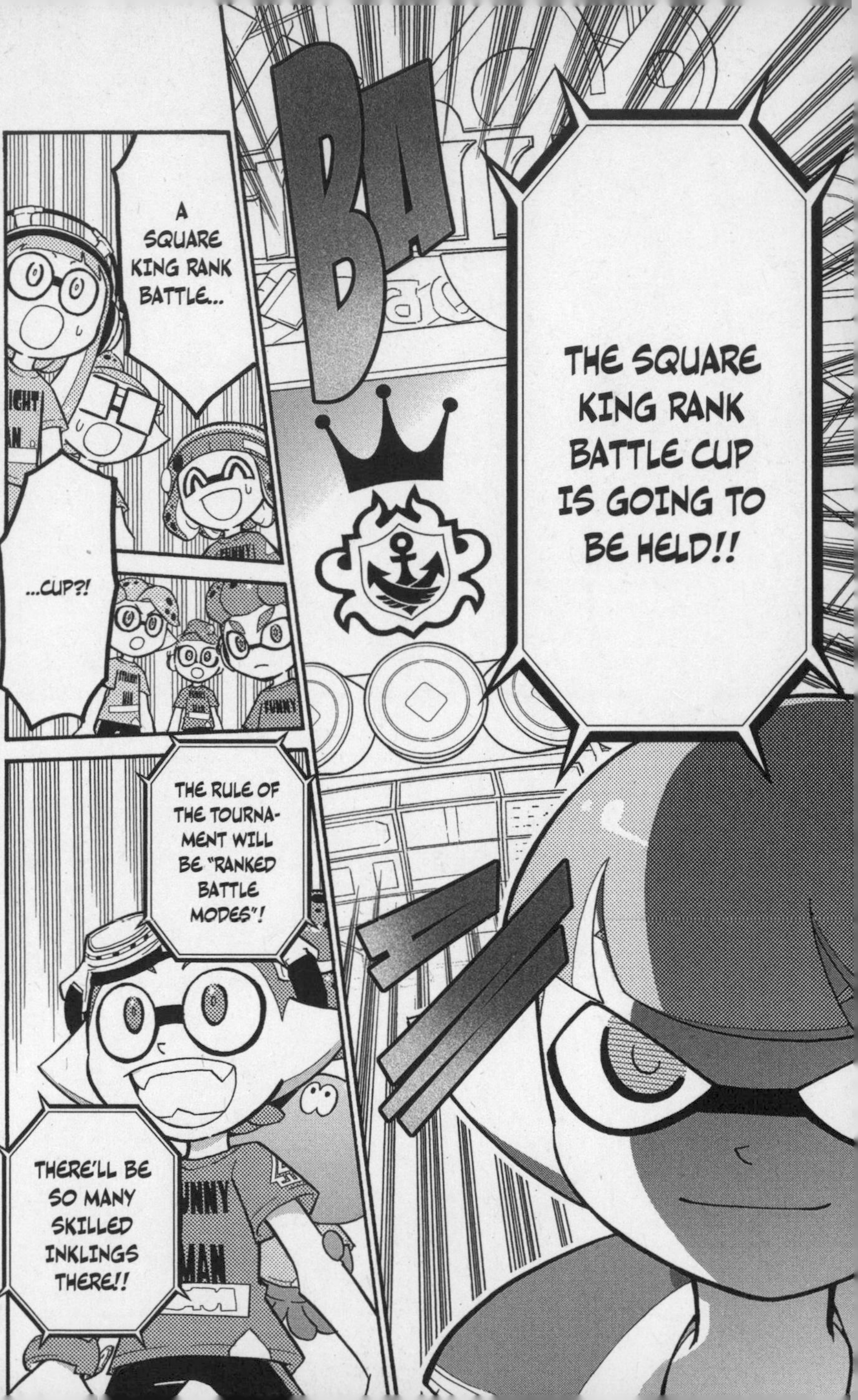
BA
THE SQUARE KING RANK BATTLE CUP IS GOING TO BE HELD!!
A SQUARE KING RANK BATTLE...
...CUP?!
THE RULE OF THE TOURNA-MENT WILL BE "RANKED BATTLE MODES"!
THERE'LL BE SO MANY SKILLED INKLINGS THERE!!

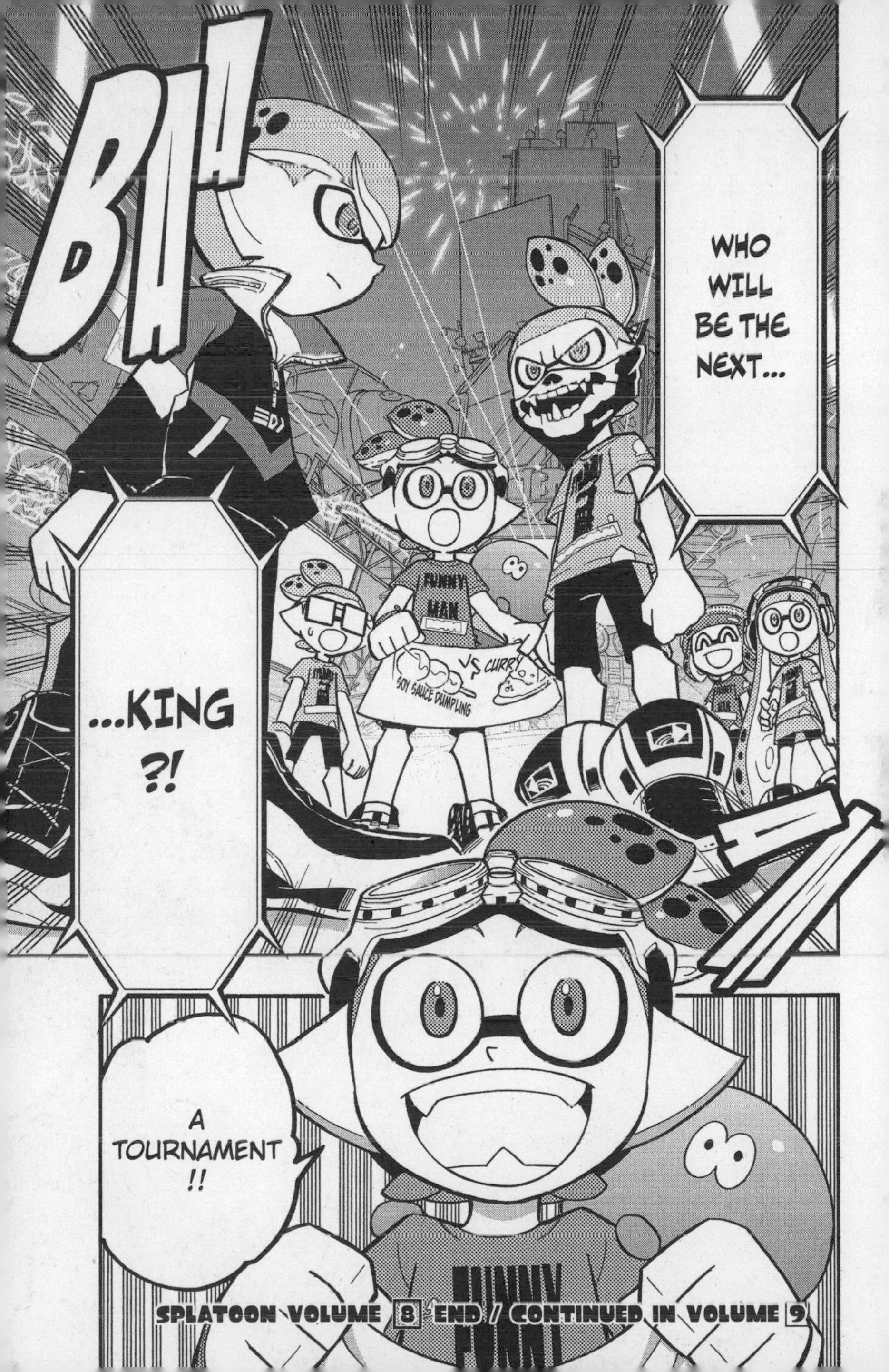
WHO WILL BE THE NEXT...
...KING ?!
BAH
FUNNY MAN
VS CURRY
SOY SAUCE DUMPLING
A TOURNAMENT !!

SPLATOON VOLUME 8 END / CONTINUED IN VOLUME 9

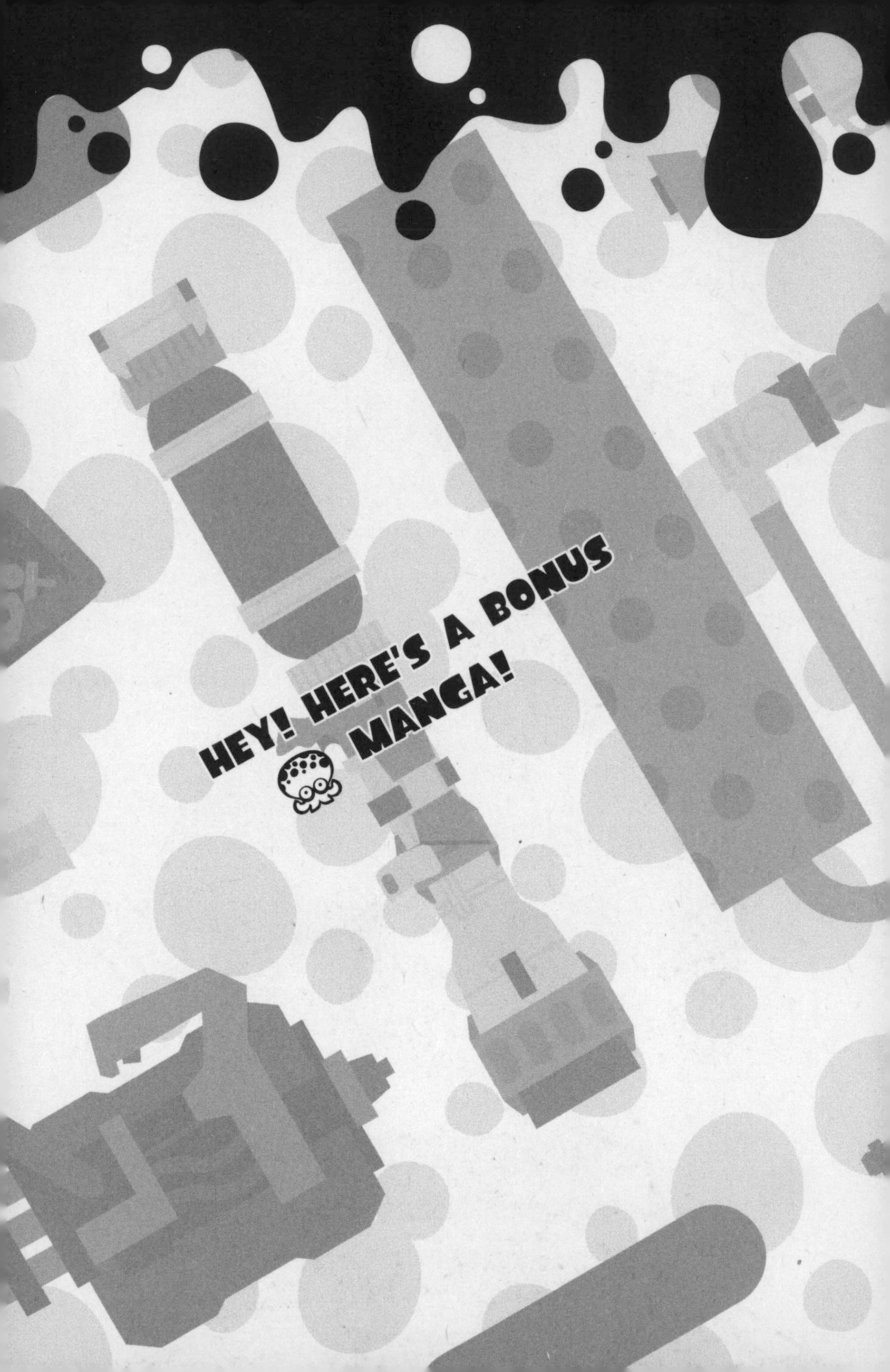
HEY! HERE'S A BONUS MANGA!

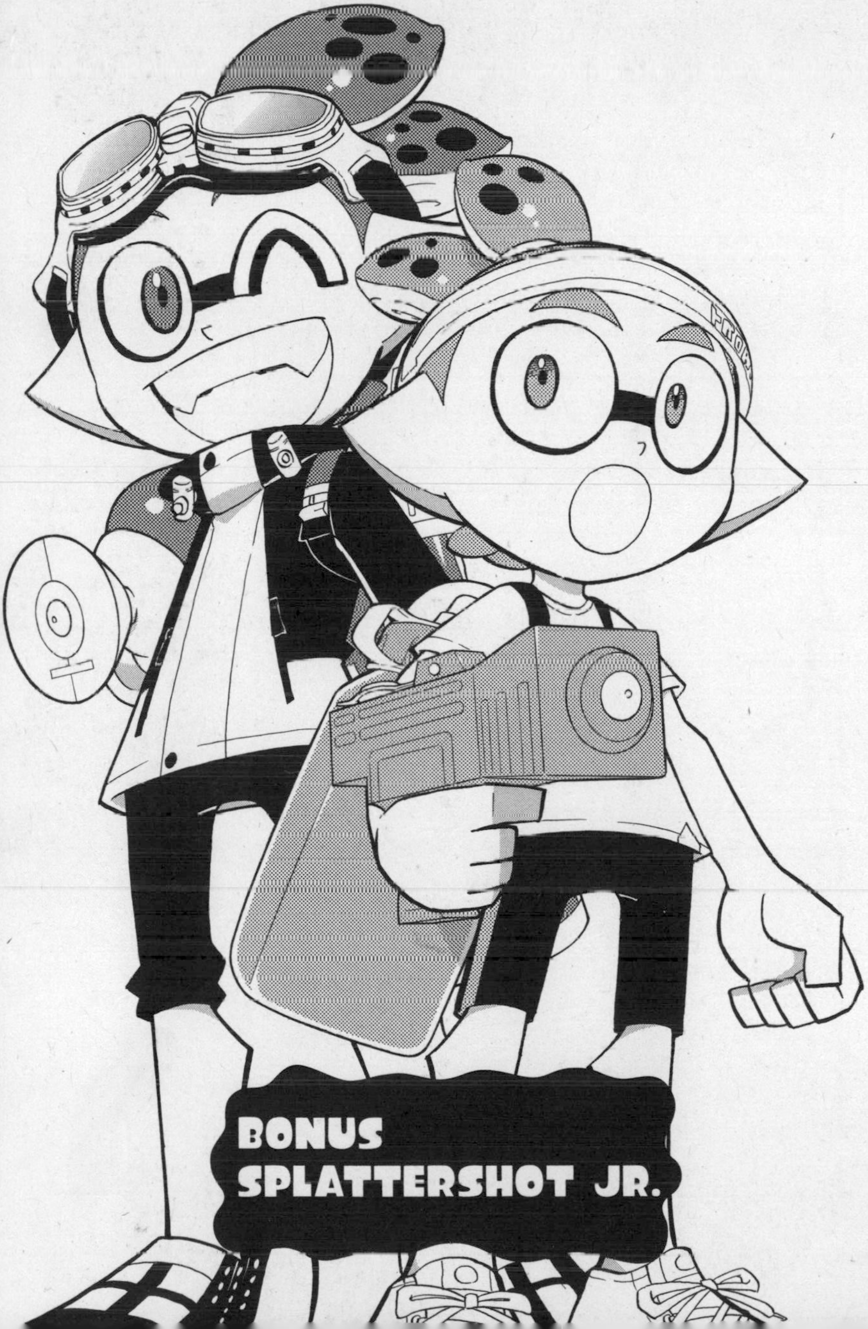

BONUS
SPLATTERSHOT JR.

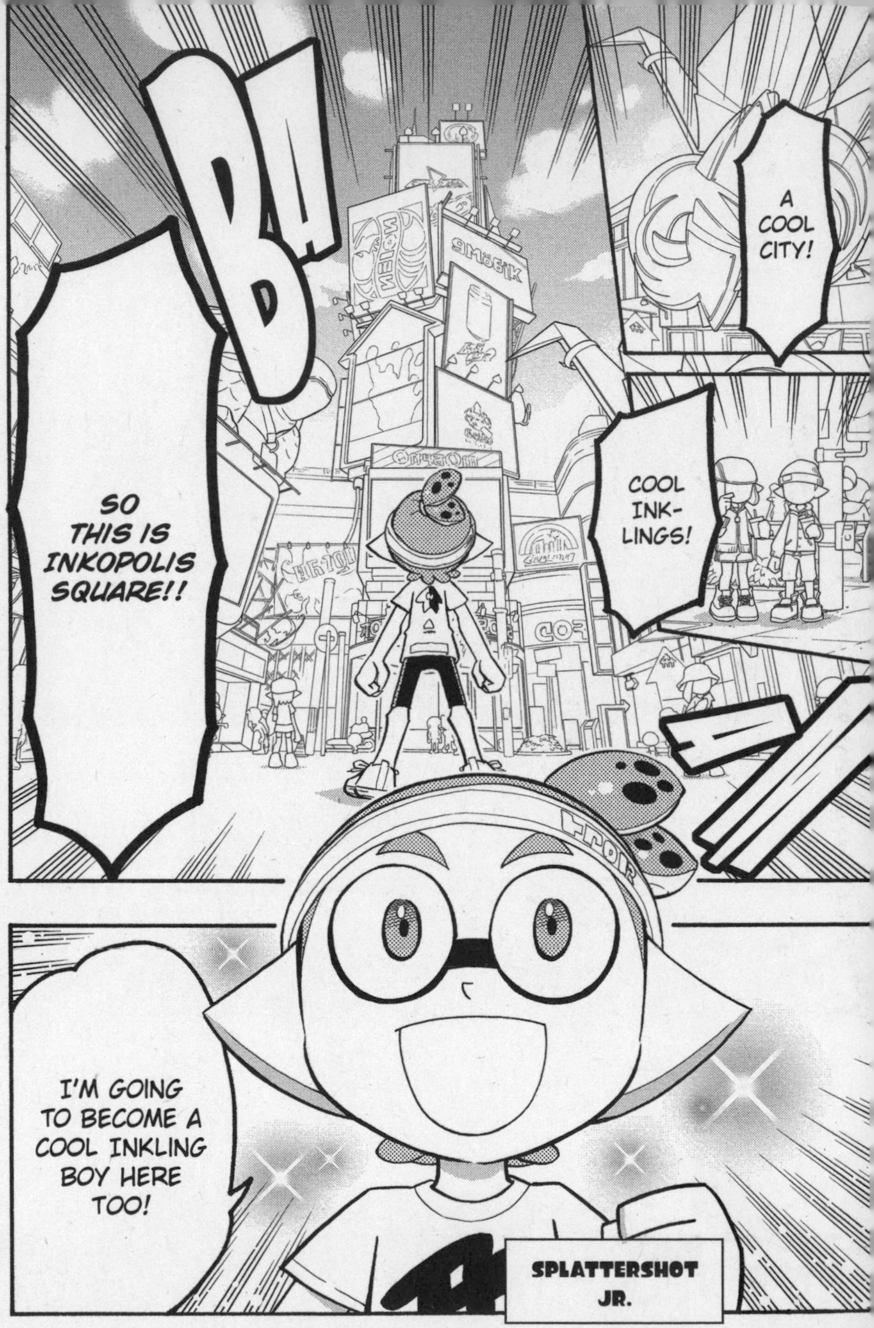
A COOL CITY!
COOL INK-LINGS!
BA
SO THIS IS INKOPOLIS SQUARE!!
I'M GOING TO BECOME A COOL INKLING BOY HERE TOO!
SPLATTERSHOT JR.

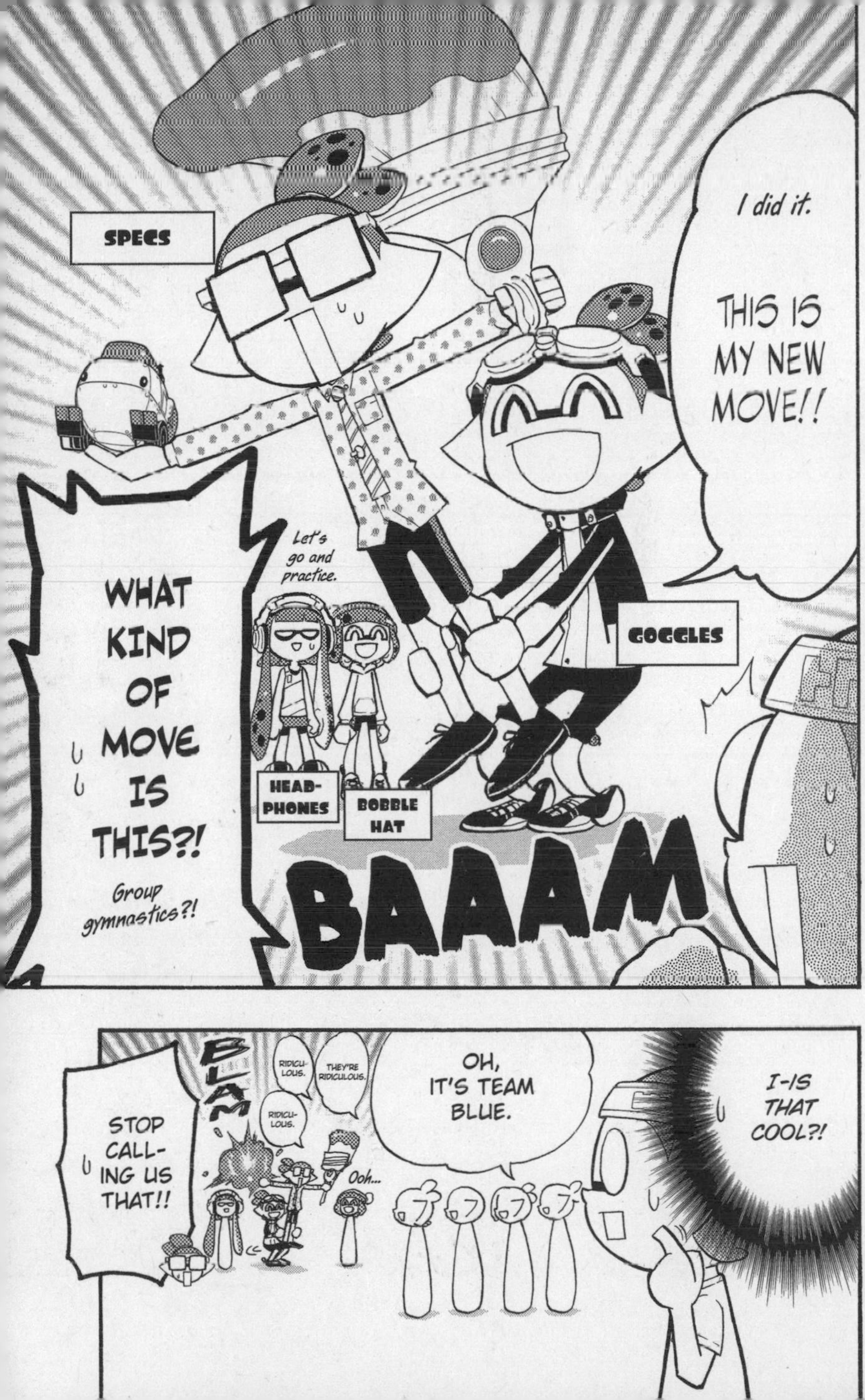
I did it.
THIS IS MY NEW MOVE!!
SPECS
GOGGLES
BAAAM
BOBBLE HAT
HEAD-PHONES
Let's go and practice.
WHAT KIND OF MOVE IS THIS?!
Group gymnastics?!
I-IS THAT COOL?!
OH, IT'S TEAM BLUE.
THEY'RE RIDICULOUS.
RIDICU-LOUS.
RIDICU-LOUS.
Ooh...
BLAM
STOP CALLING US THAT!!

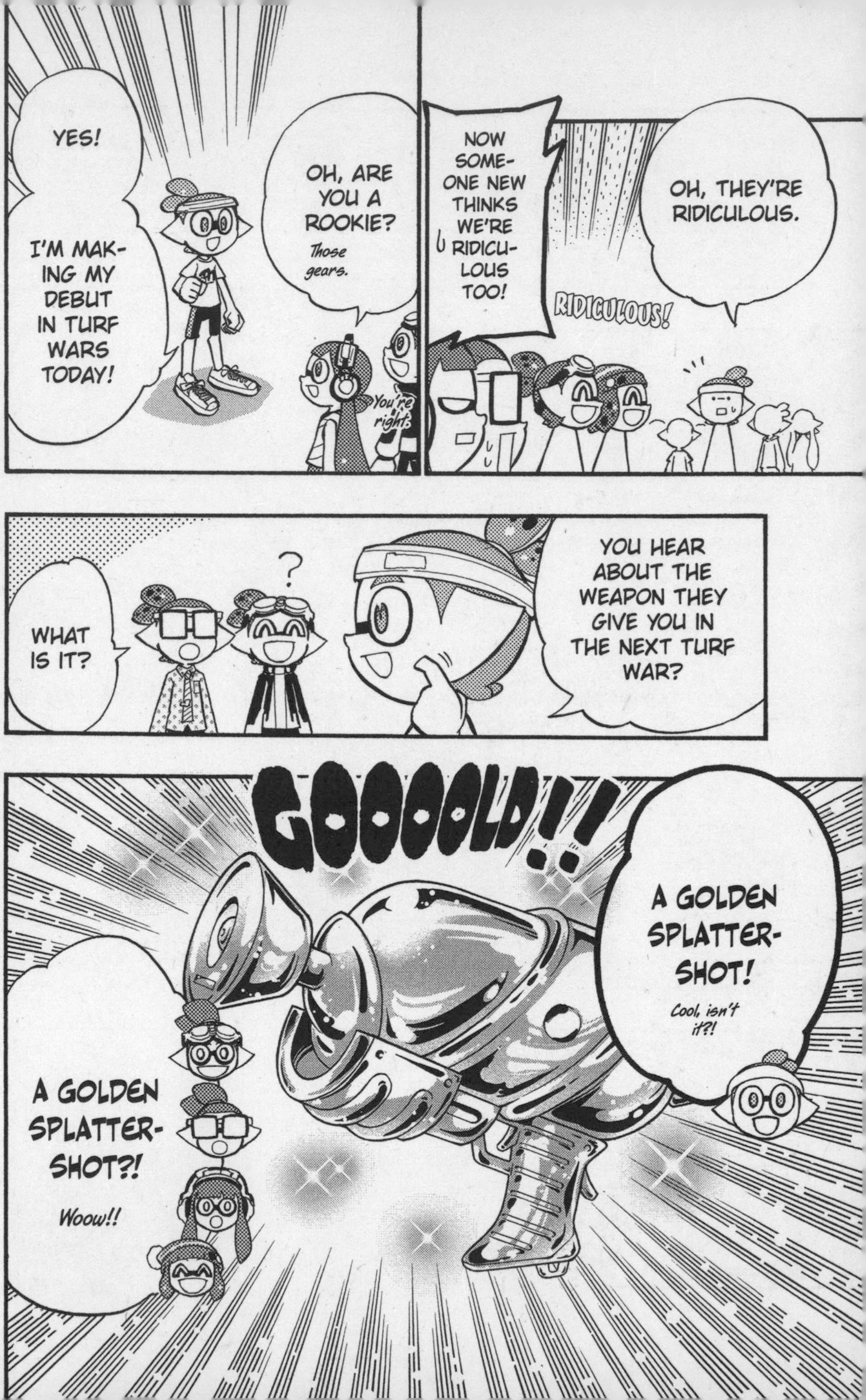
OH, THEY'RE RIDICULOUS.
RIDICULOUS!
NOW SOME-ONE NEW THINKS WE'RE RIDICU-LOUS TOO!
OH, ARE YOU A ROOKIE?
Those gears.
You're right.
YES!
I'M MAK-ING MY DEBUT IN TURF WARS TODAY!
YOU HEAR ABOUT THE WEAPON THEY GIVE YOU IN THE NEXT TURF WAR?
?
WHAT IS IT?
GOOOOLD!!
A GOLDEN SPLATTER-SHOT!
Cool, isn't it?!
A GOLDEN SPLATTER-SHOT?!
Woow!!

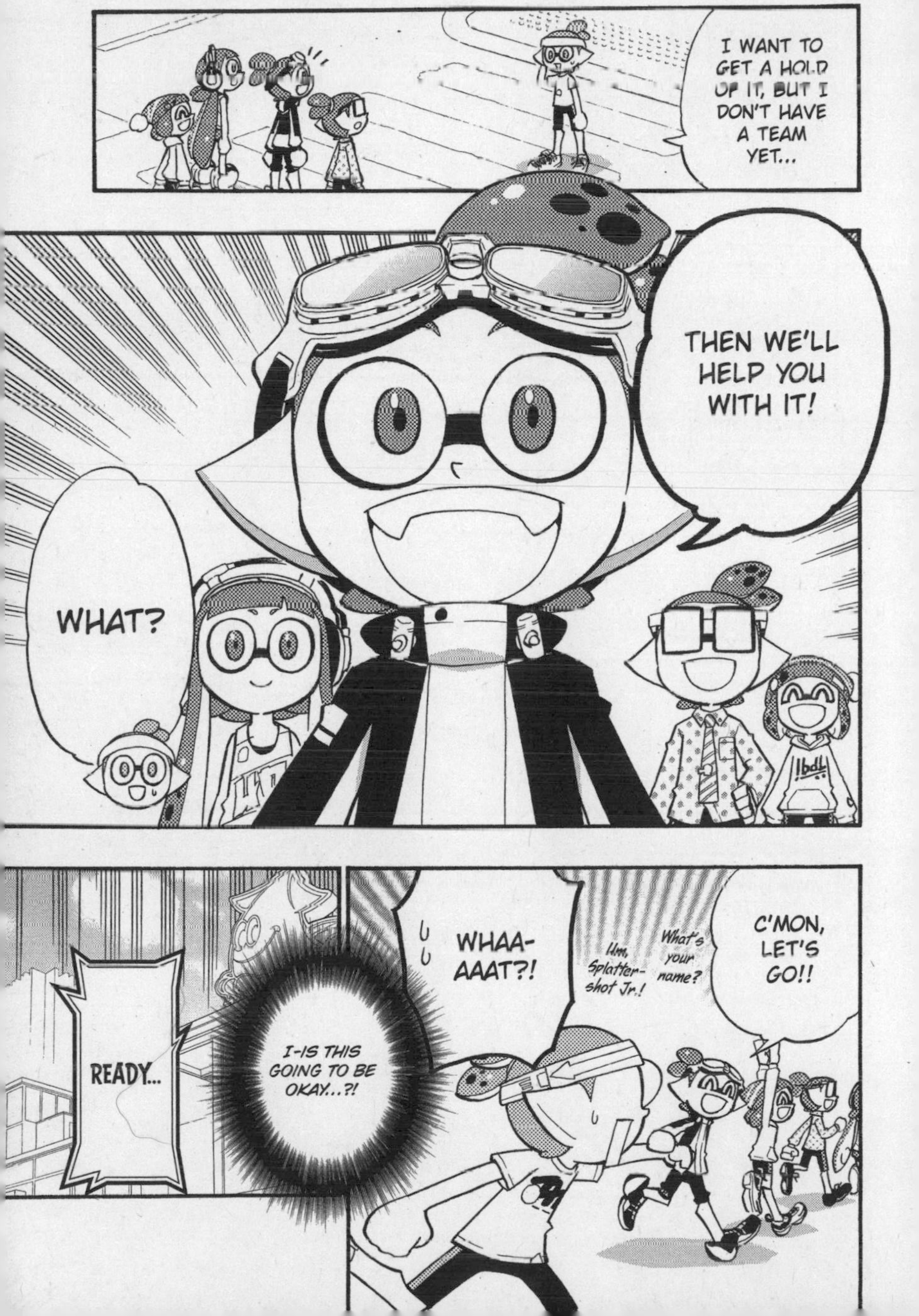
I WANT TO GET A HOLD OF IT, BUT I DON'T HAVE A TEAM YET...
THEN WE'LL HELP YOU WITH IT!
WHAT?
C'MON, LET'S GO!!
What's your name?
Um, Splatter-shot Jr.!
WHAA-AAAT?!
I-IS THIS GOING TO BE OKAY...?!
READY...

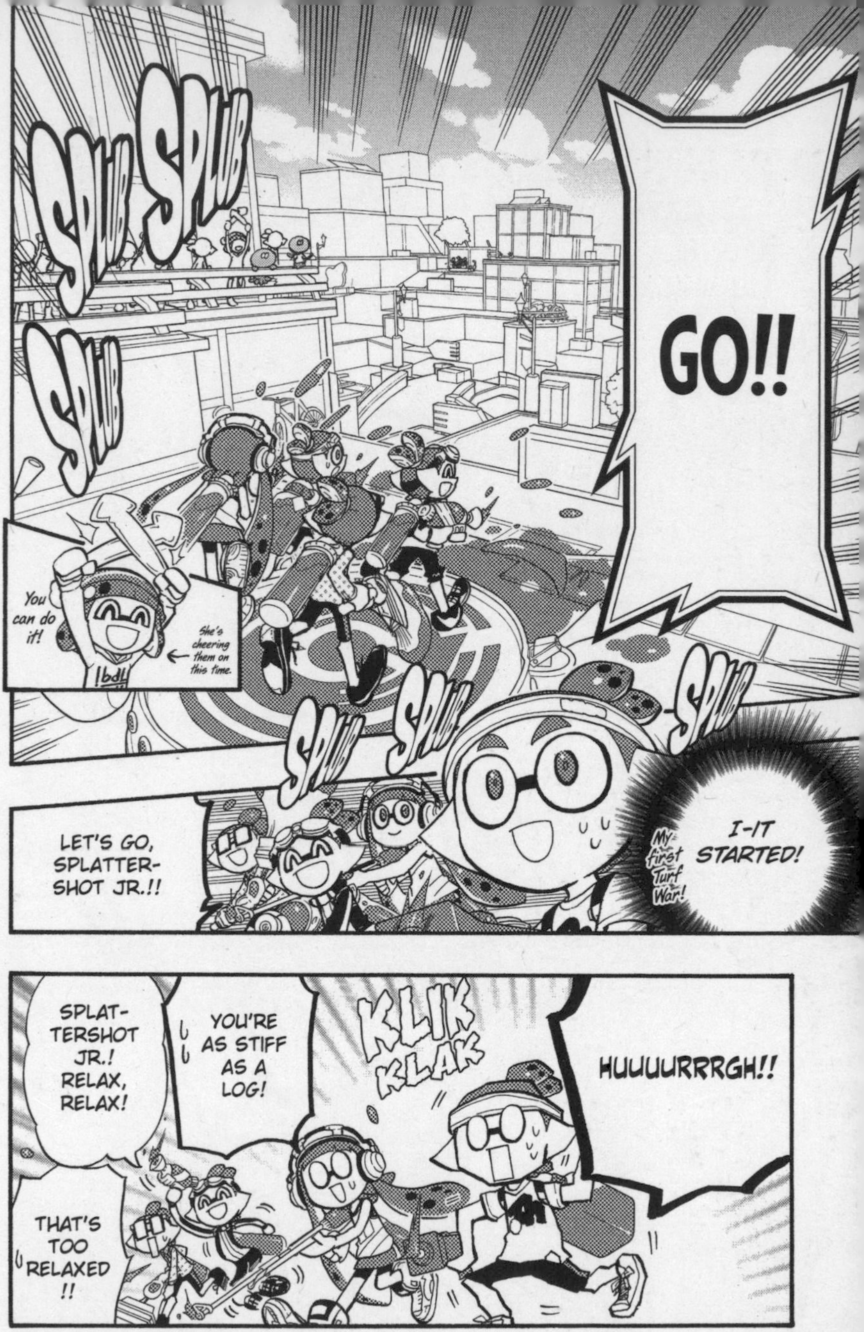
GO!!
SPLUB SPLUB
SPLUB
You can do it!
She's cheering them on this time.
SPLUB SPLUB SPLUB
I-IT STARTED!
My first Turf War!
LET'S GO, SPLATTER-SHOT JR.!!
HUUUURRRGH!!
KLIK KLAK
YOU'RE AS STIFF AS A LOG!
SPLAT-TERSHOT JR.! RELAX, RELAX!
THAT'S TOO RELAXED!!

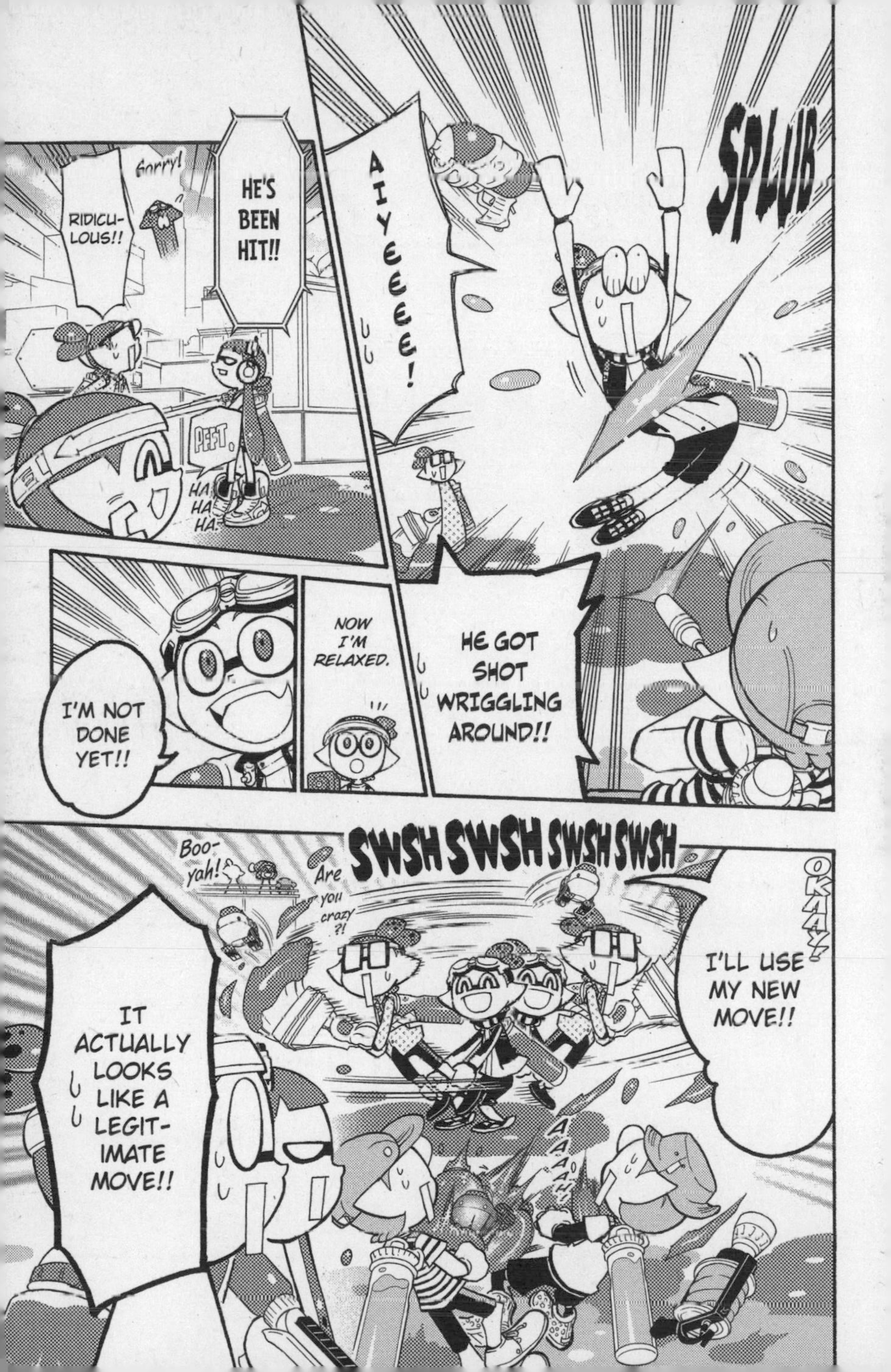
SPLUB
AIYEEEEE!
HE'S BEEN HIT!!
Sorry!
RIDICULOUS!!
PFFT
HA HA HA
HE GOT SHOT WRIGGLING AROUND!!
NOW I'M RELAXED.
I'M NOT DONE YET!!
OKAAAY!
I'LL USE MY NEW MOVE!!
SWSH SWSH SWSH SWSH
Are you crazy?!
Boo-yah!
AAAAAH!
IT ACTUALLY LOOKS LIKE A LEGITIMATE MOVE!!

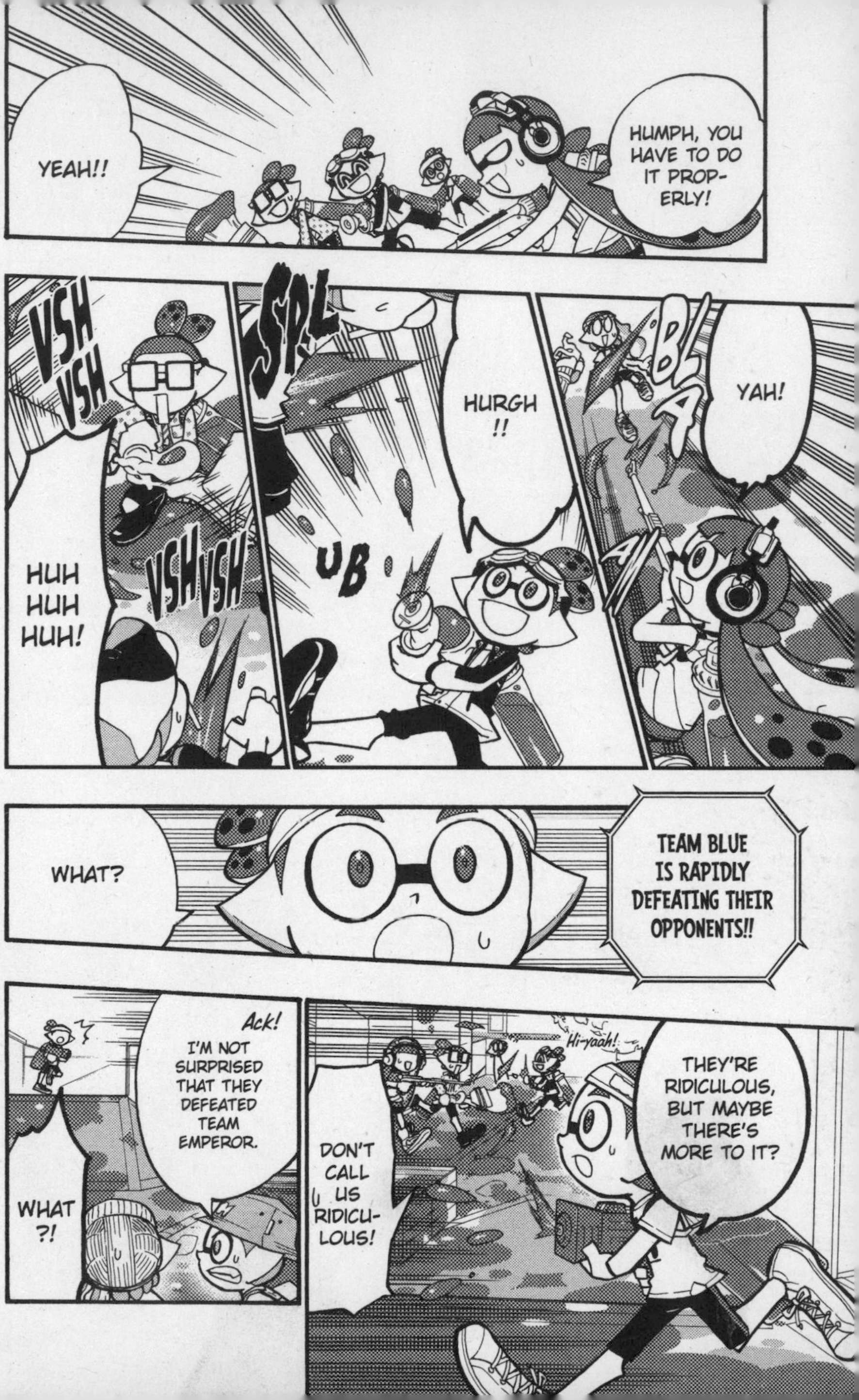
HUMPH, YOU HAVE TO DO IT PROPERLY!
YEAH!!
YAH!
BLA
A
HURGH !!
SPL
UB
VSH VSH
VSHVSH
HUH HUH HUH!
TEAM BLUE IS RAPIDLY DEFEATING THEIR OPPONENTS!!
WHAT?
Hi-yaah!
THEY'RE RIDICULOUS, BUT MAYBE THERE'S MORE TO IT?
DON'T CALL US RIDICULOUS!
Ack!
I'M NOT SURPRISED THAT THEY DEFEATED TEAM EMPEROR.
WHAT ?!

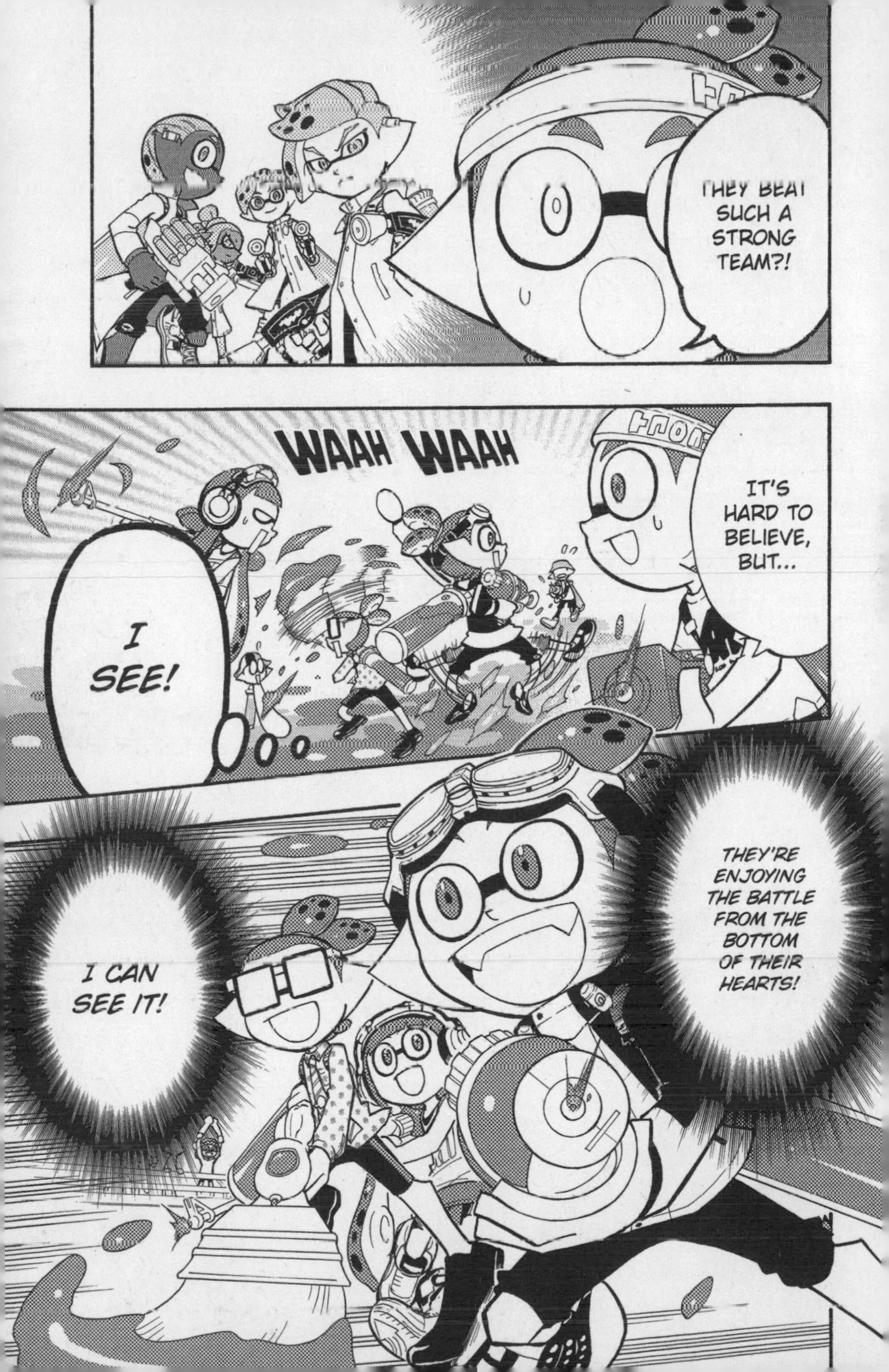
THEY BEAT SUCH A STRONG TEAM?!
IT'S HARD TO BELIEVE, BUT...
WAAH WAAH
I SEE!
THEY'RE ENJOYING THE BATTLE FROM THE BOTTOM OF THEIR HEARTS!
I CAN SEE IT!

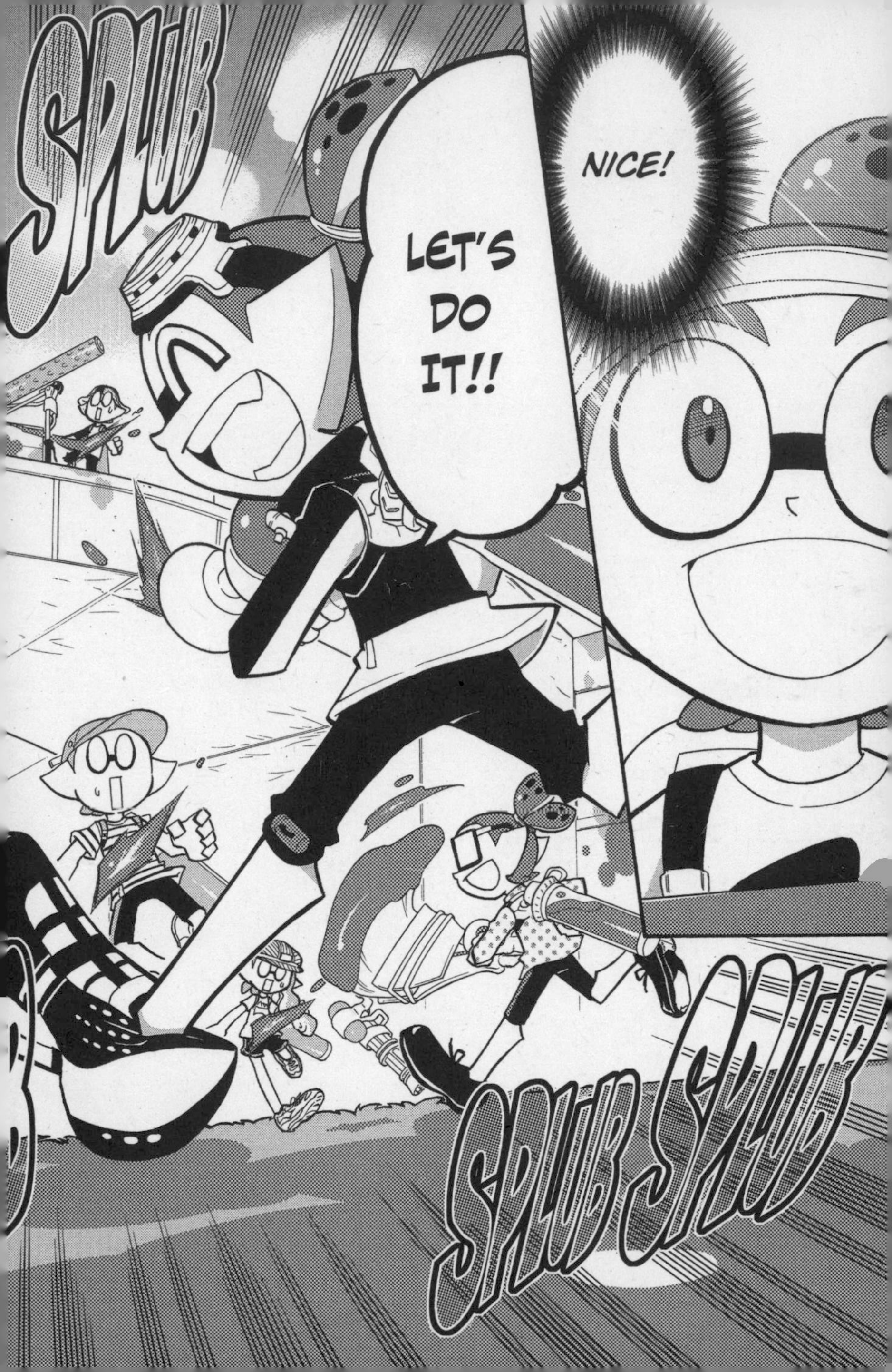
NICE!
LET'S DO IT!!
SPLUB
SPLUB SPLUB

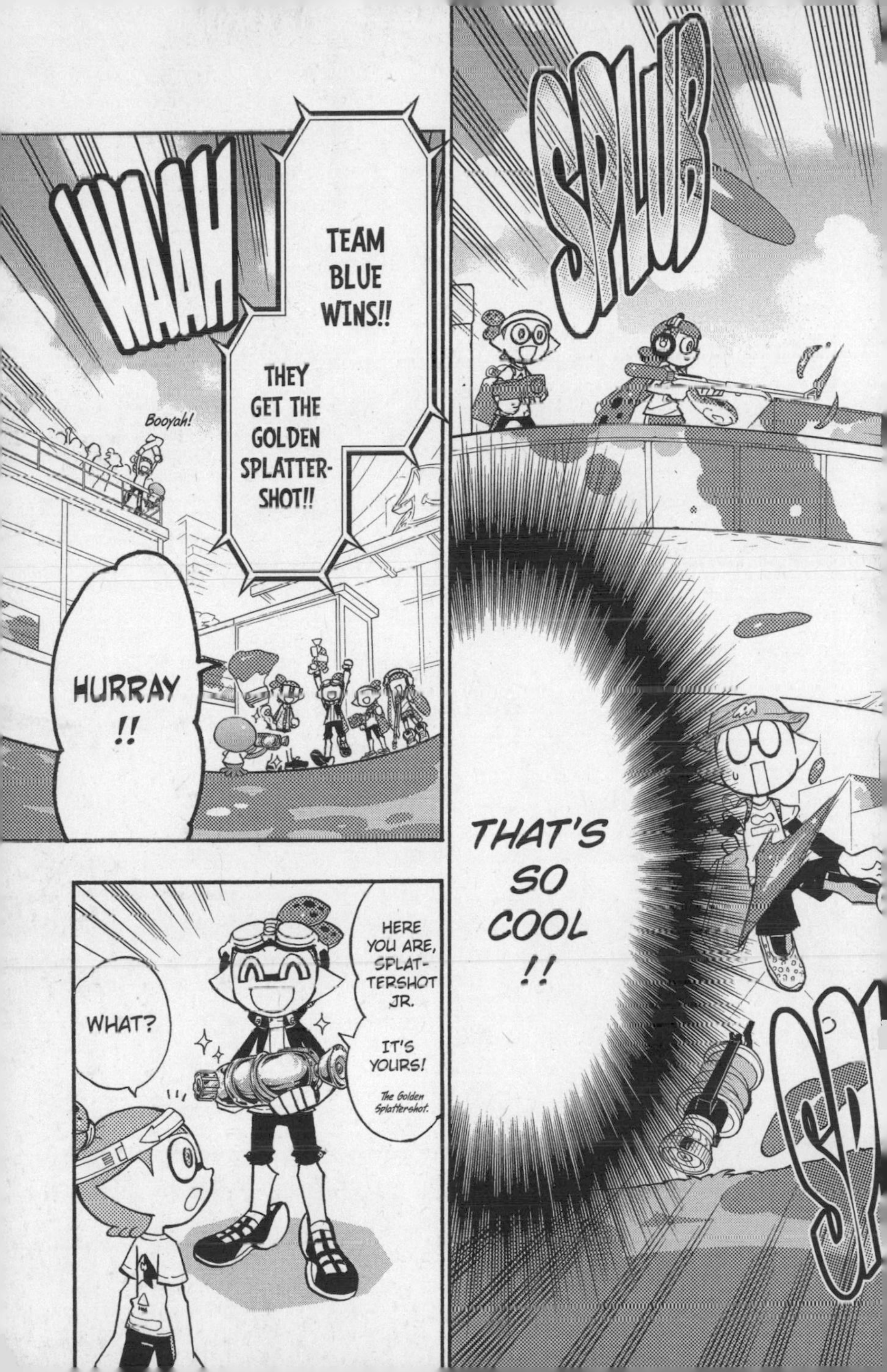
SPLUB
THAT'S SO COOL!!
WAAH
TEAM BLUE WINS!!
THEY GET THE GOLDEN SPLATTER-SHOT!!
Booyah!
HURRAY!!
HERE YOU ARE, SPLAT-TERSHOT JR.
IT'S YOURS!
The Golden Splattershot.
WHAT?

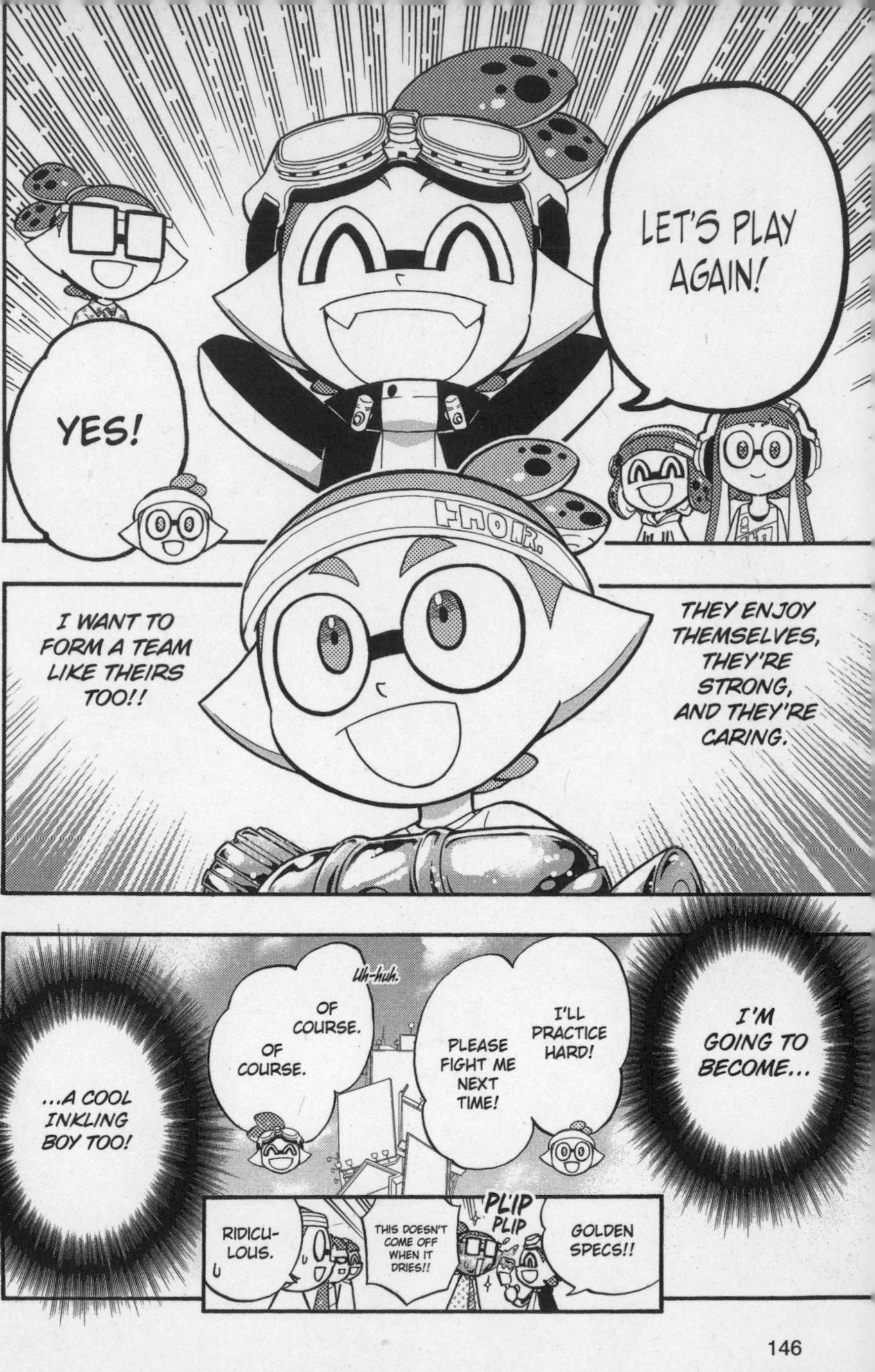
LET'S PLAY AGAIN!
YES!
THEY ENJOY THEMSELVES, THEY'RE STRONG, AND THEY'RE CARING.
I WANT TO FORM A TEAM LIKE THEIRS TOO!!
I'M GOING TO BECOME...
I'LL PRACTICE HARD!
PLEASE FIGHT ME NEXT TIME!
Uh-huh.
OF COURSE.
OF COURSE.
...A COOL INKLING BOY TOO!
GOLDEN SPECS!!
PLIP PLIP
THIS DOESN'T COME OFF WHEN IT DRIES!!
RIDICU-LOUS.

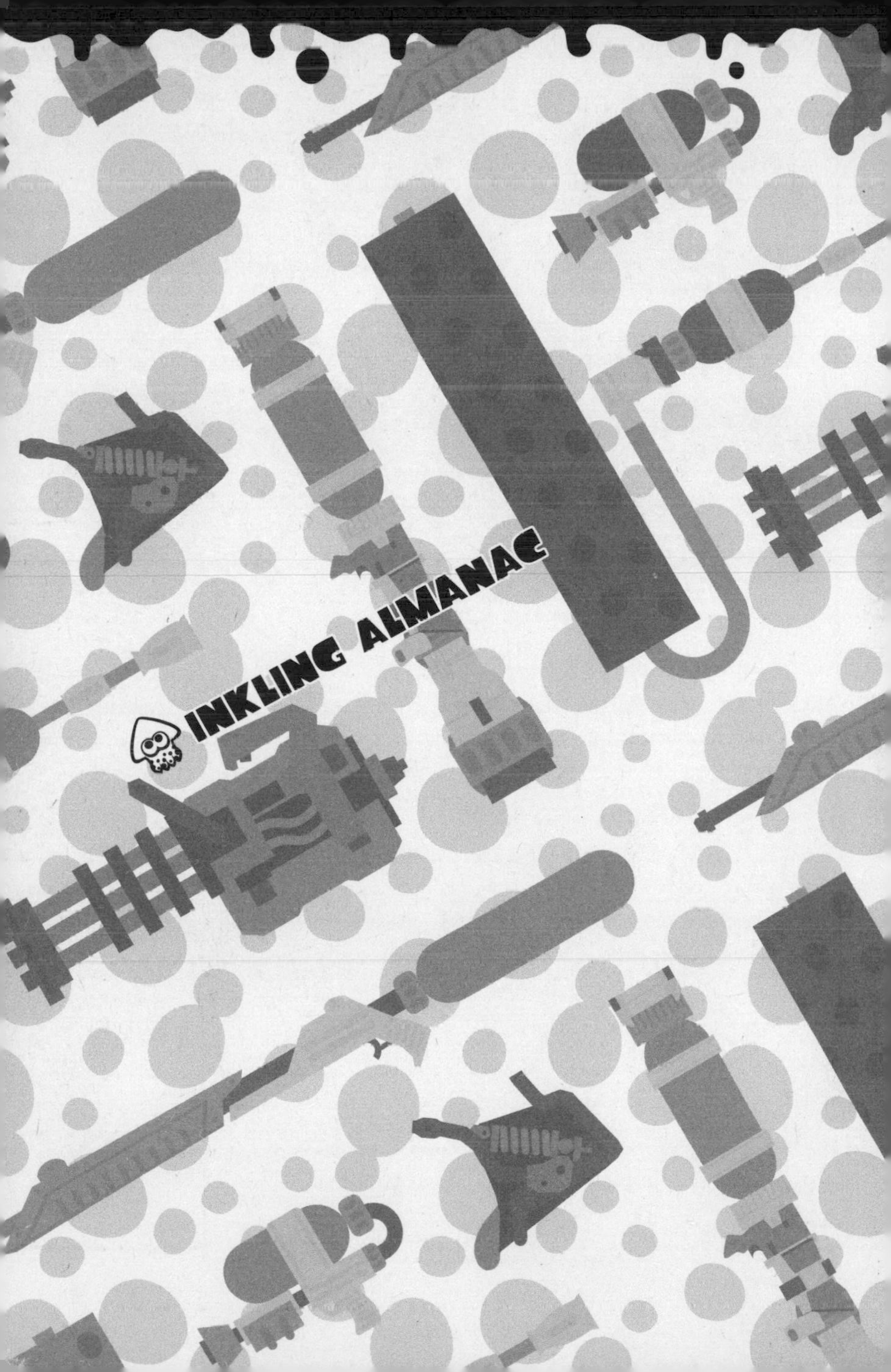
INKLING ALMANAC

ARC
EIGHT

Weapon: Blaster

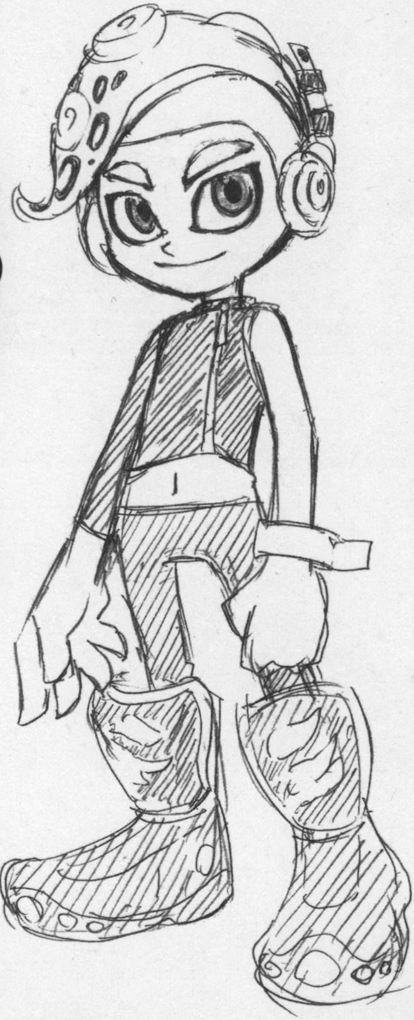

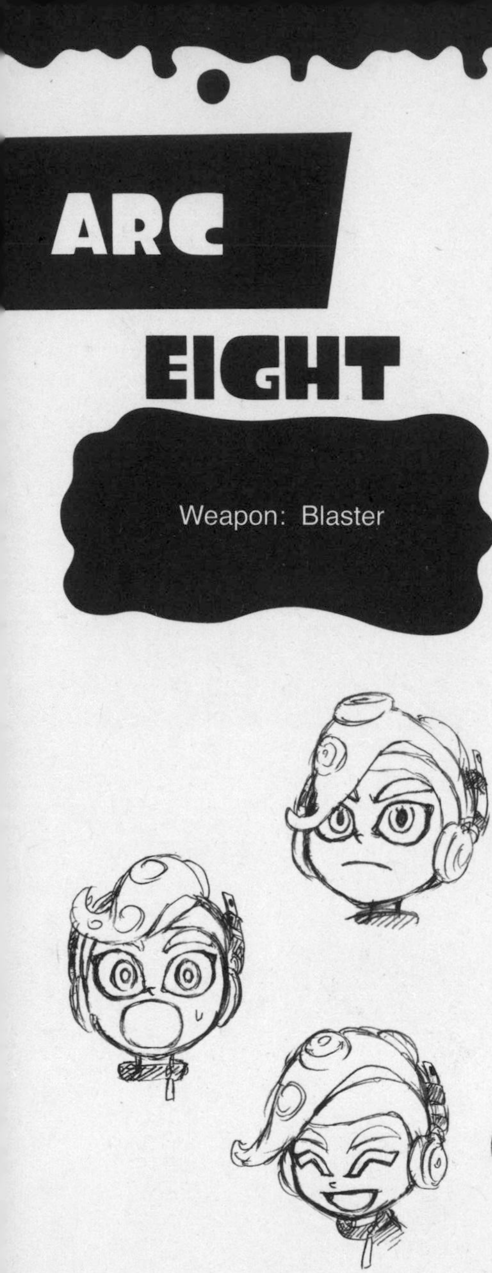

OCTO

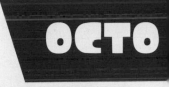

SEVEN

Weapon: Octo Shot

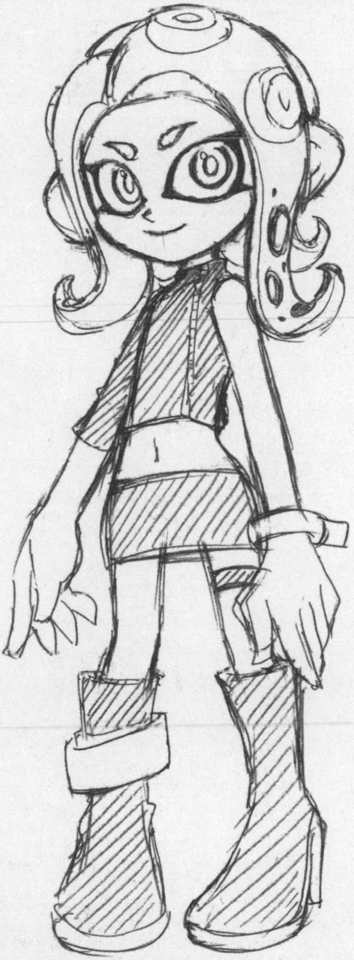

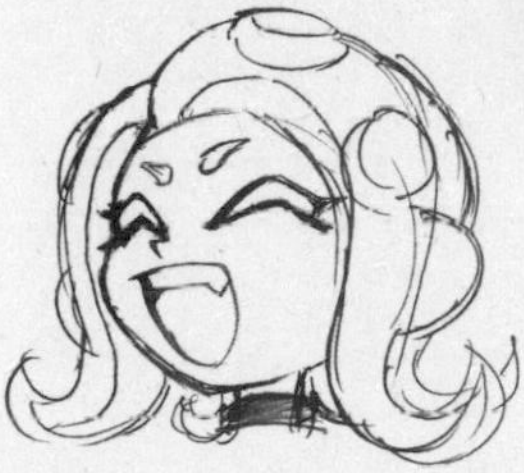

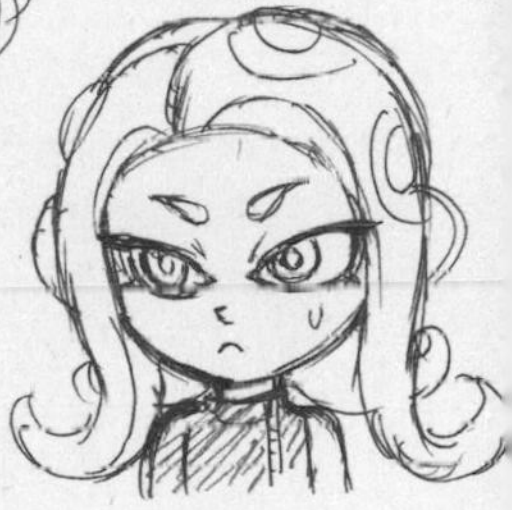

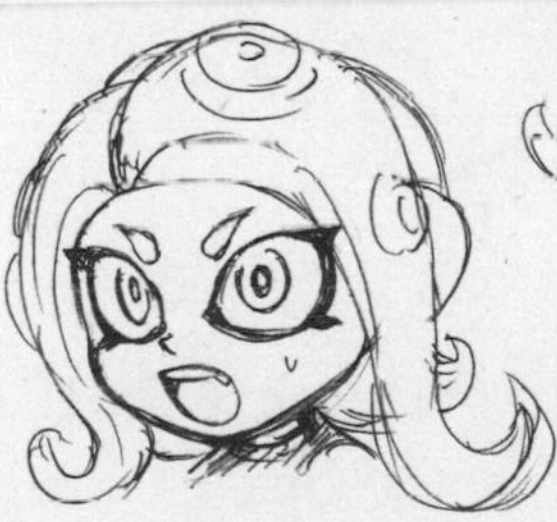

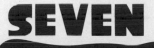

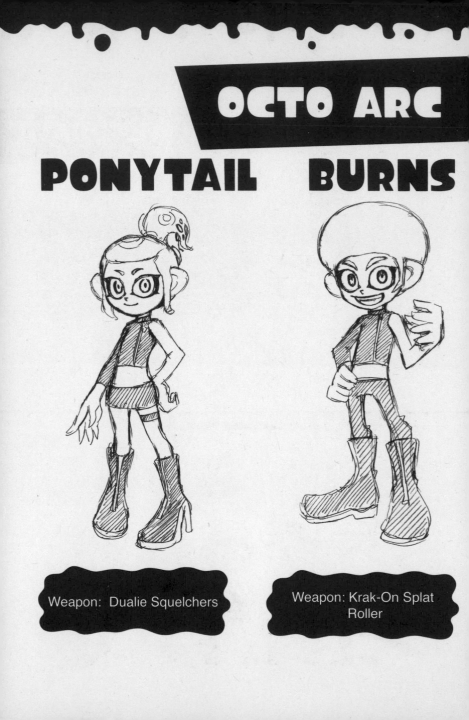

OCTO ARC

PONYTAIL

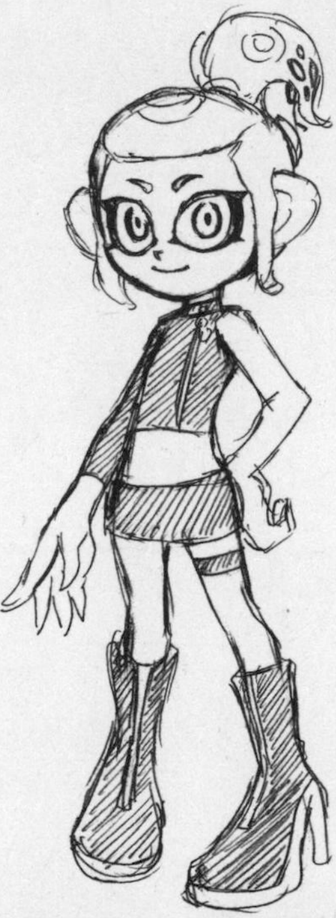

Weapon: Dualie Squelchers

BURNS

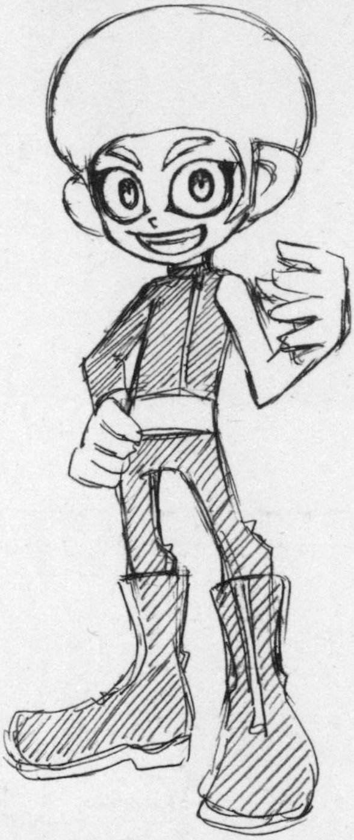

Weapon: Krak-On Splat Roller

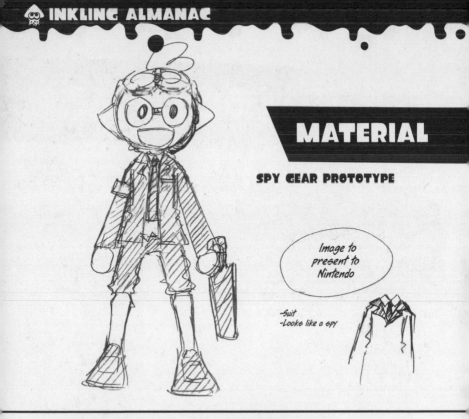

MATERIAL

SPY GEAR PROTOTYPE

Image to present to Nintendo

-Suit
-Looks like a spy

-IMAGE I RECEIVED FROM THE SQUID RESEARCH LAB

EIGHT

Weapon: Blaster
Headgear: Squidlife Headphones
Clothing: Red Cuttlegear LS
Shoes: Suede Gray Lace-Ups

INFO

• He has been influenced by Goggles and Cap'n Cuttlefish into making pickles these days.

TEAM EIGHT

(INK COLOR: MAGENTA)

PONYTAIL

BURNS

SEVEN

Weapon:	Dualie Squelchers
Headgear:	FishFry Visor
Clothing:	Squid Squad Band Tee
Shoes:	Red Hi Tops

Weapon:	Krak-On Splat Roller
Headgear:	Tennis Headbamd
Clothing:	Dakro Golden Tee
Shoes:	N-Pacer AU

Weapon:	Octo Shot Replica
Headgear:	Black FishFry Bandana
Clothing:	Annaki Drive Tee
Shoes:	Punk Cherries

INFO

· She has been interested in music bands recently.

INFO

· Eight has his memories back, but he's fond of the name Goggles gave him, so he's decided to keep it. The other three like their names too.

COSTUME TEAM BLUE

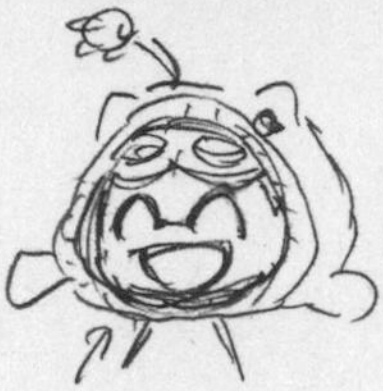

I've widened the mouth in the manga, so the expression on his face is more visible.

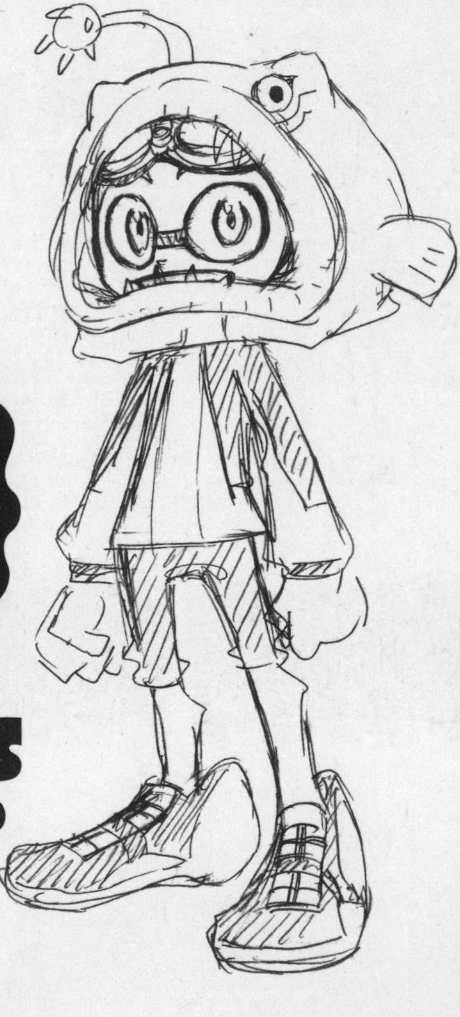

Weapon: Splattershot
Headgear: Pilot Goggles + Anglerfish Mask
Clothing: Eggplant Mountain Coat
Shoes: Hero Runner Replicas

GOGGLES
(COSTUME VERSION)

BOBBLE HAT
(COSTUME VERSION)

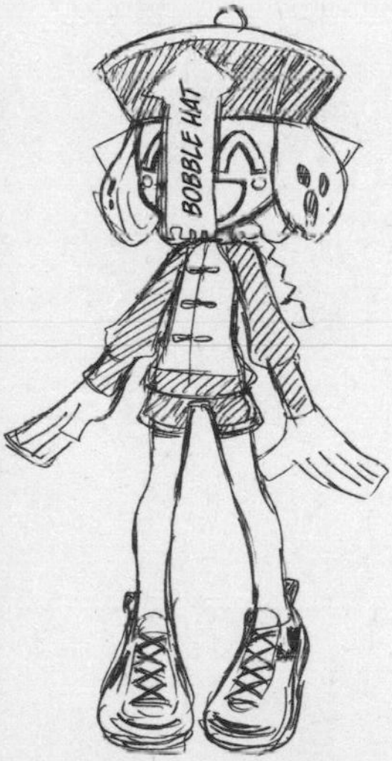
BOBBLE HAT

Weapon: Slosher
Headgear: Kyonshi Hat
Clothing: Panda Kung-Fu Zip-Up
Shoes: Purple Sea Slugs

HEADPHONES
(COSTUME VERSION)

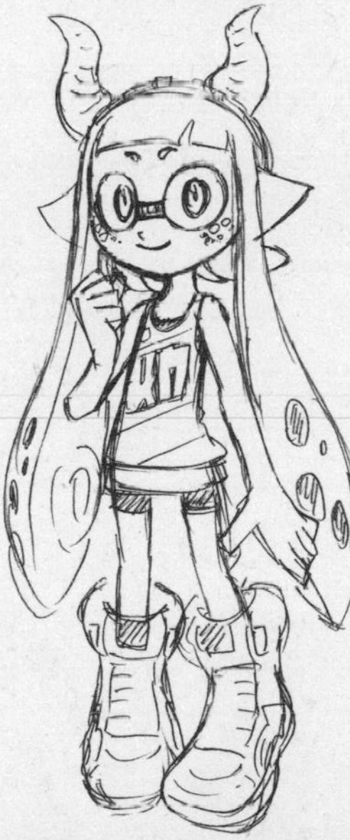

Weapon: Splat Charger
Headgear: Li'l Devil Horns
Clothing: Slash King Tank
Shoes: Red Hi-Horses

SPECS
(COSTUME VERSION)

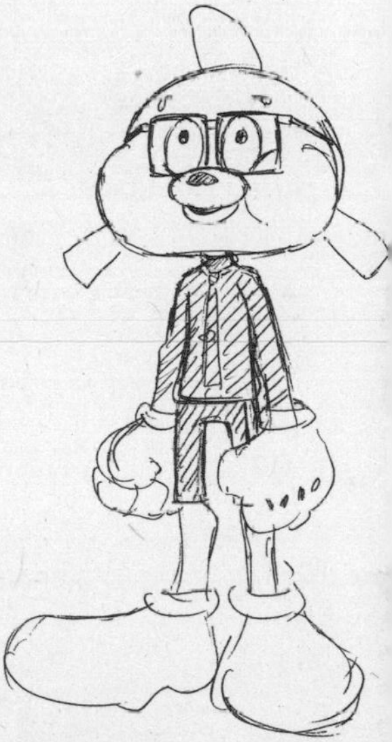

Weapon: Octobrush
Headgear: Fresh Fish Head + Retro Specs
Clothing: Fresh Fish Gloves + Baby-Jelly Shirt & Tie
Shoes: Fresh Fish Feet

SQUINJA

Weapon: Kensa Luna Blaster
Headgear: Squinja Mask
Clothing: Squinja Suit
Shoes: Squinja Boots

INFO

• He hasn't caught a cold since he started wearing costumes.

TEAM COSTUME LOVER

(INK COLOR: LIGHT PURPLE)

KNIGHT (RIDER)

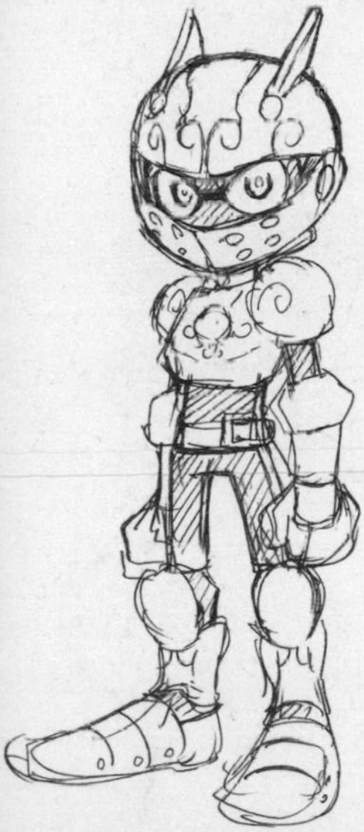

Weapon: Kensa Dynamo Roller
Headgear: Steel Helm
Clothing: Steel Platemail
Shoes: Steel Greaves

POWER ARMOR

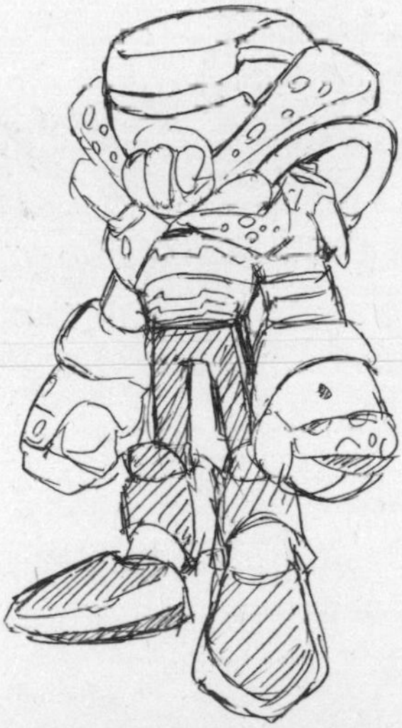

Weapon: N-ZAP '89
Headgear: Power Mask
Clothing: Power Armor
Shoes: Power Boots

ROBE

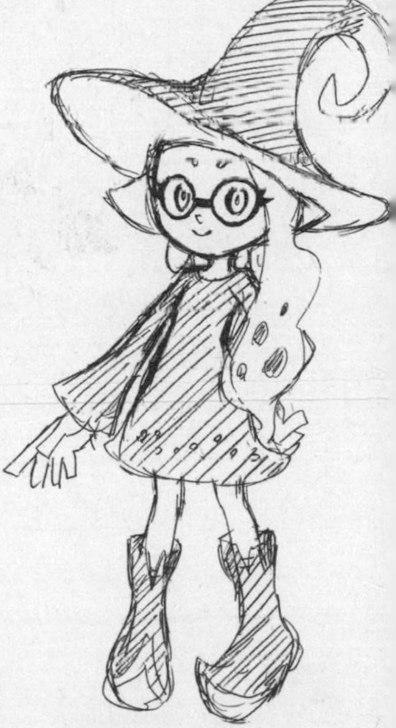

Weapon: Custom Splattershot Jr.
Headgear: Enchanted Hat
Clothing: Enchanted Robe
Shoes: Enchanted Boots

INFO

•They're always searching for a fourth member who loves to wear costumes.

SPLATTERSHOT JR. ARC

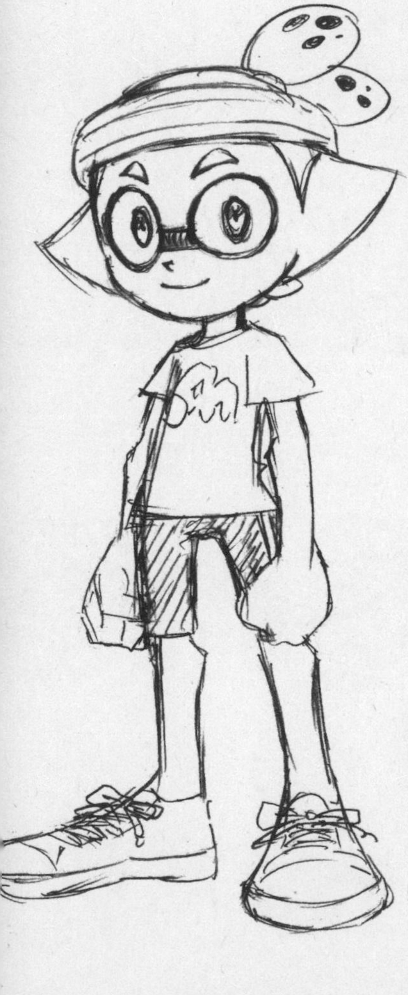

Weapon: Splattershot Jr.
Headgear: White Headband
Clothing: Basic Tee
Shoes: Cream Basics

INFO

•He keeps the Golden Splattershot in his room on display. He polishes it when he's feeling extra proud.

SPLATTER-SHOT JR.

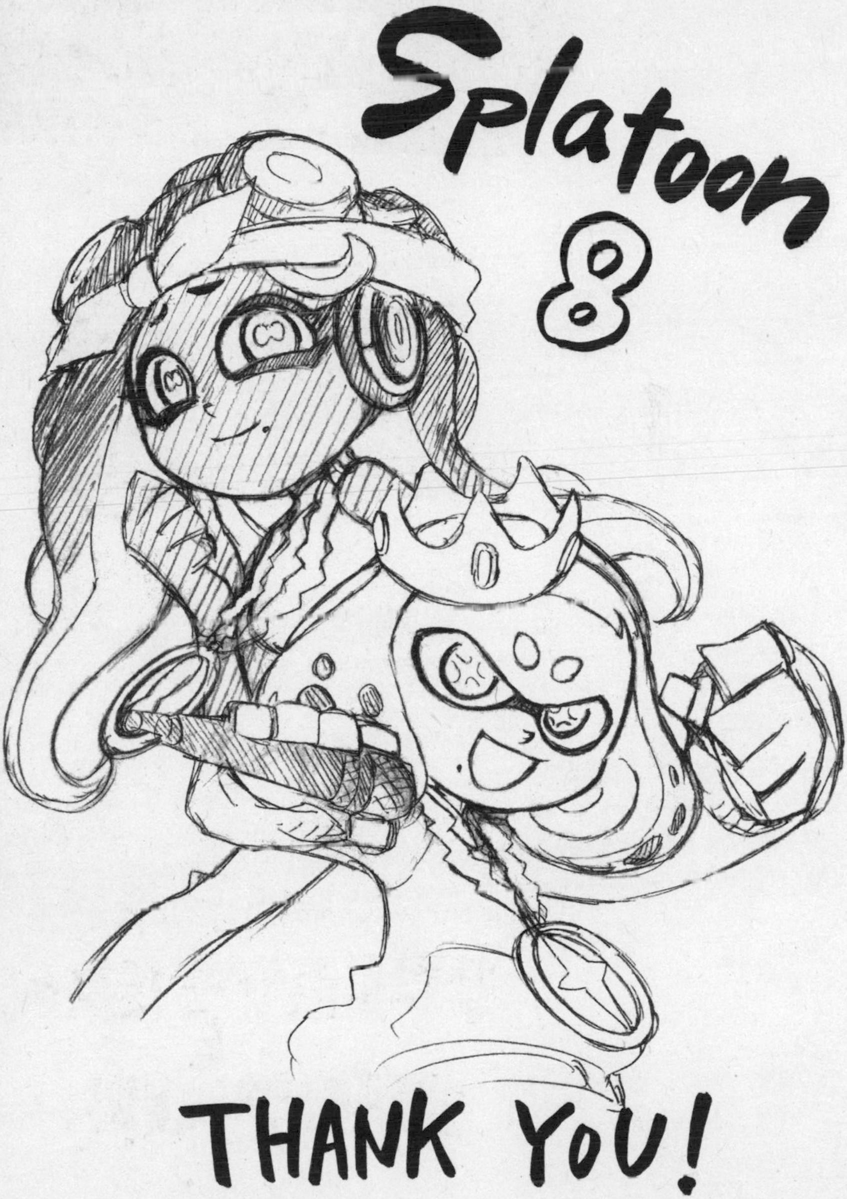
Splatoon
8
THANK YOU!

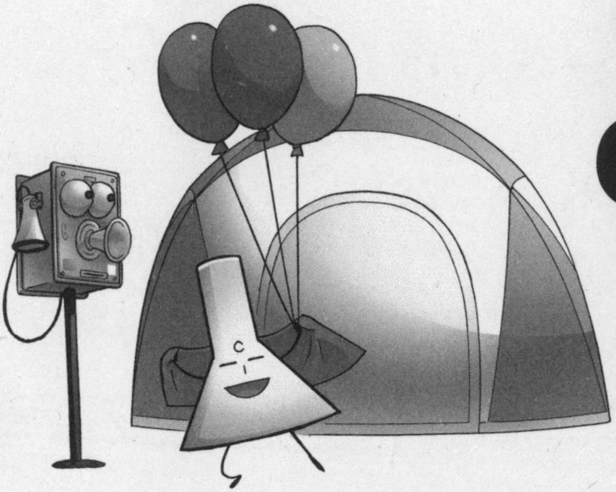

Volume 8 marks the end of the
Octo arc. Hope you enjoyed the camps,
amusement parks and Splatfests!!

Sankichi Hinodeya

Splatoon

Volume 8
VIZ Media Edition

Story and Art by
Sankichi Hinodeya

Translation **Tetsuichiro Miyaki**
English Adaptation **Jason A. Hurley**
Lettering **John Hunt**
Design **Kam Li**
Editor **Joel Enos**

TM & © 2020 Nintendo. All rights reserved.

SPLATOON Vol. 8 by Sankichi HINODEYA
© 2016 Sankichi HINODEYA
All rights reserved.
Original Japanese edition published by SHOGAKUKAN.
English translation rights in the United States of America,
Canada, the United Kingdom, Ireland, Australia and
New Zealand arranged with SHOGAKUKAN.

The stories, characters and incidents mentioned
in this publication are entirely fictional.

Original Design **100percent**

Printed in the U.S.A.

Published by VIZ Media, LLC
P.O. Box 77010
San Francisco, CA 94107

10 9 8 7 6 5 4 3 2 1
First printing, January 2020

viz.com

PARENTAL ADVISORY
SPLATOON is rated A and is suit-
able for readers of all ages.

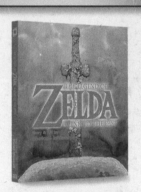

THE LEGEND OF ZELDA

LEGENDARY EDITION

STORY AND ART BY

AKIRA HIMEKAWA

The Legendary Editions of *The Legend of Zelda*™ contain two volumes of the beloved manga series, presented in a deluxe format featuring new covers and color art pieces.

From the pages of
***Nintendo Power*™ magazine,**
a full-color graphic novel
inspired by the classic
***Super Mario Bros.*™**
video games!

SUPER MARIO ADVENTURES™

Story by KENTARO TAKEKUMA   **Art by CHARLIE NOZAWA**

The peril-plagued Princess Toadstool is kidnapped by the diabolical deadbeat Bowser but super plumbers Mario and Luigi hatch a plan with their new friend Yoshi to rescue her. Are the Super Mario Bros.' plans a pipe dream? Can they stop the Koopa King before he forces the Princess to be his bride?!

Splatoon
reads from
right to
left!

This is
the end
of this
graphic
novel.